C000231522

VENDETTA

EDIE BAYLIS

Boldwood

First published in Great Britain in 2022 by Boldwood Books Ltd.

A CIP catalogue record for this book is available from the British Library.

Paperback ISBN 978-1-80280-176-7

Large Print ISBN 978-1-80280-177-4

Hardback ISBN 978-1-80280-175-0

Ebook ISBN 978-1-80280-178-1

Kindle ISBN 978-1-80280-179-8

Audio CD ISBN 978-1-80280-170-5

MP3 CD ISBN 978-1-80280-171-2

Digital audio download ISBN 978-1-80280-173-6

Boldwood Books Ltd
23 Bowerdean Street
London SW6 3TN
www.boldwoodbooks.com

For Jess – my fellow Scorpio and friend

PROLOGUE
19 JANUARY 1996

Dan Marlow didn't hide his wish to catch the barman's eye through the hatch specifically placed for shouting orders. It always paid to appear chilled out and not too intent on the job in hand. It might make him look a prize mug not having his eye on the ball, and although most people might have an aversion to making out they weren't the brightest spark, Dan did not. Doing it this way was what pulled the cash in.

'Another pint, please,' he shouted in the direction of the miserable stocky man serving the punters in the main room.

Putting away plenty of drinks was always noted too – it lulled people into a false sense of security, allowing them to assume he was half-cut.

Dan inwardly grinned. He'd got this down to a tee, but in all fairness, he'd have been happy to give this particular sit-down tonight a miss. He and Mickey had done okay for themselves around the London pubs this month, so he'd have preferred not to push his luck.

For the third time, they'd cleaned up with bells on at the Joiners Arms and their reputation in Clapham was now sailing too close to the wind to be comfortable, hence they'd had to venture further afield. Not so far afield, mind – Streatham, to be precise. But far enough away from Clapham to slow the speed of the grapevine.

South London might be a big area, but nevertheless, it was important to take this one slow, so as not to arouse suspicion.

He glanced at the intent faces around the separate room at the back of the Bricklayers Arms. There was a shedload of money up for grabs tonight, which was why Mickey had insisted they come. Personally, Dan would have preferred to wait a while longer, but what he thought rarely counted.

Dan nodded his thanks as his fresh pint was placed on the hatch, ignoring that the sullen barman sloshed two inches of his beer onto the stained wooden shelf. This would be the last drink, anyhow.

Chucking his cigarette end on the floor, Dan ground it out with his heel.

He'd pulled in a couple of small wins tonight, making sure to lose more than he'd won until the last minute, as previously agreed. Everything was going to plan. Now, seeing Mickey's barely imperceptible blink to signify the off, he waited for the cards to be dealt.

The odds had raised to a level where it was all or nothing, so it was a good job Dan knew he would clear up. Mickey was so good with his sleight of hand, so bloody expert, even knowing what would happen, Dan was yet to physically see it. The man was a genius – an absolute fucking genius.

Dan covertly scanned the huge pile of notes in the centre of the scuffed table. There was only him and one other player left – an old bloke sweating so much he looked a prize candidate for a coronary.

Knowing all eyes were on him, Dan mirrored the old man's

flash of worry on his own face as he glanced at his cards. It never paid to look confident, and he didn't much like the look of several of the people here who had already been forced to fold.

Dan concentrated on the one remaining player and sat tight as Mickey worked his magic, dealing from the bottom of the pack.

The opponent picked up his cards, his slight flinch giving Dan all the information he needed to know. The guy was fucked.

He slapped his cards face down on the table and scooped up the pile of money. 'Think this is mine,' Dan grinned, standing up. 'Cheers, fella. That's me done for tonight!'

He'd contain his glee for just a while longer until he met up with Mickey at the prearranged spot down the road. All he had to do now was leave, which shouldn't be difficult.

Mickey gathered the cards up. 'Another game, anyone?'

A squat man with a long scar down the left-hand side of his face pushed himself away from the wall and snatched the remains of the deck out of Mickey's hand. 'Let's just check these.'

Dan froze. *What the fuck was this?* He glanced at Mickey, who appeared outwardly unruffled.

The man spread the cards on the table. 'I've heard about you two from the Pig and Blanket,' he snarled. 'Yep, look! Just as I thought. This wanker has been dealing from the bottom!'

As the other men's faces twisted with rage, Mickey upended the table as a diversion. There had always been a get-out plan in the event of this happening. They'd never needed it before, but they sure as hell needed it now.

Seeing Mickey already exiting out of the small back room in the confusion, Dan started towards the door.

Slipping on the loose cards scattered on the floor, he lurched forwards and as a meaty hand closed around the back of his neck, dragging him back into the room, he could do little about it.

Shit.

Dan's mind raced. 'Wait! It's not what you think. I...'

'What about the other one?' someone yelled.

The heavy-set man with his hand around Dan's neck cast him to the beer-drenched floor. 'I don't give a toss about him. This fucker's the one with our money!'

Dan grinned, even though there was a boot across the front of his neck holding him still. 'No hard feelings, boys.' By pretending none of this was happening, he remained calm as his pockets were rifled through, relieving him of his winnings. 'You've got your money back now, so no harm done.'

The squat man leant over Dan's prone form and snarled, revealing a gap at the front of his selection of stained teeth. 'That's what you think, cunt! You've pushed your luck one time too often around these parts. We don't like cheats. I'll make sure neither of you play anywhere around here again.'

Dan's eyes widened as the man pulled a meat cleaver from his inside pocket. *Shit, shit, shit!* 'Let's not be hasty. You've got your money back now, so I...'

'Hold the fucker still!' the man snarled to the others in the room.

Dan struggled pointlessly, the grip on his arms and legs too strong. Seeing the meat cleaver rise, his eyes bulged. The last thing he lucidly recalled before the raging pain kicked in was watching with a strange, detached fascination as the fingers on his right hand were effortlessly removed.

1

ONE WEEK LATER

Marina Devlin glared at Dan downing another can of lager. She'd broached this subject several times, but he'd refused to discuss it. He'd refused to discuss *anything* this past week, and she was sick to the back teeth of it.

How she wished she'd walked away from Dan when she'd had the chance, rather than trying to prove the choice she'd made two years ago had been the right one.

She'd really liked Dan at first – *really* liked him – so she'd gone against everyone's advice to steer well clear of him, including that of her brother, who had told her time and time again that Dan was a loser only out for himself.

Marina stubbed her cigarette out and scowled. Yeah, how she wished she'd listened to Grant. Dan *was* a loser. And not just a loser, but a loser with a *gambling problem*, as well as a self-inflated sense of his own ability.

Since this belated realisation, it had been one thing after another – each episode worse than the last, leaving her further trapped. Because if she walked away now, she'd have to admit that she'd been wrong.

And she wasn't doing that.

Dan's latest idea of becoming involved with Mickey Devlin – Marina's good-for-nothing father – was the last straw.

And now *this*.

Marina's eyes tracked to the grubby bandages on Dan's hand and she shuddered. Getting his fingers cut off? How could he have allowed that to happen?

For God's sake, Grant was right. Dan was a useless, deluded bastard and all that had kept her going this past year was scheming how she could get rid of him. And not just out of her life, but out of life in *general*.

It was all she could think about.

Grabbing her cigarettes, Marina sparked up another. She might as well smoke herself to death. Why couldn't Dan have got himself killed, rather than just losing his fingers? At least it would save having to arrange it herself. Plus, as a broken-hearted girl-friend left without means, she'd be eligible for decent benefits.

That was about all she'd got going for her these days.

So much for London being paved with gold. Whoever coined that saying needed their head read!

'Are you doing breakfast?' Dan muttered, ash dropping from the end of his cigarette onto his bare chest. 'Shit!' he yelped, brushing it off with his good hand. 'Unless you fancy relieving me of my frustration?' He wrapped his arm around Marina's waist, his morning erection pushing eagerly against the small of her back.

'I'd best get up. Time's getting on.' Marina edged out of Dan's grasp. Being around him made her skin crawl. How she hated him.

Getting out of bed, she pulled her dressing gown around her nakedness and tugged her long blonde hair from the neck of the robe.

She hadn't slept a wink again last night and was still tossing and turning when dawn broke this morning. She was shattered. She had to do something about this situation.

Marina watched Dan fumbling to open another can of beer with one hand, sick of putting up with his pathetic excuses. 'What are we going to do?'

'It will be okay, you'll see.' Dan inwardly grimaced. *Every bloody day she went on about this.* He glared at the remains of his hand. Exactly what the fuck was he supposed to do? He couldn't even work in bastard McDonald's like this. Not that he had any intention of working anywhere like *that*.

It was all very well Mickey saying things would be easier once his hand had fully healed, but it was all right for him. It wasn't like *he'd* lost half of his fingers, was it? The final insult was, not only was being with Marina like shagging a corpse these days, but she'd turned into a nagging witch, which pissed him off. *Everything* pissed him off. But not quite as much as what he'd learnt last night.

Mickey might have escaped unscathed from those loons in the Bricklayers Arms, but the man was right about one thing. Now other disgruntled participants from their previous poker games were queuing up to recoup their losses, he stood to lose a hell of a lot more than just his fingers...

Dan glared back at the shorter version of his hand. At least Mickey had come up with a viable workaround. Marina wouldn't like it, but that was tough.

'Dan?' Marina repeated. 'Did you hear me? I said, what are we g...'

'I heard what you said,' Dan snapped. How could he not? Her droning on was driving him bloody mad, so he might as well just tell her the news. 'We have to leave.'

Marina frowned. 'Leave? What do you mean? Leave where?'

Dan waved his arm around the bedroom. 'Here. This place. This town.' He gritted his teeth. 'This whole bloody city!'

'What are you talking about?' Marina screeched. 'For Christ's sake, unless you've forgotten, we've got no money, so where would we go?' She paced around the room. 'It can't happen.'

Dan's face screwed into a scowl. 'It *has* to happen.'

Marina stopped pacing and glared at Dan. 'Or what? You'll leave?' That was the next best thing to him being dead. 'Go on, then! Leave! I've had enough! Off you go!'

'Fine! I will! But I don't advise that you stay. You'll end up losing those good looks of yours!' Dan snapped. 'I'll spell it out for you. It's simple! There are people after my fucking head!' He dragged the fingers of his good hand through his knotted hair. 'I discovered the extent of it last night, and it's worse than I thought. We need to go. We've got no choice.'

Marina blinked. *Lose her looks?* She wasn't losing her looks for anyone – they were all she had left.

Dan reached for Marina's hand, shrugging as she batted him away. 'Look, I know I've caused problems, but this is important. If I'm not here, they'll come for you. You don't know what these people are like. I dread to think what they'd do to a stunner like you, purely to spite me.' *Was it finally sinking into her bloody head?* 'They'll have even *more* reason to hurt you when they find out you're Mickey Devlin's daughter!'

Marina swallowed uncomfortably. *Was Dan serious?* She might have known her father would make things worse. Dan was usually the eternal optimist – another example of his delusions. But *this*...?

'Your dad said he'd lend us money,' Dan continued. 'And he...'

'I want *nothing* from him! Do you hear me? Nothing!' Marina screamed. 'Nor do I want anything off you!'

'Oh, come on, it's not all bad. Think about it. See it as a fresh start. There will be new opportunities up there and...'

Marina's heart thumped painfully. 'Where? Up where?'

'Birmingham. Mickey says we can stay with your mother.'

'My mother?' Marina screamed. 'No way! You know I won't do that. That woman, she's...'

'Listen, you stupid cow. Did you not hear me? People are coming for payback and I'm a sitting duck. *We* are sitting ducks...'

'Jesus Christ,' Marina spluttered. 'What the fuck have you done?' *How she hated him.* She'd thought things were bad ten minutes ago, but now things had surpassed even a useless hand.

'What have *I* done? It's more like...' Dan stopped as a plate smashed over his head and Marina started screaming every single obscenity she knew.

* * *

'I didn't expect to hear from you.' Grant Devlin eyed his father suspiciously. He'd worked out a long time ago their father was only out for himself. As was their bloody mother.

Why else would he and Marina have ended up in care?

It had taken Grant a long time to find a place in the world and discover something he could do well, yet the last time he'd been stupid enough to allow Marina to talk him into visiting their mother, he'd vowed never to put himself in a position again where the selfish old bitch could make him feel as worthless as he'd felt that day.

As it was, it had taken *years* to override the inferiority complex he'd had as a child, and he didn't need reminding of the time he'd felt lower than a dog's dick because neither of their parents wanted them.

To be honest, Grant had very little recollection, if any, of the day they'd been taken away. He and Marina were only dots when they'd been put into care, but he *did* remember the occasions when both he and his sister got excited about the impending visits from their mother.

Grant clenched his jaw. He'd even convinced himself she would take them home, so they could be a proper family. That way, they'd no longer have to put up with the endless digs from the other kids at school, calling them the 'ones no one wanted'.

His brow knitted. Despite the constant let-downs, he'd clung onto that bizarre hope for years. He'd been stupid and it must have been a full five years of their mother failing to turn up for one single visit before he finally accepted she was a cunt.

Thankfully, once he'd come to this realisation, it became easier to plough on with life and, by twenty-eight, he'd done all right.

Having been surrounded by violence and ne'er-do-wells since he could remember, it had been second nature to consider that a viable job prospect. And with a bit of brains, luck and damn hard work, he'd excelled in various jobs for dubious firms over the years. So much so that he now worked for himself as a freelancer – a gun for hire – accountable to no one and free to make his own choices.

He even put up with occasionally talking to his so-called father, but the man showing up unexpectedly at his local pub meant only one thing. *Trouble.*

Grant's eyes moved back to the man busy slurping the pint he'd felt obliged to stump up for. 'So, what is it you want?'

Mickey flashed his son a knowing smile. 'What have you got on at the moment, work wise?'

Grant pursed his lips. It was true he was between contracts at the moment, but he didn't imagine this man was about to offer work. Nothing he'd be interested in, anyway.

'I thought you might like to know what I've found out about your mother,' Mickey said, a sneer rolling onto his face.

Grant's eyes narrowed. 'Why the fuck would I want to know that?'

Leaning on the sticky pub table, Mickey lowered his voice. 'Because you might wish to investigate it. From what I can tell, there'll be a hefty payout in it for you...'

'I've told you before. I'm not doing your dirty work. I might be for hire, but I don't do freebies,' Grant snarled.

'I'm not asking you to!' Mickey plastered his face with fake hurt. 'It's some easy money and being as your sister's heading up that way soon...'

Grant almost knocked his own pint over. 'Marina's going to see our mother? What's that about?'

'Nothing to do with me! It was something Dan mentioned,' Mickey lied.

Grant folded his arms across his muscular chest. 'I am *not* seeing Linda Matthews again,' he said, the words hissing like steam through his gritted teeth. 'Why the hell would Marina want to visit that old bitch?' *Hadn't she learnt through experience the old cow wasn't interested?*

That last time Marina had tracked their mother down four years ago was etched into his brain. Raddled with gear, the woman was in a right state. She hadn't even bothered hiding her crack habit. Neither had she hidden that she blamed them for the mess her life was in.

Actually, it had been a case of blaming them, along with anyone else she could pull out of the hat. The list was endless.

Okay, their father had undoubtedly not helped by leaving her in the lurch, but it had been *her* who'd continued getting off her head once the social got involved and not fighting to keep hold of her children.

Mickey laughed. 'You don't like your mother very much, do you? At least you can appreciate why I fucked her off.'

Grant stood up. Just being in this man's company irritated him. 'If Marina wants to go to visit that bitch, that's her call, but I want nothing to do with it.'

Mickey pulled a newspaper cutting from his pocket. 'You may change your mind when you see this... I spotted it when I went up Brum a few months back.'

Grant snatched the clipping from Mickey's hand and unfolded it. He hardly recognised his mother. This woman looked almost *normal*. But it was her without a doubt. Posh dress or not, those were her eyes. The same eyes as those of *this* woman...

His eyes moved to the beauty standing to the side of Linda. It was a black and white photograph, but he imagined the young woman's dark hair to be the same rich shade of deep brown his mother's had once been.

The sketchy memory of his mother's hair from his childhood was nothing like the greasy, grey-streaked mess he'd last seen four years ago.

His eyes crawled back to the photo. His mother's hair didn't look greasy any more. Was it possible she'd cleaned her act up? Unlikely, but then, how come she looked so together, so normal, in this picture? And why would she be at *that* place if she was still a crack-addled whore?

The Violet Orchid Casino, Birmingham. The signage on the wall in the photograph clanged like cymbals in Grant's mind, grating like the ultimate hangover.

Samantha Reynold, recently reunited with her biological mother, Linda Matthews, enjoys a night out at her casino, the Violet Orchid, along with Sebastian Stoker and a family friend.

Who the bloody hell was Samantha Reynold? A *sister*? One that he'd never even heard of?

Grant's teeth dug into his lip, the pain failing to detract from his seething anger.

So, he and Marina had gone into care, whilst another sister lived the high life? A life granting her the ownership of a fucking casino? Somewhere that, by the looks of it, his mother was now also enjoying.

Why should she have that?

His brow furrowed further. So that was where Linda was? Living it up? This daughter was clearly one child Linda had wanted – or wanted *now*. No surprises there. Again, typical attitude of Linda.

Because that's who she was to Grant. *Linda*. Not *Mother*.

He slugged down his pint, his rage growing. Why should that skanky old bitch benefit?

For once in his life, Grant accepted that Mickey was right. He was interested in this. *Very* interested. As much as his father was a class one prick, he might be on to something.

Mickey watched Grant's expression closely. 'What do you think?'

Grant was just about to respond when the pub door burst open and one of the regulars rushed straight over.

'It's your sister. She's asking for you,' the man panted.

'What's happened?'

The man shrugged. 'Dunno. Something to do with her and the boyfriend.'

Grant yanked his leather jacket from the chair and shoved the newspaper cutting in his jeans. He looked at Mickey. 'Are you coming?'

'Nah. She's your sister. I don't want to interfere.' Mickey nodded to the pocket containing the clipping. 'Let me know what your plans are and make sure you keep me updated. Don't forget who gave you the heads up... I'll be expecting my cut.'

Ignoring his father, Grant rushed from the pub in the direction of Marina and Dan's flat. Marina was the only person in this godforsaken world that he cared about and if that wanker, Dan, had done anything to upset her, he'd rip the loser's head clean off.

He'd also speak to her about what he'd just learnt. Marina hated Linda Matthews as much as he did, and if *this* wasn't the reason she was planning to visit the old cow, then it soon would be...

2

Samantha Reynold pulled several sheets from the pile of packing paper and made quick work of carefully wrapping a plate. Laying it in the box on top of the others she'd wrapped, she glanced at Seb. His back to her, he made light work of stacking a heavy box of books on top of more boxes. 'I'm not sure why we're doing this,' she said. 'It could be weeks before the house completes. You know how drawn out these things can be.'

She looked around the open-plan living area of her Symphony Court apartment in dismay. Boxes now took up the majority of the space, leaving only an alleyway to walk through, and the general clutter and disarray was getting on her nerves.

Seb saw the frustration on Sam's face. Although they had muddled along for the last few months, alternating between staying at Sam's apartment and his above the Royal Peacock, they both wanted their own home. But very soon the place they both loved *would* be theirs.

'It won't be too much longer. I'll put the thumbscrews on and see if I can hurry it along.'

'That would be good.' Sam's feelings for Seb Stoker had not

diminished in any way since the first time she'd set eyes on him. Their unexpected whirlwind romance had survived the unsurmountable odds of being rivals in both the casinos and firms, but since the very public truce offered by Seb's father, at least the long-standing rivalries could no longer be used by anyone as bargaining chips against them.

She stared at the diamond and amethyst engagement ring on her finger. She never got bored of looking at it – the same way she never got bored of looking at Seb. And she never would. His touch, his voice – everything about him fuelled her drive for life, like the air around her.

Her world might have been turned upside down over the last year in ways that she'd never believed she could survive, yet alone be happy about, but now... now, she couldn't be happier.

'Have you heard from Gloria?' Seb asked. 'About how the kids are getting on?'

'I popped in last week to check on them, but I'm keeping a low profile. It's better for them that way, but they seem to have settled in well,' Sam said.

Allowing her newly discovered younger half-brother and sister time to adjust to living with a stranger and settle into a new school was the best thing all round. It also allowed them time to digest what had or hadn't occurred with their mother.

Turning away, Sam closed her eyes. The disappearance of her own biological mother, Linda Matthews, was the fly in the ointment in an otherwise great new life.

Making amends with Gloria, the woman Sam had always believed to be her mother, whilst trying to build a relationship with Linda – her *real* mother – as well as the crushing blow of discovering her own cousin had been behind the attacks on her casino and firm was bad enough to deal with. But then what happened with Liam...

Sam shook the thoughts away, but failed.

What she'd done to the man she'd counted as a friend, and what *he'd* done to warrant it, she'd struggled with. Had it not been for Seb, she didn't like to think how she might have coped...

Linda disappearing had been the crux. Now, having drawn a blank in locating the woman, Sam had no choice but to completely accept, or to be more correct, *almost* completely accept Linda had betrayed her too. Although it had been difficult.

Her real mother had made a choice not to be found and there was little Sam could do about it. Yet there was still a tiny part which hoped she was wrong. But the longer time went on, the more unlikely that was.

Guilt nagged – about those kids, about Linda, about *everything*...

Even contact with Vera, her mother's old friend, had trailed off. It was like Vera blamed *her* for keeping the door open for Linda, should the opportunity ever arise.

Seb watched Sam as he continued moving boxes. What he'd do for the power to take away the worries that plagued her. But whatever happened, he'd be by her side every step of the way.

Putting down the box, he wrapped his arms around her. 'You're thinking about *him* again, aren't you?' He brushed a tendril of her hair from her face. 'You had no choice, Sam. You had to do what you did.'

Sam nodded, her eyes downcast. 'Maybe, but...'

'Liam was going to *rape* you. He almost did!' Seb stopped his voice from turning into a roar. Every time he thought of that bastard, it fired his veins with hatred. *It should have been him who had finished Liam Taylor.* 'He betrayed the business, as well as you. And he most likely would have ended up killing you.'

He tilted Sam's face up. 'I would have done it if you hadn't. I *should* have. And no one will ever know what happened, you know that.'

Sam nodded. Seb and his brothers had covered her back and nothing would lead to her, but that wasn't the point. The whole thing ate away at her. Seb was hard as nails. He was used to that kind of stuff, but she wasn't.

She pressed her face against his chest, like the crisp clean scent of his shirt could somehow cleanse her mind.

The night she'd killed Liam, she'd made a vow that she would not allow anything like that to happen again – to *anyone*. And she'd sworn she would do whatever was required to achieve that.

There were too many men using physical strength or their emotional hold over women to abuse them or, like her own mother had experienced, push them into a place where they could be abused by *many*.

Sam wanted to rid the world of those kind of people, and it had since become her mission – the thing to focus on and keep her brain from imploding.

She was well aware she couldn't remove all of those bastards entirely, but she *could* use her clout and position in the city to clean some of the streets around here of this filth. And Seb had promised to help in every way to do just that.

But she was also acutely aware that Liam haunted Seb a lot more than he let on. Every time Liam came into their conversation, even if Seb controlled his words, by the way his jaw tightened and the flash of fire behind his eyes, she knew it ate away at him. That he hadn't been the one to snuff Liam from the world would always be a thorn in his side.

Sam swallowed, fear rising once again. She'd felt soiled and sullied from Liam's violation and had spent some time terrified Seb wouldn't or *couldn't* love her the same way. Every time he reacted with this suppressed hatred, it brought that raw fear rushing back. She couldn't bear any of this without Seb loving her.

As important as it was to deal with things in her own way, it was also equally important not to forget Seb's own demons.

But she wanted to move on in ways that didn't involve looking over her shoulder for when their luck ran out. Her future was with this man *here*.

As much as her power afforded, she would stop what had happened to Linda from happening to as many young girls as possible. Only then would she want to bring a child into this world. And she'd love nothing more than to have Seb's baby as part of cementing the next stage in their relationship.

Seeing Seb studying her, concern mixed with anger in his green eyes, Sam smiled. She jerked her head towards the messy room. 'Come on. Let's get on with this.'

Because that's all she could do – get on with things and forever be grateful this man loved her as much as she loved him.

* * *

Dan dragged his hand over his unshaven face as he ushered Grant into the flat's poky lounge.

'Where is she?' Grant barked. 'What have you done?'

Dan sighed. 'I haven't done anything! Marina just went batshit and attacked me with a bunch of fucking plates! Been bloody hysterical, she has, and all she kept saying was that she wanted you. I'm sure she's going mad.'

Grant glanced through to the kitchen, seeing a pile of smashed crockery on the floor. Not that it made much difference to the overall look of this place. The dump was a hole of the highest command and certainly nothing like Marina's previous flat that she'd spent a lot of time making nice before this tosser arrived on the scene.

Moving to an armchair, Dan handed Grant a can of warm lager.

'What you done there?' Grant asked suspiciously, scrutinising Dan's thickly bandaged hand.

Dan pointlessly tried to conceal his damaged hand down the side of the armchair. 'Oh, I... erm... I had a bit of a run-in with... erm...'

'With who?' Grant interrupted, his eyes narrowing. 'Who did you piss off this time?'

'Erm, just a small problem at a poker game,' Dan blathered, coming to the conclusion there was little point trying to hide it. 'I, erm, got my fingers chopped off...'

Grant spat a mouthful of tepid lager over the garish carpet. 'Your *fingers*?' And who was he doing these card blags with, as if he couldn't guess. 'I see Mickey came through this unscathed?' His rage built. Mickey hadn't mentioned a word about this just now in the pub. His father never got the hag, just left a trail of it in his wake.

'Mickey had the nous to leave quicker than me,' Dan shrugged, unsure why he was making excuses for the man.

'For fuck's sake,' Grant barked. 'How could you let this happen?'

'I didn't actually "let" it happen,' Dan gabbled, slurping at his can of lager. He needed way more beer, but he didn't dare venture out in case one of the many people after his ill-gotten gains pitched up.

He looked warily back to Grant. 'But it means there's people on my back, so I need to lie low for a while until this bother blows over.'

Grant looked at Dan, the penny dropping. 'Hold on. By any chance, is this why you're going to Birmingham?'

Dan grinned sheepishly, hoping he wouldn't get a clump. He had enough problems without Grant Devlin bashing him up. 'Well, when Mickey suggested we stay with your ma for a while, I thought it was a good idea.'

Standing up, Grant paced the room. *That sly old cunt!* Mickey was sending Dan and Marina to Brum in the hope that *he'd* follow to do his bidding? But that didn't change the most important thing...

He swung around, wanting to smash his beer can into Dan's face. 'So, what you're telling me is that you've put my sister at risk? If people are coming for you, then they'll be coming for *her* too!'

'I never thought it would turn out like this. I'm sure everything will be fine once we're out of here. Up north, I can put things right and start again,' Dan spluttered, ever optimistic.

Marina dragging things out wasn't helping. Dan needed to leave, and every hour was wasting time. If he had any sense, he'd have buggered off already, but Marina had a bit of money left on her credit cards which he could use. Plus, he didn't like cooking, so she'd be required until he could afford nightly curries.

There was also the small issue that if anything happened to Marina, Grant would rip his head off.

It hadn't been *his* plan to get people on his back. He'd been doing okay. It was *Mickey* who'd insisted on going to that last game. If they'd backed off for a while, like he'd suggested, then things would have been fine, he was sure of it.

Dan looked pleadingly at Grant. 'We really do need to leave, mate. I don't want anything to happen to Marina because of me.' Actually, he didn't much care, but it sounded better.

Grant shook his head. Dan was a prize bell-end; as much use as a chocolate fireguard; a useless prick and he rued the day his sister ever got involved with the moron. Removing Dan would be the only time he'd consider doing his job for free.

'I'm going to see Marina.' Without waiting for a reply, Grant walked down the hallway into the bedroom, finding his sister curled into a ball on the bed.

'Rena? It's Grant.' Perching on the edge, he reached out to stroke her hair.

'Oh, Grant...' Sitting up, Marina fell against Grant's chest because that's what he'd expect her to do. And she had to do what was expected. Lying here waiting for him to arrive, like she knew he would, had given her adequate time to think of a new course of action. Okay, given the circumstances, it was the *only* course of action, but this time, it would be to *her* advantage.

Playing to Grant's protectiveness of her, she knew he'd kill Dan for causing her grief, which would save *her* the hassle.

Dan would not be a problem for much longer, and getting away from where everybody knew them meant there would be the opportunity, but she needed her brother to help her achieve that.

Marina kept her face pressed against Grant's shirt so he couldn't see her dry eyes. 'We've got to leave. Dan said that if we don't then people will come for me...'

Grant's eyes narrowed. 'Nothing will happen to you, I promise. Leave Dan, I'll protect you.'

'But I *can't!*' Marina wailed, hiding her smile. *She was reeling him in.* 'I won't abandon Dan. He needs me and I love him.' The words almost choked her, but she had to keep the illusion going a little while longer. 'We're going to Birmingham...'

'I heard...'

Marina buried her face deeper in Grant's chest. *Come on, Grant. Do what I want, like you usually do...* 'I don't think I can face doing this on my own.'

'You don't have to,' Grant said, pulling the newspaper cutting from his pocket. 'Take a look at this. I'm coming with you and we're going to get some well-deserved payout.' *And Mickey could forget it if he thought he'd see a penny.*

Frowning, Marina looked at the cutting, remembering to sniff occasionally for effect. *Wait! What was this? A sister? And a rich one at that?* 'Our mother is now living it up? Am I seeing this correctly?'

Grant nodded. 'Looks like it, doesn't it? Whilst you're safely hidden from Dan's shitty exploits, I'll make it *my* business to get a payout from our mother's recent change of circumstances... And as much as it pains me, I'll put up with Dan too – but only for *your* sake.' The one person he would never let down was his sister.

Marina gave Grant one of her practised grateful smiles. If only she'd known this five minutes ago, she wouldn't have given him all that welly about loving Dan and not abandoning him. Dan could have stayed here to get murdered, whilst she went with Grant to get the money – the very *least* their tramp of a mother owed them. *Bollocks.*

But it was okay. She'd think of something. 'When are we leaving?'

* * *

'I've told you before to scrub it off,' Tom Bedworth roared, his nicotine-stained fingers pinching the girl's face as he dragged wet toilet paper across her delicate skin.

Scrubbing harder, he applied more pressure, his eyes gleaming, knowing the cheap scratchy paper would hurt. It served the silly little bitch right for not following instructions. He'd teach her. 'You shouldn't bite the hand that feeds you.'

Deb Banner stemmed the brimming tears and clenched her teeth. There was little point explaining she'd only put makeup on to hide the bruise across her cheekbone from that punter last night. It was Amelia's idea. Okay, she hadn't had to put eyeliner and mascara on too, but it was too tempting not to.

It made her feel better – makeup always did – but now it had backfired.

Deb's bottom lip wobbled. To make things worse, Chas would be even more annoyed with her now. He was already going off her – she *knew* he was. He'd been so attentive at first and all over her, but these past few months, he'd changed. Now she barely saw him and when she did, he spoke to her like dirt. It was breaking her heart.

Chas had assured her they had a future together – that they just needed extra money to make a life for themselves, hence her working here. But Deb was now wondering whether his change in attitude was *because* of the job. She'd only done it for him. She'd do *anything* for him.

'Are you even listening?' Tom yelled, his foul breath making Deb want to throw up.

She nodded. What she really wanted to do was punch Tom in the face, but she'd lose her job and then she really would be throwing everything away.

Tom unzipped his flies. 'Being as you're here, you might as well use up the five minutes I've got spare.'

Grabbing a fistful of Deb's brown hair, he twisted it in his hand, her yelp of pain only fuelling his desire for the buxom teenager. 'Get on with it, then,' he snarled, his spittle landing on her top lip.

Pushing her head down, he smiled as she scrabbled to her knees. 'Hurry up, otherwise I'll make your right cheekbone the same colour as your left.'

Tom gasped as Deb took him into her mouth. He placed his hand securely on the top of her head as she worked. 'Don't think I didn't notice that bruise. I heard you'd pissed one of your punters off. Don't be making that a habit, eh?'

Deb forced herself to think of something else other than the taste and feel of this bastard. She flitted between bursting into tears of self-loathing, frustration and pure unbridled rage.

She'd thought several times, actually, more like several *thousand* times, about walking out. Just walking out of the door past everyone, getting on the bus and going back to Frankley.

But how could she? She couldn't return to her father's, cap in hand, proving she'd failed in her quest to better herself, like she'd promised when, taking his coat, she'd walked out of his house and his life six months ago.

And worse than that, she didn't want to lose Chas. Even though he didn't seem to like her much any more, he was all she'd got left.

Deb gagged as Tom pushed himself further down her throat. Eyes watering, she steadied herself. She had to do what Tom said. The man terrified her. She had to obey him and keep things sweet, otherwise she might end up like that woman in the attic – the one who everyone knew was there, but no one was allowed to mention.

3

THREE DAYS LATER

Grant chucked his bag on the bed in the room down the hallway from Marina and Dan's and then walked to the window, peering through the yellowing net curtains through the grubby glass onto Bearwood High Street below.

Three days was all he'd had to sort a place to stay before they'd left Clapham.

He'd taken the lease on this two-bed flat above the chip shop for himself, building on the idea that Marina and Dan could shoehorn their way into Linda's flat. It would be easier to get info from inside, but discovering no trace of Linda at her last known address had put a spanner in the works. He might have known his father hadn't got up-to-date information.

He didn't mind sharing a place with his sister, but Dan?

Grant's mouth screwed into a scowl as people queued for the chip shop below, the smell of grease clinging to every fibre of the flat. Still, what did he expect? The place was cheap and staying in Birmingham wouldn't be a long-term thing.

Hearing clattering from the small kitchen, Grant made his way down the hall, a smile on his face. None of this was his sister's fault. 'Settling in okay?'

'I'm looking for mugs,' Marina said. 'Furnished this may be, but they haven't been overly generous with their fixtures and fittings, have they?'

Grant looked around the shithole which constituted a kitchen. There hadn't been a whole host of places to choose from with immediate availability. Especially at the price he was willing to pay.

'Where do you suppose Linda's gone?' Marina asked.

'No idea,' Grant shrugged. 'But you can't be that surprised?'

Marina reached to the back of the cupboard and pulled out two cracked cups, one with something unsavoury stuck to the side of it. Her nose wrinkled with distaste. 'She was living in the same place the last time we saw her.'

'Yes, but that was four years ago now, remember?' Grant added. It wasn't like he'd forget – even though he'd dearly love to. 'You heard what that bloke said when we went round earlier.'

Marina frowned. 'If what he said is correct and she hasn't been seen for six months, I wonder if I can apply for her flat? Council flats go to family, don't they?'

Grant shrugged. 'Not sure, but I expect you'd need her consent.' He raised his eyebrows. 'And we all know that's unlikely.'

Marina nodded. 'Maybe I'll try again another day. You never know...'

Grant did. *He knew*. Wherever she was, Linda Matthews would be far too busy with herself to help anyone else.

Marina's eyes narrowed. 'Linda *owes* us, Grant. We've always said that and now we've got that chance. She must be rolling in it now, courtesy of this "sister".'

Grant nodded. *Didn't he just know it*. It would have been simpler with Marina in situ at Linda's to enable him to work out how to play it, but now she'd disappeared. *Again...*

'At least we've got this place,' he said, somewhat bitterly.

'But this is yours. You don't want us under your feet.'

'It's fine,' Grant lied. *You – yes, Dan – no.* 'Stay as long as you want. Don't worry. Things will come good.'

Marina smiled coldly. 'At least I've got something to aim for now.' And Grant didn't need to know exactly everything that involved just yet. Whilst her brother still believed she had something akin to a soul, then she'd use that to her advantage.

'Where's Dan?'

'Out getting his bearings.'

Grant's teeth grated. *Course he was...* Dan would be in the pub down the bottom of the road. And that's where he was going. Not to the same pub – the less time he was around that loser, the better.

Now Marina had settled in, and so far there was no suggestion that Dickhead Dan's baggage had followed him, it was time to put the feelers out. And to do that, he needed to keep an ear to the ground. Now they were in exactly the right location, he could.

And the best places to do that were boozers.

Either way, they would reap some long-awaited rewards.

Amelia Smith pushed her way along Broad Street, her bulky frame paying for the hike from the bus station. If she hadn't been sidetracked she'd have been alert enough to get off at the right bloody stop, rather than having to drag herself the whole way from the terminal up here. Stupid cow that she was.

It wouldn't have hurt Tom to put his hand in his pocket for once and fork out for a taxi. It was bloody freezing out here.

Shivering, she pulled her thin coat around her and continued towards the Magic Bean.

Amelia pulled open the door of the late-night café, the steamed-up front windows giving the impression that it would be warm inside. Warmer than outside, anyhow.

Making her way to the counter, she glanced around the room and forced herself to smile at the sullen-looking woman eyeing her with suspicion. 'Tea, please.'

What she really wanted was a large vodka, but, by the looks of it, this place didn't serve anything like that. She glanced at the menu offering the usual: sausage and chips, egg and chips...

Her stomach rumbled. She was starving, but she wasn't here to eat. She nodded at an empty table. 'I'll be over there.'

'Take it yourself,' the woman snapped, plonking the mug of tea next to the till.

Charming, Amelia thought, reluctantly handing over a fiver, whilst calculating how much change she should get. If this miserable cow ripped her off, then she'd abandon all ideas of scouting and instead smash this old bitch in her fucking teeth.

Pocketing the change, Amelia moved to a table near the window. She'd have preferred to sit at the back near the bubbling tea urn where it was warmer, but that wouldn't afford her a view. And a view was what was needed.

Surreptitiously glancing around, she sipped the steaming tea and pulled her cigarettes from her coat pocket. There were plenty of young girls here and would be more as the evening progressed.

She knew exactly the type required and there were some here who fitted that bill.

Having exhausted the haunts down by the bus station, the decision to come to Broad Street was a bit of a gamble. The area was well known for its nightlife, but it was *expensive* nightlife; casinos, posh hotels, wine bars and upmarket clubs – not the usual area to find girls willing to ply their wares in a place like Tom Bedworth's Aurora. But lately there were lots of wannabes here – youngsters trying their luck with bagging a rich, nice-looking yuppie. But would those girls be interested in the opportunity she was offering?

Her eyes fell to a pair of young girls, their tight miniskirts no match for the temperature outside, but young enough to run with the 'beauty is pain' mentality.

Amelia's eyes then moved to the illuminated frontage and tempting opulence of the casino opposite. *The Royal Peacock*. A swish place, that. Or so she'd heard. It wasn't like she'd stepped through the door. She hardly passed decent enough to get into a Wimpy these days.

She looked down at her grubby jeans and tracksuit top underneath her thin coat. At least she wasn't working the streets any more.

Her mouth curled into a half-smile and she took another drag of her cigarette. Her promotion at the Aurora meant although she wasn't making huge amounts by running the girls and dealing with Tom's latest enterprise, at least she wasn't shagging cretins.

And bringing in the youngsters was admittedly turning over a steady coin. And the younger the better, so Tom said.

Personally, Amelia felt she should have received more kudos for her part in it. Bringing her two daughters on board at the Aurora was partly what had spawned the idea in Tom's head in the first place, but she drew the line at bringing in girls younger than sixteen. Her lips pursed. It wasn't right, was it?

At least she'd insisted *her* daughters wait until they'd turned sixteen.

People would have looked down their noses at her for allowing that, but they couldn't now her girls had come of age. No, she'd done everything a good mother should.

Amelia moved her concentration back to the two girls chain-smoking at the opposite table and tried to picture how young they'd pass for once their slap was sandblasted off. If her estimation was correct, they'd easily pass for fifteen.

Stubbing out her cigarette, Amelia wandered over. 'Hey, girls. Interested in making some decent money?'

The two teenagers made no effort to hide their contempt and one of the girls raised her eyebrows theatrically, whilst the other dissolved in a fit of giggles. 'Is she talking to us?'

'How can you tell it's a she?'

Amelia stiffened. Her immediate reaction was to punch the silly little slappers in the face, but Tom was getting twitchy and she needed to keep her position secure. Swallowing her irritation, she smiled. 'Yeah, very funny. I'm merely asking if you're interested in some work?'

'What sort of work?'

'Oh, you know...' Amelia continued, lowering her voice. 'Let's just say, I can help you cash in. Pretty girls like you know what men are like. We have a good place with...'

'If you're an example of how well it's going, I think we'll give it a miss!' the girl laughed.

The second girl stood up. 'Fuck off, you old tart. Touting your brothel or whatever it is ain't good when you look like a fat crack whore!'

Amelia's anger gave way to humiliation and before she could question her actions, she bolted from the café into the night.

4

'I'm seeing more and more of them every bloody day,' Andrew Stoker grumbled. 'It's spreading like wildfire that here is a good place to get picked up. That's not the impression we want to give.'

'Hookers will always be part of the scene,' Seb said. 'You know that.'

'Decent, classy ones, yeah, but not skanks!'

'Interesting you have such a detailed knowledge...' Seb raised an eyebrow.

'Oh, fuck off!' Andrew chucked a newspaper in his brother's direction. 'Security said there's hosts of them attempting entry lately. We can't have that.'

Seb frowned. Joking aside, that was true. It was no secret classy escorts sometimes accompanied their male companions, but tenner-a-go hookers lurking about would put the customers off. They had an elite clientele at the Royal Peacock, and he wanted to keep it that way. And there was also Sam's feelings on that subject to consider... 'If these women are hanging around outside, then we'll get some of the boys to dissuade them.'

He fixed his brother with a look. 'I don't want this mentioned to

Sam if we can help it. You know the subject's a sore point.'

Andrew nodded. 'I know Sam associates what happened to her mother as a young girl with what led to the poor cow's downfall. Don't worry, we'll do things subtly.'

'Good.' Seb leant back in his office chair. Things were going well. The Peacock's takings had remained sky high for months, the gun deals were running like clockwork, his relationship with his parents and brothers was back to normal and there had been no grief with territories.

And if all of that wasn't good enough, his relationship with Sam had gone from strength to strength. He hadn't thought it was possible to be genuinely happy, yet he was. And it was good. *More* than good.

There was only one problem and it was something which had been niggling for quite some time. He'd put it to the back of his mind, hoping a solution would materialise, but nothing had and it was time to do something about it.

Seb frowned. 'These gun deals...'

'That side of things is flying, as you know. The one due out tomorrow night is a huge one – one of the biggest yet!'

'Yep, and coupled with the extra takings from the poker tournaments, we're coining it in.'

Andrew looked at his brother with concern. 'That's good, isn't it? What's the issue?'

'The same one we've touched upon before, but now things are getting desperate. The money is fucking piling up and with no route of offloading it at the moment, it will cause big problems.' Seb forced a smile. 'I never thought I'd moan about having too much brass, but we need to find a way to spend without leaving a paper trail and we're out of options at the moment. Even the second safe at the lockup is full.'

He'd had several meetings with the firm's bean counter,

Fletcher, and at present, there was no way of safely laundering the cash. The only available way right now was to lose it forever and take the loss. That was not something that could be considered.

Andrew looked thoughtful. 'You heard what Fletcher said – we can shift it soon. A few more months, that's all.'

Seb frowned. Fletcher was a top-quality accountant who'd successfully 'lost' millions on paper over the years, but when all the usual routes of laundering the cash were saturated, they had to sit tight. 'I get that, but all that cash sitting in the safes is a beacon. If it gets found, we'd be looking at a long stretch.'

'You've probably already thought of this, but what about the house?' Andrew suggested.

'The house?'

'The one you're buying with Sam. Could you not make it a cash purchase? Explain to Sam that it's temporary...' Andrew raised his eyebrows. 'She knows the score.'

Seb listened with interest. He hadn't thought of that. But Andrew was wrong on one thing. He hadn't mentioned anything about the money backlog to Sam.

Andrew stood up. 'I'm off to check the prep for tonight's poker tournament, but think about using the house purchase.'

Andrew left the office and Seb leant back in his chair. *Andrew could be on to something.* Funding the house would help immensely with offloading a chunk of money whilst still retaining it via property. But how would he explain the reasoning behind this to Sam without making her worry? Buying the house together via 'normal' means was important to her – some semblance in their otherwise unusual world.

But the idea *was* workable.

Feeling somewhat relieved, Seb grinned. Another poker tournament on tonight as well?

Running alternate tournaments between the Peacock and the

Orchid had been Neil's idea and it was working surprisingly well. Having the family working together towards the same aim and with no hostility between his firm and the Reynolds, things couldn't be better.

Apart from moving into that house and making Sam his wife.

Not believing himself capable of loving anyone like he did her, it had been both a shock and a surprise. But one, now he'd experienced it, he wasn't letting go of.

And God forbid *anything* that threatened that.

This included keeping his nose clean. For the first time ever, there was something more than underhand dealing available. Although he'd never be straight, there was nothing to say he couldn't be as legit as a firm like his allowed.

And that he intended to aim for.

* * *

Sam frowned at the number displaying on her desk phone. She didn't recognise it. It wasn't one of the internal lines. 'Yes?' she snapped.

'What sort of a greeting is that?'

Hearing Seb's distinctive gravelly voice, Sam smiled. Just the sound of the man who sent every single one of her nerve endings alight with desire made her heart soar. 'You're ringing me from that bloody mobile again, aren't you?' she laughed. 'Every time it catches me out!' Being constantly on guard never left her. And nor should it.

She'd learnt a lot over the past few months. No longer did she shy away from the unsavoury side of things businesses like hers brought. By necessity, she'd grown into it, accepting things had to be done in ways that previously horrified her.

Trust was a rare and valuable commodity, so she'd had no

choice but to harden up. Or drown.

And drowning was not an option.

Take no shit, but be fair, and having Seb by her side made it bearable.

Seb made *everything* bearable. He was the voice of reason when she doubted herself or when she had a wobble. He was a living, breathing reminder that she had someone she trusted implicitly and someone who she now believed loved her as much as she did him.

But his unexpected call caused the age-old fear to raise its ugly head. 'Is everything all right?'

'Yeah, course! I just wanted to remind you that Neil's overseeing the poker tonight, so I'll expect you to be waiting when I get back – minus your clothes...'

Sam laughed, her cheeks burning even though Kevin sitting opposite was not party to the conversation. 'If you sort out those boxes!'

'I'll make sure of that!'

Sam grinned as the call disconnected, imagining the half-smile on Seb's lips. He would, too. And she couldn't wait. She couldn't wait to move, either. Just thinking about the home they were purchasing made her want to squeal with happiness.

When they'd first looked around the place, she'd earmarked one of the four reception rooms in particular as her favourite. She was enthralled by its original wood panelling and wall-mounted oil lamps – a beautiful and lasting reminder of the house's original character. She'd imagined how they would decorate and had bored Seb rigid, animatedly explaining in vivid detail the way she imagined it to look: the sofas with polished rounded feet and blue velvet upholstery, the scalloped backrest festooned with buttoned cushions, grouped around the centrepiece of the large room – the fireplace – its stunning painted tiles setting off the polished mahogany overmantel and wrought-iron grate. Thick velvet drapes would hang at the large window overlooking the mature garden, the afternoon sun lighting the room like magic.

And as for what would be the master bedroom, well, she had ideas for that too and...

'Have you seen this?' Kevin Stanton pushed this morning's copy of the *Mail* towards Sam, his deep-set eyes studying her intently.

Broken from her thoughts, Sam took the paper and stared at the photograph of the double-fronted detached house. *Their new house...*

Casino Couple Move to Luxurious Harborne Pad

Sebastian Stoker and Samantha Reynold, the owners of two of Birmingham's prestigious casinos, are set to shortly complete on this beautiful house.

Residents of Chase Road in Harborne, an elite and much sought-after area, will be honoured to have this well-known couple, soon to be married, as their new neighbours.

The beautiful Victorian house boasts eight bedrooms, four reception rooms, a half-acre garden, plus a large cellar converted into a gym. It's a fitting home for Seb and Sam – the perfect place for entertaining. And from the number of bedrooms, could this hint at plans to extend their family?

We at the Mail will keep you updated with further developments about our city's most glamorous couple.

'How the hell did they get wind of this?' Sam gasped. 'For God's sake! I was given assurance from the estate agents this wouldn't be made public!'

Kevin raised his eyebrows. 'Maybe it wasn't them? You know

how the press hang around. Perhaps they put two and two together and made five?'

'Then they were bloody right!' Sam snapped, scraping her fingers through her wavy hair. 'Shit, Kev, what sort of security risk is this?'

Kevin shrugged. 'It was only a matter of time before people found out.'

'I know, but we're not even there yet and they've all but given out our address!' Sam cried.

'The rest of what they said?' Kevin raised an eyebrow. 'Any truth in that? You're not, are you?'

'No!' Sam choked. 'For fuck's sake, will it get to the point where I have to publish my menstrual cycle every month to keep speculation at bay?'

She hated this. Did this mean it was too much of a risk to move?

Her jaw clenched. No. She wasn't changing her plans. She was moving to that beautiful house with the man she loved and no one would stop her.

* * *

Tom stared at Amelia, his irritation growing. 'You're telling me you're no longer willing to get your fat arse on the lookout for new flesh?' He sluiced whisky into his glass, then slammed the bottle onto his desk.

'I'm suggesting it might be better to have someone younger.' Amelia wasn't about to admit the episode in that café last night had got to her.

A sneer spread over Tom's face. 'Ah, I get it. Why didn't you just say you're too past it for anyone to take seriously?'

Embarrassment flooded Amelia's cheeks. 'I'm not past

anything!' she spluttered. 'I'm merely seeing it through a teenager's eyes.'

'You'd have a fucking job!' Tom chuckled, thoroughly enjoying himself. 'Who do you suggest, if not you?'

'What about Deb?' Chas suggested. He'd make a few extra quid if he got Deb onto this. 'I could accompany her to be on hand – at a distance, of course?'

Tom frowned and thought for a moment. Deb was more switched on than the majority of the girls. Thick as shit, half of them.

'I was thinking of Tina,' Amelia interrupted, shooting a glare at her nephew. 'She knows the ropes better than Deb.'

'No offence, love, but Tina isn't as nice looking and no matter what you dress her in, she looks fucking cheap. We don't want to come over as a doss hole,' Tom said.

Chas swallowed the urge to laugh. *What did Tom think the Aurora was?* 'Tom's right, Auntie. By hitting Broad Street, whoever does the approaching needs to look the part.'

'Broad Street?' Tom spat out a mouthful of whisky. 'Since when?' The whole point of lying low and binning off his crack dealing these last few months was to keep out of the searchlights. He hardly wanted to parade around outside the Stokers' and Reynolds' bloody headquarters openly looking for girls!

'We've brought in several girls from Digbeth already, so I've exhausted the possibilities there for the time being.' Amelia shrugged. 'Now you're concentrating on the bright young things, a lot of the youngsters congregate around the hip areas, of which Broad Street is one. What's the problem there anyway?'

'Nothing,' Tom said quickly. He hadn't divulged his business to *anyone* and it would stay that way too. 'I thought only the posh lot went there.'

'It's the place to be,' Amelia insisted.

'So, shall we give Deb a go at trying her hand?' Chas asked.

'Or Tina?' Amelia pushed. As much as Chas was family, she was beginning to rue the day she'd extended her kindness to her nephew. She hadn't got him a bloody job here so he could encroach on everything she'd lined up for herself and her daughters. He could fuck off if that was his plan.

Tom finished the remains of his whisky. 'We'll go with Deb. She'll have to put her slap back on, though.' He skimmed down the list of bookings and slapped Chas on the back. 'You did well with her, but as she's the favourite at the moment, I could do without giving her the night off. However, we have to speculate to accumulate.'

'Understood.' Chas stood up. 'I'll go and brief her.'

'No, I'll do that,' Tom said. That would give him another go with the girl whilst reminding her how grateful she should be for this additional responsibility. 'But in the meantime...' He jerked his head towards the safe. 'Isn't it time you medicated the woman upstairs, Amelia?'

Amelia nodded, her teeth clenched. Working with Tom was deteriorating. He'd started speaking to her like shit and treating her like a skivvy. She needed a rapid rethink if she wanted her own situation to be as viable as it had started.

Moving to the safe, she reluctantly pulled out a bag of heroin and crack, plus the kit needed to cook it.

She was getting heartily tired of Tom's insistence she dose that woman up to the eyeballs. Six months now that woman had been in the attic, yet not a word of explanation had been offered as to who she was and why she was the only one afforded the luxury of free gear, yet the only one not permitted to leave the confines of her room.

Amelia didn't like it. It wasn't right, but what could she do if she wanted to keep her job?

5

'I knew it!' Andrew muttered, putting the phone down. 'I had the feeling something would kick off.'

Halfway out of the office he shared with his brother, Neil paused, not liking the scowl on his twin's face. 'What's up?'

'The croupier on table sixteen suspected one of the punters was being fly and flagged it up with security. Daz is holding them in the pen.'

Neil kept pace with Andrew as he strode along the corridor and opened the door leading to the steps that led to the basement. The metal stairs were a vivid contrast to the plush carpet covering all the other staircases in the Peacock, but these ones didn't need to be dressed like the rest of the place. No customers came this way, unless they were in the shit. And, by the sounds of it, these ones were. 'How many of them are there?'

'Just two, as far as I can gather.'

Neil inwardly sighed. Andrew's face meant business. There was a deep-seated hatred for table cheats – something their father had stamped out – and it wasn't good to think it might become rife once more.

Andrew entered the small, sparsely furnished room, empty except for a few wooden chairs and a strip light fixed to the ceiling. 'Are these them?'

He glanced at Daz. As head of casino security, Daz Ellis was a beast of a man – not the sort anyone would wish to be on the wrong side of. A valued member of the Stoker firm, he did a sterling job of keeping the arseholes away.

Daz poked the seated man in the back of the head with his thick finger. 'The croupier caught this geezer sliding his own card into his hand.'

'I was doing no such thing!' the man barked, his pointed chin jutting out in defiance. 'Your croupier needs training if she believes that to be the case.'

Grabbing the slim man around the throat, Andrew lifted him off the chair. 'All of our croupiers are fully trained, so be careful what you insinuate.' His green eyes scorched the man's face, then he turned his attention back to Daz. 'Has he been searched?'

'Not yet.'

Andrew nodded. Security dealt with most aggro themselves, short of fraud. *That*, the Stokers personally dealt with. He looked the well-dressed man up and down in contempt. 'Turn your pockets out.'

'I beg your pardon?' the man spluttered, his face a picture of indignation. 'How dare you drag me into this cell-like room and treat me like a common criminal and th...'

'Shut the fuck up!' Andrew slammed the man against the wall. They had a reputation to uphold. The Peacock was serious business with serious players, not a shithole for card sharks.

'This room's like a cell because it doubles up as one for wankers like you.' His teeth glinted in the harsh glare of the fluorescent strip light. 'Plus, it's soundproofed...'

'Wait, you...'

'He said shut it!' Neil shoved his hands deep into the man's trouser pockets, finding nothing apart from money and a packet of cigarettes.

Andrew spun the man around, crushing his face against the wall and pulled his suit jacket from his slightly built frame. Chucking the jacket to Neil, he glanced at the man's female companion as she casually inspected her long fingernails. 'You don't appear too bothered about your boyfriend, love,' he smiled. 'I take it he *is* your boyfriend?'

The woman shrugged, not looking up.

'I thought as much,' Andrew sneered. 'I can tell them a mile off.' He jerked his head at Daz. 'Get this hooker out of here. Exit her out the back.'

Lumbering his massive frame across the room, Daz effortlessly lifted the woman from the chair, her stiletto heels scraping as she scrabbled to keep contact with the floor.

The man, still squashed against the wall, sagged in defeat as the secret pocket in the lining of his suit jacket was ripped open.

'Yep, here they are.' Neil threw a handful of playing cards onto the wooden table.

Andrew forced the man's head within inches of the cards. 'What do we have here? Ace of Spades, King of Clubs, Queen of... yeah, here... Queen of Hearts and oh, what a surprise – another ace...'

He held a card up to the light, scrutinising it. 'Not a bad replica of our embossed deck, mate, but not *that* good.' He then grabbed the money retrieved from the man's trouser pockets. 'This will be returned to our till.'

The man's muffled protests were ignored as Andrew smashed him cleanly in the jaw with a right hook.

Flying across the room, the man landed in a heap on the floor. 'You're lucky I'm in a good mood, otherwise you would have lost your fucking hands.' Andrew smiled nastily. 'Try this again *anywhere* around here and I'll make sure you do.'

Wiping his hands, Andrew left the room with Neil, leaving Daz to expel the man from the building on his return. 'For God's sake,' he muttered. 'It's all very well doing these tournaments, but I warned you waiving membership for these occasions might mean an influx of tossers. If this keeps happening, then I'll vote it's knocked on the head. I'm not having sharks and street hookers in here. I'll brief the staff on what to look for and let Seb know what's gone on.'

Neil nodded, disappointment bubbling. He'd wanted the tournaments to be successful. It had been the first idea he'd had for the business. He'd been sure it was a winner, but now it looked like he might have been wrong.

* * *

Seb wrapped his arms around Sam's slim waist from behind, planting his lips along the soft skin of her shoulder.

He could spend every second of every day with his nose pressed against her skin, smelling the gorgeous scent which primed him every time. Like an addict, he could never get enough.

He turned her around. 'For the final time, don't let what was printed bother you. Everyone will know where we live sooner rather than later, so why does it matter? Let them get on with it.'

'I just hate having no privacy,' Sam moaned. 'I want my personal life to be just that – *private*. Like normal people.'

Seb laughed. 'But that's just it. Whatever "normal" is, that's not us!'

Sam pursed her lips. *Didn't she know it.* Her life was anything but bog-standard, but that didn't mean she had to like *this*. 'We're not film stars, so why the hell should we not have privacy?'

Seb shrugged. 'Part and parcel. It's been like this my whole life. I forget you're not as used to this as me.'

Sam let Seb top up her wine. It was true. Although her father had regularly featured in the paper, sponsored various businesses and opened places with scissors and ribbons, as far as she could recall, there wasn't a single time when their home life or family privacy had been intruded upon. The only time she'd *ever* had press attention was during the yearly parties her parents threw for her birthday.

But that had all changed. Since taking over the running of the Violet Orchid, she'd been public property, with every facet of her life up for public consumption. From the very public revelation of her real birth mother, photographing her in the club, speculating over everything, to now printing an article about their new home? It was all too much.

Seb pulled Sam back into his arms. 'We're about to complete on the house we both want, so don't let a story in the *Mail* ruin that.' He nodded at the pile of boxes stacked in just about every available space. 'Besides, I'm not living in this chaos any longer than necessary.' He pressed his lips to hers. 'Don't let it get to you. It means nothing.'

Sam smiled weakly. Seb was right, but even so, it *did* get to her.

'We'll play them at their own game,' Seb added, his eyes sparkling. 'We'll put them in a position where there will be no need for speculation or digging around for titbits.'

Sam frowned. 'How do you mean?'

'The first thing we'll do once we complete is throw a house-warming party. We'll invite everyone, *including* the press,' Seb grinned. '*That* way, the nosy bastards can get a good look at whatever they want for themselves and then they can fuck off. Ta-dah!'

Sam couldn't help but laugh as Seb picked up his ringing mobile. Whatever the issue, he had the ability to somehow make it right. Another reason why she loved this man like no other.

6

Chas rolled off Deb, the movement a good excuse to glance at his watch. There was no doubt she was tasty and when he'd set his sights on her months ago in Frankley, it was because he wanted in at the place his Aunt Amelia worked at. He knew someone like Deb would be just the ticket, but he hadn't counted on it being so all-consuming.

His eyes narrowed. The girl was pathetic. Considering she had blokes crawling all over her the entire day and night, he'd have thought she wouldn't be quite so desperate. But it wasn't any old bloke she wanted. It was just *him*.

It was doing his head in.

Once he'd got her at the Aurora, that should have been the end of it, but she insisted on clinging to the belief they were together. It was ridiculous, but he had to play along. He didn't want anything jeopardising his position.

'What do you think of the extra work?' Chas propped himself up on his elbows. It was important to pretend her opinion was important, rather than let on everything had already been decided.

Deb pouted her full lips. 'I don't know... I mean, I'm not sure I want to convince other girls to work here.'

Chas dug his nails into his palms. 'Why not? I thought you wanted to make things work between us?'

Deb sat up, wide-eyed. 'I *do*! I just meant, well, the job isn't how you said it would be... How *I* thought it would be and...'

'For fuck's sake!' Chas barked, getting out of bed. 'Perhaps you don't want to make things work between us?'

'I *do*,' Deb pleaded. 'I just worry that you're going off me... That these men...'

'We all have to make sacrifices,' Chas lied, scrutinising Deb with cold eyes.

'Okay, tell me what I need to do,' Deb said hollowly. Chas had been so attentive – so *nice* at the start, but now...

He was all she'd got. He'd said they had a future together, so whether she was comfortable about this latest thing or not was irrelevant. If it made him happy and made things better, then she'd do anything.

* * *

Dan eyed Marina as he shovelled forkfuls of Pot Noodle into his mouth. 'You're quiet.' Hitting a clump of dry noodles and rock-hard powdery bits, he glared into the plastic pot. This hadn't even been stirred properly. He needed something to soak up the collection of pints he'd put away this afternoon down the Pack Horse and this thing was in no way hitting the sides.

Marina scrubbed at stubborn clods of something nameless clinging to the single kitchen worktop. 'I've a lot on my mind.'

'It's not money again, is it?' Dan muttered. 'I told you I'm working on that.' *And he was.* He'd learnt lots from the folks down the pub. The

Brummies weren't suspicious like the Londoners. This lot up here had accepted him into the fold with open arms. It was the perfect playground to coin it in. Right friendly and everything. So friendly, he'd been invited to a sit-down tomorrow night at the Whistling Pig.

'Being as you mentioned it, what *are* you planning on doing for money?' Marina knew what *she* was planning, but she wasn't telling him.

Dan rolled his eyes, his concentration fixated on the dry Pot Noodle. *Here we go.* 'As it happens, I've been invited to a game tomorrow.'

Marina slammed her scourer down. 'Are you serious? We came up here to get away from people you'd ripped off, now you're doing it again?'

Dan flapped his one intact hand. 'It's just a game. Nothing else.' *But it would be... soon.* Because as well as checking out the places holding under the counter sit-downs, he'd also learnt of the big places where major money exchanged hands. To get into those, he needed a decent amount of running capital and tomorrow's game was a step closer to that. Like Mickey said – *'work your way into new opportunities'.*

And *this* time, Dan had a good feeling about it.

Wandering into the kitchen, Grant overheard the tail end of the conversation. He looked at Dan with disdain. 'You're not trying your shit in the big casinos, are you?'

'No,' Dan laughed. 'Not yet, anyway.'

'Well, do us all a favour. When or *if* you go down that road, pick any of them, apart from the Violet Orchid.'

A clump of noodles dropped from Dan's fork as it hovered halfway to his mouth. 'Why?'

'Because I'm planning to get a job there and I wouldn't want to have to break your fucking legs, would I?' Except Grant would *love* to break Dan's legs. One at a time. Slowly and very painfully. Grant winked at Marina.

Dan didn't need to know that his and Marina's new sister owned the Violet Orchid.

Neither would he mention that he'd been watching some of the security leaving of an evening and now knew *exactly* who to approach for a job.

* * *

'I thought it would be easier to pop in rather than relay this over the phone.' Seb took a seat in Sam's office, then helped himself to a whisky from the decanter.

'I've just had a meeting with Andrew, Neil and security. There was an instance of sharking last night, so we need a plan that both clubs operate. We also have another problem which seems to be growing...'

He looked to Kevin chewing the end of his pen and then to Sam. *He had to level with her.* 'Hookers... and I don't mean escorts, I mean *hookers!*'

'We don't have a problem with that here,' Sam snapped. 'And I don't intend for there to be one either!' She wasn't having people in her casino whose sole purpose was to take advantage of women. *Or in the vicinity. People like Liam... People of the ilk who had been party to ruining her mother's life...*

Realising she'd reacted sharply, she squeezed Seb's hand. She didn't want him to know how much some things still gnawed away at her. Him being unable to be transparent, regardless of his good intentions, would be the worst. 'What I mean is that it's important to keep things running as they are now, without anything altering it.'

Seb concealed his concern. He wouldn't have Sam upset. 'It will be fine as long as we nip it in the bud.'

'When did these street hookers start coming into the Peacock?' Kevin asked.

'It's not so much a problem *in* the Peacock, although the woman accompanying the card shark last night was one, but they're congregating outside in the general area,' Seb explained. 'It's easy enough to stop them from entering the casino. We just pull the non-member poker nights.'

'But the tournaments we've had so far have worked really well,' Sam cried. 'I don't want to stop those unless we have to.'

Seb knocked back his whisky and poured another. 'We've already briefed our staff on what to look out for so they can flag these people up before they get as far as a table. That and put more security on. Our teams will move the women outside as well,' Seb explained. 'I suggest you do the same.'

'I'll get onto that now.' Kevin stood up.

'Thanks, Kev,' Sam smiled as he left the office.

The minute the door closed, Seb pulled Sam onto his lap. 'By the way, I had a call from the estate agent. We're due to complete tomorrow.'

Sam squealed with delight, the worry over Seb's other news temporarily forgotten.

7

'What happened there?' Grant peered through the windows of the Ring O Bells at the cordoned-off site opposite. Each time the traffic queuing for the Horsefair roundabout cleared, it exposed the demolished building, leaving a gap in the closely packed surroundings.

He didn't actually care about the place, but it was a good excuse to get into a conversation. And that was what he needed.

He stubbed his cigarette out, then swivelled around to face the men sitting on the adjacent bench seat.

This was the pair who had exited the back of the Violet Orchid on the occasions he'd kept watch. They knew what went on around here because they looked like him – men who did a certain kind of job for a living. *After all, it took one to know one...*

A man with cold grey eyes scrutinised Grant. 'What's it to you?'

Grant shrugged. 'Nothing. Just wondered.'

'You're not from round here?'

Brilliant analysis, Grant thought, hearing that question for the hundredth time over the past couple of days. 'I'm up from London.'

'Passing through?'

Grant knew they were weighing him up. That was okay. He'd got them talking and in turn, they had to suss him out. He'd be doing exactly the same thing in their position. He wasn't in their position, but he *had* been, and he would be again. He was counting on it.

He slugged down the rest of his pint. 'I've just moved here. At least for the time being. I'm between jobs, but that happens, being freelance. I'm Trevor, by the way.' Grant stuck his hand out as the two men exchanged glances.

'I'm Craig and this,' Craig jerked his head, 'is Stu. Freelance, you say? What is it you do?'

Grant sucked his bottom lip and winked. He knew how to play it. 'This and that. Nothing I can mention, if you get my drift? I've worked for a couple of London firms and several private companies...' That was all he needed to say. They knew what he did for his money, the same way as he knew what *they* did for theirs. Like an invisible tattoo, it glowed behind the eyes if one knew where to look. *The unspoken badge of membership.*

Picking up his empty glass, Grant gestured towards the bar. 'Pint?'

Receiving nods, he walked away, giving the men the chance for an ad hoc discussion, undertaken with gestures and mannerisms rather than words, because walls frequently had ears.

He'd got nothing to lose by making himself quietly available, but *everything* to lose if things stopped here.

Grant pulled cash out of his pocket and placed it on the wet beer towel. One good thing about not being in London was the cost of beer. He got three pints up here for the price of one back home.

Grouping the drinks, he picked his way back to the table. His next move was to steer away from questions aimed at him. He looked back to the building site. 'So, what happened?'

Stu raised an eyebrow. 'It was reported as an electrical fire.'

'Hmm, I find there's a lot of those sometimes,' Grant grinned. Picking up his pint, he casually slurped at it.

They knew.

He'd leave it there and wait for an in, because he'd get one. Maybe not right now, but very shortly.

* * *

Taking a deep breath, Marina walked around the side of the vast building, glancing behind her as she went. Her brother was scouting for an in to the Orchid again tonight and she didn't want to bump into him because then she'd have to explain herself and she didn't want to do that – primarily because she hadn't worked out exactly what she was going to do just yet.

Dan wasn't an issue – he'd be at that pub and wouldn't know or care where she was. No one would be back for hours.

Grant doing the leg work of finding out where Linda was hiding was all very well, but as she'd been so stupid to make out that she was sticking by Dan, she couldn't just casually drop it into the conversation that she wanted him to get rid of the man.

Aside from not wanting to be bludgeoned to death in her bed because of Dan's debts, Marina wanted him out of her life for *good* and waiting at the bus stop this morning, listening to teenagers chatting, gave her an idea of how she could do just that...

She looked up at the looming hulk of the building, hearing the muffled buzz and strange vibration. It wasn't like she was going inside. From what she'd heard about the Dome, at twenty-seven, she was *far* too old.

Marina hurried into the shadows. There should be a couple of dealers hanging around somewhere.

Sensing people she couldn't see, an unwanted fluttering of

anxiety ran over her. Taking a deep breath, she sat on a low wall and looked around the dimly lit area, aiming to appear relaxed.

'After some Molly?'

Marina's head shot up. She stared at the man, his hands digging deep into a pair of dark tracksuit bottoms, the hood of his top concealing most of his face.

'What else have you got?' Ecstasy was too good for Dan. He'd enjoy it too much and, unless she was ultra-lucky, it wouldn't kill him either. No, she needed something that would work. *Big time.* 'I'm looking to zone out completely.'

'Some brown?'

Marina frowned. *What did she want?* She needed something to hit Dan between the eyes without him having a clue.

'Pills?' the man pushed.

'I ain't much good at taking pills,' Marina said. When the man shrugged and made to walk off, she panicked. She couldn't sit here all night. 'Hey, you must have *something* that would zonk me out?'

'Ketamine?' the man suggested. 'It's in a bottle and tastes like shit, but it will zonk you out. Go easy on the booze, though. They don't mix well.'

Marina smiled and shoved her hand in her pocket for money. 'Go on, then.'

Coupled with enough booze, ketamine should fuck Dan up enough not to stop, or even *notice*, her caving his head in. And if it didn't, then she'd throw her hands up and ask Grant to finish it. She'd make out it was self-defence or something. *Easy.*

Besides, she was counting on Grant utilising his tricks of the trade to get rid of the body afterwards. He'd have no choice but to help her once things were at that point.

Shoving the small bottle in her pocket, Marina hurried away.

Moving through the subway, she resisted the urge to glance over her shoulder and continued through the warren of underground passageways, the tiled walls and dim light creating a mire of shadows.

This whole place was a rat run, but now she had a starting point and the gear, she was getting somewhere. A step closer to payback for one name on the list.

Stuffing her hand into her pocket, her freezing cold fingers struggled to grip her cigarette packet. Lighting one, she continued in the direction she hoped was correct.

Marina climbed the steps, pleased to be out of the subway onto Broad Street.

She glanced around. She couldn't wait any longer to see the place this 'surprise' sister of theirs owned. Especially after the added insult of that article in yesterday's paper. How come Samantha Reynold was so important to make headlines merely because she'd bought a bloody house?

Marina gazed up at the pristine frontage of the Violet Orchid casino and her mouth fell open. It was a thousand times better than she'd imagined.

Her usually pretty features twisted into an ugly sneer. *How fair was this?*

It wasn't. Neither was it right. None of it was bloody right.

This woman – Samantha-bloody-Reynold – had it all; the posh casino, the hunky boyfriend, tons of money and, by the sounds of it, a posh fucking house as well.

And what did *she* have? A dive of a stinking flat above a chippy in Bearwood with her brother and her useless one-handed boyfriend?

She'd been previously planning Dan's demise and dreaming of smashing her useless mother's teeth down her throat, then making a fresh start in Birmingham. That was until she'd discovered this woman – her sister, born of the same crack whore – had somehow attained the opposite of what *she'd* got.

Now she'd got *more* people to get even with.

Realising she could no longer feel her fingers, Marina dropped her cigarette butt and crossed the road towards a café. She'd have a warm-up, then make her way back to the dump she now lived in.

Perhaps, aside from riling herself further from being right in front of this centre of opulence, it would explain what made Samantha Reynold so damn different?

Because whatever the woman had, she should learn to be less selfish and share.

8

With relief to be behind the heavy metal doors of one of their many lockups, Seb dumped the holdall on the top of the cabinet, the resounding thud echoing around the large expanse.

Bloody heavy that was, but it wasn't surprising, considering the amount of wedge it contained.

He wiped the light sheen of sweat from his brow with the back of his sleeve. Although he was used to carting extortionate amounts of money across the city after deals such as these, he'd never once got a tug or been jumped. But there was always a first time for everything and so the relief of reaching the safety of the lockup never failed to be welcoming.

Taking a swig from the bottle of water he'd had the foresight to bring, Seb was grateful to slake his thirst. He was parched.

He unzipped the bag and pulled out several neatly bundled wads of fifty-pound notes. Each one contained a grand. This had to be the biggest deal yet. The money was yet to be counted, but they were past checking that sort of thing during deals with the Irish. Both parties knew their relationship would come to an end if either side pulled a fast one and that wasn't beneficial to anyone.

Six hundred grand in this bag. *Six hundred bloody grand!*

Unlocking the metal cabinet, Seb entered the code for the safe and pulled open the steel door. He stared at the crammed contents. There had to be over two million stuffed in here already. And this didn't include their normal takings from the casino.

At least that wedge ran through the bank. A decent amount of the firm's money had to, otherwise it would be too suspicious. And yeah, he resented losing a percentage of that to the taxman, but keeping them off his back was the most important thing.

But this lot – all this extra couldn't be easily explained. No firm had such massive and random increases in takings, unless there was a dodgy reason. But having more than used their quota of routes to plough money without causing anyone grief, they were stuck for the time being.

Seb frowned. There wasn't enough room in this safe for this new haul. He opened the adjoining safe, wincing at the equal lack of space.

He knew Andrew felt he was being overly cautious with his reticence to wait, but he'd got wind there were random audits coming his way from the tax office and customs combined and he didn't want to fall party to one of those!

Seb's mouth twisted. *Random, my arse*, he thought. That lot loved digging around casinos and the like, knowing damned well there were usually other facets involved with businesses such as theirs.

Well, those bastards wouldn't get their grasping mitts on any more of the firm's money. He handed over enough to them, as it was. Overcautious he may be, but he'd rather that than end up broke and spending the next however many years in the nick.

Even more so now he had a life to look forward to with Sam.

Seb's mouth curled into a smile. Maybe they'd even have a couple of kids a few years from now?

This thought both pleased and excited him and he wanted not only his firm, brothers and parents, but his additional and hopefully soon to be *extended* family to be covered forever more. He would do everything in his power to make that happen. But that prospect was looking dubious, unless he could think of how to move some of this money on.

Opening the third safe in the row of cabinets spanning half the back wall, Seb shoved the holdall safely at the bottom. At least there was room in this one, but that wouldn't last long. The house purchase would clear that money in the holdall, plus he'd used a few grand on the furniture he'd ordered, but that was only a drop in the ocean. What about the bloody rest?

Slamming the door and hearing the lock set, Seb grabbed his car keys. He'd planned to talk to Sam about the house this afternoon, but she'd been so excited about the coming completion, he hadn't wanted to dampen her joy. But now he'd gone ahead without speaking to her.

Flicking the lights off, he dragged the metal doors of the lockup closed and crunched across the gravel to his car.

Cancelling the mortgage at the last minute had come as a surprise to the bank, but Chamberlains had been more than happy to do the deal with cash. And that was all sorted for tomorrow.

It meant another trip back here, but better that than risk lugging around half a million on his person in the interim.

Seb made good time through Erdington. He'd see how the night's poker tournament was going at the Peacock and then head home and explain the change of plans to Sam.

* * *

Deb glanced at herself in the window. It made such a difference looking like she used to, rather than how Tom made her dress for the punters' benefit.

Even though the glass was steamed up, Deb's reflection was clear. Even her hair looked decent, not that silly little girl thing she did when working. Even being out on a freezing cold night was better than putting up with those grotesque men pawing her.

She glanced at the bottom of the tight fitting yet elegant knee-length dress protruding from under her fitted leather jacket. It looked the part and sure, they were nice clothes – just not what she'd have picked herself.

She'd have much rather worn her wax jacket.

Her heart sank. That green jacket of her father's, although she'd hated it at first, thinking it a stinking ugly thing, she was now glad she'd taken it with her when leaving his house. It was the only thing left from her previous existence. Plus, it was warm.

Deb pulled open the café door and walked up to the counter. Ordering a Diet Coke, she glanced around for somewhere to sit.

Her nerves fluttered. There were plenty of people that, at first glance, might be what Tom was looking for, but how did she approach this? She'd thought it was sorted in her head, but faced with the situation, her confidence deserted her.

What if she broached the subject with the wrong people? She might get her face smashed up and then her ability to earn money would be ruined. Things would never work out with Chas then.

The beginnings of tears pricked at the back of Deb's eyes as she took her drink over to the table. She had to remember the plan. *She could do this. Have faith.*

Plonking herself down, she pulled out her cigarettes, willing her fingers not to shake from cold and nerves.

Lighting one, she exhaled slowly, watching the blue smoke curl upwards to mix with the layer of fug collecting below the ceiling like a suspended raincloud.

Look for girls acting sophisticated, but wearing clothes purchased from the market. Act casual, confident and friendly. Weigh up the surroundings and get into conversation. Don't be pushy. Pay attention to detail. Never give out any personal details and no direct information about the Aurora.

Feeling marginally better, Deb took a sip of her Coke and glanced out of the window.

Whether she could see him or not, Chas was within watching distance, clocking her.

She looked around the café, her attention sharpening at a group of three girls seated at the other end of the large window who could be possibilities.

Stubbing out her cigarette, Deb went to light another, scowling to find the lighter's wheel slipping in her fingers.

'Here you go.'

Deb looked up, finding a woman holding out a lighter. 'Thanks,' she muttered, lighting the cigarette.

'Are you okay?'

Deb smiled at the blonde woman at the next table. She had to be in her late twenties, nowhere near Tom's brief, which was a shame because she was very pretty. 'I'm late meeting my boyfriend and I think he must have given up,' she blathered then looked away. She had to keep her concentration on the ball.

Out of the corner of her eye she saw the three girls getting up. Maybe she could catch up with them outside?

Her heart thumped. What should she do? Chas had said not to leave the café under *any* circumstances until the hour was up and then she had to walk down the road along the route they'd agreed so he could pick her up. But what if this was her only chance to get these girls on board?

She'd risk it. She had to. She couldn't miss an opportunity.

'You off?' the blonde woman smiled.

'I think I've just spotted my boyfriend,' Deb lied, nodding in the direction of the illuminated frontage of the casino opposite.

'Have a good night,' the woman said as Deb scuttled from the café.

* * *

'You stupid, stupid fucker!' Amelia wrenched half a bag of frozen peas from the small freezer in her office, kept for purposes exactly like *this*.

She hadn't expected her bloody nephew to be such a thick dolt.

Sharply sucking in her breath so not to launch into a tirade of further abuse in front of the girl, she wrapped the peas in a tea towel and pressed them against Deb's eye.

She'd quite like not to bother covering them so the silly tart got cold burn, but she couldn't risk any more damage to the little cow's face.

The girl was a pretty one and as much as she'd like the slut out of the way, giving open access for Tina to progress, neither could she afford to antagonise the situation with Tom.

Amelia glared at Deb, her sobs now reduced to muffled sniffling. 'Oh, for God's sake, girl! Enough of the histrionics! With any luck, these peas will do the trick before the swelling takes hold and no one will be any the wiser.'

Like Tom. Because if the girl's face ended up looking like she'd been in the ring, there would be hell to pay. She fixed her glare back to Chas. 'Anything to say for yourself?'

'She went against instructions,' Chas muttered. 'The stupid bitch left the café and legged it across the road. I thought she was doing a fucking runner. How the hell do you think it felt sitting on my hands waiting, whilst she chatted. It was hardly like I could drag her into the car in front of everyone, was it? Though if she'd been one minute longer, I would have.'

'I was trying to do what was asked,' Deb sobbed, her hand reaching out to touch the sleeve of Chas's leather jacket.

Chas jerked his arm away. 'Asked? You weren't asked. You were fucking told! You were also told what *not* to do!'

Amelia pulled Deb back into the chair so she could keep the bag of peas in place. 'And what *was* achieved because I'm yet to hear?'

Chas slumped back in his seat like a sulky child. Furious, he was. Bloody furious. Was everyone out to make him look like a twat? He wasn't having it. Not from Deb, not from his aunt, not by *any* of them. 'Yeah, Deb, did you achieve what was "asked", as you like to see it? Where are those three tarts you were pally with because I don't see them.' He made a big deal of looking around Amelia's tiny office under the stairs that was little more than a cupboard.

Deb wiped a trail of snot from under her nose with her sleeve, still reeling that Chas – the man she loved – had struck her. 'I said I would get them well-paid work. I didn't say where, but I think they got the gist. They seemed to, anyway.'

'You *think*? They *seemed*?' Amelia barked. 'They either did or they didn't! Which one is it? Christ almighty!' Pulling the bag of peas from Deb's face, she yanked open the freezer drawer and slung them back in.

'I-I've arranged to meet them tomorrow night at seven, then I'll bring them here. That was right, wasn't it?' Deb said, scared to explain what she'd arranged. She'd got this so wrong. She'd thought everyone would be pleased. She'd thought she'd done well.

'You're expecting another night off?' Amelia yelled. 'Bleeding hell! Tom will go tits!'

'But he said not to mention the Aurora!' Deb countered. 'How could I do anything else, if I couldn't do that? I had to give them the chance to think about what I'd said.'

'Don't be bloody smart,' Amelia screamed. 'Let's hope for your sake the sluts are there tomorrow and also that Tom don't find out you went against the rules.'

'I didn't mean to. I wasn't trying to run off,' Deb pleaded. 'Why would I do that? I'm with Chas and...'

'You stupid slag!' Chas roared, jumping from the seat. 'I can't stand this bullshit. You're not with me, Deb, and never have been. You're just one of many, so quit thinking you're something special.'

Deb stared at Chas like he'd slapped her again, but this time harder. 'W-what?'

'You heard,' Chas sneered. 'Now clean yourself up and get out of that dress before you trash that too. It looks like you'll be needing it tomorrow night as well.'

As Chas stalked from the office, Deb broke down into a fresh round of sobs. 'He didn't mean that, did he?' she whimpered.

Amelia folded her arms over her ample chest. 'Oh, he meant it all right. I still can't believe you thought otherwise. Listen, girl, you can't be this stupid. It's about time you fucking wised up, otherwise you'll drown in this game.'

Deb blinked. She didn't want to be in this game. She never had. She was only doing it because it was what Chas wanted and it would enable them to be together.

The crawling sensation of having made a very wrong decision slithered into her veins. A decision that would now be very difficult to get out of.

9

In Chamberlains estate agents, Sam fidgeted impatiently. All she wanted to do was get everything signed and leave, but it was a prerequisite that the staff fawned over them, rather than getting on with the paperwork.

She glanced at the two women sitting at the desk, staring at Seb. They might as well have their tongues hanging out, it was so obvious.

Sam instinctively rested her hand on Seb's thigh as he continued the necessary conversation with Mr Chamberlain. Seb knew how to play to the crowd, that was for sure, but she had no need to stake her claim on him. Seb only had eyes for her, even when his face cracked into one of his showstopping smiles as a woman brought over yet another cup of tea.

'Are you not drinking your tea, Miss Reynold?'

Mr Chamberlain's voice shook Sam from her internal musings. 'If you don't mind, I'd rather get on,' she replied tersely. 'We're eager to get this wrapped up.'

She ignored the hint of amusement on Seb's face. He was

always telling her she needed more patience. *Like he was a fine one to talk!*

'Oh yes, yes, of course,' Mr Chamberlain blustered, shuffling the paperwork over the desk. 'You must both be extremely busy. I'm very grateful you've taken the time to come in here today at short notice.'

Sam smiled through gritted teeth, but as Mr Chamberlain lined up the pages to sign, handing the pen firstly to Seb, excitement fluttered once more. She couldn't wait to get into their new house.

Interrupted by Seb's nudging, Sam looked up, seeing the pen poised in his fingers.

'Are you signing, or what?'

Grinning, Sam hastily scrawled her name on the countless sheets of paperwork.

Mr Chamberlain clapped his hands together and gave Seb a nod. 'You're all set. The house is yours.'

'The keys?' Sam frowned.

'Oh, I've already got them,' Seb said, glancing at Mr Chamberlain. He'd planned to tell Sam he'd swapped the funding of the house, he really had, but there just hadn't been the time and he didn't want to spoil anything.

He knew she'd only worry that the house didn't belong to *either* of them, but the Royal Peacock. It was only temporary. As soon as the usual routes for laundering the cash freed up, they'd take the money out of the house and fund it themselves, the way they'd planned.

'Just before you go...' With a flourish, Mr Chamberlain's arm moved in the direction of two staff who headed towards them with a huge bouquet of flowers and a magnum of Champagne. 'You've been wonderful clients and it's been both a pleasure and a privilege helping you find the home of your dreams.'

'Oh! Erm... thank you.' Noticing the group of press outside, Sam shot a look at Seb. *She knew it...*

'If you'd be so good as to pose for a photograph outside the office,' Mr Chamberlain simpered. 'Having the endorsement of Seb Stoker and Sam Reynold will do wonders for the business.'

'No problem.' Seb gave Sam a wink and steered her out of the door in front of the waiting photographers.

* * *

Sam screamed with delight as Seb scooped her into his arms and carried her up to the door of the house. 'We're not married yet!' she cried, her excitement at bursting point.

'We will be soon!' Pulling the key from his pocket, Seb inserted it into the ornate brass lock. 'Anyway, you don't have to be newlywed to carry your woman over the threshold!'

As the big wooden door opened, Seb placed Sam down on the Minton tiled floor and looked around, his happiness accentuated further by the joy on Sam's face.

Sam spun around in the large hallway, drinking in the Victorian features: the coving around the ceiling; the ornate arches and the beautiful stained-glass window shining a multitude of coloured lights onto the walls.

She ran her hand along the carved balustrade at the bottom of one of the two staircases, her eyes following the carpet secured by brass stair rods up to the first floor. 'It's as perfect as I remembered,' she said, wrapping her arms around Seb's neck.

Giving Sam a lingering kiss, Seb then grinned. 'Which room shall we christen first?'

'On what? We haven't got any furniture yet. When are we arranging to get our stuff moved?'

Seb's green eyes sparkled with delight. Grabbing Sam's hand, he pulled her in the direction of her favourite reception room.

Sam gasped with amazement as Seb opened the door, her mouth gaping with surprise. 'Oh, my God! How... how?'

The room was furnished *exactly* the way she'd told Seb she imagined it.

'You see?' Seb laughed. 'I *do* listen.'

'Oh, Seb,' Sam gushed. 'I love it! How on earth did you get all of this in here for today?'

Seb winked. 'You'd be surprised what persuasion can do, as well as twisting Chamberlain's arm to release the keys early.' *Plus a hefty wedge of cash, but he'd pay four times over to make Sam happy. He'd bottle her expression if he could.*

'You mean you had the keys all along!' Sam gasped.

'Only since yesterday,' Seb laughed. 'But before you slap me, we still had to sign all that paperwork.' *And casually shove a holdall full of cash into the greedy twat Chamberlain's hand...*

Sam perched on the edge of a sofa and ran her finger over the soft velvet cushions. She couldn't be annoyed with him. 'What a wonderful surprise! I can't believe you've done this all for me!'

'I've only done this room and one bedroom,' Seb said. 'I figured you'd want to do the rest yourself.'

'You've done one of the bedrooms too?' Sam jumped off the sofa in excitement. 'Let me see.'

'My pleasure!' Grabbing Sam's hand, Seb pulled her from the reception room up the staircase, the sound of her excited giggling making his heart swell.

Hardly able to contain her anticipation, Sam flung open the master bedroom door, her heart thudding in her chest. She gasped with delight. 'Oh, Seb! It's wonderful!'

A four-poster emperor bed sat against the centre of the left-hand wall, the luxuriant cream velvet drapes edged with green tasselled piping. Matching bedside tables sat either side and a huge shaggy rug lay in the centre of the room on the polished floorboards.

Sam's eyes could barely move fast enough to take in all of the detail Seb had taken pains to include, like the multicoloured chandelier hanging from a thick brass chain in the centre of the ceiling; the rainbow-coloured glass looking like every jewel she could imagine. It was the one, the *very one* she'd drooled over in a magazine.

In a half-trance, she wandered across to the floor-length window taking up the majority of one wall and gazed out over the white metal balcony across their beautiful garden. It contained a selection of flowering plants and shrubs. Although it was winter, she could imagine the cacophony of colour spring would bring and when the thirty-foot magnolia tree blossomed, that would be a spectacle she could barely wait for.

Her eyes filled with tears. She was so lucky. So lucky to have this wonderful place, to have Seb – the man who would be her husband; to have the casino; to have this life. By God, it was just perfect!

'Hey! You're supposed to be pleased!' Seb folded his arms around Sam's waist. 'This wasn't supposed to make you cry!'

Turning around, Sam wrapped her arms around Seb's neck. 'I *am* happy. So happy! I love you so much.'

'Not as much as I love you, Samantha,' Seb murmured, his lips on her throat. 'Now, let's get this bed christened. It will make my excellent thoughtfulness worthwhile.'

Winking, he led Sam over to the four-poster and pulled her on top of him.

10

Deb could have cried as she applied her eyeliner with a shaking hand. This was the third time she'd messed it up and time was ticking. She hadn't even showered since her last punter and every time she moved, she got a waft of his smell, his body odour clinging to her skin.

Swallowing down the rising nausea, she scrutinised her face in the mirror. Her eye was a little swollen, but thanks to the frozen peas, it wasn't too noticeable.

Deb replaced the lid of her eyeliner and closed her eyes in desperation. She felt like her heart had been ripped out and shoved back in the wrong way.

Now she had to get in the car with Chas, knowing that everything she'd believed was a lie.

All night, she'd lain awake, hoping he'd come to apologise; explain he'd been angry, was sorry for hitting her and hadn't meant what he'd said. But, of course, he hadn't. And neither would he.

Smoothing down her purple dress, she slipped her jacket on.

This was like déjà vu. Couldn't she backtrack to yesterday and change the course of the future?

If she had the choice, would she go back to yesterday, or return to a point before she'd made the decision to do any of this?

Deb looked around the small room which she called her own. The bright curtains hanging at the windows failed to hide the blown leaking panes of grubby glass, or stop the draught from the rotten wooden frames.

She got up from the unmade bed. She should change it, but she didn't have time. And neither did she want the smell she knew the sheets would stink of on her hands or *anywhere* on her.

She had to somehow convince those girls that working here was a good idea? Could she really do that? Did it matter? Did anything matter any more?

Deb bit her bottom lip. If she started crying, she didn't think she would stop. Plus, she'd be late.

Picking up her handbag, she left the room and locked the door behind her. Chas said the other girls helped themselves, that's why he looked after her earnings.

Her lip trembled. She hadn't seen a penny of any of the money she'd earned over the last six months. She hadn't even questioned Chas holding onto it.

Stupid. Without a bloody doubt it had been stupid.

Chas wouldn't give her that money now. In fact, he'd *never* had any intention of doing so. That was now very obvious.

Feeling even more dejected, Deb walked down the long landing, her stilettos clacking on the bare wooden floorboards. Rounding the corner to the first staircase, she walked slap bang into another girl.

'Watch where you're going, you stupid cow!' Tina hissed.

'Sorry...' Deb muttered.

Not long ago, she'd have retaliated with a mouthful, but she was too weary to bother. Where had the cocky, confident girl she'd been not many months ago disappeared to?

Gone forever, she suspected. Evaporated. *A bit like everything else...*

But if she didn't get back out there and do what Tom wanted, things would get even worse.

* * *

Marina concealed the spite threatening to drip from her pores to drench the newspaper in front of her.

For years, she'd learnt to hide what she really felt about the outside world. But aside from the time she'd spent locked inside her own head, her brain full to the brim with the never-ending stream of ideas, resentments, wants and needs – the only thing fuelling her with the drive to keep breathing was keeping hold of the belief that one day, her chance would come.

And now it had.

She stared at Dan, her face twisting into a grimace. The way he lounged in the chair staring at the TV, scratching himself with what was left of his stubby hand, made her sick.

Her hand moved to the pocket of her jeans, feeling the tell-tale outline of the vial she'd scored last night, then she moved her gaze to Grant opposite at the small kitchen table. Remembering what she was supposed to be doing, she glanced back at the picture of Samantha Reynold's new house. 'Aren't they lucky!' she said sarcastically.

Grant grunted. 'Lucky isn't the word.'

Marina smiled inwardly, hardly able to wait until Grant put his plan into motion. 'Do you think you'll land a job there?'

'Why not?'

'What do you intend to do?' Marina asked. *Because it had better be good.*

'Get on side with our lovely "sister", that's what. I'll find out where Linda is and then get money from the pair of them. If Samantha can treat our mother like royalty, then she can do the same for us! I'm going back over to that pub to see if those blokes from the Orchid will offer me a job.'

'And if they don't? What then?'

'They will,' Grant insisted. He jerked his head at Dan. 'Is he staying with you?'

Marina shrugged despondently. 'Unlikely. He's got that card game, remember?'

'You shouldn't be on your own until we're sure no one has followed him up here.' He glared in Dan's direction. 'Look, I'll give things a miss tonight and stay with you. This stuff can wait for another day.'

Marina gasped. 'Don't do that! I'll be fine. We need to get things moving with our plan. Or should I say *your* plan.' She wrung her hands together, playing the young, benighted sister – the one Grant felt duty bound to look after. 'I'm not much use for anything, am I?'

'Don't be crazy. Course you are!' Grant insisted, pulling his sister in for a hug.

Marina could smile openly now she was pressed against Grant's chest. Her attention slid back to Samantha Reynold's house, shoving its wealth and privilege in her face in a taunting reminder. 'Carry on with your plan. I could do with some good news.'

Grant studied Marina for what felt like an hour. 'If you're sure you'll be okay?'

Marina smiled. 'I'll be fine.'

She pretended to be consumed with reading a magazine until

Grant finally left the flat. She hadn't thought he'd ever go. She glanced at her watch, her eyes tracking back to Dan on the sofa. He hadn't moved an inch, the lazy bastard.

The need to rid him from her life thrummed in an ever-increasing rhythm. Every second he breathed the same air became more insulting than the last.

She fished the small vial out of her pocket and turned it around in her fingers, staring at the label on the bottle.

Could she get away with doing this now? This was the first opportunity to have Dan on his own since she'd got the gear. How long would it be before there was another chance?

Marina's fingers stumbled over the cap, her clammy hands slipping, but at the sudden sound of the doorbell, she shoved the bottle back into her pocket and jumped from the chair, her face twisting into a scowl as Dan stumbled off the sofa, pushing past her.

'I'm off now,' Dan called whilst Marina followed him up the hallway.

Marina remained silent as Dan left without a backward glance. *Bastard. He might well have escaped for tonight, but he wouldn't next time.*

At least now she could plough more thought into it. There was no point being too eager and making silly mistakes that could otherwise be avoided.

She shoved her feet into her boots. In the meantime, she'd go out herself.

* * *

Deb stared out of the window of Chas's car into the rushing darkness as they sped along the Hagley Road towards Broad Street. Despite everything, the urge to reach over and touch his hand was immense, as was the intoxicating scent of his aftershave – the smell of which she'd always loved. But she dared not. He'd made his position clear.

Deb instead concentrated on keeping her teeth from chattering. Despite the leather jacket, this dress wasn't doing her any favours in the bitter temperature, especially as the car's heating stayed resolutely set on zero.

She didn't want to do this. There was no way she wanted to be responsible for talking those girls into the same position she was in. But what could she do?

Like another slap to the face, the realisation sunk into her brain. She was trapped. And they – Chas, Tom and Amelia – knew it. They'd be watching her like a hawk to make sure she toed the line.

Deb sucked in her rapidly tightening breath, the situation crushing her lungs.

'You'd best do a good job.' Chas's voice made Deb flinch. 'No pissing about or pulling fast ones. You'd better deliver!'

'I will,' Deb muttered, the words sticking in her dry throat. *And she would.* She had to because if she didn't, then she suspected things would get a lot worse. Instead of allowing the rising panic to escalate, she would do what they wanted, whilst she formulated a plan as to how to get away from this.

Without her even noticing, they arrived opposite the Royal Peacock and she lurched forward when Chas slammed the brakes on.

'There they are,' he said. 'Over there.'

Deb's eyes darted towards the front of the casino, seeing the girls from yesterday. Her heart sank. She'd hoped they wouldn't turn up. Now she was about to condemn these girls – all vivacious and with something to prove, like she herself had been not so long ago – to a life of misery.

'Did you hear me?' Chas gripped Deb's arm. 'Do what we agreed.' Grabbing her face, he twisted her head so she was forced to look him in the eye. 'I'll be waiting and watching. Once you're ready, walk around the back and I'll come and pick you all up.'

Releasing his grip, Chas watched Deb stumble from the car and quickly cross the road towards the girls.

11

Listening to security, Seb's brows knitted. 'They're there now?'

Daz nodded. 'They were when I came back in to find you. A whole bunch of them loitering around.' His mouth curled in distaste. 'We've moved several groups on, one of them twice, but they keep coming back.'

Seb ran his hands over his cleanly shaven chin with frustration. He'd been just about to leave. So much for him and Sam spending their first night together relaxing in their new home. 'Can't Andrew deal with this?'

Daz shook his head. 'Andrew and Neil are sorting a delivery out. What should our next move be?'

His walkie-talkie suddenly crackled into life. *'Group One returned. Suspicious activity also present with different group.'*

Seb frowned. If Andrew and Neil didn't return from the delivery soon, he'd have to hang around even longer for the tournament to end. *For Christ's sake.*

Getting up, he and Daz moved down the corridor to the small operations room where the extensive CCTV system was monitored.

A man jumped to attention the moment they pushed into the room. 'Show me,' Seb muttered, pulling a chair up in front of the row of monitors.

The man pressed a series of buttons. 'There's this one.' Changing the monitor's display from four split screens into one, he homed in on a specific camera. 'This lot have been moved on twice.'

Seb squinted at the grainy black and white footage of a group of seven women. Skimpily dressed in cheap Lycra skirts, the women leant up against the Peacock's wall – *his* casino. He scowled at the woman nearest the entrance, her leg against the brickwork, her long bleached blonde hair straggling down over rolls of fat spilling from a dark-coloured boob tube.

He peered closer at her over-tight miniskirt that left little to the imagination. 'Christ,' he muttered. *Even Neil would struggle with her!*

'See what they do.' The man zoomed out to show a wider perspective.

Seb recognised two men approaching as regular members of the Peacock and watched as the women, including the knickerless one, pushed themselves away from the wall, impeding the first man's route up the casino steps.

The blonde draped herself over the man and he struggled to extract himself. Turning on his heels, he promptly walked in the opposite direction, closely followed by the rest of his group. 'This is no good,' Seb growled, his annoyance mounting. 'How many times did you say you'd moved that lot on?'

'Twice,' Daz confirmed. 'As you can see, they're hell-bent on staying. Shall I bring them in?'

Seb shook his head. 'Not yet.' Manhandling women was not something he wanted to do or even order his men to undertake. No doubt there would be press lurking, eager to photograph his staff dragging women off the street. By the looks of it, he was losing enough customers as it was. 'If they won't listen to any of you, perhaps they'll listen to me?'

And, in the event there were press hanging around waiting for an opportunity to cast aspersion, they'd be less likely to accuse *him* of anything untoward than a member of his security.

After that, he'd call Neil to tell him to get his arse back here, pronto. That's what mobiles were for, wasn't it? Neil could cash up the tournament and go over to the lockup because *he* was having time with Sam tonight one way or another.

Turning on his heels, Seb made his way back down the staff corridor to the casino reception and the pavement outside.

* * *

Pulling the collar of his thick overcoat higher, Kevin kept a brisk pace towards the Ring O Bells with Craig and Stu.

He could have done without walking in this weather, but it allowed the chance to talk without the rest of the team overhearing.

Kev turned his back against the gusting wind to light his cigarette.

It wasn't like there was anything to hide – he'd already briefed the team to keep an eye out for certain 'ladies' using the frontage as a fruitful pickup point. Judging by what he'd glimpsed as they'd left tonight, it looked like that was indeed becoming popular.

Although they had a good team, it was imperative his boys weren't spread too thinly, especially now extra security was needed for Sam's ill-timed housewarming party. He had to check out Stu and Craig's suggestion before word got out of a job up for grabs, otherwise he'd have a list as long as his arm of his present staff's brothers and other family members clamouring for the position.

He may well need one of them yet, but he preferred to see what this man was like first. 'You reckon this bloke will be in here tonight?'

Craig shrugged. 'I got the impression he would.'

Kevin wouldn't usually employ a stranger – these sorts of jobs were almost always done via personal recommendation – but they needed fresh blood. Stu and Craig knew what they were about and knew how to spot a like-minded person.

'This guy's from London?' Kev probed as they neared the Ring O Bells.

Craig nodded. 'Not sure which part, though. Like I said, he's worked for several firms and personal contracts. A freelancer.'

'And he didn't say which firms or who,' Stu added.

Kev chucked his fag end down and stuffed his hands deep into his pockets. That the man hadn't name-dropped was a good indication of merit. The term 'freelancer' spoke volumes too and spelt out very strongly that he was a gun for hire. Although that wasn't what was required at present, someone with those credentials and good enough to go it alone was useful to know. 'What made him leave London?'

'He didn't say and I didn't ask.' Opening the door to the pub, Craig glanced around, giving an abrupt nod in the direction of a well-built blond man sitting alone in the far corner. 'He's over there.'

Kevin gestured to the bar. 'I'll get these in. You go over. No point wasting time.'

Grant appeared nonplussed as the two men from the Violet Orchid approached. He knew they'd come. Sooner than expected too. He surreptitiously glanced at the third man at the bar. 'Hey, fellas,' he said casually as they reached his table. 'Another night off?'

'Something like that,' Craig said. 'Mind if we join you? We have a proposition for you...'

* * *

Marina couldn't be altogether sure why she'd returned to the Magic Bean tonight, other than a strong feeling she should explore the possibility of her alternative plan.

She tapped her lighter against the side of her mug of tea, her eyes trained on the Royal Peacock's entrance. Ideally, she'd have preferred a view of the Orchid, but this would have to do.

Marina recalled the photograph of Samantha's house in the paper, the mere memory making her angrier. But that was okay because she needed to remain angry.

It wasn't difficult.

Her jaw was stiff from clenching her teeth. Thinking of that over-privileged cow made her almost as furious as knowing Dan was playing the big 'I am' at a card game. But now she'd had this new idea, Dan's demise was on the backburner. He wasn't off the hook by any stretch of the imagination, but *this* pushed everything else into second place.

Yep, Dan wasn't first on the list any more because she had a new primary target.

Samantha.

Grant's aim to get money off their spoilt bitch sister was much appreciated, but she wanted *more* than that. She wanted to make Samantha Reynold's life a misery and to force the pampered cow to experience what it felt like for her life to fall apart.

She turned her empty mug around on the sticky Formica table, scowling at the piles of crumbs left by the previous customers.

How exactly would she screw Samantha's life up?

Marina frowned. She wasn't sure, but the first port of call was to get within striking distance.

Her eyes brightened. She could drug Samantha and make her admit she'd taken everything for herself. Then she'd kill the bitch!

She grinned, her excitement mounting. It would be easy to source more ketamine for when it got to Dan's turn, but first she needed to get into the Orchid.

How? A job? As a customer? Accompanying Grant?

No, he'd never allow it. Grant wanted this cut and dried.

'Are you sitting there with the same drink all night?' a voice said. 'This ain't a soup kitchen.'

Marina smiled sweetly at the hatchet-faced woman from behind the counter standing in front of her, arms folded over her massive chest. 'I'll have another tea, if you don't mind?'

'Hmph. Come and get it then. I ain't a fucking waitress.'

What was she, then? Marina glared at the woman's retreating back before following to the counter. Slamming her money down, she snatched the fresh mug of tea, not wasting a thank you on the rude cow.

Returning to the table, she twisted around in the plastic chair, her attention back on the casino opposite.

In the short space of time she'd been here, she'd have to have been blind not to notice the security coming out to move on women. No shred of a doubt, *they* were prostitutes.

Her lips twitched into a smile. And by the looks of it, they'd been busy for the last century. *What a bloody mess.*

The Peacock was Samantha's boyfriend's club, was it not? She couldn't quite see the front of the Orchid from where she sat, but the place must be getting the same issue. It was amusing that the area immediately surrounding her darling sister's casino should be going downhill.

Her attention sharpened further as she watched a big man wearing a suit stride down the entrance steps of the Peacock, followed by an even bigger man. She watched the two men approach the old tarts, the younger, more attractive man entering into a conversation with one of them.

Surely a top-looking man dressed to the nines wouldn't sport with any of those old crones?

She peered through the condensation of the window to get a closer look. *It was him!* The guy in the newspaper.

Sebastian Stoker.

Marina's heart picked up a drum-like rhythm, bitterness raging.

Marina watched as the women reluctantly moved away, leaving a smug smile on the perfectly structured face of Sebastian Stoker. The very same fucking handsome mug Samantha woke up to every day in their new, luxurious, posh, fucking bastard, perfect house.

Whilst she'd got... Dan...

Anger towards the sister she'd never known exploded. That thief was probably, at this very minute, plying her slut of a mother with caviar-topped canapés.

Linda-fucking-Matthews had no doubt inveigled an invitation to live at that newly purchased house with the perfect couple.

Marina's teeth grated. It made her sick. It really did.

Picking up her cigarettes, she lit another, her mind trawling the raging swamp of ideas of how to get into the Orchid as the fine backside of Seb Stoker moved up the steps into the Peacock's lobby, his pet monkey following.

Half-heartedly looking back to the group of young girls, Marina paid little attention to a car blasting the horn.

She probably wouldn't have even noticed anything amiss if she hadn't clocked that flash of pure panic across a girl's face.

This panic was only visible for a split second before it was hidden back underneath the trowelled-on makeup, but Marina had seen it.

Plus, she recognised the girl. It was the very same one who'd been in this café last night, who, on spotting her 'boyfriend', dodged the traffic to reach the group of girls on the other side of the busy road. The *same* group of girls that, if she wasn't mistaken, had also been in here.

Marina had had the feeling something suspect was going on last night and she'd been right. That girl was lying through her teeth. And now she had a pretty good idea of why...

She watched with interest as the red VW Golf continued down Broad Street, immediately followed by the girl and her band of newly acquired tarts, their stilettos clattering along the pavement until they were completely out of view.

12

Happily accepting the new pint balanced on the unsteady tabletop, Dan couldn't help but smile. His smile was for several reasons: one – he was out of earshot of Marina's nagging; two – he'd made a tidy packet at this sit-down and was on track to pocket more before the night was out; three – even though the beer was flat, it was cheap; and last but not least, it was another night not having to ignore death stares from Grant.

Dan glanced at his hand of cards, his top lip curling into a sneer at the stumps of his fingers. *That* was his only fuck-up and not something that would be repeated.

Playing his cards, he felt confident enough to relax.

Turning his attention back to the game, Dan was pleased to see that he'd cleaned up on this round too. He scraped the pile of money from the centre of the table using his good hand. 'Another round, gents?'

Amid much muttering and shaking of heads, the other players got to their feet and shuffled off. 'I take it that's a "no", then?' he laughed, winking at Col and Baz.

Meeting these two in the first pub he'd set foot in on coming to

Birmingham had been a godsend. Col and Baz knew all the places to go where he could make some dosh with his card playing skills and that was a much-needed bonus.

'Probably a good job. You'll get a bad rep. Where the hell did you learn to play like that anyway?' Col asked, suitably impressed.

'Let's just say I learnt from a master,' Dan boasted. Not that he'd tell Mickey Devlin that.

He eagerly stuffed his latest winnings in his pocket. Even these two mugs were too fucking thick to notice his sleight of hand. Now he had enough dosh to go to a casino. A wide smile split his face. 'So, tell me lads. What do you know about the Broad Street casinos?'

'Broad Street?' Baz raised his eyebrows – or rather *eyebrow*. 'There's several. The main ones are the Orchid and Peacock.'

'Stay clear of those,' Col chimed in. 'They're owned by the Stokers and the Reynolds.' He leaned across the table and lowered his voice. 'The Stokers are psychos and some of their people drink here, so be careful what you say.'

'Plus the head Stoker is shagging the bird who runs the Orchid firm,' Baz added.

'A woman runs a place?' Dan scoffed.

'It won't be a laughing matter if they catch you saying that, mate.' Col slurped at his tepid beer and pointedly eyed the missing fingers on Dan's hand. 'It looks like you've already pissed people off in the past...'

'I ain't bothered,' Dan bragged. 'I'm from London, remember? I've seen it all!' *The Violet Orchid was also the place Grant said he was going for a job. Interesting.*

'Those gaffs are expensive too,' Col added. 'To be honest, you'd be better off trying your luck at another place I know of. It's a casino of sorts, but with *extras*.' He gave Dan a knowing wink. 'A couple of decent lookers there too.'

Dan sat forward, suddenly open to this possibility. 'Where's this?'

'It's down the Hagley Road. It's called the Aurora.'

'Get your coats then, boys,' Dan grinned, finishing his pint. 'Let's go and pay this Aurora place a visit.'

* * *

'Well, that was hard work,' Neil griped. Walking behind the bar, he helped himself to a second double whisky.

Squeezing past the barman busy emptying drip trays, he glanced around the now empty casino. 'Thank God we've got no stragglers tonight.'

That accident in the Queensway had caused havoc getting through town, the traffic snarled up in every single direction. The delivery might have gone to plan, but he hadn't counted on being back so bloody late.

Andrew followed Neil to a table, watching his brother place his drink down and pull out his cigarettes. 'What are you doing? Have you forgotten about getting the takings to the lockup?'

Neil's lighter paused halfway to his mouth. 'Oh, come on! It's almost 3 a.m. and I'm knackered. I'll do it tomorrow.'

'No, you fucking won't!' Andrew snapped. 'Seb said the money had to move tonight and you assured him it would.'

Leaning on the table, he lowered his voice. 'You know he's jumpy about cash being left around here and I agree with him.'

Neil knocked back his whisky, then nodded towards his now empty glass. 'It won't hurt waiting until the morning. I'm too tired to drive and I've had a few.'

'These tournaments were *your* idea. We're all tired, so pull your fucking weight!' Andrew glanced over to one of the runners. 'Simon?' he shouted. 'You free to take Neil to the lockup?'

'Sure,' Simon replied, pleased to be tasked with chauffeuring a member of the inner circle. 'I'll bring the van round.'

Neil grimaced. 'For fuck's sake. Give us the codes then. I haven't got one for the third safe.'

As Andrew whispered the numbers, Neil grabbed a pen, about to write them on his hand.

'Don't do that, you idiot!' Andrew hissed. 'Send yourself a text on your new mobile and then delete it.'

Neil rolled his eyes and begrudgingly stabbed in the numbers on the text. 'Happy now?'

Helping himself to a further whisky for good measure, he slugged it down in one, then shrugged his jacket on. 'Suppose I'd better go.'

* * *

Neil didn't want a conversation with Simon. In his opinion, the bloke was a muppet. Trapped in a van going to Erdington at 3 a.m. listening to this man rattle on wasn't his idea of a great time.

'Another good night then? Great idea of yours, those tournaments,' Simon said brightly.

Neil grunted. He *had* thought it a good idea, but judging by these latest problems, he didn't hold much hope they would continue. And that pissed him off. There would be plenty of 'I-told-you-so's about waiving membership on those nights, thanks to this growing influx of hookers and sharks.

Neil's eyes moved to the holdall between his feet in the footwell. Surely they could find a way to resolve this without binning off the idea? It brought in shedloads of money, after all.

'Is it any good?'

Neil scowled. *What the fuck was Simon going on about now?* Realising the runner was referring to the mobile phone in his hand, he sighed. 'They're a pain in the bloody arse!'

For instance, if he hadn't got one, Seb couldn't have called him halfway through the delivery, telling him he had to do *this*. He could have had a few more drinks and gone to bed. But no. Instead, he was *here*...

'Oh, but I'd love to hav...'

'Can we just get to the fucking lockup?' Neil snapped.

Simon promptly quietened and continued up the road. Taking the next turn, he pulled into the industrial estate. 'We're here now.'

Neil grabbed the holdall. *Fuck. The bloody code!*

Scrabbling with his mobile, he stabbed the buttons to bring the screen to life. He hated this thing. He didn't understand it and didn't want to, either.

Opening the text message he'd sent himself, Neil memorised the numbers, hoping he wouldn't need to look again. He couldn't stand fiddling about with the bloody thing. 'Keep the engine running. I'll be two minutes.'

Fumbling to shove the phone towards his jacket pocket, Neil reached for the door and jumped from the van.

Switching on the cab light, Simon pulled his newspaper off the dashboard and was just about to flick through the sports section when he saw something out of the corner of his eye.

Reaching into the footwell, he picked up Neil's mobile and went to place the phone on the dashboard, but noticed the screen was still on.

He didn't mean to look at the text message on display. All he was trying to do was to put the phone to sleep, but he couldn't help seeing what was on there, could he?

Feeling honoured to witness inner circle inside information, Simon glowed with pride. Putting the phone to sleep, he placed it safely on the dashboard ready for Neil's return.

13

Dan woke up with a head stuffed full of mouldy socks. At least that was what it felt like.

Forcing open his eyes, it took a few minutes to adjust to the unfamiliar room. Seeing a stranger's bare back next to him in the creaky old bed, confusion spiralled. And then it hit him.

He was still at that place from last night.

The recollection of winning more games of poker in the dingy room downstairs, along with retiring for a 'celebration' with one of the girls, gained clarity.

His eyes moved to the right, the movement starting a chain reaction of thumping pain. Whatever was in the 'complimentary' drinks must have been paint stripper.

With difficulty, he sat up, a smile forming on his lips. He'd won a nice packet, he remembered now. Add that to what he'd made at the Whistling Pig and it had been a top night's work. Plus, he'd got a shag. And from the bits he could remember, the girl wasn't too ugly either.

All in all, a good night.

Hang on...

Panic bubbled, starting in the soles of Dan's feet. He'd had a whole wedge of cash, but the memory of coming upstairs last night was sketchy to say the least. *Was his money still there?*

Ignoring the pounding in his head, Dan jumped from the bed and grabbed his jeans and jacket from the floor. He stuffed his hand into the pockets, feverishly rooting around for the wads of cash, his heart pounding to find nothing.

Shit! He'd been turned over. Done.

Tugging his jeans on, he wiped the rapidly forming sweat off his forehead with the back of his arm, then closed his eyes in despair. It must have been this tart. Or one of her mates. They must have all been in it together, the trampy little fucking...

'Are you off? Don't let the security catch you. It costs more to stay overnight,' Tina said, turning over.

Dan started towards the bed, his face twisted with rage, then stopped.

'Don't forget this,' Tina said, holding out a bag of money. 'You were dropping it everywhere last night, so I shoved it in here for you.'

Snatching the bag, Dan could have fallen to his knees with relief.

Tina studied the man. 'I haven't pinched any of it!' She'd wanted to, but if this bloke favoured her, he'd become a regular and then she'd get extras. The guy wasn't short of cash and someone like *this* she'd like to see more of.

Dan continued staring into the bag, a mixture of relief and mistrust rolling around his head, when banging suddenly sounded from the ceiling above. 'What's that?'

Tina shrugged. 'Just some mad woman. I've never seen her, even though she's been there for months.' She leant forward conspiringly. 'We all reckon she's locked in there.'

'Oh, come on!' Dan snorted.

'Seriously!' Tina cried. 'All the other girls think she's deformed or something.'

In reality, she had no clue who or why that woman was upstairs, apart from that her mother dealt with her and she wailed and banged a lot. But even her mother was tight-lipped about it.

Dan pulled his jacket on. 'Right, I'm off.'

Tina pouted coquettishly like she'd seen the others do. 'Will we be seeing you again?'

'You just might,' Dan winked, looking at Tina properly. *And why not?* The girl wasn't bad. Not a patch on Marina, but she didn't whine, which made her a thousand times more attractive. But not as attractive as making money like *this* on a regular basis.

Taking a quick look up and down the landing to make sure the coast was clear, Dan strode along the creaky wooden boards.

* * *

'I want you to tell me exactly who you had in your fucking room all night.' Tom stared at Tina perching on the end of her bed, the picture of sweetness and light.

The little tramp was taking the mick. If she wasn't Amelia's daughter, then he'd sling the cow out here and now.

If he hadn't been stuck on the bog having a dump, he'd have grabbed that man sneaking up the landing by the collar and made him cough up the going rate for spending longer than booked with one of his girls. Taking liberties, it was.

'I weren't hiding him. We fell asleep,' Tina cried.

'A likely story. You know the rules. How much extra did you filch?'

Tina jumped backwards as Tom strode towards her. 'Nothing, I swear!'

Tom sneered inwardly. He didn't have time for Tina's games –
for *anyone's* games. 'You must think I'm fucking stupid or...'

'Tom, seriously!' Tina pressed. 'That guy is minted!'

'What the fuck are you talking about? He looked like a dosser.'

Tina smiled knowingly. 'He had three grand in his pocket. I
could have pinched the lot.'

Tom looked at Tina aghast. 'That's supposed to be good? Why
the hell didn't you nick it, you stupid bi...'

'Because I want him to come back. *You'll* want him to come
back.' Tina sat forward and began to talk.

For once, Tom decided to allow Tina the benefit of touching
him and didn't attempt to stop her roving hands. Leaning back in
the seat, he closed his eyes and let her talk whilst her hands
brought him relief.

* * *

Grant poured the milk he'd just bought from the corner shop into
his tea. 'You okay, sis?'

Marina forced a smile. *No, she wasn't. How could she be?* She
stared back at the latest article in the paper, on page two, no less.

There she was again. Samantha Reynold, gazing adoringly up
at the strong jaw of Seb Stoker, her perfectly manicured hand on
his chest. He proudly held a set of keys aloft, his other arm protectively around Sam's shoulders.

How fucking perfect.

Marina could hardly read the accompanying article, her eyes
had narrowed so much.

Joy for Birmingham's Glamorous Couple

Chamberlains Estate Agents made Seb Stoker and Sam Reynold the happiest couple in the city as they picked up the keys for their Harborne home.

Looking a picture of excitement, the couple cannot wait to get settled in their beautiful new house.

'We'd best get cracking with moving in ready for our house-warming party,' Seb Stoker joked. 'That's if I don't get side-tracked by my gorgeous fiancée.'

Congratulations, Seb and Sam, from everyone at the Birmingham Mail.

Marina tossed the paper across the table. Weren't they just so perfect, so happy, so bloody *everything*...

Congratulations, Seb and Sam, my arse, she stewed.

'You should see your face!' Grant laughed.

'They make me fucking sick!' Marina hissed. In fact, they angered her even more than Dan did. And that was saying something.

She glared at Dan's outline slumped on the sofa in the lounge.

That sorry excuse of a man thought she'd be livid over his absence last night. He'd sloped in, giving her spiel that he'd got trolleyed and fallen asleep at Col's, but she'd been too busy hiding the disappointment that he hadn't been murdered, run over or inexplicably died from unexpected natural causes during the night.

It wasn't like she cared if he didn't come back. The less time she had to look at him, the better. Neither was she impressed with the wad of money he said he'd won. It would only be a third of the real amount... 'At least *he's* happy...' she muttered.

'Fucking cock!' Grant spat. As long as Dan stayed out of the way, he'd ignore the fool. There were more important things to think about. One in particular that he hadn't yet had chance to tell Marina about. 'By the way... I'm in.'

Marina frowned. 'In?'

'At the Orchid,' Grant grinned. 'The head security honcho came to find me last night.'

Marina smiled, although she didn't know whether she was happy for Grant to be around Miss-Bloody-Perfect-Reynold or not. Regardless of how much money might be in it for them, she wanted to hurt the bitch, not help her. *Other things were sometimes more important.* 'When do you start?'

'Tonight.' Grant placed his mug of tea on the offending newspaper. 'I'm meeting this sister of ours later.' He was already wondering how to conceal his hatred for the woman. 'I haven't told you the best bit yet. That article...'

'Don't!' Marina snapped. 'I'm fucking sick of hearing about how happy and perfect they are!'

'Ah...' Grant raised his finger and eyebrows simultaneously. 'That's what I'm trying to say. Apart from them wanting me to help police a hooker problem around the casinos, I'll be part of the security for their housewarming party. I'll have direct access to Samantha's life.'

Marina sat back, resentment stirring once more. So, even Grant would experience the high life, albeit via secondary means, whereas *she'd* be still stuck here with...

A smirk twitched in the corner of her mouth with the sudden glimmer of a tweak to her embryonic idea. With some clever planning and bit of luck, it could work. And if it did, it would be *fantastic.*

Grant's brow furrowed. 'What? You're scheming, I can tell. What are you thinking?'

Marina smiled. 'I'm not sure yet, but I will soon.'

14

'I spotted it, but wasn't close enough to react,' Andrew seethed, his eyes focused on the playback of last night's security footage. 'There!' Pressing pause, he rewound a few frames and pointed at the screen. 'That lot.'

Seb leant closer. 'What, a bunch of young girls?'

'But in just a second...' Andrew let the tape continue, zooming out of the picture to show the passing traffic. 'Here.' Pausing the tape, he poked the screen. 'That car.'

Seb folded his arms. 'I haven't a clue what you're rattling on about.'

'We were on the way back from sorting that delivery last night when I saw those girls rushing down the side road that runs off Broad Street by us.'

'Right?' Seb said uninterestedly, more bothered with the latest amount of cash that he had to offload.

'We'd just turned into our underground car park when the car stopped behind,' Andrew continued. 'One of the girls was terrified. She got in, but the others didn't.' He pointed back to the grainy image on the small monitor. 'It was *this* car.'

He zoomed in further. 'Bollocks. I can't make out the reg. It was a red VW Golf, though.' His face morphed into a scowl. 'By the time I'd got round the barrier, the car had gone and the remaining girls had legged it.'

Neil rolled his eyes. 'It was probably their dad. It's none of our business anyway.'

'It wasn't their dad, I can tell you that!' Andrew spat.

Seb studied Andrew intently. 'What are you saying?'

Andrew turned to face his brothers. 'I'm saying, I reckon someone's pimping young girls around here.'

Neil laughed. 'Just because Seb got rid of those old trouts last night, it doesn't mean everyone around here is a hooker! It's not our business.'

'You may well take the piss, but I'm certain of it,' Andrew barked. 'I don't like that sort of shit. They were only young. It ain't on.'

Seb scowled. 'If that sort of thing is happening right under our noses, then it *does* make it our bloody business.' And this would be the *last* thing Sam wanted to hear.

He jerked his head at the CCTV monitor. 'Keep an eye out tonight for that car and the girls. I'll throw the sick bastard in the canal myself!'

He turned away from the screen and back to his brothers. 'On to this party – the catering and everything else is sorted for Tuesday. Sam is providing a couple of security guys and she's meeting a new man tonight that Kevin Stanton has taken on too, but I need to do likewise with a couple of our guys.'

Neil raised an eyebrow. 'Are you expecting trouble?'

'No,' Seb laughed. 'I've only invited the press and local businesses, but even so, I don't want any of our stuff pinched. Plus, I want no gatecrashers.' He turned to Neil. 'Did you put that cash into the lockup last night?'

'Yeah, but I could have done without doing it at three in the bloody morning!'

'Neil whined so much I had to get one of the runners to give him a fucking lift!' Andrew jibed.

'Yeah, all right,' Neil snapped. 'But what's going on with these poker tournaments? Are they being scrapped?'

Seb folded his arms. 'No one's got any intention of scrapping *anything*. I know there's an escalating problem with those women and, from what I've just heard, it could be worse than we thought, but we'll deal with it.'

And he *would* deal with it. If Andrew was correct and nonces were hanging around his club, that was not happening under any circumstances.

* * *

Casually walking up Broad Street, Marina hoped no one was watching her, otherwise they'd know she'd been up and down the same hundred yards about forty-five times.

It was another bitterly cold night and she was frozen to death. Even with the tyrant behind the counter, it was tempting to take refuge back in the Magic Bean, but doing so meant she wouldn't be ready to pounce the moment the opportunity arose.

And she hoped the opportunity *did* arise soon before she succumbed to hypothermia.

Without making it obvious, Marina glanced at the women congregating along the street, coming to the conclusion they must have built-in antifreeze to withstand hanging around for hours dressed in barely-there clothes. Or maybe they'd taken enough gear to ensure they felt nothing?

She didn't know and, personally, didn't care.

But what she *did* care about was whether that girl would show up. Marina needed to find her because what she'd got in mind was the most brilliant way of twisting the knife and hitting Samantha Reynold where it would hurt most.

Marina continued past the Violet Orchid, not glancing at it out of principle. She had to keep her mind on what she was here to do tonight. Allowing that place and the person within it to rub salt into the open festering wound was not helpful.

But finding that girl would be.

Reaching level with the Royal Peacock, Marina kept her line of sight fixed ahead, whilst watching out of the corner of her eye as security moved women along again, like the previous night.

Swallowing her mirth, she continued. She'd walk a bit further, then make an about turn. A few more circuits and she'd have to accept the girl wasn't showing tonight.

Wait! Was that her?

Stopping abruptly, she craned her neck over the never-ending crawl of traffic, focusing on the young woman standing alone.

It was her!

Without further hesitation, Marina dodged between the slow-moving vehicles, ignoring the car horns and angry shouts.

'Hi again!' Marina said brightly, quickly reaching the pavement on the other side. 'We met in that café the other night.' She pointed in the direction of the Magic Bean. 'Did you find your boyfriend?'

'I, erm... yes, I...' Deb lied, her voice trailing off.

Marina frowned at the girl's eyes darting around. She was either off her tits or plain terrified. She suspected it was the latter. Whoever governed the silly cow had tabs on her movements. But no manner of skanky pimp would put a kybosh on *her* plans.

She must use the girl's fear to her advantage. She took hold of her arm. 'Come with me.'

'No! No, I can't!' Deb pulled against Marina's grip.

'I'm not kidnapping you, for Christ's sake,' Marina said, keeping her hold. 'I'm worried about you.' She nodded towards the Magic Bean not ten yards away. 'Let me buy you a coffee. At least warm up a bit?'

Deb hesitated, her mind spinning. She *was* cold and this lady seemed nice, but Chas... he'd go crazy if she disappeared... *Five minutes wouldn't hurt, would it?*

'Come on,' Marina urged gently. 'You'll catch your death standing here like this.'

Against her better judgement, Deb found herself nodding. Teeth chattering, she allowed herself to be guided in the direction of the café. Her top lip trembled, the unexpected kindness having the power to almost tip her over the edge.

If there had been another alternative to coming up to the attic himself, then Tom would have taken it, but having stupidly sent Amelia to deal with the cheap lager delivery from Bookers, he'd had little choice. It wasn't like he could get any of the others to do it.

Irritably undoing the padlock on the door, Tom barged into the room, gagging as the overpowering stench of unwashed bodies and excrement assailed him.

'Jesus Christ,' he muttered, his eyes adjusting to the darkness. He could just about make out the shape of the figure on the bed in the dingy top floor room. He could definitely smell it.

What the fuck had possessed him to keep Linda Matthews here? Why hadn't he just killed her when he'd had the chance? No one had come looking for her and no one would. Everyone believed she'd done a runner.

But what had seemed the safest option had fast turned into a royal pain in the arse, not to mention a drain on his resources.

As the howling grew louder, Tom stared at the syringe in his hand. Taking a deep breath, he approached the bed. 'Good evening, you raddled old bitch!' he spat, setting up the kit needed to deliver heroin into Linda's scrawny arm.

'Tom?' Linda gasped, her voice weak and raspy. 'Is that you?'

Tom didn't reply, he just grabbed Linda's wrist and wrenched her arm out, searching amongst the many track marks for a space.

Pulling heroin into the syringe, he held it between his teeth whilst he fashioned a tourniquet around the stick-thin upper arm. How bloody ridiculous to even think this *thing*, this tart, would lend any clout in making Samantha Reynold pay for her safe release. Now, because of his stupidity, he hadn't even dared it be let known that he had the old cow in his possession.

'You need to sort yourself out.' Tom tightened the tourniquet, wishing more than ever it was around Linda's neck. 'I can't keep funding your habit. You need to start earning!'

He glared at Linda's grey face; drool hanging from the corner of her mouth and dark circles around her sunken eyes. *What bloke in his right mind would pay for this?*

'I will, Tom,' Linda groaned. 'I just need a bit more gear and then I'll be on it, I promise.'

No, you won't, Tom thought. After this, she'd be back off on one again, safely out of the way for another few hours. Because no one could discover Linda here.

His eyes narrowed as he stuck the needle into one of the few remaining veins that hadn't collapsed.

It wasn't so much the other girls who were the problem. None of them would dare question him and neither would Amelia open her trap, but that incident this morning had flagged up just how risky this was becoming.

That punter of Tina's who'd had the fucking cheek to overstay his welcome could have gone walkabout.

He hadn't, but the point remained the same. He *could* have and an outsider finding a wailing woman wouldn't look good. What if the bloke felt the need to say something to someone?

Tom jammed the plunger of the syringe down harder than he should, receiving a small rush of satisfaction as Linda's eyes rolled as the drug surged up her veins. *It would be a shame if she overdosed...*

But what Tina had told him of that man earlier had been interesting. The drunken boasts of card sharking exploits and leaving London because of it; how he'd all but cleaned up at the sit-down at the Whistling Pig and fleeced the wasted losers downstairs...

Interesting. And if that man returned – which Tina was sure he would – there were some options on offer.

Tom could either wait for the man to rip off more of his customers, then arrange for him to get conveniently mugged on the way out, or he could send him to the Orchid to rip off Samantha Reynold. *Or both.*

If he couldn't get his hands on his daughter's money himself, there was nothing stopping him from getting someone else to do it for him, was there?

Wondering why he was still standing next to this creature in the attic now he'd done his duty, Tom pulled the needle from Linda's vein and released the tourniquet.

Chucking a packet of cream crackers on the bed, he left the room, the urge to breathe untainted air more important than bothering to check whether the woman was still breathing.

15

Grant followed Kevin up the corridor, his nerves buzzing. He felt his hatred rising but had to keep it under wraps. *There was Samantha Reynold!*

'Ah, Sam! I'm glad I've caught you.' Kevin made his way towards Sam. 'Got a moment?'

Locking up for the evening, Sam turned, the key still in her office door. 'Erm, well, I...'

'I thought now would be a good time for you to meet Trevor Jensen. Trevor's our new man.' Kevin extended his arm in Grant's direction. 'He has plenty of experience that will come in handy.'

'Pleased to meet you, Trevor,' Sam smiled. She had planned to have an early one tonight, hoping to have some time with Seb. They'd been like ships passing in the night the last couple of days and the lack of time together grated. Still, Kevin had taken Trevor Jensen on in response to her requirement for additional security, so she must accommodate him.

She unlocked her office door. 'Please, come in.'

Grant smiled. So this was his sister? He stared at her bright smile and wanted to punch the teeth out of the self-assured spoilt bitch's head. 'I don't want to hinder you from going home, Miss Reynold,' he said, his voice treacly-pleasant.

'It's not a problem, and please call me Sam.' Sam moved into her office. 'Take a seat.' She remained standing as the men sat down. 'Can I get either of you a drink?'

'I'm fine, thank you,' Grant replied, hiding his surprise. *She was offering to get them a drink?* What sort of a setup was this? Wasn't she supposed to be the boss? *Oh, this would be so easy.*

'I've been giving Trevor the low down of why we want his services. Perhaps a step down from what he's accustomed to, but extremely beneficial to us.' Kevin glanced at the man sitting to his right. Craig and Stu had done well spotting this one. The man was astute, forward-thinking and knew how everything worked. He was getting on well with the other enforcers already.

'You're too kind, Kevin,' Grant laughed, pretending to be bashful. The twat was right, though. He knew his stuff and yeah, this might be a step down – on the *surface* – but to him, the end result would more than outweigh job satisfaction.

And what about *her*?

It wasn't difficult to study Samantha without her knowledge. That was part and parcel of his job after all – one he was extremely good at, even if he said so himself. He hadn't known what to expect, but *this* wasn't it. He wasn't sure why either, she just wasn't...

Silly, really. It wasn't like she'd be wearing a plaque stating, 'I've robbed my siblings of their dues', or 'Our mother preferred me', or 'I'm a selfish, greedy cunt', was it?

Sam smiled again. 'Trevor, I hear you'll be one of the men policing my event on Tuesday?'

'I will be indeed, Miss Reynold. Sorry, Sam... I guarantee you'll have no unwanted people inside or outside your house. The same applies here the rest of the time.'

'I've filled Trevor in about the escalating "women" problem,' Kevin explained.

'I've been booked many times for my ability to deal with issues subtly and without fuss,' Grant said cryptically. 'There will be no public interest stories for the press to get wind of.'

'That's good to hear,' Sam said, already liking Trevor Jensen. 'The press seem to enjoy reporting every facet of our lives – business and personal – so we don't want any adverse publicity.'

Grant nodded. 'Understood. Leave it to me.' He really hoped that tosser, Dan, defied him and came to try his luck here. He'd love nothing more than to rip the twat to shreds under the guise of working. 'From what I've seen so far, you've got a good team and I'm happy to be able to join it.'

Kevin stood up. 'Let's leave Sam to get off home and I'll fill you in with the schedules.'

Sam stopped Kevin as they moved to leave the office. 'Could I just have a quick word about something separate?'

Kevin nodded. 'Of course. Make your way back to the team room, Trev. I'll join you shortly.'

* * *

Marina had listened to everything Deb said. Not that she'd said much. Nothing that gave her any further information as to what the girl was really up to, but she hadn't expected anything else. Furthermore, she didn't need Deb to spell out what the problem in her life was. She'd already worked that one out.

Marina didn't give a toss. All she had to do was *pretend* that she did – at least until she worked out how to play it.

She eyed the young girl. She looked depressed, but she'd scrub up. She noted Deb's hands, white with cold, gradually regaining their colour from being wrapped around her steaming mug of tea. *She had to play this softly.*

'I can see you're far from happy and before you ask, I ain't a cop, so relax.' Marina slowly lit a cigarette, then offered the packet to Deb. 'I can guess what you're involved in, or should I say, what you've been *forced* into, so enough said on that.'

Deb felt slightly better now the feeling was returning to her toes. 'Then why...?'

'Why have I brought you here, or why am I being nice to you?'

'Both...' Deb said, her voice small.

'Because I want to help you. By helping you, it helps me. I want you to do something and if you do this, shall we say, "job"...' Marina saw a distinct change in countenance wash over Deb's face. The barriers had gone up, the defeat returning. *She must keep her on side.* 'When I say "job", I don't mean in the vein of your *usual* job...'

The colour flooding Deb's cheeks showed Marina she'd hit the nail on the head. 'You'll be paid a large amount of money for one evening's work. This money will give you the means to leave whatever trouble you are in.'

Deb blinked. *Had she heard correctly?* This had to be a setup. Had this woman been sent by Amelia or Chas, or even Tom, to see if she could be filched to work elsewhere?

'Look, girl.' Marina's voice sharpened. 'I don't run a brothel and neither do I personally want your services – not *that* way, at least.' She softened her expression. 'I just need someone to help me with something and I'm offering you that chance because, by the looks of it, you're as happy as I am right now.'

Sighing, she stood up. 'But I'm obviously wasting my time. I apologise if I've offended you.'

Watching Marina pick up her handbag from the table and turn

to walk away, Deb grabbed her arm. 'Wait!' she cried, her voice shaky. 'W-what would I need to do?'

Even Amelia's snarky comments and the death stares from her ugly daughter couldn't remove the small glimmer of possibility – *hope*, even, the type Deb had been sure had disappeared forever – from burning quietly at the back of her mind. It proved there was a small part within her which felt she owed herself the chance to change the situation she'd allowed herself; that *Chas* had allowed her to believe she deserved and was trapped in.

Deb clumped up the stairs towards her room, closing her ears to the wailing from upstairs. Whoever that was on the floor above, she wished they'd shut the hell up.

Her resolve burnt brighter. This place was fucked up; these *people* were fucked up, but this was her chance – one she'd given up hope to even think existed, let alone would ever come. But it had. And she had to do it. She just *had* to.

Ignoring the now plaintive and anguished wailing, Deb let herself into her room and slammed the door, glad it acted as a partial sound barrier.

Placing her handbag down, she stripped off the same stupid dress she'd been told to wear and put on a pair of leggings and a T-shirt before slumping on the bed.

She stared at the damp wall. What if what that woman wanted her to do wasn't even real? After all, it was unusual to offer that sort of money for doing, well, barely anything.

Could the opportunity possibly be kosher?

Deb's heart plummeted. She had no idea who those people were that the woman – Stacey – had mentioned. She rummaged in her handbag and stared at the phone number scrawled on a paper napkin from the Magic Bean.

Stacey must be involved in serious shit to have that sort of cash to chuck around on what she described as 'getting her own back'.

Deb's slight shoulders shrugged. What did it matter? If she pulled it off, then she'd have enough money to disappear from this city for good. She could start again elsewhere and somehow forget that this dreadful period in her life had ever occurred.

Deb folded the napkin and placed it safely back in her handbag.

She didn't need any more time to think about it. She'd take the chance. If it turned out to be a load of old bollocks spouted by a madwoman, then so be it, but she had nothing to lose by finding out for definite.

She looked around the room that had been her prison for the last six months.

If this wasn't a windup, then she wouldn't have much longer to spend here with these – these *people*. And that alone was worth *everything*.

Deb smiled for the first time in ages. Whatever happened, this had given her a spark of her old self back. And she would hold on tightly to that before it drained out of her again.

16

'Where's *he* gone?' Grant nodded to the vacant space on the sofa. The full ashtray and the empty cans of lager overflowing from the bin underlined Dan had been present not too long ago.

'The pub? The casino? To shag a tart? Who knows?' Marina spat. 'As long as he isn't here, that's fine by me!'

Frowning, Grant stared at his sister. 'I thought you wanted to support him? Stick by him because you *love* him?' The word 'love' spat through his teeth.

'Yeah, well...' Marina shrugged. 'Anyway, we've got more important things to concentrate on now.' It wasn't like Grant was going to do his brotherly duty and throw Dan out of the window, otherwise he'd have got rid of the twat by now.

Disappointing, but it was her own fault for encouraging his opinion. An oversight on her behalf. That's if Grant even thought much about her any more, being as he was so wrapped up with the Orchid. 'I would have thought you'd be out by now? Aren't you working tonight?' Marina snapped.

'For God's sake,' Grant sighed. 'I thought you'd have been

pleased that I'm getting on well with everyone and been made party to the ins and outs.'

'Isn't that nice!' Marina sniped.

'Like I told you last night, I overheard Sam and Kevin talking about Stoker putting his money in a lockup, so all we need to do is find exactly where the place is.'

'Sam now, is it?' Marina swung around. 'Why are you so pally? This is supposed to be about getting our own back on our mother and our oh-so-perfect sister, isn't it? You know, the one who's had everything, whilst we've had *nothing!*'

'There will be millions in those safes which is ours for the taking,' Grant cried. 'Or it will be very soon...'

Marina's lips pursed into an extremely thin line. 'But I want personal payback as well as financial. I want that bitch's life ruined for what she's taken from us!'

'But Sam hasn't personally taken *anything!*' Grant barked. 'Our mother did that. I just want the money and I don't give a fuck whose it is. Besides, Sam's marrying Stoker, so what we take from him, we take from *her* too.'

Turning her back on her brother, Marina stared out of the window down into the darkness of the street. Taking money from Samantha's boyfriend wasn't the same as ruining *her* greedy spoilt life. How dare Samantha Reynold have the perfect life with a perfect house, a perfect man and tons of money. 'Why are you standing up for her?'

Grant watched his sister closely. 'I'm not standing up for her! I'm getting the fucking money! What else do you suggest we do?'

'Revenge, that's what!' Picking up the overflowing bin, Marina threw it into the corner of the lounge, the empty beer cans rolling across the grubby carpet. She leant against the windowsill and inhaled deeply. She had to tone this down. Without Grant's help, she was shagged. 'I'm sorry,' she said, putting on her little-girl-lost look. 'This is getting to me. I...'

'I understand.' Grant enveloped his sister in a hug. 'Look, within a few weeks, if not sooner, I'm confident I can get my hands on that money and then we'll be able to start a new life.'

He looked into Marina's face. 'That can be anywhere we like. Surely that's worth more than screwing up someone's happiness? Doing that won't get us a new life, will it?'

Marina squeezed a couple of tears out. Keeping her face downcast, she nodded. 'You're right.' *No, he wasn't. The money wasn't all she needed.*

She'd thought Grant was on the same page, but he wasn't. She was glad she hadn't told him what she'd planned because from what she'd just heard, he'd try to dissuade her. And that would *not* happen.

She smiled weakly. 'Hadn't you best get going? You don't want to be late.'

'If you're sure you're okay?' Grant said, not entirely convinced Marina was all right at all.

* * *

Tom barged into Deb's room. 'Amelia told me about you sloping back in last night with no one – no leads or anything. *Again.*'

Deb backed towards the headboard of her bed. 'I tried, but there was no one about last night. I...'

'Don't give me shit!' Tom pointed his yellowing finger an inch from Deb's eye. 'Are you taking the piss? We're losing money each time you come back empty handed. This ain't no holiday camp!'

Deb swallowed hard. *Didn't she just know it.* She was glad she'd phoned Stacey to tell her she'd accept her offer this morning. All she could do now was hope that it came good because she couldn't deal with this any more. Or rather, *wouldn't*.

At least the glimmer of resolve she'd found hadn't deserted her, even if everything else had.

'Is that a smirk?' Tom grabbed Deb's face, his fingers squashing her cheeks. 'Do you know how easy it would be for me to cut you from here...' Sticking his finger into her skin, he dragged it across her cheek, under her nose and across her other cheek, '... to here? I'll tell you, shall I? *Very* fucking easy!'

He threw Deb back on the bed. 'So, what are you going to do about it?'

'I'll go out tonight and find some more people,' Deb mumbled, avoiding looking at Tom.

'What?' Tom yelled. 'I can't hear you!'

'I said, I'll go out again tonight and fi...'

'Not tonight, you won't.' Tom grinned savagely. 'You've lost sight of your main line of work, so...'

Banging and wailing from above started in earnest, interrupting Tom. Grabbing one of Deb's stilettos off the floor, he whacked it against the ceiling, flakes of Artex crumbling onto the bed. 'Shut your noise, you rancid old whore!' he screamed.

'Who... who is that?' Deb asked before she could stop herself.

Tom waited for Linda's crying to stop, stared at the shoe in disgust and tossed it back on the floor. '*That* is someone who didn't do what they were told.' His eyes glinted in the afternoon light as he jerked his head at the ceiling. 'That's how *you'll* end up if you keep wasting my fucking time.'

Pleased to see Deb's horror, he stormed to the door. 'Oh, and as I was saying before I was rudely interrupted, you're not going out tonight. You're the sole entertainment for a group booking.' He shot her a glare. 'Make sure you wear your school uniform.'

* * *

Andrew stared at the screen. 'Maybe you're right.' He tapped his pen against the CCTV monitor. 'That girl I saw the other night getting into the car isn't around. Perhaps it was nothing.'

Neil pulled up a chair. 'Have you got the footage from the other night to hand?'

Andrew frowned. 'Yeah, it's here. Why?' He scrolled through the relevant dates and times of the footage.

'I thought I saw her last night, but I can't be sure.' Neil watched closely as Andrew played the relevant recording.

'There!' Andrew said, pausing the playback.

'Zoom in.' Neil peered closer. 'Yep, that's her.'

Andrew sat back. 'Why didn't you say? You heard what Seb said.'

Neil nodded. 'I know, but she was the other side of the road, so I wasn't sure. But seeing this, it's definitely her.'

Andrew exhaled loudly. *Proof of an underage racket going on under their noses was not what he'd wanted.* 'You're sure it's the same one?'

'As sure as I can be. She went in that café opposite with another woman.'

Andrew rubbed the beginnings of stubble on his chin. 'Which woman?'

'How do I know?' Neil exclaimed. 'A blonde. Older than *her.* Couldn't see much else from where I was.'

'I wonder if that's who's running those girls?'

'It could be innocent?' Neil countered.

'It could, but let's keep a close eye,' Andrew said. 'My instincts are telling me it's no good.' Pushing his chair away from the monitors, the castors squeaked on the tiled floor. 'I meant to ask, did you delete that text the other night with the safe code on?'

'Of course I did!' Neil snapped. 'I'm not stupid.'

17

In the Whistling Pig, Dan drank his pint, happy to have spent the day successfully avoiding Marina and her bloody brother.

Since the minute Marina had woken, he'd kept out of the way. It hadn't been difficult. Both her and Grant seemed distracted and so, after pretending to do 'useful' things, he'd escaped at the first available opportunity for a well-deserved pint or two.

Actually, he'd had about ten pints and there was still room for more. Even no one wanting to play poker tonight didn't bother him. This lot would forget about him cleaning up soon enough and then they'd be well up for it again.

Nothing like the Londoners, thank God.

Yep. Definitely a good move all round coming to Brum. Plus, he'd got that tasty little chick at the Aurora to pay another visit to...

Unsteadily placing his pint down, Dan turned to Baz. 'Fancy a trip up the Hagley Road later?'

Baz raised his eyebrows. 'What again? You planning to skint them out again?'

'Nah,' Dan laughed. 'I was thinking more along the lines of utilising the "extras" on offer again...'

'You must be mad!' Baz cried. 'With a bird like yours at home, I'm not sure why you'd want to!' From the small glimpse he'd got of that woman when they picked Dan up the other night, she was a bloody stunner!

Dan kept his face from screwing into a grimace. He wasn't admitting his alleged missus wouldn't even shag him any more. 'A change never hurts.'

Dan immersed himself with finishing his pint. That bitch and her freako brother were planning something. They thought him a bloody dimwit, but he wasn't. Their whispered conversations and the looks they shot one another showed they were up to something. Something that didn't include *him*.

Let the pair of inbred fuckers get on with it because their stupid assumption that he took notice of fuck all would be their big mistake.

Oh, yes, whilst pretending to be engrossed in a nonsensical TV programme, he'd seen Grant jerk his head at Marina to follow him out of the lounge.

And what had he done? Exactly what any other rational member of the human race would. He'd followed them.

Dan had heard every bloody word through the balsa wood walls of the shithole flat. And it had made exceptionally fascinating listening.

So they were planning to lift the money out of the safe? *Stoker's safe?*

What he'd heard gave him the impetus to decide he would go for exactly what *they* were going for. He didn't know how yet, but whatever happened, he intended to beat them to it.

All he had to do was keep listening to their hush-hush conversations and in the meantime, maybe it was time to pay the place a visit himself to see the lie of the land?

'Cheers, mate,' Dan said as Col deposited a fresh pint in front of him. He struggled to find his cigarettes through the pile of empties stacking up on the table and scowled at the barman perched on a stool, busy reading the paper, the lazy bastard. 'I was thinking of trying my hand at the Royal Peacock soon. What do you think?'

'I was going to say which hand, but you've only got one!' Col said, creasing into drunken laughter.

'Yeah, very funny,' Dan muttered. 'I'm serious. I want to go to the Peacock.'

'Oh, come on! It costs a fucking fortune for membership in those places,' Baz reasoned. 'You're better off sticking with the pubs, mate.'

Dan frowned. 'But didn't you say there are certain days when you don't need membership?'

'The poker tournaments?' Baz shrugged. 'Yeah, but I'm fucked if I know when they are.' He glanced around the ramshackle bar. 'But *he* does...'

Dan saw a man leaning worryingly close to a woman at least thirty years his senior. With beer goggles that thick, he surely couldn't be reliable?

'Simon?' Baz shouted.

'I thought you said to give that lot from the Peacock who drink here a wide berth? Now he's coming over...' Dan hissed, seeing the man staggering across the sticky carpet.

'I meant the enforcers. Simon's a runner. He ain't nobody, just a drunk twat.' Baz smiled as the man approached. 'All right, mate? Can you tell my pal what night the Peacock's tournaments are?'

Simon flopped down onto a stool and helped himself to Baz's pint. 'They alternate between our club and the Orchid on Tuesday nights.'

Baz didn't miss the turd drinking *his* pint or referring to the

Peacock as 'our' club. *In his dreams...* 'And you don't need membership?'

'Nah, not on poker nights,' Simon replied, now deciding to help himself to one of Dan's fags. He extended his hand. 'Interested, are you? I'm Simon, by the way.'

'Dan,' Dan muttered, the man already bugging him. He watched Simon sway from left to right. With any luck, he'd topple off the fucking stool.

'This Tuesday's tournament is at the Orchid, but if you fancy checking out the Peacock, I'll get you a VIP pass for the members' stuff. I can arrange most things,' Simon boasted.

'Oh, have a day off!' Baz chuckled. 'Next thing you'll be telling us you're off on hols with the Stokers!'

Simon stared at Baz indignantly. 'As a matter of fact, I'm an integral part of the firm!' Grinning, he lowered his voice. 'I get told things only for the inner circle...'

Baz rolled his eyes. 'Righto!'

Simon stared hard at Baz, then turned to Dan. 'If Neil Stoker trusts me enough to give me the code for their bloody safes, then I think you can take it that we're on good terms.'

Ignoring Baz's snort of derision, Dan's pulse ramped up. This might be bullshit, but the guy was pissed and clearly loved to boast, so it could be true. *And if it was...* 'Let me get you another beer in, Simon.'

Wrapping her arms around Seb's neck, Sam pressed her lips to his. 'I hardly see you any more.'

Seb forced a smile. 'Business is hectic at the moment, which is good in many ways, but bad in others. Namely *this*...' He pulled Sam back against him.

'Sorry! I didn't mean to interrupt.' Grant entered the staff corridor, seeing a flash of menace stir behind the eyes of the man with Sam Reynold. *No guesses who that was...*

'Ah, Trevor!' Sam cried. 'This is my fiancé, Seb Stoker. Seb, this is our latest security man, Trevor Jensen.' Even after several months, referring to Seb as her fiancé sent shivers down her spine. The only better thing would be the day she could call him her husband.

'Mr Stoker.' Grant stuck his hand in Seb's direction. 'It's good to meet you. I'm on the team doing the security at your party.'

Seb shook the man's hand. *So this was the guy Kevin Stanton had employed?*

He covertly looked the man up and down. Well-built and tall, with confident, astute eyes... Sam had gone on and on about the list of credentials this bloke had – a freelancer in London.

'I hear you're from the big smoke?' Seb's green gaze coldly scrutinised the man. 'Change of scenery moving to Brum, was it?'

'Something like that,' Grant shrugged. 'It depends how long I'm needed as to how long I stick around.' *And how long it takes me to work out how to empty your safe...*

'Hopefully you'll stick around permanently,' Sam said. 'I think you're a great addition to the team.'

In the handful of times she'd met him, it surprised her just how much she liked Trevor Jensen. He wasn't cocky and she'd seen how well he'd gelled with the other enforcers. Kevin only had good things to say about him, too.

Seb's face remained passive, but underneath the cogs turned. He could see the way this man looked at Sam and he didn't appreciate it. It was too overfamiliar for his liking.

'I'd best get on.' Nodding politely, Grant moved towards the enforcement team room.

Sam waited for the footsteps to disappear before she spoke. 'You could have made more of an effort. Trevor's only just started.'

'I was pleasant.'

Sam straightened Seb's tie. 'Don't give me that! I know you, Seb Stoker, and you gave him *that* look.' She made light of it, but hoped Seb wasn't going back down the road of suspecting everyone. *They were past that now, weren't they?*

'I'm not convinced,' Seb said. 'He's new, yet he's doing security at ours on Tuesday? I'm surprised you're okay with that.'

'Why wouldn't I be?' Sam asked. 'Kevin thinks Trevor's perfect with his specific set of credentials.'

Seb shrugged. 'That's as maybe, but why would someone like that move from London?'

'How should I know?' Sam wrapped her arms back around Seb's waist. 'I'm just grateful another man's been sourced who fits the bill. Now forget about that...' She traced her finger down Seb's jaw. 'Shall we sneak ten minutes in my office?'

Seb unwrapped Sam's arms. 'I'd love to, but I want to catch my accountant before he disappears for the night. I'll see you at home.'

Disappointed, Sam watched Seb walk down the corridor, her brow creasing. He hadn't been himself the last few days. Hopefully the party on Tuesday would give him the chance to unwind and relax.

* * *

Dan was thoroughly enjoying himself. He swigged from a tumbler of house vodka and drunkenly squeezed the breast of the girl comfortably perched on his lap.

She could sit here as long as she liked. The way she was grinding against his groin was having a tantalising effect, even though he was wasted. One thing he wouldn't be wasting was this insistent hard-on.

'You're my good luck mascot, Tamsin,' he slurred.

'I'm Tina, remember?' Tina eagerly stroked Dan's thigh, whilst keeping a firm eye on where he stuffed his winnings. 'You're very good at cards.' She winked suggestively. 'It's not the only thing you're good at either, if I remember rightly...'

Dan glowed with pride. 'You'll get a repeat of that later, if you play your cards right.' He laughed loudly. 'Play your cards right. Oh, I'm good, me, eh?'

'Aren't you just!' Tina cooed, already bored shitless. She glanced at Tom sitting on the other side of the room, clocking every move she made. She'd promised she'd point out this guy the next time he showed up and she had.

Tina inwardly glowed. She was important for once and would get 20 per cent of anything she filched from this man. 'Let me top up your drink,' she insisted, sliding off Dan's lap.

Turning, she leant over to pour more vodka, her cleavage in Dan's face. 'Careful!' she scolded teasingly as he sloshed his drink down her tiny skirt. 'I'll have to take this off if I get soaked.'

Laughing loudly, Dan grabbed Tina by the hip and pulled her towards him, burying his face in her chest.

Tina jokingly pushed Dan away. 'Are you sure you can afford me? Do your winnings amount to *that* much?'

Staggering to his feet, Dan held his glass at a precarious angle. Tipping more vodka down the front of his T-shirt, he banged his fist against his chest. 'Afford it? Course I can fucking afford it! There'll be lots more coming soon, that I can promise you!'

Tina risked another glance in Tom's direction before wrapping her arms around Dan's neck. She batted her badly applied fake lashes. 'Are you sure about that? You'll skint everyone out around here, the way you've been going, and then what will you do?'

'That won't be an issue. The amount of money in some places is immense!' Dan's grin split wider. And he would have it all. Now he was privy to stuff they weren't, Marina and Grant were too late, the stupid deluded fools.

'Ooh, are you planning to try your hand at one of those places up Broad Street?' Tina asked sweetly. Maybe she could accompany him? She'd always wanted to go in one of those swish casinos. 'Which one are you a member of?'

'Never you mind.' Tina's awe bolstered Dan's ego no end. He gulped down a huge mouthful of the vodka. 'Anyway, I don't need to be a member.' He tapped the end of his nose. 'Put it this way, I've got inside information and I know where they keep their money...'

Tina kept her fake amazement in place. 'Wow! You must be really cool to be in with people like that!'

Dan drunkenly arched an eyebrow. 'Who said I'm in with them? They ain't my friends, but their fucking money is!' He laughed maniacally and swayed even more unsteadily.

Tina guided Dan back into his seat. 'Sit there and I'll fetch a fresh bottle.'

She skittered over to the bar, giving Tom a sideways look. As expected, he followed her behind the makeshift counter. 'Did you hear that?' she hissed as she rooted around for a new vodka bottle.

Tom nodded. *He'd heard, all right.* Under the cover of the bar, he grabbed Tina's wrist. 'Get yourself upstairs with him before he passes out. I want more information.'

'What do you mean?' Tina stared at the painful grip Tom had of her wrist.

'I mean, find out what *he* meant. It's not fucking difficult. Is he planning a job or talking crap? I need to know.' Tom's eyes narrowed into slits. 'This is your chance to fucking prove your worth, so I suggest you take it.'

18

Amelia smiled smugly at Tina. From what her daughter had just said, Tom should be mightily impressed with her detective skills.

Maybe now Tom would realise he'd made a mistake with Deb – who had so far brought nothing to the table – and should have given that task to Tina instead?

Chas was slipping in Tom's estimation quicker than a lead balloon too. It served the silly bastard right for treading on her toes. This was *her* gig and Chas had no right to ride roughshod over it the way he had.

Under the guise of preparing the first dose of the day for the woman upstairs, Amelia glanced between Tom and Tina, seeing Tom's brain whirring at ten to the dozen. 'You've done really well there, Tina,' she said loudly.

Tom looked up sharply, as if he'd forgotten he wasn't alone. 'Better than well, I'd say.'

In fact, she'd done *more* than well. He found himself smiling at Tina before he remembered himself. It would do no one any good to forget their place.

Tina preened, over the moon to be on the receiving end of Tom

Bedworth's admiration. 'It was easy. I could hardly stop him once he got started,' she enthused. 'He couldn't wait to impress me.'

Tom frowned. It seemed a bit too simple that this Dan geezer should come in here spilling his guts about his plan to do a job on the Stokers. Who in their right mind broadcast that if they wanted to live?

But if it was real...

'Dan knows the codes for the safes and everything!' Tina continued.

Tom eyed Tina curiously. *She had to be exaggerating, surely?* 'What are they, then?'

'Well, erm, he didn't exactly say. Not yet... but...'

'Ah, just as I thought – it's bollocks,' Tom snapped. 'There's no way someone would know something like that. I mean, who the fuck is he? Where would he have got that information from?'

Tina shrugged. 'He seemed certain to me. He was right chuffed about getting one over on his girlfriend. It's her who's planning the job.'

Tom sat back. 'You're telling me this is down to some bird?' He sighed. 'What a waste of bloody time.' He'd thought for a split second then there could be a hint of truth in this. 'He's having you on.'

Tina shook her head frantically. 'No, I don't think so. It's not just his girlfriend. Her brother has just started work at the Orchid and Dan overhears things.'

Tom's senses prickled. 'His girlfriend's *brother* works at the Orchid?'

Tina nodded enthusiastically. 'Yes and Dan hates him. He hates his girlfriend too. He only came to Birmingham with her because he had no choice, but now he knows they're planning this job and he knows the safes' codes and they don't, he's sticking around.'

'And why would Dan know these codes?' Tom folded his arms defensively. 'Psychic, is he?'

Tina shrugged. 'He said he heard it from one of the Peacock's runners.'

Tom mulled this over further. If he was going to use this guy to get somewhere, then the man would need to keep his trap shut in future. He kept the smirk from crawling back onto his face. 'When is this bloke coming here again?'

'Dunno. He's going to the Orchid on Tuesday for the poker tournament,' Tina said casually. 'He reckons it will be a good night, being as the main people will be tied up at some housewarming party. His girlfriend's brother is doing the security there too.'

A sharp influx of elation jolted through Tom's veins at this additional snippet of information. *Housewarming party?* He'd heard about that in the paper. He quickly got to his feet. 'I need to see this Dan pronto.'

'I don't know when he...'

'I need a conversation with him,' Tom barked.

Amelia glanced from Tom to Tina. 'Tina can't be expected to know when the man will be back,' she reasoned.

'She should have made fucking sure before he left!' Tom paced around his desk, then reined himself in. Shoving a smile over the scowl, he put his arm around Tina and kissed her forehead in a rare display of affection. 'You did great, girl, and I'm counting on you to continue doing so.'

This was the best thing that had happened in *months*.

Maybe his luck hadn't abandoned him after all?

He jerked his head at the syringe in Amelia's hand. 'Get a move on delivering that. We don't want the noise putting people off, do we?'

* * *

Looking over her shoulder, her ears finely tuned for movement, Marina slipped along the hallway to Grant's room. He'd be out most, if not the *whole* day, plus the evening, no doubt pandering to Samantha Reynold's wishes.

'Doing that won't get us a new life, will it?' she muttered sarcastically, bitterly remembering Grant's words from yesterday.

Yes, it would. *Partly.*

Killing Samantha would mean removing her mother's favourite daughter. Linda may be keeping a low profile, but she was somewhere behind the scenes benefiting from all that Samantha could offer.

Not for long, the sneaky old bitch.

Marina's beautiful face twisted into a snarl. That old witch had already showed her face once in connection with Samantha, as that photo from the paper Grant had shown her proved.

The stupid old cow might have disappeared from her previous location and not been seen for a while, but she'd clearly washed her hands of all her old cronies because she'd had a better offer, courtesy of Samantha.

Well, Samantha, Marina thought, opening Grant's wardrobe. *You might have fooled my brother, but you don't fool me.*

Getting on her knees, Marina rooted around in the bottom of the wardrobe, pulling out several pairs of her brother's boots. *His kit must be stashed in here somewhere.*

She knew him well enough to know that he wouldn't go *anywhere* empty handed.

Ruining Samantha's life, breaking her heart and then killing her would also trash that skank of a bitch mother's plans. What she'd lined up to claw from her preferred daughter with her druggie, grasping hands would turn to dust once the source of her newfound wealth and lifestyle was no more.

Bingo – two birds with one stone.

Grant might have forgotten their shitty childhood, but *she* hadn't.

Marina smiled as her fingers touched a suitcase behind spare bedding at the back end of the wardrobe. Holding her breath, she pulled it out, sure to note the exact position of everything around it.

She paused, double-checking Dan was still otherwise engaged with whatever shit he was glued to on the box and, satisfied all was well, opened the suitcase.

She moved the neatly folded jumpers to one side.

Yep. There it was...

Her eyes locked onto the outline of the Beretta securely wrapped at the bottom of the case and she ran her hand over it just to make sure. She didn't want to risk unwrapping it; not until she needed it, because she'd never be able to replace it in the identical way Grant had done.

Because then he'd know...

And he couldn't know until the very last minute.

Marina bit her lip. She'd expected Grant to embrace this part of the task as much as her, but now that wouldn't happen. At least, not at the moment. But he'd see sense by the time this part came to fruition.

Replacing the jumpers, she zipped up the suitcase and meticulously put everything back in place.

Now her mind was at rest over the gun being available, she could concentrate on the first part. And that would happen on Tuesday.

Yes, she'd need Grant's help with that, but that was okay. He'd do as she said. He always did.

Marina stood up, wincing from kneeling on the wooden bedroom floor and pulled the door behind her, ensuring she left it ajar the inch it was to start with.

The first part of Tuesday's plan began tonight.

* * *

Seb stared at the piece of paper in his hand. *What a bloody nightmare.*

In a way, it would have been easier not to know exactly how much backlog of money they'd got, but Fletcher had confirmed last night, thanks to his contact in the tax office, that the Peacock was definitely due for an impromptu audit and investigation. He had to think about this. And think about it fast.

He stared at the scribbled notes he'd made once more. Just under three and a half million pounds excess and more coming in every day.

'Neil saw that young girl again the night before last. She wasn't there last night, but...' Andrew frowned at the concern on Seb's face. 'Is everything all right?'

Seb sighed and placed his piece of paper on the desk. 'No, not really.' He chewed his inner cheek. 'This tax and customs thing. I've had it on good authority that we're on the list for a full audit.'

'Shit!' Neil looked first to Seb then Andrew. 'Does that mean...?'

'That they'll investigate and search our properties and list all the assets? Yes, it does,' Seb said.

'Then we have to move the safes from the lockups,' Neil gasped.

'Where to? Who do you trust to hold that cash? Customs could land on us tomorrow or in six months,' Andrew cried. 'It's not like they'll tell us. Even if we did trust someone to hold the cash, we can't expect them to do so for that length of time.'

'At the end of the day, Customs know we've got a hell of a lot more than what we declare. They just need to prove it.' Seb grimaced. 'And at this rate, they will!'

'It also rules out any more big purchases we could make around now. Am I right?'

'You got it. And let's face it, there's only so many things you can buy with a suitcase full of cash.'

'At least you offloaded some on the house.'

'A drop in the ocean,' Seb said glumly. 'Christ, we've never had so much excess cash waiting to be laundered. It's a fucking disaster!' Seb snatched up his ringing phone and cut the call, leaving the receiver off the hook.

'Could you not put a chunk through the Orchid?' Andrew asked.

Seb shook his head. 'No. And even if I could, I *wouldn't*. It would just pass the problem on to Sam, or we'd all get done for laundering.' He stared back at the paper. 'Plus, I haven't mentioned anything about this. I don't want her worrying.'

'What's the plan then?'

Seb sighed. 'I haven't got a fucking clue. And that's what's bothering me more than anything.'

19

Sam walked along the street, her jaw set. She glanced at people as she passed – shoppers and businessmen, but tonight would tell a different story.

And it was a story she was not liking.

Nearing the Peacock, she upped her pace. Why hadn't Seb answered his phone? She could have done without having to come here. Although Seb was absent from his office, she just had to hope he was in the Peacock somewhere because she had to talk to him. From what she'd just been told, a resolution must be discussed.

Her brow creased. She was not having that sort of thing go on in front of her nose or *anywhere* if she could help it and could barely believe Seb had failed to mention this could be such a big problem.

And if it was, then it was something they were duty bound to deal with.

Sam yanked open the heavy door of the Peacock. No door staff during the afternoon. Approaching the reception desk, she forced a smile. 'Hi, Serena. Do you know where Seb is?' she asked brightly, despite her black mood.

'Good afternoon, Miss Reynold,' the receptionist beamed, her sylphlike hand pointing in the direction of the staff corridor. 'Mr Stoker's in his office.'

'I'll pop down then,' Sam said, not waiting for permission. Walking to the corridor, she frowned. *If Seb was in his office, why hadn't he answered his landline?*

She shouldn't have had to learn about this from Kevin. Seb should have told her of his and the firm's concerns. Why did everyone else know, apart from her?

Striding down the corridor, Sam tried to be rational. Maybe Seb hadn't wanted to say anything until he had definite answers. He knew how much this subject angered her and the deep-seated hatred she held for it.

Her personal obsession had spawned a hatred for the people governing vulnerable and impressionable youngsters and if she could stop one girl being dragged into a life of misery, then it was better than nothing.

Reaching Seb's office, Sam tapped on the door and walked straight in. 'Seb? Are you... oh!'

The abrupt silence that fell at her arrival and Seb shoving paperwork into the drawer of his desk made Sam freeze. She looked from Seb to Andrew and then Neil. 'Am I interrupting something?'

'Sam!' Seb got to his feet and shut the desk drawer. 'Is every-thing all right?'

'I could ask you the same!' Sam replied, suspicion brewing.

'Just busy, that's all.' Seb kissed Sam on the cheek and gestured for her to sit down.

Sam lowered herself down into the chair. What was Seb hiding? What were they *all* hiding? They'd immediately fallen into silence as she'd opened the door. She'd long since removed her lack of trust where Seb was concerned, but his behaviour the past couple of days did not sit comfortably.

She looked between the Stokers, refusing to allow her mind to run away with itself. 'I got no answer from your phone... I just had a meeting with Kevin and he mentioned an issue with possible underage pimping?' She looked directly at Seb. 'Why haven't you mentioned this to me?'

'It was me,' Neil cut in. 'I asked Kevin if he or any of his staff had noticed anything this last week.'

Seb glared at Neil. 'And I didn't mention it because we weren't sure.'

'You don't need to skirt around this with me because of my mother's past.'

Seb held his hands up – anything to deflect from the accusatory list of figures in his desk drawer. 'I know it's difficult. I admit I didn't want to have to go down that road unless we knew what, if anything, we were dealing with.'

'And we still don't know,' Andrew added. 'We're just keeping an eye out for certain people we have suspicions about. It's not a big deal.'

'Plus, there's nothing to report,' Neil added. 'We'd have told you if there was.'

Sam wanted to point out that they should have done so, *regardless* of whether there was anything to report or not, but she kept it to herself. It would only make it look like she was on the defensive. Perhaps she was? But whether she appreciated the sentiment or not, Seb had her best interests at heart, she supposed.

* * *

Slamming the gear stick into third, Chas shot off from the lights and continued up the Hagley Road, squeezing up the side of a double decker on his left without losing his wing mirror to either that or the oncoming traffic.

He glanced at Deb out of the corner of his eye. Thankfully, since he'd made it clear they had no future, she'd backed off. But she'd backed off a bit too easily. On one hand, this was good, but he did wonder why she'd taken it on the chin so well.

Maybe it was like Amelia said – the silly cow had realised it was pointless? But that didn't mean she was exempt from instructions. If Deb thought she'd get away with making him look a mug for the umpteenth time, he'd sling the ungrateful little slag into a layby.

His eyes narrowed. She must be stupid to think he wouldn't notice she'd sloped off the other night. He'd only got out of the car to nip up an alley for a piss, but when he got back, she was nowhere to be seen. He'd been gone less than two bloody minutes. Was she so thick to play him after what had happened last time?

Oh, she might have said she was chatting to some likely contenders, but he didn't believe it.

Chas glared at the side of Deb's head as she stared out of the window, his face screwing into a scowl as they approached Broad Street. She was hardly the best advertisement for the Aurora with a face like a slapped fish. 'You'd better pull on a better attitude than the one you've got if you want anyone to give you the time of day.'

Chas's voice jolted Deb from the imaginary world she'd put herself into. She could feel his eyes burning into her, but that was fine. Whatever marks his glaring might sear into her skin just added to the new bruise she'd concealed under layers of makeup.

But no amount of makeup could hide last night from her memory.

She shuddered, refraining from touching her swollen cheek-bone. Those men had probably been the worst yet. And that was saying something. The five middle-aged 'businessmen' on a work trip from Sheffield had thought it would be amusing to pass her around like a doll whilst they laughed, joked and slapped her around.

Deb closed her eyes with revulsion. The only way she'd stopped herself from screaming was the hope of shortly getting out of this whole setup.

If she couldn't, then she didn't know what she'd do.

She continued staring out of the passenger window as the Hagley Road turned into Broad Street and fought to quell the forming tears. She couldn't carry on like this. If she couldn't end it, then it would end *her*.

Her new-found resolve was slipping, but she wouldn't let it. She *couldn't*.

If Stacey wasn't here tonight or this came to nothing, then she'd rather be dead...

'Did you hear what I said?' Chas's hand moved from the gear stick to grip Deb's leg, his fingers digging into her thigh.

Yelping, Deb tried easing Chas's grasp. 'You're hurting me,' she whimpered, hating herself for sounding so desperate.

Chas swerved to the side of the road behind a row of taxis and yanked the handbrake on. 'I can't see the point of this.' He wrenched his hand from Deb's grip. 'If you go out there like this, you'll get nowhere. I'll not have you make me look like a prick in front of Tom again. I might as well take you straight back to the Aurora.'

'No!' Deb shouted, surprised she'd got the energy. She couldn't miss meeting Stacey – it was her only ticket out of here.

Seeing the shock of her outburst morph into rage on Chas's face, she rapidly weighed up the situation. 'What I mean is, I won't let you down. N-no one gave me time to explain before. I was making headway the other night and then the girl got scared. I got nervous because the time before I was due to meet you was running out and this girl must have picked up on that.'

Chas frowned. 'You shouldn't be so transparent. That's your fault.'

Deb nodded meekly. 'I know. I'm scared I'll upset you and... I just want to please everyone...' She smiled weakly, wishing she could spit in his lying face. 'It puts me off, knowing you're watching me.'

'Oh, don't be pathetic!' Chas sneered. 'I watch you because you can't be trusted!'

Deb stared, wide-eyed. 'When did I ever betray you? I didn't, Chas, you know that.' The words stuck in her throat, but she forced them out regardless. 'It's been difficult since you... you dumped me...'

'There was nothing to dump, you stupid cow!' Chas barked. 'Best you don't let me down tonight.' Leaning over, he opened Deb's door. 'Off you go. Perhaps if you do well tonight, then I won't think so badly of you.'

Holding back her relief, Deb scrambled from the car. 'Shall I meet you in the usual place?'

Chas nodded. 'I'll be around somewhere. Wait somewhere obvious and keep an eye out. You've got an hour. Make it count.'

Pulling the door shut, Chas grinned, watching Deb jump back onto the pavement. The thick cow needed to be quick if she didn't want her fingers lopped off.

He slammed the car into first and continued up Broad Street. Deb would go out of her way to do well tonight.

He laughed out loud. She wouldn't dare try to pull a fast one. He'd broken her too much for that.

For once, he could ditch sitting in a fucking freezing car policing the stupid cow and instead go to that boozer around the corner for a pint in the warm.

* * *

Grant stood over the map of the layout of Sam's house. It was bloody massive and that felt like yet another insult.

This act of pretending to be part of the team protecting the woman was aggravating beyond words. Digging his nails into his palms, he reminded himself that it was necessary in order to wheedle his way into Sam's trust and her life. It wouldn't be forever. But now he had a definite plan of getting money by lifting Stoker's safes, it made everything palatable – even *this*.

Yet Marina worried him. Her wish to remove Samantha wasn't part of the plan. Well, it might have been had it been the only viable solution, but it wasn't. There was a lot at stake here and doing that would cause unwanted issues. Like *big* ones.

As a newcomer to the Orchid security, if Sam was suddenly offed, who would be the prime suspect?

His jaw clenched. Yep. *Him*.

Why bring that sort of bother? A huge amount of money was up for grabs without adding additional grief.

Marina must not lose track of this. The only important outcome was to receive their financial dues – not anything else. Wiping out Sam's boyfriend's money would have a knock-on effect and was good enough retaliation as far as he was concerned.

The other major problem here was Stoker.

'Is everything clear?' Kevin tapped his pen on the map. 'You both know what part you'll be policing?' He looked between both men. 'Trevor, you're dealing with the front door and the guest list, and Stu, you're doing the back entrance and garden.'

Grant pretended to be interested. The brief was simple enough, but he wanted info that wasn't on the map and never would be. 'What's Stoker like? I met him yesterday and I don't think he liked me very much.'

Kevin grunted. 'Seb's a tough nut, but he's okay.'

'Yeah, but he stared at me like I was trying to get into Sam

Reynold's knickers!' *And that was not something on the agenda.* Sam Reynold was undoubtedly gorgeous, but she was his sister, for God's sake.

'Stoker has been really good for Sam and for the Orchid in general these past few months,' Kevin scowled. 'Strange, you may think, considering the Stokers have long since been rivals.'

Grant nodded. 'Strange isn't the word...'

Kevin folded his arms and perched his big frame on the edge of the desk. 'There's a lot of things you don't understand. Not long ago, something happened which could have ended *very* differently, so Seb Stoker is doing his job in every way.' He fixed Grant with a long stare. 'That's all I'll say on the matter.'

Grant raised his hands in submission. 'I meant no offence. Just getting the lie of the land, that's all. Us Londoners aren't great at wording things,' he grinned, attempting to make light.

Placated, Kevin nodded. 'Okay, so coming back to Tuesday...'

Grant leaned back over the large map on the desk and pretended to knuckle down to the coming task.

20

Holding the newspaper cutting, Deb gaped at the man in the photograph. '*Him*?' It was weird enough what this woman was asking for, but to *this* guy? 'W-what's this about?'

Marina's mouth twitched at one corner. 'That, you don't need to know. All you need to know is what you need to do.'

Deb read the accompanying article again. She had never seen this man before. She couldn't say she knew much about casinos either, but she had *heard* of the Stokers and the Reynolds. *Everybody had.*

'Stacey, I don't know about this. I...'

'What's the problem?' Marina hissed. 'This should be water off a duck's back for someone in your trade! Oh, and you'll need these...' She passed a carrier bag across the table.

'W-what's this?' Deb asked.

'Don't look in it here!' Marina hissed. 'It's a uniform you'll need to wear, plus the stuff to do the business. I'll explain the details in a moment.'

Deb blinked, fear bubbling. Stacey had been so kind and eager to help, but now she'd changed. 'But this is one of the Stokers and not just that, he's the head of th…'

'Keep your fucking voice down!' Marina dug her fingers into Deb's arm. Her eyes darted around the café. It was stupid talking about this with people around. And now, after all her planning, this stupid little tart was getting cold feet?

Keeping hold of Deb's arm, she stood up. 'Let's go for a walk.'

'But I…'

'*Now!*' Marina kept her smile in place, but her tone was harsh.

Realising she had little choice, Deb rose from the table and followed Marina out of the café onto Broad Street.

Keeping a firm grip, Marina began walking. 'Link your arm through mine and smile.'

Deb struggled to keep up. Chas would be watching, and he'd see her walking off with this woman. She'd be in even more shit now. 'Stacey, I…'

Marina stopped. 'Your pimp has gone around the corner, so he's not watching you. He's in a pub down there somewhere.' She casually pointed down the road. 'I presume that's what's bothering you, so stop flapping and listen.'

Deb swallowed, the horrible realisation hitting her between the eyes, probably for the first time.

Chas *was* a pimp.

The urge to run back to her father, despite everything, surged. Why had she evaded the glaring truth by toning it down, like it made her situation better?

Deb felt like crying with shame. *She was a prostitute.* And she was luring other girls just like her into that awful Aurora.

Marina watched the emotions crashing over Deb's face. The girl really was deluded. 'Look, I know what you do, but I also know you don't want to be in that position.' She tried to be reasonable as she pulled Deb along. 'I'm not judging you. I'm giving you the chance to change your life, so I suggest you grab it. This will be the only time, though, I can promise you that.'

'But what if I get caught...?'

'You won't,' Marina snapped. 'Otherwise, as well as the prick in the red VW Golf, you'll have me on your back!' Her mouth twisted into a sneer. 'And believe me, you don't want that!' She patted Deb's shoulder. 'Right, like I said, keep smiling and walking and I'll tell you exactly what to do.'

Deb's legs felt like concrete as she walked on, her mind racing. Now she was even more trapped, but if one evening's work meant she could escape from everything, then didn't that justify it?

Whether it did or not, she had to do it.

* * *

Neil had taken the opportunity to nip to the off-licence to buy a packet of fags. They were cheaper than in the Peacock's rip-off vending machines.

His ad hoc excursion was also an excuse to check the lie of the land. There had been little call for security to move congregating women on tonight, and whilst that was a positive sign amid the concern over underage pimping, he wanted to see for himself.

Neil was about fifty yards away from the Peacock when he did a double take. *Wasn't that the girl he'd seen the other night?*

He craned his neck through the line of traffic, unable to get a clear view to the other side of the road.

There was another woman too and she looked like the one he'd seen with the younger girl on Friday night.

Neil looked from left to right, then frantically picked his way across the road. It was *definitely* the same girl.

'Hey!' he yelled, clocking the girl look in his direction, whilst the older woman hurried off the opposite way.

Reaching the other side of the road, he upped his pace, scouring the pavement ahead to make sure he didn't lose the girl. 'Wait!'

Forcing himself to break into a run, Neil closed the gap.

'Get off!' Deb screamed, panic cascading as the man grabbed her arm.

'I'm not attacking you!' Neil glanced around, aware that people were staring at him. *This didn't look good.* 'I just want to talk to you.'

Jerking away, Deb pulled her jacket tightly around her, her need to escape this stranger intense. 'Leave me alone!' she cried, her eyes darting around. *Where was Stacey?*

'Are you all right?' Neil frowned. The girl paused, giving him time to actually look at her. The kid couldn't be more than sixteen! And was that a bruise on her cheek?

'What is it to you?' Deb snapped, anger coming to the fore. Was everyone the same? All wanting to get into her knickers? Her hand brushed her pocket where the packet Stacey had given her sat. 'I'm not working tonight.' *And soon she wouldn't be doing this ever again.*

Neil's eyes narrowed. 'Don't insult me, you silly girl. I'm not interested in kids, but I *am* interested in who is sending you out. We've seen you before.'

Deb faltered. *Who had seen her before?*

She looked at the man in front of her properly – a handsome bloke with piercing green eyes and distinctive features... Very similar looking to that other man... The man Stacey wanted her to...

Shit! This was one of the Stokers! Her heart pounded. What was it he'd said? *They'd seen her before?* How could she do what was required now? She'd be recognised.

Neil watched the girl's face with interest. 'Tell me who is making you do this.'

'I don't know what you're talking about,' Deb blustered, turning away. 'You've mistaken me for someone else. I...'

'I don't think so. You just said you weren't "working" tonight, so I'm not wrong on *why* you're here. Who did that?' Neil pointed to Deb's slightly swollen cheekbone.

Deb self-consciously raised her hand to her face. 'No one... I...'

'Who's that woman you were just with? Does she make you do this?' Neil pressed. 'Or the guy in the red car?'

Deb paled. *Red car? Shit. Shit. Shit!* 'Please! I need to go.'

Turning on her heels, she moved along the pavement far quicker than she thought possible. She risked a glance over her shoulder, horrified to see the man following her.

'Wait!' Neil roared.

Deb wasn't waiting. Chas would kill her for this. As would Stacey when she realised her plan was ruined.

Spotting Chas's car on the other side of the road, Deb skittered through the traffic, never believing she'd be so glad to see the man who had broken her heart, used her and treated her like shit. Pulling open the door, she clambered into the passenger seat.

'You stupid cunt!' Chas barked. 'Where the fuck have you been? I've been looking for you for ten minutes!'

Now clearing the other side of the road, Neil raced up to the car. The car Andrew had pointed out on the CCTV footage. *The red VW Golf...*

This bastard was something to do with all of this and he'd be finding out exactly what.

Seeing the hand of the male driver crushing the girl's face into the headrest, Neil banged on the window. 'Oi!' he yelled, pulling at the car door.

The girl's terrified eyes darted over, meeting with his for a split second. 'Let her out!' Neil screamed, the driver's hand now around the girl's throat. He had to get that girl away.

He pulled at the passenger door handle again. Finding it locked, he banged on the red metal. He couldn't break the glass with her sitting so close. Rushing around the other side, Neil reached for the driver's door. He'd put this window through, not giving a fuck if he cut the bastard behind the wheel. 'You! Let that girl out!'

His elbow was against the glass when the car screeched off and Neil could do nothing but jump out of way.

Ignoring the people staring at him, he straightened the sleeves of his suit jacket and casually crossed the road as if all was normal.

Bollocks!

But he had got a clear look at the man and needed to get back to the Peacock and jot down the car's registration plate before it disappeared from his memory.

As unpalatable as it was, there was now no way of pretending there wasn't an issue with young girls being controlled for unsavoury means around here.

21

Sam poured a fresh cup of tea, enjoying the morning light filtering through the tall sash window into the wood-panelled breakfast room. She looked across at Seb. 'Want a top-up?'

'No, thanks,' Seb muttered distractedly.

'There's people arriving in the morning to do the decorations for the party tomorrow,' Sam said brightly, aware things had been a little strained between her and Seb since her impromptu arrival at the Peacock yesterday. 'The caterers will be here about five.'

Everyone could do with a well-earned break. Especially Seb. But there was something missing; something she would have loved to have been able to arrange. Her brows furrowed. 'I wish I could have located Linda and invited her. She'd love this house.'

'Hmm,' Seb grunted.

'I know you believe she's turned me over, but I still don't believe that's the case.' Sam sipped her steaming tea. 'And it's not just a case of wishful thinking, before you say that. It's a genuine instinct.'

'Nice that's all you've got to worry about! For God's sake, I wish you'd just accept that Linda used you,' Seb snapped, getting up.

Immediately regretting his words, he bent down and planted a kiss on the side of Sam's neck. 'Sorry. I didn't mean to snap.'

Sam turned around in her seat, hurt by Seb's words. For days now, he'd been uncharacteristically off with her. 'What's going on? Have there been additional things happening with the prostitute problem? I know you think I'm cross for not being kept in the loop, but you'd tell me, wouldn't you? I know I get upset about how Linda was treated when she was young, and sometimes I let what Liam tried to do affect me, but...' She frowned. 'Is it that you'd rather not have this party? You haven't been yourself for days and...'

'Everything's fine,' Seb said hastily. 'I'm just overworked. Now I've got to dash.' He winked at Sam in his usual way and left the room before the smile could slide from his face in front of her, bristling yet again at the mere mention of that bastard Liam's name.

Sam heard Seb's car start, the tyres crunching on the long gravelled driveway. He might have just turned on the charm, but *something* was bothering him.

Cold slithered up her spine. Was it Liam again? She'd just seen his eyes flash when she'd mentioned him a moment ago, so was it that which was playing on Seb's mind?

Seb had told her time and time again the attack hadn't been her fault, but if that was the case, why did it make him so angry? And angry with *her*, it seemed.

There was only so long she could keep brushing his hurtful comments under the carpet. And the thought that he might not feel the same way about her any more cut her to the quick.

Sam gathered the breakfast plates together. Maybe Andrew would know what was worrying Seb? She wouldn't ask anything until after the party, though, and could only hope Seb was in a good mood tomorrow night – especially with the press in attendance. They'd pick up on unrest straight away.

Taking the plates into the kitchen, Sam stared out of the window into the garden. Maybe they should cancel the housewarming? Short of Neil and Andrew, everyone else invited were business associates and the press. It wasn't really what she'd had in mind, but Seb had insisted.

Sam glanced at her reflection in the kitchen window. The party was organised now and it was too late in the day to cancel.

* * *

Tom wasn't sure if he'd heard correctly. 'She was talking to *who*?'

Chas shrugged. 'I can never tell which one is which, but it was definitely one of the Stoker twins she was talking to when I arrived to pick her up.'

Tom's eyes narrowed. 'Why would you "arrive to pick Deb up"? Aren't you watching her *all* the time?'

'It's just a turn of phrase,' Chas spluttered, realising he'd dropped himself in it.

'Then how long was she talking to this Stoker for?' Tom pushed. 'And why?' He had to be careful. No one knew of his history with the Stokers, and he must keep it that way.

'Erm, I'm not sure. As I turned the car around, I lost sight of her,' Chas lied. There he was thinking it was safe to go to the boozer. By the looks of it, that little slut had dropped him in it yet again.

Leaving his poky little office, Tom loped up the stairs, his jaw clenched. If that little tart had brought trouble to his door, he'd kill her. He'd rip her to shreds, bit by fucking bit. He hadn't remained in the shadows, losing out hand over fist, only to get a possible in to some long-awaited money via this Dan punter, just to be dropped in it by Deb, the stupid slag!

Reaching Deb's bedroom door, Tom didn't knock; he didn't even use his hands. He was too angry to touch anything with his fingers, short of pushing the tart's eyeballs through their sockets into her head to rattle around inside her empty skull like marbles.

Raising his foot, Tom booted the door open. As it thudded loudly against the inside wall, he lurched over to the petrified figure on the bed. 'You stupid cow!' he roared, his fist grasping Deb's hair. 'What the fuck do you think you're playing at?'

Howling in pain, Deb stared at Tom, terrified. 'I haven't done anyth...'

'Why were you speaking to a Stoker?' Tom snarled, his bared teeth inches from Deb's face, spittle spraying over her cheek. He twisted the fistful of hair. 'You fucking tell me everything now! Understand?'

Deb nodded as much as the limitations of her burning scalp allowed. She opened her mouth, but all that escaped was yelping.

Tom squashed his index finger into Deb's open mouth, pushing into the corners. '*This* is where I will cut you if you don't tell me what was said.' Seeing the abject panic on the girl's face, Tom felt better. *She'd talk.*

Throwing her back with force, he removed his grip. 'Speak.'

Deb brushed the tears from her eyes with shaking fingers, her mind scrambling for what to say. It had to be believable. Tom would kill her otherwise.

'For the last time, why were you talking to a Stoker?' Tom's voice was hoarse, his breathing laboured.

'I-I don't know any Stokers...' Deb stuttered. 'Which ma...?'

'Don't pretend you don't know who they are,' Tom spat, his temper heading over the line. '*Everybody* knows those cunts!'

Deb blinked, desperate to come up with something feasible.

Whatever was going on with Tom and those people was a big deal, but she could hardly tell him about Stacey and what she'd agreed to do. Tom would also then know she planned to leg it away from him and his band of perverts.

'Chas was there!' Tom's eyes bulged out of their sockets. 'Stoker was screaming at him to let you go, so why was that? Tell me!'

Despite Deb's escalating terror, resolve glimmered. 'That man when I got into the car?' she blathered, frantically thinking on her feet. 'I didn't know who he was.'

Tom looked at the ceiling in mock despair, then his eyes narrowed menacingly. 'You didn't know who he w...?'

'I didn't!' Deb screamed. 'I swear!' She held her hands up, like they would stop the coming onslaught. 'I've heard of the Stokers, but I didn't know what they looked like.'

Sensing a slight pause in Tom's advance, she continued. 'A man approached *me*, asking if I'd seen a girl called Joan and...'

'Bollocks!' Tom raged, making Deb jump for the third time. 'Utter bollocks! Why the fuck would he bang on Chas's car, telling him to let you go then? What have you said about me?'

As much as it sickened her, Deb clutched Tom's sleeve and looked up at him beseechingly. 'Chas jumped on me the minute I got in the car. His hands were around my throat and he was screaming at me. He went berserk in front of that man.'

Tom paused. *Chas had roughed the girl up in front of a Stoker? The stupid...*

Seeing Tom's hesitancy, Deb jumped on the opportunity. 'Chas was screaming at me and asking why I was talking to him, but I didn't say a word about you or anyone!' She clutched Tom's sleeve harder. 'Why would I? The man just asked about Joan.'

'Who the fuck is Joan?' Tom shrugged Deb's hand from his shirt, his mind whirring.

'I-I've no idea,' Deb stammered. 'I just said I didn't know. I got in the car and then Chas started on me. That's when the man started shouting. He must have seen Chas attacking me. Why would I have said anything about you, Tom? I wouldn't, I promise I wouldn't.'

Deb saw Tom's shoulders sag, like someone had opened a valve. She held her breath, daring to hope he believed her. *Did he?* Part of it was true. She hadn't said anything about Tom or the Aurora.

Tom stared at Deb crouching on the bed. Why *would* she have said anything about him or this place? The fact is, even *she* wasn't that stupid. Adrenaline pulsed. *This was that fuckwit Chas's fault.*

Tom was sure he would have a cardiac arrest. He knew the Stokers hated violence towards women and if one of them had seen Chas giving Deb a slap, they'd have intervened.

He closed his eyes in horror. Chas had flagged himself up to the Stokers, which conversely meant it could lead back to *him*... He didn't want that at any time, and certainly not as he was poised to pull off the job of the bloody century!

His attention swung back to Deb. 'Which Stoker was it?'

Deb shook her head. 'I have no idea.'

Still not daring to breathe, she watched Tom's horrible face twist into an indescribable expression before he walked out of the room without uttering another word.

It was only then that she dared to take in a large lungful of air.

22

'Of course you can still do it,' Marina spat. 'Nothing has changed. Just keep out of everybody's way until you get the chance you need.' If Deb got caught up in any shit after that point, that was *her* problem. As long as the damage was done, that was fine.

'Get there for 9 p.m. tomorrow and go to the front entrance. Blend in with the waitresses,' she continued. 'There will be a tall blond security man on the door. He'll let you in. I'll meet you the next day in the Magic Bean at 8 p.m. and pay you, okay?'

Without wanting to hear further bleating, Marina slammed the phone down.

She plonked herself down in the armchair and scowled at an empty Big Mac carton, a couple of dried-up fries and a gherkin slice stuck to the coffee table. Swiping the mess onto the floor with a satisfying clatter, she kicked the overflowing ashtray on top of the clutter.

Now she had to instruct Grant to let the girl in. What with his obsession with doing nothing other than steal Stoker's money, she'd have to think of a justifiable reason for her request. One that

wouldn't offend his new-found sensitivity towards Samantha-fuck-
ing-Reynold.

She rolled her eyes. Grant saying he'd found out from some of
the other guys that not so long ago Samantha had been attacked
and almost raped by a friend was no big deal. Neither was the bullshit that word had it she'd killed the man herself.

Grant really was embarrassing himself if he'd fallen for that
rubbish. Samantha Reynold didn't have it in her to say boo to a
goose, let alone dispatch someone. It was more likely she'd been
throwing herself at this so-called friend and then cried wolf when
she got found out, the cheap slag.

'Who was that?'

Marina swung around to find Dan standing in the lounge doorway. 'Who was what?'

'On the phone?' Dan walked into the room, his tracksuit
bottoms sitting low on his hips. 'You were on the phone. Who were
you talking to?'

Marina glared at Dan's visible bum crack. Could he be any
more revolting? Maybe she should have rid herself of him first?

No. This was *way* more important.

Besides, with how Grant was at the moment, she wasn't sure
whether he'd even help her on that score any more. No matter.
She'd do everything herself if needs be. She was doing this – *all* of
it, come hell or high water.

'Marina?'

'What?' Marina barked. She'd blocked Dan out there for a
moment and now he'd bloody ruined it.

'The phone?'

'Why do you care? It's just someone I'm going for a drink with
at the weekend,' Marina lied.

Dan raised an eyebrow. 'Who? You don't know anyone around
here.'

Standing up, Marina folded her arms across her chest – mainly to stop herself from punching Dan in the face. 'How would you know? I've barely seen you since we've been here! Why are you still here, anyway? Shouldn't you be in the pub by now, like you usually are?'

'Keep your hair on!' Dan retorted. 'Just making conversation.'

'Well, don't!'

'And in answer to your question, I'm going out shortly.' And Dan knew *exactly* where he was going. He'd pay the Aurora another visit. He hadn't been since Saturday – two whole days without having a good time and being around people who thought he was cool. Like that nice little Tina chick.

He'd have gone back last night if he could, but instead he'd gone to the Whistling Pig to see if that pisshead, Simon, had turned up with his promised VIP pass. Unsurprisingly, there had been no sign of him.

A pass for the Peacock was neither here nor there. Not now he was heading to the Orchid for that poker tournament tomorrow instead.

Dan waited for Marina to grill him further, but she'd flounced out of the room. Hearing her footsteps stamping up the hallway, he dashed over to her handbag and pulled out her purse, quickly extracting her credit card that still had a few hundred quid on it.

Providing the bitch hadn't spent anything recently, it would give him a float. He was buggered if he was dipping into his working capital from the last few wins, presently safely concealed in the shoebox on the top of the wardrobe.

Marina deserved to cough up for lying, anyway. And that's what she was doing. *Lying.* He'd heard her on the phone saying something about keeping out of everybody's way and about the blond security man. *Grant?*

Dan's eyes narrowed. Whatever Grant and Marina were up to

was irrelevant because he'd get to those safes long before they did. Thanks to Simon, *he* had the codes and he very much doubted that *they* did.

* * *

Sam hadn't meant to get waylaid. Trevor Jensen had only come in to double-check the guest list for tomorrow, but they'd got sidetracked. The man was so easy to chat to, she'd almost forgotten she barely knew him or that there were countless other things to do. It had also taken her mind off what could be troubling Seb.

Grant watched Sam laugh at his last remark about the misery of Tube trains and what a relief it was not to use them any more. He'd fed her a whole load of crap about his prior life in the smoke; an imaginary ex, whom he still missed, his parents who lived in Streatham, and a brother who worked for the Highways. It was easy fabricating a life that didn't exist.

He hadn't expected Sam to be so easy to get along with. He'd expected her to be up her own backside and to hate her as much as he'd thought he would. But he didn't. And the more he spoke to her, the more he thought she was all right.

But he had to stop staring at her. Her eyes were the same as his and Linda Matthews's eyes. It was obvious, but that was only because he *knew*.

Despite Sam's laughter, Grant also sensed sadness under the surface. 'Forgive me if this is out of turn, but are you all right? You seem on edge. Are there additional people you're expecting trouble from at the party that I need to know about?'

Sam's face fell and she flapped her hand dismissively. 'No, it's just the whole thing has ended up as more of a press exercise than anything else.' She rolled her eyes. 'As far as I'm concerned, parties should be for friends and family and instead, this is business associates and reporters!'

At this, she grinned mischievously. 'Inviting the press was Seb's idea to stop them nosing about. I feel like leaving a dead body half-sticking out of the wardrobe just to give them a story!'

Grant laughed heartily – *genuinely*. Sam was down to earth and funny, with no airs or graces. And dare he say it, he found himself quite liking her. 'You mentioned family? Aren't your parents going?'

Sam paled. 'My father died several months ago... A car accident...' *A car accident that wasn't a car accident...*

'I'm really sorry. I had no idea,' Grant exclaimed.

Sam shrugged, blinking away the mist that formed in her eyes every time she thought of the man she'd believed be her father. 'It's okay. Not from being round here, you wouldn't have known.'

She laughed to deflect her sadness. 'Why do you think I'm running this place? This time last year, I was a graphic designer. I'm telling you now, Trevor, life was a lot simpler then!'

'I can imagine!' Grant returned the laugh, but mainly to hide further surprise. *Sam had control of the Orchid only because she'd had to?* 'That change must have been difficult.'

Sam nodded thoughtfully. 'It was. At first, especially. Call it a baptism of fire!'

'What about your mother?'

'Which one?' Sam muttered.

Grant frowned. He'd seen the photo of Sam and Linda in the paper, clear as day. 'I... erm...'

Sam grimaced. 'It's a long story.' She picked at her manicured nails. 'Put it this way, I'd only recently been made aware of my real mother, but now I've lost contact, which, to be honest, is disappointing.'

'At least you didn't get binned off to shitty kids' homes and got adoptive parents who gave you *this*! The rest of us got a pile of crap,' Grant snapped.

Sam frowned. 'I thought you just said your parents lived in Streatham? Were you adopted, then?'

Grant blinked. *Shit.* He'd been so shocked by Sam's unexpected revelation about Linda, he'd forgotten who he was supposed to be. *Stupid, stupid.*

He pulled himself together. *Don't lose sight of what you're doing.* This was to get his hands on money, not to gain another sister.

'No, my folks *do* live in Streatham. I meant, you hear stories of kids ending up in bad places and having a hard time of it,' he mumbled.

Sam stared at Grant curiously. What had she been thinking by discussing her personal business with a stranger? Her mind must be overloaded. Trevor Jensen may be easy to chat to, but it stopped *here*. 'Okay, well, I think that's enough on that subject. My story's not interesting anyway.'

Grant looked at Sam, her barriers firmly back in place. He'd been uncharacteristically lax there, but he didn't think he'd blown it.

But what she'd said *had* been interesting. *More* than interesting. If Linda wasn't in the picture, then both he, and *especially* Marina, were wrong in their assumptions.

Grant was about to speak again when the phone rang.

'Samantha Reynold.' Sam aimlessly ran her finger along the curled length of the telephone cord. 'Hi, Kevin... Oh, I'm not sure... I'll check with Seb later.' Her finger now traced the outline of the phone itself. 'He's not there today... He's gone with Andrew over to Erdington... Yeah, they're doing something at the lockups...'

Grant's ears pricked up, but continued flicking through his wallet, pretending to act disinterested. *So, Stoker's lockups were in Erdington?*

'I'll confirm as soon as I can... Okay...' Sam replaced the receiver and sighed. 'Sorry about that. It was Kevin checking how many of Seb's security will be joining you and Stu tomorrow.'

Her business-like tone signified the previous conversation was now firmly closed. 'Okay, so back to the guest list. Are there any other questions about tomorrow?'

Grant shook his head, his mind ticking over in the background.

He didn't know Erdington at all, but it shouldn't be difficult to pinpoint where Stoker's lockups could be. And in one of those lockups were the safes...

His brain ricocheted with ideas. He was unaware of the ins and outs of Sam's story, but knew enough now that she wasn't the person he'd presumed. And he suspected by the glimpses he caught now and then behind the eyes, so similar to his own, there were more skeletons in her closet. What the lads had told him of her history had both shocked and surprised him.

Sam Reynold may have the Orchid, but her life was way less straightforward and privileged than he'd assumed.

Sam stood up, signifying their time was at a close, and Grant quickly got to his feet. 'I'll be off then,' he smiled. 'And don't worry. We'll make sure everything runs smoothly for you and Mr Stoker tomorrow.'

'Thank you, Trevor.' Sam smiled stiffly. She waited for him to vacate the office, then sat back in her chair and put her head in her hands.

Something was brewing – she could smell it in the air; taste it on the end of her tongue.

* * *

'For fuck's sake!' Chas muttered, tripping on a shoe on the first-floor landing. *Did these tarts have to spread their mess out of their bloody rooms?*

He'd been hoping to catch Tom to find out what bullshit excuse that silly cow had thought of this time to excuse being slap bang in a conversation with a Stoker.

He smirked. He might not know the history between Tom and the Stokers, but there was definitely a problem there, so he'd love to have witnessed the round of abuse Deb copped for associating with one of them.

Tom certainly hadn't been happy when he'd stomped off in search of her this morning and the muffled yelling through the ceiling would have been heard from Redditch!

It was only the pain of Chas's stubbed toe which stopped him from chuckling, imagining Deb cowering from Tom's wrath. With any luck he'd thrown her out already, the two-faced, useless bitch.

Deb should be grateful that *he* hadn't punched her teeth down her throat. She could have made it look like he'd *condoned* her talking to a Stoker. At least Tom knew that wasn't the case and would have put the girl straight for her slackness.

He continued down the rickety stairs to the ground floor. Now Deb was exiting stage left, he might suggest to Tom that things revert to *him* going on the lookout for talent again. He'd done all right before, hadn't he?

Rounding the corner at the bottom of the stairs, Chas playfully slapped the backside of one of the girls on her way up to her room. He might pay her a quick visit later. He hadn't sampled that one yet.

'Can I have a word?'

Swinging around to see Tom in the doorway, Chas grinned. 'I was just coming to find you!' He sauntered into the office and, without invitation, plonked himself down in a chair. 'I hope Deb got a round of fucks for her stupidity! How did she take being binned off after her epic screw-up? I already told her she was lucky she hadn't already been banged up in the attic with that loon.'

Tom inwardly flinched. Chas had been snooping around up there, had he? Discussing Linda with his bloody aunt, no doubt! Chas was a goddamn liability and he wasn't standing for it. 'Don't forget to take that with you.'

Chas's eyes darted to his grey holdall. 'That's my bag! What's that do...'

'You're out of here,' Tom snarled. Moving closer, he grabbed the lapels of Chas's jacket. 'I guess I'll have to tell you why, being as you're too fucking thick to work it out yourself! Apart from being a nosy bastard, you've alerted the fucking Stokers, you prick. You're lucky I don't kill you!'

In shock, Chas's hand moved to stop Tom from reaching for his throat.

Tom shook with rage. This snarky bastard had the fucking cheek to swan in here acting like everyone else was in the wrong? Being fucking clever?

'I-I don't understand,' Chas gibbered, the manic rage in Tom's eyes underlining a side of the man he hadn't seen to this extent before. Certainly not to *him*. 'Deb was the one wh...'

'You stupid cunt!' Tom roared, his hand bypassing Chas's grasping fingers and locking tightly around his throat. 'It was *you* who might have brought the attention of the Stokers to my door, not her. How could you be so fucking thick?' His eyes bulged, spit flying. 'The Stokers hate wankers who knock birds about and you go and half-strangle that silly cow in front of one of them?'

'B-but I...'

'Shut it!' Tom hissed. Pulling his pocketknife from his jacket, he flipped it open and pressed it against the pulsing vein in Chas's neck. 'I should finish you now for the shit you could land me in!'

Chas scrambled to grab hold of something – *anything* – to give him traction against this unexpected assault. Tom was stronger than he'd given him credit for. 'It was Deb. She's...'

'She's nothing!' Tom spat. 'She knows fuck all! This is on *you*. You moron! You utter fucking piece of...'

'It's okay, the Stokers don't know me!' Chas spluttered. 'Even if I did accidentally piss that geezer off, he won't know I work for you or th...'

'You *don't* work for me!' Tom yelled. 'As far as I'm concerned, you never have. Christ! They could trace you here by your car or...'

'But...'

'I said, *shut it!*' Tom screamed. Yanking the knife from Chas's throat, he held it across his open mouth and pressed down hard. 'You sit here grinning like a cunt? This is the only smile you'll ever see from now on!'

Chas felt very little as the blade cut deep into the flesh at the corners of his mouth and across his cheeks. In fact, he couldn't comprehend at first why blood was flowing. That was until the pain kicked in. '*Aaargh!*' he screamed, panic engulfing him.

His flailing arms only caused the knife to dig deeper. He tried to speak and reason with this madman, but he couldn't form anything but garbled sounds.

'I'm trying to deal with that woman in the attic and all I can hear from down here is screaming, so what the fuck's goin... Oh, my Christ!' Amelia shrieked as she burst into the office. She stared in horror at her nephew – a gash turning his mouth into a gaping, bleeding yawn. 'For the love of God, Tom, what have you done?'

Amelia's outburst jolted Tom back to reality. He stared at her coldly. 'You need to stop flapping your gums about what's in the attic! Now get this piece of shit out of here. Drive him and his fucking car either into the bastard canal or drop him at the hospital anonymously. He's your family, so *you* decide.' His eyes narrowed. 'Whatever you do, don't hang around or bring anyone back here with you, otherwise you'll be following him.'

Wiping his bloodied hands down his jeans, Tom fished a ten-pound note from his pocket and threw it at Amelia. 'Leave him and his fucking car at your chosen place and get yourself a taxi.'

He then glared at Chas, frozen in shock. 'You've got ten seconds to get out before I cut your tongue clean out of your fucking head.'

With Amelia's help, Chas staggered from the room and down the hallway, his hands held over his mouth failing to stop the blood from dripping onto the floorboards.

Keeping the toilet door less than an inch ajar, Deb pressed herself against the wood and watched, her whole body shaking as the whimpering, disfigured man she'd once thought was her boyfriend, hurried past.

23

Tom swilled vodka around his glass. Taking Chas's gross negligence out on his face had been a fantastic stress buster and one which he'd immensely enjoyed.

Okay, so it didn't remove the worry that the Stokers could be on the lookout, but he must remain rational. If they *were*, they'd be on the lookout for Chas, not *him*. And now neither Chas nor his clapped-out motor were anywhere to be seen, there was absolutely nothing linking back to *him*.

It was all good.

Now he could properly concentrate on this new opportunity and work out exactly how to play it.

He watched Tina fawning over Dan, like he'd instructed. Dan's presence meant he could move forward, but how, he wasn't quite sure. It all depended on how receptive this man was and which way *he* played it from here.

Tom frowned. He'd talk to the bloke, but should he go down the road of threats, or a business arrangement? After all, *he* had the nous as well as local knowledge, whereas this London prick did not.

He focused on the missing digits on Dan's right hand. That didn't look too promising as to the man's ability either.

Getting up from his seat, Tom wandered across the Aurora's gambling room, ignoring the other punters. He was even less interested in them tonight than usual.

Reaching the table where Tina sat on Dan's lap, her hands roving suspiciously under the table, Tom signalled for her to disappear. 'You must be Dan,' he said. 'I'm the owner of the Aurora.'

Extending his hand, Tom tried not to cringe as he took hold of the stumpy fingers. 'Would you spare me five minutes of your time? I'd like to speak to you about something. In my office, perhaps?'

* * *

Dan followed Tom, uncomfortable with the stain on the office floor that looked suspiciously like blood...

'Look,' he began, taking a seat in the offered chair. 'I don't want any trouble. If this is about staying over on Friday without paying extra, it wasn't on purpose. I crashed out.' He shoved his good hand in his pocket and pulled out his wallet. 'I'll pay for it now.'

Tom decided that being blatant was the best way to go. 'That was noted, yes, but as you're such a good customer, it's not a problem.' He smiled slowly. 'Actually, I wanted to speak to you about your proposed idea of undertaking a very risky job on the Stokers.'

Dan almost choked. What the fuck had he said the other night? That he was going to rob Stoker's safe? *Oh shit, shit, shit! How pissed had he been?*

Sweat broke out on his palms and beaded across the back of his neck. *Christ, how should he play this? Weren't all these casinos in on stuff together?*

His eyes darted back to Tom. This guy could have already informed the Stokers of his plans...

Dan tried to make his surprise look authentic, but suspected he'd failed miserably, instead revealing the distinctive look of someone who was terrified – probably because he was. Even though he tried to stop himself, his hands nervously wrung together – as best as they could with half of one missing... 'Th-there must be some kind of confusion. I was wasted on Saturday and obviously talking shit.'

Tom studied Dan carefully. The guy was shitting it. He could tell a mile off that he was lying, too. This fucker *was* planning to lift the brass all right, but if he thought he wouldn't be sharing it now he'd opened his gob...

'A word of advice. If we'll be working together, you really need to be in control of your mouth.' He tapped the side of his temple. 'There's a lot of truth in the saying, "careless talk costs lives", remember!'

Dan opened his mouth, then shut it again. *Working together?*

Placing his elbows on the desk, Tom leant closer. 'Bringing me on board will ensure several things. One – I make sure the Stokers and no one else gets wind of your schemes. Two – I'll share with you my many years' experience of the ins and outs of this city, who's in it and how they work.'

Dan remained silent. Was this bloke suggesting if he didn't split the money then he'd drop him in it? His eyes narrowed. If this guy thought he'd give up half the pickings...

'I know what you're thinking,' Tom said casually. 'Another problem you have is being extremely readable. Something else we'll have to work on.' A smile twitched at the corners of his mouth. 'But you're right. If you want to go ahead with this unhindered, then you'll be doing so with me!'

Dan clenched his jaw. *So, there was little choice?*

'But,' Tom continued, 'the Stokers are no friends of mine. The very opposite, in fact, but if you don't take my offer, then I'll have no compunction in handing you over to them, enemies or not.' *Would he hell! But Dan didn't need to know that.*

Dan accepted the fresh vodka Tom poured and stared miserably at the chipped glass. Okay, so this wasn't part of the plan, but would it really hurt to have two heads on this, rather than his alone? Tom knew Birmingham and what went on behind the scenes and if the man had beef with the Stokers, there would be more impetus to ensure it was pulled off successfully.

Dan chewed his lip. He might not have a lot of choice, but in retrospect, it wasn't such a bad idea.

Tom had the pleasure of seeing Dan's silent acceptance and kept his well-practised stance of nonchalance in place, as if this wasn't a big deal. Of course it was a big deal. It was a *huge* fucking deal.

He sipped his vodka. 'Tina tells me your brother works at the Orchid and is part of the security at Stoker's shindig tomorrow?'

'Grant ain't my brother,' Dan snapped defensively. 'My girl-friend – if you can call her that – he's *her* brother.'

Tom nodded casually. 'Whatever, just tell me what this Grant person has got against the Stokers. Why come from London to hit on them?'

Dan shrugged. 'I dunno, but we had to get away from London because...' He glanced at the remains of his fingers. 'I've a few people after me down there and my missus has family up here, so...'

Tom eyed Dan's hand for the second time and hoped the man's judgement had improved since whatever he'd done to piss London off. 'And these people? Are they still after you?'

Dan shook his head. 'Nah. They don't know where I've gone. I'm starting afresh up here.'

'Back to what your missus and her brother have got against the Stokers...?'

'I'm damned if I know, but what I *do* know is they've got an issue with their mother. We were supposed to be staying with her, but she'd done a runner some months ago.' He rolled his eyes. 'I can't say I was upset. She's a junkie bitch.'

'Right and...?' Tom hissed, getting impatient. *He didn't want this prick's life story.*

Dan leant forward, creasing paperwork on Tom's desk with his sleeve. 'Marina – that's my missus – she reckons the mother is living it up with a sister they didn't even know existed until the other week. I don't know much else, but they want money. Grant overheard the sister talking about where Stoker keeps his cash.'

Tom stared at Dan confused. 'How does this sister know Stoker?'

'Because she's shagging him! Their new sister's only that tart who runs the Orchid.' Dan smiled nastily. 'They think I don't know, but I hear most of what Marina and Grant say.'

'Samantha Reynold is their *half-sister*?' Tom refrained from screaming with both delight and amazement. *Oh, this was getting better.* This meant Linda was the 'junkie bitch' upstairs in his attic? Whatever knowledge he had about *that* he was keeping well and truly to himself.

Dan grimaced. 'I haven't a clue who Samantha is, and I don't fucking care! I hate Marina and I hate Grant. All I want is to get the money they're planning to rob before they do and then I'm getting away from the pair of them.'

Tom handed Dan the vodka bottle. 'You'd best pour yourself another one. It will be a long night discussing this.'

24

Slamming the phone down, Sam stormed to the basement, her heels clacking down the stone steps. Finding the door to the room Kevin had asked her to come to locked, she banged on it impatiently.

'What's going on?' she cried when Stu opened the door. Pushing past, Sam stepped inside, seeing a bloodied man secured to a chair.

When he'd called, Kevin said they'd pulled this man in because he'd been seen with a group of girls and matched the description Neil Stoker had given them.

Her eyes darted over the slim-framed man, blood from his smashed nose congealing in his patchy brown stubble to gloop around the acne scars pitting his chin. Wearing a black or dark navy tracksuit, difficult to tell which in the artificial illumination from the overhead strip light, the man stared up through the swelling slits of his bruised eyes.

Whoever this was, he'd taken a good pasting and by the look on Trevor Jensen's face, there was still more to come.

Sam turned to Stu, watching from his perch on the edge of the work top. 'This is him, I take it?'

Receiving Stu's nod, Sam moved her attention back to the man in the chair, the cable ties around his wrists already having dug thick grooves into his skin. Anger flared. *He deserved his hands to fall off, the dirty bastard.*

She stepped forward, her disgust mounting. 'What have you got to say for yourself, you piece of shit?' she spat. 'What gives you the right to groom young girls? I'll tell you what it gives you. *This!*'

Raising her hand, Sam slapped the man around the face. 'You're pimping girls barely out of school and think you can do this on my turf?' Staring at her stinging hand, her stomach turning at the man's blood on her palm, she hastily wiped her hand on her trousers.

'What's it got to do with you?' the man croaked, his voice thick with drugs. 'Jealous because you're not getting any?'

'I don't think that was the correct answer.' Grant kicked the man hard in the chest with his boot, the chair toppling backwards, landing the man on the floor with a thud. A horrible crunching sound echoed around the room as he followed up with a deft kick to the ribs.

'I'll tell you who I am.' Sam stepped over the groaning man. 'I own this place. This is my territory and therefore my business!' *This piece of crap, this filthy bastard thought he could groom young girls on her doorstep?*

Almost panting with rage, she averted her eyes from the creature on the floor, her spiralling fury scaring her. 'Just finish him off,' she hissed. 'Or shall I remove his balls first?' It was like watching herself in a film. These words, this rage, didn't even sound like her.

'Wait!' the man gibbered. 'I shouldn't have said that, but I ain't no nonce. I...'

'Don't fucking lie!' Sam motioned for the man to be sat back upright.

'Look!' the guy spluttered as Grant yanked both him and the chair up by his hair. 'I'm not pimping anyone. I...'

'You're telling me that girl I saw you grab ain't no hooker?' Stu barked. 'She is! I've seen her several times.' He bent over the frightened man. 'Where's your car?'

'What car? I haven't got a car. I can't even drive! And that girl, she's my fucking girlfriend and...'

'Don't all pimps say that?' Sam cut in. 'We all know what you were doing.'

'Okay, okay.' The man coughed out part of a tooth and spat it onto the floor. 'She'd pissed me off and yes, she's a hooker, but I ain't no pimp!'

'Stop wasting my time,' Sam scoffed. 'Where do you take these girls once you've recruited them?'

'I told you, I don't! I work at the fucking fish market!' The man's eyes darted between Grant, Stu and Sam. 'Belinda's a hooker, yeah, but that's her choice. I don't know the others, I swear. They're Belinda's mates. I grabbed Belinda because she fucked off tonight with my gear and I ain't having that. It's *my* gear and I need it.'

Sam looked at Stu. 'This *is* the guy you were told to bring in?'

Stu fidgeted uncomfortably. 'He matched the description.'

Sam reeled. *This might not even be the correct person?* They couldn't turn on some bloke having a row with his missus. She wanted to get to the bottom of who was recruiting these young girls, nothing else.

'This is all he's got on him.' Grant indicated a small bag of heroin on the table, along with a key fob and a cheap green plastic lighter.

As the steel door banged for the second time, Stu opened it, revealing Kevin and Neil Stoker.

'Him!' Kevin pushed into the room and pointed to the man in the chair.

Neil gave an abrupt shake of his head. 'That's not the bloke.'

'For Christ's sake! Get him out of here!' Sam cried.

She stalked back over to the man. 'Think yourself lucky,' she hissed. 'I don't want to see you or your girlfriend on Broad Street *ever* again, otherwise I'll change my mind. Do you understand?'

Receiving a hasty nod from the trussed man, Sam left the room.

Moving down the corridor, she raked her fingers through her hair, then stopped, remembering they were covered in that man's blood.

Shit. She'd almost had that man killed. Her hatred for nonces was one thing, but if she was aiming it at the wrong targets, then it was getting out of control.

Slamming her office door closed, she leant against the wall, her heart thumping. She'd refused to become like everyone else and treat life as cheap, and what had she just very nearly done?

Shaking, Sam stumbled to her desk. She didn't like this. She didn't like how this was changing her.

Picking up the phone, she dialled Seb's office line. He'd calm her speeding thoughts.

As the phone continually rang out, she eventually replaced the receiver, her heart sinking.

* * *

Deb kept her smile in place as the man she'd just pleasured vacated her room. She then ran to the washbasin in the corner to sluice cold water over her face.

Leaning against the sink, she stared at the rusted juddering tap. Water wouldn't wash the trace of that revolting man away.

Nothing ever did, but it was a ritual she'd developed over the past few months – one small thing to cleanse herself.

Going through the motions had been easier than usual tonight – only because her mind was crammed with what she'd seen happen to Chas and the spiralling need to get away from this hellhole.

Deb should be happy that Chas had received his comeuppance, but she wasn't. It merely underlined that this place, these people, were more dangerous than ever.

She gritted her teeth as the wailing and shouting from above became louder. It had been going on for *hours* tonight. It never went on this long. Someone had to do something for that woman. Shouldn't she be in a mental hospital or something?

Deb had heard all the rumours about the woman in the attic being mentally unstable, but this wasn't right. None of it was right. Didn't Amelia tend to this woman, whoever she was? But it had been hours since Amelia had disappeared with Chas.

Perhaps Tom had killed them both?

Feeling sick with dread, she moved to the door, listening for movement. Dare she go and look? What happened if she ran into Tom?

It was no good. She had to go and see what was going on. She'd go even more stir-crazy if she listened to this never-ending noise.

Heart pounding, Deb slipped from the room, the noise from above increasing without the additional layer of the door. She tiptoed along the landing and crept up to the attic, holding her breath in case one of the tired old steps made a tell-tale creak alerting someone to her presence.

But no one would hear over this racket, would they?

Her inquisitiveness overtaking logic, Deb continued to the top of the narrow stairs, the attic landing virtually pitch black.

She faltered, seeing a crack of light spilling from a room at the far end. The noise was ear-splitting. It sounded like a tortured animal, and it was coming from in *there...*

With her heart in her mouth, Deb edged along the corridor, stealing a furtive glance over her shoulder. If she was caught nosing around where no one was allowed to go, then she would face possibly worse consequences than Chas. She should go back downstairs, she knew that, but she had to know what was going on.

This person, however ill or deformed, may have hurt herself, and with Amelia or Tom nowhere to be seen, what sort of person did it make her, if she didn't try to help?

Reaching the door, Deb steadied herself against the doorjamb and, with trepidation, inched in line with the crack of the door.

Before she collapsed on the legs that had turned to jelly at the sight in front of her, Deb stumbled into the room.

* * *

'I'm telling you, she lost it!' Neil's brow knitted with concern. 'I've never seen Sam like that. She was all set to have the guy offloaded!'

Andrew raised his eyebrows. 'Why the fuck did Kevin give the go-ahead for a random loser to be pulled in? Did you not give him specific details?'

'Of course I bloody did! I don't know how they got it so wrong! Word will spread and...'

'For Christ's sake!' Seb smacked his fist on the desk, the reverberation shaking his empty crystal glass. 'I'm sick of this.'

The nonces bothered him – bothered him a *lot* – but stressing the woman he adored into making bad judgements bothered him more.

It wasn't like he couldn't understand why Sam had blown her stack. With Linda's history, her reaction wasn't surprising. Sam might think she concealed how much her mother's past bothered her, but he knew it haunted her every single day.

His personal failure in locating Linda made it worse. He'd let Sam down and that was the *last* thing he'd ever wanted to do. He wanted to be the one to put everything right and give her everything she needed.

Yet now he was on the cusp of the shit hitting the fan and because of all of this cash, he might lose everything. What good would that be to Sam? What good would it be for anyone? Yet all anyone seemed bothered about was this other issue.

'Just find the fucking bloke! In the meantime, does no one understand that *we're* in the shit unless we find a way to get rid of this cash?'

Snatching the decanter, Seb poured himself another whisky. He'd finally got everything he wanted in life; a woman he loved, a successful firm, a beautiful house and an upcoming wedding, yet now he'd attained that, it was all at risk.

And the latest meeting he'd had with the accountant tonight underlined this.

Andrew exchanged a look of concern with Neil. *This wasn't like Seb.* 'I know things are difficult with this money, but we'll sort it. We always do,' he said.

Seb slugged down his whisky and remained silent. Ever optimistic, his brothers. And no, it was always *him* who sorted everything, not them.

Then there were all the things he *hadn't* been able to sort: Liam attacking Sam and her having to avenge it. *He* should have been the one to do that.

And Gary – his youngest brother – getting murdered that he'd failed to stop, or even *avenge*.

The list was growing, and Seb despised letting Sam down. Letting *everyone* down.

He shoved his finger in his collar to relieve the building heat.

And now, on top of everything, he'd ignored the phone when it rang. He'd seen it was Sam, but he'd been talking to the accountant and couldn't face lying to her, saying he was fine when he wasn't.

But now he knew why she'd called and he'd blanked her. *Christ*. This wasn't how things were supposed to be.

'Look, there's no harm done,' Neil reasoned. 'That bloke will say fuck all and we'll find out who's behind this seedy crap. Andrew's right about the money too – it will work itself out.'

Standing up, he slapped Seb on the shoulder. 'Don't stress, bruv. You've got your housewarming tomorrow, so let's just have a laugh and take the piss out of the press, eh? The rest can wait another day for once.'

Seb nodded, even though he was far from convinced. He didn't want to take the piss out of the press, nor did he want a bastard party. Neil and Andrew couldn't see the wood for the trees.

However, the party was one thing that he didn't have to let Sam down on.

25

Amelia nodded in response and waited as the girl loitering in the doorway left. She could have been saying she'd just murdered someone for all the attention she'd paid her.

But then, if that girl had murdered someone, it wasn't all that different to what *she'd* been doing.

All this time, she'd shoved the nagging doubts and questions over her own life, the life of her daughters, and those of the girls she'd encouraged to work in Tom Bedworth's Aurora to one side. The excuses she'd meted out in Tom's defence in order to justify what she turned a blind eye to had flowed off the tip of her tongue. It had been simple convincing herself that she had it good, but now, like an epiphany, there was no way of dressing it up any more.

Nothing justified what she'd witnessed tonight, nor excused how she'd dumped her own flesh and blood in a hospital car park and simply walked away...

Yes, she'd left Chas in his own car, barely conscious and permanently disfigured, making it clear that he was not to utter a single word. He'd been 'lucky' to have been spared.

Amelia's hand covered her mouth as nausea rolled once more.

Chas could have bled to death by now and all she'd been bothered about was following Tom's instructions to get back to the Aurora – both to keep on his good side and to cover her own arse.

Now, sitting here in this cupboard under the stairs that was allegedly her office, the cold light of truth dawned.

It wasn't a pleasant awakening.

Amelia knew Tom was a tosser, but she hadn't until today accepted *quite* how much of a tosser he was. And this wasn't just because of what he'd done to Chas – her nephew wasn't that much different to Tom in his way of thinking and how he treated people, but the way *Tom* treated those girls and how he'd brainwashed *her* into thinking this setup was all right was something else.

She'd accepted so many things without question and what she had questioned, she'd excused.

But it stopped here. It *had* to.

Whatever happened, Amelia no longer wanted to be a part of it.

Suddenly aware someone else was standing in the doorway, her head jerked up, her eyes wide like a scared rabbit.

Deb. Someone *else* she'd blamed, when yet again, it was people like Tom and Chas who were at fault.

Deb timidly stepped into the room. 'A-are you all right?'

This sudden and unexpected kindness surprised Amelia. She pushed the feeling away before it snowballed and she collapsed in tears for what she had lost and what could never be regained. 'What's it to you?' she snapped, immediately resenting herself for being on the attack. This girl needed a break rather than more abuse. 'Sorry,' she muttered, pulling herself together. 'What can I help you with?'

Glancing over her shoulder, Deb squeezed herself into the cupboard-like space, sure Tom would pounce on her from behind any minute and drag her off to be chained like an animal, the same as that other woman.

After seeing what she'd seen in the attic, she'd wanted to barricade herself in her room, not caring how much she despised being in there. *Anything* was better to avoid the same fate, but staying in her room only prolonged the agony of being trapped. She had no chance of changing her situation unless she stepped out there and arranged it so that she could do what she'd agreed with Stacey.

That alone could get her murdered, but by doing nothing, that fate, or *worse*, was guaranteed.

This way, however risky, offered a sliver of hope.

At the girl's continued silence, Amelia looked at Deb's pale features. A vast difference to the vivacious teen Chas had brought here six months ago. 'I asked you what you wanted,' she said, refraining from screaming out loud for her to go away and leave her alone.

'I've got bookings tomorrow, but I really need to go out,' Deb blurted before her nerve deserted her. 'I wouldn't ask, but it's important.'

Amelia pursed her lips. At this very moment in time, she'd happily tell the girl to run for her life and never come back, but she had to get a clear head before she made decisions. *Best to pretend that nothing was amiss.* 'There's no way you can go out on a jolly if you've got bookings, you know that.'

Deb bit her lip, her mind searching for excuses. 'Please. It's not a jolly, I've got an appointment and I need to go.'

Amelia frowned. Her bastard nephew hadn't got this girl up the spout as a parting shot, had he? She nodded at Deb's belly. 'You're not...?'

Getting the gist, Deb thought about agreeing for a split second, then changed her mind. This way was less likely to be discovered and also give her more clout to avoid serving the punters. 'I'm not pregnant, but...' She looked at the floor. 'I think... I think Chas might have... erm... infected me with something...'

Amelia's eyes narrowed. 'How do you know, the amount of men you've had?' *See! She was doing it again. What made her immediately jump to Chas's defence?*

'I-it must have been him,' Deb spluttered, her face turning the shade of a beetroot. 'He's the only one who refused to wear a condom.' She sniffed for effect. 'He said I was being selfish and did it anyway and now... now...'

'Yes, okay.' Amelia held her hand up. 'I get the drift.' *Typical of Chas – selfish to the end.* She stared at Deb, pity for the girl growing. She wouldn't have that shit of a nephew of hers render this poor wench infertile with one of his foul diseases. 'You've got an appointment, you say?'

'There's a late-night clinic on Tuesdays,' Deb said, hoping Amelia didn't check. She didn't know if there was any such clinic. 'I was going to ask Chas for a lift, but I can't find him.'

Seeing Amelia blanch, Deb immediately wished she hadn't added that last bit. She didn't even know why she had. For some inexplicable reason, she'd wanted to see Amelia's reaction.

'Chas is busy. I'll give you money for a taxi.' Amelia pulled a small cash box from the drawer.

Deb blinked in amazement. 'Thank you, but what about Tom? He'll want me to work and...'

'Don't worry about that. I'll cover for you.'

Deb felt like throwing her arms around Amelia's neck and hugging her. 'You'd do that for me? Won't you get in trouble?'

Amelia shook her head. 'If Tom notices you're not here, I'll think of something. You have to get yourself sorted. STDs can be nasty.'

'Thank you,' Deb said, gratefully accepting the ten-pound note, barely able to contain her relief. Now she could do what she'd promised Stacey. Although that brought its own set of terrors, it *did* mean she was one step closer to being out of here for good.

Turning, she went to leave the room. 'That woman upstairs...'

Amelia flinched. *Shit!* What with Chas being attacked this afternoon, she'd completely forgotten. She'd been about to dose her up when she'd raced down here to find out what all the noise was about. *Had she left the door open?* 'What about her?' she snapped. 'Have you been up there?'

'No!' Deb lied. She couldn't have Amelia turn on her, not now she'd given her a pass for tomorrow. She certainly wasn't going to admit what she'd seen. 'She's just been making a hell of a row these past few hours, that's all.'

Amelia nodded. 'I'll deal with her now.' *Fuck, fuck, fuck!* She wasn't keeping that poor cow up there any more. She wasn't doing any of it. All of this had to stop.

Deb's teeth chattered uncontrollably, knowing if she was caught trying to escape, she could be in for the same fate as that woman in the attic, but she'd had to look in that room. She'd just *had* to, but that smell, the state of that woman chained to the metal bed frame, the cuffs around her stick-thin wrists digging into the thin flesh causing deep and infected welts was a sight to behold.

There was barely a space on the woman's arm that wasn't scarred with puncture marks. Half of those were also infected; stinking yellow pus oozing from the raised track marks.

Bile rose up her throat.

The woman wasn't disfigured or psychotic either – not like the rumours said. She was a *prisoner*, drugged to the hilt and, from what she could gather, had been that way for months.

And Amelia was party to this?

She had to escape and *really* get away, rather than hide in the shadows somewhere in the city. Because Tom would find her, she knew he would.

26

Grant eyed Marina warily. 'You can't drop this on me and expect me to accept it without an adequate explanation.'

Marina sighed. She knew Grant would question this, but she didn't expect him to be *quite* so difficult. 'Just for once in your life, can you not trust me?' she snapped. 'I know you think I'm pointless and hopeless and...'

'You know I don't think that,' Grant interrupted. 'You're my sister and I'd do anything for you, but you need to tell me *why.*'

'Because you don't want to upset Samantha? Is that it? Prefer her to me now, do you? This party and whether she has a good time are more important than what I need? What *we* need?'

Grant paced the kitchen. He had to be at Sam's house in an hour and he'd been hoping to have a scoot around the place before playing doorman. 'Don't be ridiculous. What's got into you? I can't afford to scupper our plans. I need to keep them onside so I can get what we're owed and then get out of this dump!'

'*Our* plans?' Marina screeched, her eyes narrowing. 'You mean *yours.*' She waved her arms theatrically. 'When does anything *I* say count?' *Quick, change tack.* 'Does it ever cross your mind that I'd like to have some input into this?' She sagged dejectedly. 'It's always *you* who does all the work. I'm trying to help.'

Grant glanced at his watch for the second time. 'If you want me to add someone to the guest list, then you at least have to tell me why. I don't want anyone jeopardising things. I know where the lockups are now. I even had a look myself after work the other night. All we need is a schedule of when it's safe to attempt the break, then we're ready to go.'

Marina inwardly screamed. Grant wasn't listening. *Perhaps this would do?* She placed her hand on his arm. 'Why do you think I've arranged this?' She smiled convincingly. 'The girl I want you to let in, I've briefed her to listen to anything the Stokers say. Party or not, they'll discuss business at some point during the evening and she'll be around to hear it.'

Not quite the true reason, but the only feasible one that would make sense to Grant.

'You've told a random woman what we're doing?' Grant gasped. 'If that's the case, we might as well forget everything!'

Marina laughed. 'See! You automatically presume I'm stupid. Of course I haven't done that. I'm paying her to listen. That's why I want her listed as a waitress. You said there are caterers and wait-resses tonight, so what's the problem?'

Grant frowned. 'This could cause more problems than it's worth. I'll be there to hear anything th...'

'You'll be on the *door*,' Marina cried. 'This girl can mingle between the Stokers, their associates, *all* of them. Oh, please, Grant. Let me help.'

Grant raised an eyebrow. 'You say you're paying her? You mean, *I* am?'

Marina smiled, the smile that always twisted her brother around her little finger. 'Oh, come on! It's not like we won't have lots of money soon. You never know, she might hear something that could speed things up.'

Grant rolled his eyes. He didn't like this, but if it made Marina feel better, then he'd do it. She'd had so many disappointments lately. 'Okay, okay. What's her name?'

Marina beamed. *Got him.* 'Deb Banner.' And Deb wouldn't be mingling with anyone. Her instructions were simple. Two jobs – the first, then the other. Aside from that – stay completely out of the way until the relevant opportunities arise.

'I'll put her on the list.' Grant stared at Marina. 'I hope for both our sakes this friend of yours doesn't screw up.'

Marina laughed. 'What is there to screw up? She's only going to be an extra pair of ears.'

And the rest...

* * *

Sam straightened her black dress and centred the diamond solitaire in the hollow of her throat. Slipping in the matching diamond drop earrings, she then attached one of her dainty orchid clips into the side of her hair, leaving long glossy waves to cascade around her bare shoulders.

She glanced back in her dressing room mirror and blotted her lipstick with a tissue. She was ready and so was everything else.

The caterers had been here for hours, and the planners had done a stunning job of decorating the reception rooms. The house looked perfect and more than ready to accept the host of people coming tonight.

She only wished those people included those *she* wanted here. Instead, she'd have to pose for countless press photographs. That's if Seb even turned up.

Sam's heart lurched, not for the first time today. Seb had gone out earlier under the proviso of not being long, but it was almost seven o'clock and he still wasn't back. The guests would arrive soon, so what was she supposed to say if he was nowhere to be seen?

She'd wanted to discuss what had happened last night; the way she'd lost it with that man. She knew Seb must have been told about it. He'd always taken her concerns on board – the only one to rationalise things in her ever-speeding mind – but last night he'd been dismissive, like she shouldn't waste her time worrying about it.

Well, she *was* worrying about it. She'd behaved like a callous hard bitch to that man and it bothered her.

But what bothered her more was Seb masking his real mood. They hadn't even made love for three days, which was unheard of. Each time she'd instigated it, needing his closeness and touch, he'd found an excuse. *Why?*

Where was he? Would he be in a weird mood again, or worse – not even show up for his own party?

A light tap on the door made Sam look up. 'Yes?'

As Trevor walked into the room, she couldn't help but sigh dejectedly.

'Blimey, I'm not that much of a disappointment, am I?' Grant grinned. 'I've come to tell you that your guests are arriving. We're stalling them with parking at the moment, but what do you want me to do with them?'

'I take it Seb isn't here yet?'

Grant shook his head. 'Not yet. Is there a problem?'

'There will be if he doesn't show up soon,' Sam snapped, slipping her lipstick into a clutch bag. 'How could he do this to me? How am I supposed to explain his absence to our business associates and the bloody press?'

'He's probably turning into the drive as we speak,' Grant said good-naturedly.

Blinking to rid her eyes of the burn of tears, Sam stared at the ceiling. 'God, I hope he's okay.'

Grant moved closer to Sam. 'Is something wrong?' He thought about putting his hand on her shoulder and then thought better of it. *Come on, Sam, tell me what's eating you.*

'Something is, but I don't know what,' Sam blurted. 'Dealing with all these people alone and being a laughing-stock is the last thing I need.'

This time, Grant *did* lay his hand on Sam's shoulder. She might have luxury and money, yet her life was far from rosy.

Not for the first time over the last day or two, he questioned his plan about turning Sam and Stoker over. 'You won't be a laughing-stock, you'll be fine. Seb will be here soon.' He nodded decisively. 'Come down, smile and give them the hostess treatment. Say Seb's been held up but will be here shortly, and I'll make sure the girls get the drinks flowing.'

Sam faltered. 'What if he *doesn't* turn up? What if something's happened?'

'Like what?' Grant asked. 'What do *you* think could have happened?'

Sam shook her head. 'I don't know. I trust nothing and no one these days.'

Grant smiled, but inside, his conscience stuttered – an unfamiliar feeling. Gaining Sam's confidence was a step in the right direction. It was what he'd wanted, but now his initial plans didn't sit right. He actually *liked* this woman and, more strangely, was developing a certain amount of respect for Stoker. From what he'd gathered from the others on the team, Seb had ruffled feathers in his own camp in the past over his relationship with Sam, so the man had moved mountains to look after Sam's interests. And that was important.

Grant found himself wondering what it would be like if he was honest about who he really was before swiftly pulling his mind back on track. *That could not happen.* He had to remember where his loyalties lay – and they were with Marina. They had to be.

He'd already let Marina's plant in along with the serving staff – the nervous little fake waitress was downstairs, ready to go. He needed to remember that. 'Come on, Sam. Mr Stoker will be here soon, I'm sure.'

Sam stood up and grabbed her clutch bag. 'You're right! I'm overreacting. Thanks for talking sense into me, Trevor.'

'No problem. Anytime. Anyway, I'd best get myself back down there.' Grant looked back on his way out of the room, seeing the worry still firmly etched across Sam's face, and suspected that it may now reflect his own.

27

Seb knocked back another whisky. Out of all the glasses he'd had so far tonight, this was the first he'd actually enjoyed.

Topping his glass up, he waited until the accountant left the office before speaking. 'Finally, we're getting somewhere.' *Not ideal, admittedly, but it was the only thing left to do.*

Andrew rubbed his chin thoughtfully. 'I have to say, I'm surprised you'd want to go down *that* road.'

'You're not the only one!' Neil muttered. 'How can we be sure we can trust them?'

Seb finished his drink and reached for the bottle once more. 'The simple answer is we can't, but we're running out of time.'

'But the *Irish*?' Andrew exclaimed. 'Christ, Seb! They're our main point of supply. If it goes wrong or they turn us over, then what?'

Seb turned his whisky glass around on the table, looking into the brown liquid, like it contained the answers. It was bad enough swallowing his cock to ask a favour of the Irish in the first place – and a *huge* favour at that. It wasn't an enviable position, but he'd exhausted all other possibilities and it was the lesser of two evils. 'I had to get something lined up.'

Neil frowned. 'Yes, but...'

'But nothing!' Seb barked. 'It's our only option, unless you can think of something better?' He looked between his brothers, the ensuing silence proving his point. 'If something more palatable presents itself over the next two weeks, then we'll change tack. Nothing's set in stone yet. I've merely tested the water to see if they'd do it. And they will.'

'Okay.' Andrew leant back in his chair. 'Let's say, for argument's sake, that we do this and we *don't* get turned over, then how much will this favour cost us?'

Seb drained his glass. 'That's yet to be negotiated...' *A pretty penny, he didn't doubt.* 'The most important thing is that Fletcher agrees it's feasible and will lose, on the surface, around two million of the excess.'

Neil frowned. 'But will it be fast enough? Like Fletcher said, the time the Irish require to set this up may be too long. What happens if Mr Taxman comes digging in the interim?'

'It's better than the options we had this time yesterday, which were none!' Seb snapped. 'No, it's not ideal – far from it, but right now, it's all we've got.' For the first time since this money issue came to light, he felt like there might be light at the end of the tunnel, so it would take a lot more than Neil and Andrew looking on the downside to dampen his better mood.

'Right, but we still need to lose the rest short term.' Andrew rested his chin in his hands. 'If we take a chance with the Irish and complicate our business arrangements, then it's also time to call on Sam to hold the remainder.'

Seb topped up his drink. 'I told you, I want Sam kept out of this. I will not jeopardise her business.'

'I agree with Andrew, Seb,' Neil said. 'It's time to ask for Sam's help. She'll do it for us and I'd rather the small risk to the Orchid than bring another firm onto the list of people we'll be beholden to.'

'It's not like she'll be expected to hold the majority,' Andrew added. 'There's only about another million to hide. It would be different if we were asking her to shoulder the full amount.'

Seb took time screwing the cap on the whisky bottle to think. *Maybe they had a point?* Sam would not be pleased when she realised the Peacock was in schtuck and she hadn't been asked to help. She'd made him promise there would be no secrets, so maybe it was time he levelled with her?

The main thing was that the weight hanging around his neck had now lifted with the prospect of having a workaround, even if it meant involving the Irish. 'Okay, I'll speak to her.'

Andrew nodded. 'Good. When?'

'Not tonight. I'm in too good a mood to have t... Oh, shit!' Seb looked at his watch. 'Fuck! The housewarming! I should have left ages ago.' He got to his feet, wavering slightly. 'Bollocks! The guests will be arriving by now. She'll kill me for this!'

Neil laughed. 'And there's a prime example of why we haven't got ourselves attached to a woman.'

'Yeah, but she's not just a *woman*. And I wouldn't have it any other way!' Seb grinned.

'Come on.' Andrew grabbed his car keys. 'We'd best get a shift on. *I'll* drive, the amount you've put away.'

* * *

Still stinging from the earful he'd received from Sam over his mess-up yesterday, Kevin wasn't in the best of moods. Operating a skeleton staff of security with a poker tournament going on, thanks to the ill-timed housewarming party, wasn't helping either.

He'd let Sam down over that identification and it bothered him, not only because he'd failed to check who he'd instructed the boys to interrogate, but because Sam had been so livid.

He hadn't realised quite how much of a sensitive topic this was for her until he'd seen her out-of-character reaction. She'd been about to have the man exterminated and that had taken him by surprise.

No one could abide nonce wankers, but to have a *personal* connection made things so much worse. Now Neil Stoker had filled him in on Sam's biological mother's history, he understood her obsession.

Kevin scowled at the upcoming rotas on his desk.

He'd let Sam down big time. His slackness had made it look like she'd screwed up.

Nailing the bastard she had her sights set on was now *his* mission. So much so that he'd pulled off half his available men to actively scout the area and when his men next eyeballed a likely contender or a red VW Golf, he'd personally make sure it was the correct target before it went any further. He would not embarrass Sam again.

Kevin's head snapped up with a knock to the door. 'Yeah?'

Craig entered Kevin's office. 'We've got a suspicious one in tonight!'

Kevin inwardly sighed. 'Go on.'

Craig's huge frame filled half of the room. 'There's a guy who no one's seen before. A smarmy fucker – bit weird looking.'

'I don't give a fuck what he looks like. What's he done?'

'Nothing as yet,' Craig said, 'but the croupier flagged him up for being a possible card shark. He's won two sit-downs already.'

Kevin shrugged. 'It's not unusual to win two games. It's a tournament night!'

'There's something about him that's not the ticket. He's, well... odd... and he's wearing gloves... it's fucking weird, if you ask me.'

'Gloves?'

'Yeah, those weird fabric white ones – think of Michael Jackson or the sort worn when handling priceless artefacts or posh books, sort of thing. Know what I mean?'

Kevin sighed impatiently. No, he didn't know what Craig meant and neither did he want to. He hadn't got time for this.

'I think one of us should keep tabs on him.'

'We haven't got the manpower for that tonight,' Kevin snapped. 'Half the shift are outside policing; two are working that party and the ones left, including you, are monitoring the casino. We can't take one of you off to watch Gloveman!' And he wasn't pulling in one of the men from outside to monitor someone who looked like he 'might' play dirty at 'some point'.

It wasn't best use of his men and would only cause more unrest if he sanctioned that. 'If the situation changes, then let me know, but only if it does,' he continued. 'And that doesn't mean purposely standing there waiting for it.'

Craig shrugged his huge shoulders. 'Okay. You're the boss.'

Kevin nodded. He *was* the boss of the enforcers. *For now.* But if he didn't regain Sam's trust, he suspected that might not last much longer.

Once Craig left the office, Kevin picked up his walkie-talkie. 'Any sightings on the VW Golf?'

The machine crackled loudly, the feedback making him wince. Although the line was marred with interference, he still heard there had been no sightings of the man, the girl on the list, or anything untoward. There even seemed less of the 'women of the night' this evening than usual.

They were probably all at Sam and Seb Stoker's party, Kevin thought bitterly.

Even though he had to run things here tonight, he strongly suspected he wouldn't have been invited anyway.

28

'Who are you?' The girl looked Deb up and down curiously. 'I haven't seen you before.'

'I'm Deb. The agency sent me,' Deb said, quickly recalling the brief Stacey had gone over so many times. She willed herself not to let her nerves get the better of her. 'I got a call this morning asking if I could waitress here tonight. Someone's off sick.'

The girl pursed her lips. 'I bet that's Shaz, the lazy cow. She's missing out, though, because this is a right posh place, ain't it?' She looked about appreciatively.

'Yes, it's really nice,' Deb agreed, wishing this girl would go away so she could think.

The girl nodded at the trays set out on the vast expanse of worktop. 'I'm Sasha, by the way. I suppose we'd best get a move on getting these drinks out. Do you want to take red or white?'

'I don't mind,' Deb shrugged, when in reality, she didn't want to do any of them. *Whisky*, Marina had said. There were no trays of whisky, so how was she supposed to do this?

She watched Sasha pick up one of the large silver trays and sashay out of the kitchen. Aside from not knowing how she would carry one of those trays without sending the dainty-stemmed wine glasses toppling everywhere like dominos, how she would put one foot in front of the other *and* hold the tray was even more worrying.

Deb was sure the buzzing of her overfiring nerve endings was audible. The music from the other room needed to be a lot louder than the comfortable background tunes to drown out the cacophony going on inside her.

The same question pressed back into her mind. *What had she agreed to do this for?*

She was sure she would pass out from fright before the required opening presented itself. That's if it ever did. And she had to get the first part of the instructions done before that could happen.

But *how*?

She wondered if she could conceal herself in one of the cupboards? Even two units of this massive kitchen were bigger than any entire kitchen she'd ever seen.

Her mind trailed back to the two-ring electric hob at her father's. How she longed to be back in the relative safety of that little house. Its memory and the life it held now seemed a million years ago.

Deb couldn't help but stare at the shiny granite work surfaces, the polished chrome of the taps and the solid oak cupboards that looked like something straight out of a magazine. A large range cooker inset within the original chimney breast, the mantle above covered with brightly coloured tins and jars, looked like an advert and the large window in front of the double butler sink showcased one of the biggest gardens she'd ever seen.

Deb heard the chatter and laughter coming from the other rooms, but it was overshadowed by the incessant thumping of her own heartbeat banging relentlessly in her ears.

She hadn't been anywhere else in the house yet and had been too nervous to take in any of her surroundings when she'd arrived. She'd blindly followed the other girls from Top Notch Catering, not daring to avert her eyes from the black heels of the girl in front as they'd been directed to the large kitchen at the end of the hallway.

The tall, blond guy on the door was just like Stacey said. He hadn't batted an eyelid when she'd given her name. The only hint he knew who she was the look he'd given her as he'd instructed her to follow the others – the emphasis on the word 'follow'.

But now what?

Her hand moved to the pocket of her white apron over her neat black pencil skirt.

That stuff was still there. She didn't know why she kept checking. Probably because she wished it *wasn't* there, so she could leave. On the other hand, she was scared it might disappear because then she'd fail. She'd get no money and end up like the woman in the attic.

Deb stared at the tray of drinks waiting for her to serve to the guests like a waitress should.

But she wasn't a waitress, and she was terrified.

How could she get into the midst of everything without being noticed?

The majority of people wouldn't give her a second glance, but that man from the other night – the one who'd kicked off the trouble between Tom and Chas – must be here. He was one of the Stokers, so he had to be here *somewhere*. And there was a good chance he would recognise her.

If he recognised her, then...

Deb's mind span towards the point of no return.

Perspiration stuck her white blouse to her back. She had to go and find a suitable opportunity for part one of her task.

Deb succeeded in making as few trips as possible into the main house. Only twice she'd ventured from the kitchen into the reception rooms and both of those times were enough to push her into a state of unbridled angst. And she still hadn't had a glimpse of the one person she needed to find.

The rest of the time, she'd got away with being the one to remain in the kitchen, loading and unloading the dishwasher to keep the fast-disappearing trays of drinks replenished and lined up, ready for the other waitresses to serve.

The party was now in full swing and everyone was working on full power to keep the guests in drinks and nibbles. It had been so hectic this past hour, she'd barely had time to worry about what she still needed to do.

'Bloody hell! It's crazy out there!' Sasha said, her eyes twinkling. 'I'd love to grab one of those eligible geezers. It would do wonders for my bank balance, not to mention my street cred!'

Deb tried to look interested, but it was taking all of her concentration to pour the drinks.

'You should get one of the others to do that and come and check out the talent,' Sasha enthused. 'Fuck me! There's twins and all. Plus the head honcho... No wonder that Samantha bird looks so happy. I would too, with him in my bed!'

Deb's heart skipped as Sasha's words sank in. *The Stokers? They were here?* 'When did they arrive? Last I heard, people were wondering where they were.'

She hoped her question sounded casual, but felt the colour

moving to her cheeks, like voicing anything exposed her intentions.

'They've been here about half an hour. We've all been flipping coins to see which one of us gets to serve them,' Sasha laughed.

'Nice looking, eh?' Deb played the game. 'I'll go myself next time. Where are they?'

'The main man is in the front reception room. You won't get much of a look in with him, though. He's surrounded by the press and, of course, Samantha-stunning-Reynold. The others are in the back room.' Sasha grabbed a glass from one of the newly stocked trays and downed the red wine. 'Ah, that's better!' She smacked her lips enthusiastically. 'A glass of this is probably the equivalent of a month's wages for us, so I'm helping myself to a few!'

Deb stared at the empty glass in Sasha's hand and resisted the urge to have one herself.

Seb Stoker had been here half an hour? She had to weigh things up *now* because if she didn't get part one of the plan done, things would go wrong.

Her heart thumped harder. She had to make sure she wasn't spotted by that brother – whichever one it was who had seen her before. But how would she get a window with Seb Stoker or enough of a gap to do what was needed? She hadn't even located any whisky yet...

As Sasha skittered off with another tray, Deb rooted through the cupboards. What if the spirits were kept in a fancy cabinet in one of the other rooms? Didn't posh places do that?

Sweat building, she yanked open the heavy door of a floor-to-ceiling larder. The slide-out shelving held more fancy jars and bottles of pickles and marinade, sea salt and spices than she'd ever seen.

On the bottom shelf stood three bottles of whisky.

Glancing over her shoulder, Deb grabbed one of the bottles and stared at it.

Glenfiddich Thirty-Year-Old Single Malt.

'What are you doing?'

Deb span around to see one of the caterers – a snotty-looking woman in her mid-thirties. 'Erm, Mr Stoker requested a whisky.'

The woman pursed her lips. 'Hmm, well you'd better find a proper whisky glass. Take it in on one of those small trays over there. Anyone else wanting spirits?'

'Not that I'm aware of,' Deb blabbered.

The woman stomped over to a glass-fronted unit. 'I'm sure Mr Stoker keeps his preferred glass in the cabinet in the drawing room, but you can't interrupt to root around cupboards like an imbecile. Take one from here.'

Seeing the confusion on Deb's face, the woman harrumphed loudly as she pulled a crystal tumbler from the cupboard. 'Oh, for God's sake. Do they not teach you *anything* these days?'

Snatching the glass, Deb mumbled her thanks and turned back to unscrew the whisky, praying the bottle didn't slip through her clammy hands.

* * *

Sam smiled for the umpteenth photograph of the evening. She felt like screaming. Instead, she looked at Seb adoringly, like she was supposed to for the flashbulbs, becoming steadily more impatient as to when he would explain why not only had he arrived half an hour after the party had started, but also why at least *part* of his lateness was down to drinking somewhere other than here.

There hadn't been one opportunity to ask him what had gone on. And something *had* because he might fool the press and the rest of the people with his perfected act, but he wasn't fooling *her*.

Maintaining the image of the perfect couple as they moved for a photograph in front of the floor-to-ceiling velvet curtains framing the French doors, Sam hissed, 'Are you going to tell me what's going on?'

Seb kept his trademark smile directed at the camera. 'Not now, but later, okay? Everything is going to be fine, I promise,' he whispered, steadying himself against the wall.

He knew time was running out to lay his cards on the table and tell Sam what a thin line he was treading with this excess money situation. He should have told her from the beginning because she was starting to question whether the mood hanging around him like a bad smell was something to do with her. And that was not what he wanted her to think. *Ever.*

The very last thing he wanted Sam to think was that he couldn't keep the wolves from the door. He wanted her to feel secure with him, but tonight was not the time, nor the place.

She'd understand when he explained. Very soon, he would be able to breathe easy and enjoy life.

He planted a kiss on Sam's cheek, his lips moving to linger on her ear lobe. 'Fancy fucking this lot off and going upstairs?' he murmured.

Sam grinned despite her annoyance. 'I doubt whether you'd be up for the job after the amount you've put away!'

'You cheeky mare!' Seb laughed, glancing up at the waitress hovering behind Sam. 'Yes, love?'

'You asked for a whisky, sir?'

Seb stared at the tumbler on the small silver tray the girl held. 'I didn't, but I'm long overdue one.' He picked the glass from the tray and grinned. 'Cheers!'

Sam elbowed Seb in the ribs as the girl scurried away. 'I wish you wouldn't tease those people.'

'I wasn't!' Seb winked. 'I genuinely didn't ask for a whisky, but I can't stand this fucking wine bollocks, so I'm having it.' He drank greedily from the glass. 'Ah, that's better! Hey, I hope those girls aren't dishing out my best whisky to everybody!'

'If it runs out so you can't drink any more, then I'll be glad!' Sam scolded, only half joking, but feeling a little more optimistic over Seb's recent moods.

29

Half an hour later, Deb was still shaking. How long would that stuff take to kick in? What if it didn't? Had Stacey even thought of that? What if the man collapsed downstairs and there wasn't the opportunity to undertake part two?

Giving in to temptation, Deb snatched an untouched glass of wine and gulped it down. She must be insane drinking a random drink after what *she'd* done, but then again, she must be mad getting involved with this in the first place – there were far too many variables.

When *this* happens, do *that* and then once *that* happens, wait for *this*, then do *that...*

What if none of it happened? Or they happened, but in a different order?

What if she got caught?

Deb's brain sped through possible scenarios. Stacey had been adamant things were likely to run in a certain order. *'I know men,'* she'd said. *'The minute Stoker feels less than compos mentis, he'll make himself scarce, rather than risk embarrassing himself in front of his cronies.'*

But anything could happen and who would be in the firing line if or *when* it did?

Easy – *her...*

Deb's breath hitched. She stood to be caught whatever happened. How had she have ever thought this feasible?

Calm down, she urged herself, her eyes darting to another glass of wine that could easily have her name on it.

She had to get a grip. How could she know when it was her cue to move onto part two by hiding in here?

She'd accomplished part one. She hadn't been stopped, questioned or gunned down. No one was any the wiser. The same applied to the rest if she didn't fall apart.

She gritted her teeth. *Come on*, she repeated, the mantra soothing her frayed nerve endings. *This is your only way out of your fucked-up life. You owe these people nothing. Absolutely nothing.*

Look at them – they'd got everything, whilst she had nothing.

To reiterate this important point to aid her internal argument, she looked around the vast kitchen once more, concentrating on the expensive, up-to-date equipment and gadgets.

'These people would sell you for a quid quicker than you could click your fingers.' Stacey's words echoed in Deb's brain. *'The Stokers are the sort to force girls and women into lives like yours. You can be the one to show them it's unacceptable and won't be tolerated.'*

Deb's throat tightened. Stacey was right. These people were criminals and benefited by using others for their own gain. She was doing everyone a favour.

Feeling bolstered, Deb moved towards the kitchen door, only to walk straight into someone. 'Sorry,' she gasped, her eyes trailing up a tall man.

'Should you be helping yourself to the guests' wine?' the man said frostily. 'Who are you here with?'

'T-top Notch Catering. I...' *This was one of the security. Shit.*

Quickly, think. Think! 'I'm sorry, I'm just so thirsty. I haven't stopped tonight and...'

'There's a fucking tap over there,' the man barked. 'Top Notch, you say?' He looked Deb up and down. 'I haven't seen you serving food and drinks.'

'I-I've been keeping the trays topped up,' Deb floundered, her knees going weak. *She'd been sprung. Fuck, fuck, fuck! She'd failed... Now she'd...*

Grant appeared in the doorway. 'What's the issue, Stu?'

'This girl.' Stu nodded towards Deb. 'Is she on the trade list, Trev? She's been lurking in here half the evening, and I just caught her downing a fucking drink!'

Grant glared at the girl Marina had insisted he allow entry to. What use was she with eavesdropping if she'd been hiding in the kitchen? Still, he had to keep up the act. 'Yeah, I let her in. She's on the list.' He glared at Deb as he pulled the guest list from his pocket. 'I'll double check anyway. What's your name again?'

'D-Deb. Deb Banner,' Deb spluttered. This guy must know what she was here to do if Marina had sorted it with him?

Grant scoured the names. 'It's fine, Stu. She's on here.'

Nodding abruptly, Stu walked back to his position, leaving Grant to grab Deb's arm. 'Why the fuck are you lurking in here? Get back out and do what you're supposed to be doing. Grab a tray and fucking mingle!'

Deb didn't need telling twice. Rushing to grab more drinks, she all but ran out of the room, trying her best not to think about being in the thick of things.

As her legs propelled her unwillingly towards the room where she had last seen Sebastian Stoker, Deb made the decision to make herself as invisible as possible and hope to hell that the opportunity for part two presented itself sooner rather than later.

* * *

'Where the bloody hell is Neil?' Seb slurred loudly. 'Is he still talking to that boring bastard from Shipley's?'

'Shh!' Sam nudged Seb, making him sway precariously. 'You're shouting.'

'I'm not shouting, am I?' Seb shouted. 'Am I shouting?' He frowned, his face contorting with the effort it took to move his muscles.

'You're bladdered!' Sam said. 'Go and sober up!'

'I am *not* drunk!' Seb protested. Overbalancing, his elbow knocked a candlestick from the mantlepiece, the crash causing a moment of stunned silence before the chatter resumed.

'Please, Seb,' Sam begged. 'The press will love this. You're staggering and I'm sure everyone heard you say Bill Shipley was boring. You've drunk too much!'

Seb laughed loudly. 'Oh, lighten up! I'm fine!' *But he wasn't.* Okay, so he'd had a few before getting here and was well known for drinking more than a rugby team without showing any effect, but for once, he was really feeling it. Over the last ten minutes, it had hit him like an earthquake. And it was getting steadily worse.

He went to brush a lock of Sam's hair from her face but couldn't coordinate his hand. *Shit.* Maybe he *should* go out of the way for a bit?

Sam scowled. This really was the worst. Was it not bad enough that Seb had turned up late, only to embarrass himself by getting wasted? These people would love nothing more than having mud to sling.

He'd insisted on inviting people from businesses on the strip, as well as the press – shoving the point home that they'd survived the long-standing bitter rivalry between the Reynolds and Stokers –

but for him to turn up in a state and act like a clown did nothing but undermine them, both as a couple *and* their firms.

How bloody much had he put away? Either way, she wasn't letting him scupper the evening.

Catching Andrew's eye, Sam beckoned him over. 'Get Seb upstairs for a while,' she hissed, gesturing to the murmuring press, hovering like vultures. 'They're waiting for something to happen...'

Andrew glanced at the gathering press and eyed Seb once again. 'How's he got himself in this state?'

'You tell me,' Sam snapped.

'He had a few during our meeting, but not enough to get mullered. You know he doesn't get out of control.'

'It seems there's a first for everything,' Sam countered, utterly fed up. Tonight was a disaster. 'I'll check on him in an hour. If he's sobered up by then, he'll be okay to come back down.'

Andrew nodded. 'Go and divert the press as much as you can.'

'Whaddya doing?' Seb yelled when Andrew grabbed his arm.

Without further hesitation, Sam hurried in the direction of the circling photographers, a smile plastered on her face, her mind scrambling for something to interest them other than a drunk Seb Stoker.

'Excuse me,' she said, pushing past the young waitress loitering in the doorway with the tray of drinks.

Pressed against the back hallway, Deb attempted to blend in with the curtains. She stared at the staircase looming in front of her.

It had been ten minutes since Seb Stoker had been ushered upstairs. She'd seen it from the doorway and had been frozen in terror, thinking the man with Seb was the same one who'd banged on Chas's car. But he wasn't. Similar but *not* the same. It was the other twin, but it had still been far too close for comfort.

Once she'd seen the twin return from upstairs and Samantha still avidly entertaining the press, Deb knew it was time to make her move.

As far as she knew, no one had seen her slip out here. She hoped not anyway.

Looking back to the stairs, the noise of blood rushed frantically through her veins whooshing loudly in her ears.

This was it. She would either achieve what she was sent to do or the whole thing would crash around her.

On shaky legs, she moved up the staircase, glancing back to the ground floor as she went. This must be what was classed as a 'servants' staircase'. Did this lead to the same part of the house as the main one? That one led off from the square reception hallway at the front of the house – the area where all the guests were. No one and nothing was down here, short of a door to a cellar and a couple of storerooms. Even the kitchen was back up this corridor.

Deb reached the top of the stairs, the landing shrouded in darkness.

Where would Seb Stoker be?

Heart thumping, she crept along the landing, pausing outside the first door. She gingerly turned the brass doorknob and gently pushed. *Nothing in there.*

Tiptoeing to the next door, Deb's lungs remained rigid, scared to pull air into them in case it was too loud. She had to find this man, do what was needed and then sit and wait for someone to come looking.

And that was the very worst part...

She had to purposely wait to be discovered... That instruction was clear.

'It will be Samantha,' Stacey had said, adamant her theory was correct. *'I guarantee she'll check on him.'*

Deb peeped inside the next room and then moved on.

What if Seb Stoker was on the third floor? She'd never have time...

Swallowing down the rising panic, Deb pushed the third door open and light spilled onto the dark landing.

There he is...

Deb's eyes tracked to the man slumped across the most beautiful bed she'd ever seen. Her pulse raced.

Pushing herself into automated mode, Deb slipped into the room and shut the door behind her, still not daring to breathe.

What if he woke up? Had Stacey thought of that?

Suddenly, the present situation became clear. It didn't matter what happened to *her* as long as the job was done. She was expendable.

Whether Stacey cared about what happened in the aftermath or not, *she* did. This was her *only* chance to change her life and she was taking it regardless.

Deb's resolve strengthened. She had nothing to lose. If it went pear-shaped, then it went pear-shaped. She'd rather be dead than continue at the Aurora.

Making sure the empty vial of ketamine was still safely stowed in the apron pocket, she pulled at her clothes. Tugging her sweat-soaked blouse off, she let it drop to the floor and then slipped her pencil skirt from her hips to pool around her ankles.

Deb moved to the bed in her underwear and swallowed nervously.

She hadn't taken on board just how attractive Seb Stoker was. She'd seen photos in the paper many a time and had agreed with the girls drooling over his pictures that he was easy on the eye. But in real life, he was more than that.

The man was absolutely drop-dead gorgeous.

And now she had to take this gorgeous specimen's clothes off without him stirring?

Deb's shaking fingers hovered over the buttons of Seb's crisply starched dress shirt.

What you waiting for? she asked herself. *These people use girls like you. He deserves this – they all do.*

Her eyes moved back to Seb's face, his eyes shut, his breathing slight, yet deep.

Taking a deep breath, Deb unbuttoned his shirt, then undid the leather belt around his waist. He didn't move a muscle.

Gaining confidence, she paused, training her ears for any hint of movement.

Nothing. Right, come on.

Realising nothing would rouse Seb Stoker from his drug-induced slumber, Deb didn't mess about inching his clothes from his body. Yanking his trousers off the bottom of his feet, she paused, transfixed with the fine physique underneath the man's clothes.

Regaining her concentration, with effort she rolled him onto his side and yanked the bedspread and sheets out from under him.

Now all she had to do was get into the bed and wait, listening carefully for when someone approached. Then she'd get into position, ready to escape as fast as possible.

* * *

Craig had seen enough. He'd heeded Kevin's instructions of not monitoring the strange, gloved man, but now croupiers on three separate tables had flagged this man up, he'd made the decision to personally watch what Gloveman did during his next game.

He'd allotted thirty minutes, nothing more.

Propping himself up at the bar, despite his menacing size, he was adept for keeping a low profile. And by doing just that, he saw the man slip a card from the end of his sleeve.

That was it. Low staff or not, he was pulling this one in.

Striding over to table twenty-two, Craig laid his meaty hand on Gloveman's shoulder. 'Excuse me, sir?'

Dan looked up, the irritation of being disturbed from rounding tonight's winnings off dissolving with the sight of a man-monster looming behind him.

It was okay. He'd play this cool.

A casual smile slithered across his face. 'Yes?' Dan replied courteously.

'Would you mind accompanying me to the office for a moment?' Craig said. His voice was pleasant enough, but anyone worth their salt knew the innocent-sounding question was a clear order.

Dan faltered. He could do this one of two ways: kick up a stink, or collapse into a pile of terrified flesh at the prospect of being carted off by this bruiser. Or he could manufacture a combination of the two? But he needed to hurry and decide because he still hadn't answered, nor moved one way or the other.

He couldn't afford to balls up because it would get back to the bird that ran this place and that, in turn, would get back to Stoker...

Dan didn't want his face becoming known – especially with what he had planned.

Bollocks.

'What seems to be the problem?' Dan's voice was steady and calm. 'Don't tell me that my winnings from table twenty were miscalculated?' He sighed theatrically, rolling his eyes at the croupier.

'Accompany me, please,' Craig repeated, wanting to avoid manhandling this muppet out of his seat in front of the other customers.

'Is it so important that this can't wait until after this game?' Dan asked, suddenly feeling rather sick. 'We're at a crucial point.' His next hand would clear £4K and he didn't want to miss that.

Craig's bullhead blocked out the illumination of the green ceramic light overhead as he bent down. '*Now*, sir,' he hissed, his voice low.

Dan placed his cards on the table and smiled at the other players. 'My apologies, gents. It seems I've no choice but to fold.' He cut Craig a stare for good measure before getting to his feet. 'I hope you've got a good reason for this,' he said as he was frogmarched out of the games room.

Surely this bozo didn't know the rules of poker? The last two croupiers weren't members of MENSA, that much was obvious, so it must be something else.

Perhaps Grant had been murdered during a random fight at Stoker's party?

Unlikely, Dan thought. He wouldn't be that lucky. Besides, this lot didn't know of his connection to Grant.

A glimmer of an idea formed. Maybe that was it. Maybe he should tell them? They weren't likely to accuse one of their staff's relatives of being on the fiddle, were they?

* * *

'They're asking questions about Seb's absence again,' Sam whispered to Andrew. 'I keep telling them he's taking urgent business calls, but they won't leave it. I'm going to have to check on him and see if he's in any fit state to rejoin.' She looked over to the waiting journalist. 'A shot of Andrew at the bottom of the stairs, perhaps?'

'Oh, great...' Andrew muttered, watching the photographer make his way over. 'Cheers for that!'

'Only fair you should take some of the strain.' Sam grinned mischievously before quickly moving up the stairs.

It was only then that her smile dropped. Her face ached from pretending everything was all right. She'd fended off Seb's absence, but she was damned if she was doing it *all* bloody evening.

She approached the bedroom, her hand twisting the doorknob. Seb owed her a good explanation for getting so wasted and leaving her to...

Stopping in the doorway, the image burnt onto her eyeballs. 'What the...?'

In slow motion, the scene moved frame by frame: a semi-naked woman clambering off Seb, a look of shock etched on her pretty face...

Sam remained frozen, unable to move. *This couldn't be happening.*

Her eyes followed the figure scrabbling to pull a black skirt over narrow hips and picking a white blouse from the crumpled pile of discarded clothes on the floor. *Seb's clothes...*

The woman held the blouse over her chest, her spare hand reaching for a white apron.

A waitress? Seb had just slept with a waitress? And she wasn't even a woman – this creature was a mere slip of a girl.

The man she'd vowed to marry had slept with a *teenager*? In their home? In their bed?

Bile tracked up Sam's throat. Coming to her senses, her eyes narrowed. 'Who the fuck are you?' she screamed, lurching forward.

Yelping, the girl backed towards the bed. 'I'm sorry. It's not...'

'Not what it looks like?' Sam lunged for the girl, her eyes blazing. Her gaze then darted towards Seb.

'You bastard!' she screamed, her hands flying towards Seb. She yanked the sheet away. He was butt naked.

Her heart pounded with rage like never before, not knowing who to go for first – him, or his tart.

Sam's head turned towards the sudden movement. 'Oh, no you don't!' she roared. Grabbing the girl's hair, she dragged her to the floor. 'Tell me what the fuck you're playing at!'

With difficulty, Seb pushed himself up the pillow and looked around the room in bewilderment. 'Sam? Is that you? Wh...?'

'You can shut the fuck up!' Sam's slit-like eyes swung towards Seb. First she'd deal with this slut and then she'd deal with *him*.

31

Grant raced up the stairs, unsure what had happened, short of distinctively hearing Sam Reynold's raised voice. He might have known the second he'd gone for a piss one of the guests would take the opportunity to slip upstairs. He should have held off using the bog until Stu had done his rounds of the garden.

His mind whirred. This wouldn't do him any favours. He'd promised no one would slip past him. Why tonight of all bastard nights?

Thundering up the landing, Grant heard footsteps behind him. Now Stu and the other security had decided to wake up, had they?

Reaching the bedroom where Sam's shouting was coming from, his hand reached for the doorknob, finding the two Stoker brothers and a photographer behind him.

Christ, could this get any worse? Kevin would have his nuts on a stick for this, but for now, the only thing was to make sure Sam was unharmed and remove the intruder.

Barging the door open, Grant slammed into the room, Andrew and Neil behind him.

'What in God's name is going on?' Andrew yelled as a half-naked girl ducked past them down the landing.

'This bastard!' Sam pointed to Seb. 'That's what's gone on!'

Grant's head darted around. That girl – she was the one Marina had sent. *What the fuck?* 'Oi!' he yelled, turning on his heels. He had to stop her. It had only been a couple of seconds. He could still catch her.

'Come back here!' he roared. Racing back down the landing, he barged into a photographer busy clicking his camera at the girl's back as she hurried down the stairs.

Clearing two steps at a time, Grant kept his eyes on Deb as she skittered through people in the reception hall, their once lively chatter now reduced to silence.

The only noise was the sound of glasses smashing on the Minton tiled floor after being knocked from guests' hands as the escaping girl fled.

* * *

Kevin didn't think he could stand anything else going wrong tonight. The main aim was to concentrate on finding that nonce, but now Craig had brought in that bloke he'd mentioned earlier, despite everything that he'd said?

Staring at the receiver, he felt like slamming it down. 'You've got definite proof of that? If it's just suspicion surrounding th...'

Pausing as Craig explained, Kevin's heart sank. 'Okay, then there's no choice... Yep... Hold fire and keep him there. I'll get in touch with her now.'

Replacing the phone, Kevin leant back in the chair and picked up his cigarettes.

Great. Tonight of all nights, in the middle of Sam's party, he'd have to call to tell her there was an instance of sharking. This time at the Orchid.

It would be a night he was in charge, wouldn't it? Like he needed to be party to anything else to let Sam down on...

Kevin picked the receiver back up, dialling Sam's home number. He had to tell her whether he liked it or not. She was the one to give the orders on what to do with fraud cases, not him.

He waited as the phone rang out. *Surely someone would have answered by now?*

Cutting the call, he redialled, only for the same thing to happen.

Shrugging his shoulders, Kevin flicked through his address book, his thick finger running down the line of names under 'S'.

Stopping on Andrew Stoker's mobile number, he jabbed the digits into the phone.

If Sam wasn't available, then Andrew could give her the message.

Two rings was all it took.

'Andrew? It's Kevin... Sorry to bother you... I can't get hold of Sam... There's a problem at the tournament. We've got a shark and... *What?*'

Kevin's mouth dropped open. 'Fuck...' he muttered. 'Yes, I hear you... What do you want me to do with this bloke we're holding?' He frowned. 'Completely? Okay... Yes, I will. Let me know if Sam needs anything.'

Replacing the receiver, Kevin stubbed his cigarette out. It seemed the Orchid wasn't the only place things had gone haywire tonight.

Although Andrew Stoker hadn't gone into details, whatever had happened at the party must be bad if the hater of card sharks himself said to let the prick they'd got here, go.

Craig wouldn't like it, but orders were orders. And in Sam's absence, an order from a Stoker was the next best thing.

* * *

With a mouthful of dirt, Deb lay face down, grateful that Samantha Reynold's garden had an abundance of bushes and beds offering cover.

Lying perfectly still, she imagined she could hear the movement of earthworms in the soil below. She was so silent, she was sure her heart had stopped.

Her stomach then lurched hearing a nearby voice. It sounded like that security guard who Stacey knew. Or was it one of the others?

Seeing the beam of torchlight in the distance, Deb closed her eyes. If it was that same security guard, would he help aid her escape?

But he'd been chasing her down the stairs... It was only the mass of people congregating in the reception hall which had granted enough confusion for her to get a head start and evade the pursuit.

Nausea rolled with the increasing suspicion the security guard had not been aware of the brief she'd been instructed to do.

Hearing the familiar pounding of her heart again was a slight comfort. This noise, which had been strangely absent for a while, reminded her that she wasn't dead. *Yet...*

And that man – Seb Stoker... The whole Stoker firm would be after her now. As would Samantha Reynold.

Stacey had somehow pre-empted the whole situation perfectly. It had run like clockwork.

Tears stung Deb's eyes. She didn't think she'd ever seen anyone look so angry or betrayed as Samantha Reynold.

The worst thing was, Seb Stoker had done nothing. Nothing at all. And to be fair, neither had *she*. All she'd done was make it *look* like something had happened.

Deb shuddered. Now she had the two most dangerous firms in Birmingham on her case. She was dead meat if she didn't get away from here.

Lifting her head, Deb peered through tiny gaps in the rhodo-dendron bush. She couldn't see the flickers of torches any longer, nor hear shouting. She could hear nothing but her own heartbeat and the rustle of the wind. But she could sense people in the immediate vicinity – maybe not close by, but *somewhere* – poised and ready for any movement.

Deb screwed her eyes shut and slumped back to the wet ground. How long would she have to lie here? These weren't the sort of people who would give up easily. She was already chilled to the bone and it wouldn't be long before the relentless temperature of the February night rendered her frozen.

A fresh wave of panic overtook her. The mounting desperation to be free of the Aurora and all that went with it, driving her to this insanity, had made her forget to question one major part – what to do *after* she'd completed the job. Stacey had told her to meet her back at the Magic Bean, but that was tomorrow. What was she supposed to do until then? Where was she to go?

Deb's fingernails cut into her palms as a creeping sense of desolation flooded her. 'Please tell me I haven't done all of this for nothing,' she whispered into the darkness. The thought was too awful to contemplate.

She felt like screaming. Why the hell hadn't she had the brains to sort this out beforehand? How could she have been so bloody stupid?

Gingerly, she pushed herself up onto her knees and peered above the bush. She couldn't stay here any longer. As much as the thought was abysmal, she had no choice but to return to the Aurora until tomorrow.

She'd go back, act normal and arrange to go back out tomorrow night, under the guise of scouting. She could only hope Amelia had covered for her long absence tonight.

It was all she could cling to, anyway.

Taking a deep breath, Deb crept from the bushes and headed down the garden in the opposite direction of the house. There had to be a hedge, fence or wall to climb over. And once she'd done that, she would find the main road, or *any* road, to lead her back to the place she dreaded.

* * *

It had taken a while for Dan to stop shaking. Although he'd kept his cool whilst locked in that suspiciously soundproof-looking room in the basement of the Orchid whilst a man the size of an Olympic wrestler glared ferociously at him, the minute he'd been allowed to walk out of there, the pent-up fear had escaped, draining from his pores.

Slapping a tenner in the taxi driver's hand, Dan clambered from the car, thankful his legs still worked. However, they didn't feel too stable.

He could have walked from Broad Street, but he wasn't certain he'd have made it to the Aurora. He could also have gone back to the flat, but being as all the pubs were now shut, the only place he could think of offering a stiff drink away from Marina's nagging witch-like voice was here.

Besides, he wanted to tell Tom what he'd learnt. It wasn't much, but the information should be appreciated. Anything to take his mind off how close he'd come to not only getting a pasting, but possibly ruining his plans entirely.

Dan banged on the Aurora's door, glancing over his shoulder just to make sure no one had followed him, then looked down at his feet, double-checking he hadn't dreamt that he'd walked away with both legs intact.

What about his hands?

Nope – nothing else lost. Luck had been on his side tonight, but there was no way he could go to the Orchid again now. He could only hope going through security footage wasn't part of those bozos' job descriptions, otherwise Grant would see he'd been there. And worse, got collared. *Almost.*

'All right?' Dan pushed past the Chinese girl opening the door and made his way down to the backroom, like it was his own house.

He signalled for a drink and plonked himself down in a chair, his eyes scouring the room for Tina. He could do with a bit of relaxation.

'Thanks,' he muttered as his drink was deposited on the table in front of him and struggled to pull his cigarettes from his jacket pocket. *Stop fucking shaking*, he snarled inwardly.

'Ah, Dan!' Tom strode across the room. 'I didn't expect to see you in here tonight.'

Dan jumped at Tom's bellowing voice. The smile across the man's face wasn't reflected in his eyes as he jerked his head in the direction of the office.

He dutifully got up, making sure to take the large glass of house vodka with him, glumly accepting that his wish of getting some relief with Tina was unlikely. The last time he'd been in Tom's office, he'd been in there *hours*.

Tom kicked the office door shut the second Dan was over the threshold and gestured for him to take a seat. 'That party at Stoker and Reynold's has finished early. What news have you got?'

'Well, I... erm... don't have any news on that yet,' Dan reluctantly explained. 'I haven't seen Grant. I've been at the Orchid.'

Tom bristled. 'The Orchid? What the fuck did you go there for? Did I not tell you to keep a low profile? All we need to concentrate on is th...'

'Yes, but I wanted to check it out,' Dan cut in hastily. 'I knew there would be minimum staff because of the party, so it was the ideal time to go. They were so thin on the ground, I could have done that place over single-handedly!' *Lies, but needs must.* He held his hand up, his confidence returning. 'Besides, it was part of my original plan to have a look.'

He smiled. Tom could do nothing without the codes for the safes and he wasn't giving those up just yet. Not until it was the right time. But he wasn't going to mention the close call in the basement with a bulldog bouncer. Tom didn't need to know about that. Anyway, that was a mere blip and not worth discussing.

Seeing Tom's face gliding into a snarl, Dan continued. 'I know what I'm doing and you'll be glad I went.' He took a leisurely gulp of his vodka. 'Something kicked off at the housewarming party...'

Tom sat forward, his attention now fully piqued. 'What? What happened?'

Dan grinned. 'Not sure yet, but I will do. I came straight from the Orchid to here and...'

'You mean you left a direct trail from the Orchid to this place?' Tom gasped. *Was this bloke an utter cretin?*

'Relax!' Dan flapped his stumpy hand. 'They weren't interested in what I was doing, believe me!' *Not after that phone call...* Without that coming in at a very opportune moment, he strongly suspected he wouldn't be here at all. 'I positioned myself in earshot of one of the security.'

'Get to the point!' Tom muttered, his irritation growing exponentially.

'I overheard him on the phone. Something had happened at the party. He didn't look pleased.'

'That's it?' Tom spat. 'That could be *anything*! You've risked everything for that?'

'Nah, it's something big, I can tell.' Dan grinned. And if Tom knew he'd been let off for sharking, then he'd realise it *had* to be something big. 'I just popped in on my way back to the flat,' he lied. 'I'll keep my ear to the ground when Grant gets back tonight.'

His mouth cracked into a wide smile, even though he'd now have to put up with Marina. 'I get the feeling that whatever has gone on will take up a lot of their concentration over the next few days, so we need to get ready to move on the lockups.'

Tom scrutinised Dan. He'd thought he was saddled with this poxy setup and this alone for the foreseeable future until this bloke had stumbled into his life. He was like a lucky penny. *But was he full of shit or not?* The man didn't have a bloody inkling of his personal connection with Sam Reynold, so had no reason for fabrication.

Either way, he had to run with it – the man was holding all the cards – *literally*.

Tom frowned, the effort of thinking becoming increasingly tiresome. From Amelia's recent attitude and things in general lately, the Aurora was going down the pan. They were running out of new faces and the takings were down. On top of that, he had to offload that bitch in the attic – she was taking up too much room and resources.

As soon as he got his hands on this long-awaited dough, he'd be out of this dump and out of this cursed hole of a country. Everyone could rot in hell as far as he was concerned.

Hearing somebody scuttle past, Tom didn't even bother rushing to peer out of his office door like he normally would. This was way more important than anything the tarts were doing. Little did they know, their time earning from his premises was limited.

Instead, he slapped Dan on the back, prepared to give him the benefit of the doubt. 'Right, son, get your arse back to your shithole of a flat and discover what's gone down tonight. Keep your ears finely tuned for any whiff of the Stokers' planned movements over the next few days because that's when I'm expecting to move on this.' Tom leant over the table, not far from Dan, his face splitting into a sinister smile. 'Got it?'

Dan nodded and got up from the chair as casually as he could manage.

32

Light streamed through the open curtains of the back bedroom, but whether it was four, six or 10 a.m., Sam had no idea. Time meant nothing. The remainder of last night – one of the worst nights of her life – had merged into the next day. She hadn't had a wink of sleep. Nor had she expected any.

How would she sleep again now her life, or what she'd *believed* to be her life, was in tatters?

The man she loved with her whole heart, the one who'd stood by her – them against the world – had broken every bit of the trust she'd given him.

She could barely begin to think about what had happened. In many respects, it felt like a bad dream.

If only it was...

Sam's scratchy eyes, puffy from the tears she'd shed, stared at the collection of jumbled furniture in the bedroom. This was one of the many spare rooms yet to be decorated and sorted out. One that now never would be.

The exact memory, after screaming at Neil or Andrew to get everybody out of her house last night, was sketchy. She vaguely remembered hearing the noise of the people downstairs gradually fading to silence as they left.

She also remembered screaming at Seb to 'get the fuck out', just as she'd launched her engagement ring in his face.

She didn't know if she'd hit him, scratched his eyes out or what, but she'd wanted to, she knew that.

She couldn't recall Seb leaving, but he had.

The only clear thing in her mind was the burning need to be out of that bedroom, away from everybody and everything. That bedroom she'd loved, which now could never be anything other than a reminder of when her heart had imploded.

How could Seb do this? And with that young girl?

Everybody would know about this, but even the prospect of public humiliation was nothing compared to what *really* mattered.

She'd trusted Seb with everything. She'd believed him. She'd *truly* believed he was the one.

That she'd been so wrong hurt so much that she could hardly pull the air into her lungs.

The question was, where did she go from here? How could she carry on?

There was only one real option.

Standing up, the lack of sleep making her sway, Sam pulled a holdall from the suitcases stacked against the far wall. There were some of her clothes in this room – stuff she hadn't yet sorted or put away. She'd take some of those. There was no way she was setting foot back into *that* bedroom again. The same reason why she couldn't remain in this house.

Shoving clothes into the holdall, she looked down into the garden. So, she'd been right? The sense that something was brewing this last week – that constant prodding at the back of her mind telling her something bad was on the horizon – had finally shown itself.

Seb's strange attitude had been down to this. He wasn't happy with their life together. *With her.*

Whether this thing with that slip of a girl had been going on beforehand or not was irrelevant. Either way, it showed what they'd had as a couple was nothing like what she'd believed.

Sam swiped away the single tear rolling down her face with the back of her hand. At least she'd had the sense not to sell her apartment. Now she needed it more than ever.

* * *

'What the fuck were you thinking?' Neil raged, slamming the morning paper down in front of Seb. 'How could you be so stupid?'

Seb rubbed the fresh growth of stubble on his chin. 'I've already told you. I know nothing about any of this.' He glared at Neil defiantly. 'It's a setup!'

'Setup?' Neil cried. 'At least have the decency to admit it! Even *I* wouldn't try to worm my way out of this! Why the hell do you think you're back in your old flat, rather than your house?'

Seb sighed, his head pounding. He wasn't sure why he was back in the flat. His memory of last night was nothing more than a grey mist. He never got so drunk as to lose control. It was too dangerous in his position. *Something was very wrong with this situation.*

He turned back to the front page of the *Birmingham Mail*, his anger fast turning back to bewilderment and shock.

City Casino Boss Party Shame

Sebastian Stoker took the term 'playing away from home' to another level last night. On Tuesday evening, the house-warming celebrations of glamorous couple and city's favourites, Samantha Reynold and Seb Stoker, took on a sour note. After a long absence from the party by Stoker, excused by his fiancée as urgent business calls, he was discovered in an upstairs bedroom in a compromising position with an unknown woman.

We have attempted but failed to make contact with Ms Reynold this morning for comment, but it can only be imagined how devastated Samantha must feel to discover her fiancé's indiscretions going on under her very own roof and in front of so many influential business associates and journalists.

This wasn't the best decision for Stoker to make as head of the Royal Peacock casino and the Stokers' city firm.

A partygoer, who wishes to remain anonymous, stated: 'All we heard was Sam screaming blue murder, then a half-naked girl ran from the house. I doubt there will be a wedding after this...'

That's the question on the lips of many people in Birmingham this morning, as well as what this means for the future relationship between the two once rival firms.

Seb inwardly groaned at the photograph showing the bare back of a young woman halfway down the stairs of his house; the faces of stunned guests in the reception hallway looking up in shock.

He continued reading:

The identity of the woman in question is unknown, but she is described as being around 5' 3", with shoulder-length brown hair, a slim-build and roughly seventeen years of age. It is believed she is a worker from the company who supplied the catering for the party.

If anyone has information concerning the identity of the

mystery young lady or if she would like to get in touch with us
herself, we will gladly hear her side of the story.

Screwing up the paper, Seb threw it onto the table. 'This is
ridiculous! I don't know this woman!' Nor did he want to. No
matter what state he'd been in, he'd *never* betray Sam. Not in that
way. Not in *any* way.

Sam was the best thing to have ever happened to him.

He gulped from a large glass of water, his mouth parched.
'Where's Sam? I need to speak to her.'

Andrew shoved his hand in his pocket, retrieving Sam's
engagement ring. 'You don't remember this bouncing off your
head, then?'

Taking the ring, Seb stared at it. 'Sam believes this bullshit?
Oh, for f...'

'Quit the bullshit! Sam walked in on you!' Neil yelled. 'She saw
it with her own eyes! We *all* did!'

'*What?*' Seb roared. *Were they actually saying this was true?* That
he'd slept with this woman? This teenager? It wasn't possible. He
wouldn't have. He would never... 'I have to see Sam,' he croaked,
getting to his feet. '*Now!*'

'She won't want to see you! That much I *do* know,' Andrew said.

Sinking back into the chair, Seb put his head in his hands. *This
couldn't be happening.*

Andrew looked at Neil. 'Come on. We need to speak to Kevin.
There was an issue at the Orchid last night and being as I called
the shots, I'd better find out the result.'

Seb didn't raise his head as his brothers left the flat. Normally,
he'd want to know *exactly* what had gone down, but today, the
singular and only thing in his frazzled mind was Sam. He had to
put things right. He couldn't lose her.

33

Grant watched Marina eagerly reading the front of the *Birmingham Mail* and blocked the lounge doorway with his frame. 'I want an explanation,' he said, eyeing his sister's rapturous face.

Marina giggled – the sound strange and high-pitched. 'This is brilliant!' she murmured, her mouth curling into a smile. 'It couldn't have gone better.'

Adrenaline pulsed in Grant's veins. 'Are you listening? I got no sense from you last night and you're no more coherent today!' Striding over to the sofa, he snatched the paper from Marina's hands. 'Tell me what's going on!'

Marina looked up, the flash of irritation quickly masked by batting her eyelashes. 'What do you mean?'

'Don't give me that!' Grant snarled. 'This girl who Sam discovered in the sack with Stoker was the one *you* sent in.' His finger stabbed the image of the girl. 'This could ruin everything! How could she drop us in it like this? You said she knew what to do!'

Marina's lips twitched into a smirk as Grant stormed across the room, his fist connecting with the wall.

'I knew this was a bad idea,' Grant raged. 'I wasn't happy about it in the first place. All that girl has done is arouse suspicion. Even Stu questioned who she was before this happened. Now, they'll check who let her in and see it was me. Whatever information she may have heard is bloody pointless now and all because she got sidetracked. On top of that, what she's done has very probably ruined Sam's relationship with Stoker.'

His teeth grated. From what he'd seen of Sam afterwards, it wasn't only her relationship that was in pieces – her face had reflected her life imploding. And that he didn't like. Whatever Marina thought, Sam didn't deserve this. 'The stupid girl didn't do what she was supposed to do. You should never have involved her.'

Marina's smirk grew wider. 'That's where you're wrong. She did *everything* she was supposed to do.' She recovered the newspaper from the floor and stared at the article again, her gratification increasing. The whole city would be laughing at Samantha Reynold by now. *It was perfect.*

Grant opened his mouth, then shut it again. He watched his sister scouring the words, soaking up the implications with glee. He could not believe this! 'Are you saying you set this up?'

Snatching the paper, he pulled Marina off the sofa by her sleeve. 'You staged this?'

Marina shrugged her arm from Grant's grip and glared at him defiantly. 'So what?' she spat. 'I told you only a few days ago that I wanted that bitch's life ruined, and I meant it.' She laughed shrilly. 'All I did was get that silly tart to dope Stoker's drink and then shag him. I knew the spoilt bitch would check on him like a paranoid fishwife and I was right! She must be gutted, and this is just the start!'

'We agreed to just go for the safe, nothing else!' Grant raged. 'All we needed was a schedule of the Stoker movements to get a clear run!'

'*You* agreed, not me!' Marina shot back. 'I want personal

payback as well as money. I want every single fucking thing that matters in that spoiled cow's life trashed.'

Grant sighed. 'I've had enough of this madness. You think that ruining Sam's relationship with Stoker puts right what our mother did by dumping us? Get real.'

'I'm real, all right. And yes, ruining Samantha's relationship with lover boy *does* make me feel better. See?' Marina pointed to her wide smile. 'I'm happy – *very* happy. This will cause a knock-on effect. Her whole life will crumble and then boom! It will be over!'

'Christ!' Grant barked. 'You must be deranged! Sam's not stupid. Before long, she'll work out this was a setup, so all you've done is make things difficult. *And* you lied to me!'

'I wonder why...' Squaring up to Grant, Marina jabbed her finger at his face. 'It's obvious you think Samantha is the bee's knees. For all your promises, you're on *her* side, not mine. I knew you'd turn. You probably want to screw her yourself!'

Grant grabbed Marina by the shoulders and slammed her into the wall. 'What's the matter with you? That's disgusting! She's our sister! How c...'

'She's no sister of ours. *I'm* your sister. Me!' Marina screamed. 'I'll not be passed over for her, do you understand?'

Grant couldn't help but laugh. 'This is ludicrous! You know it's not like that. Stop being crazy!'

'But you're starting to take her side. You act like you care what happens to her. Why? You're changing, Grant, and I don't like it.'

Grant sighed. It might be true that he liked Sam Reynold, but it didn't change the end result. 'Look, we said we'd get the money and that still stands. See sense! As long as this stunt you've pulled doesn't scupper anything, we can move on the haul in a couple of days.'

'But I've done you a favour. By doing this, I've deflected their concentration,' Marina hissed, her eyes blazing. 'The next part will *guarantee* the whole firm's mind is elsewhere!'

'What next part?' Grant sniped. 'Haven't you caused enough suspicion? What's your "brilliant" idea this time around?'

Marina swung around, her eyes bright. 'Easy. You're going to kill her!'

Grant's mouth fell open. 'Kill *Sam*? That's not part of the plan. What about the money? What about our mother? She's the one wh...'

'Kill her too if you like. In fact, that would be even better!' Marina laughed. 'And yeah, I want money, but I want this more. Samantha has taken everything we should have had.'

'You're losing the plot, Marina. I can't just kill the woman!'

'Why not?' Marina screamed. 'Isn't that what you do? You're a fucking hitman! What's the difference?' Sweat broke out on her brow. 'Christ, Grant, just do your fucking job!'

Grant's temper flared. 'I may be a gun for hire, but this is personal. I have no reason to kill Sam. We're getting the money and then we're out of here. That's the end of it.'

He paced the room, looking back as he reached the door. 'For God's sake, sort yourself out! I need someone on side here, not someone chucking around this sort of shit and causing problems.'

Striding up the hallway, Grant grabbed his jacket. Marina had lost the plot big style. She'd become a liability. The only thing to do was to get his hands on this cash and get everyone the hell out of here.

But somewhere within him, the gnawing notion grew that people who really didn't deserve it were being targeted. And that didn't sit comfortably.

As much as Marina wouldn't accept it, Sam was their *sister* – their blood.

It was this which clouded Grant's mind so much as he left the flat that he failed to notice Dan lurking in the bedroom doorway.

Shutting the attic door, Amelia scraped the tears from her face with her pudgy forearm, before leaning against the landing wall, her head pounding. The sound of her teeth grating echoed within her ears, but nowhere near loud enough to drown out the screeching coming from the room she'd just left.

Two days since she'd given that poor bitch any drugs and, yes, the woman was suffering cold turkey, but the decision had been made and that decision was final.

She'd left enough food and water to see the woman through and she'd also loosened the wrist cuffs. The sad old cow was so thin, she could slip them off without unlocking them, but it was up to her to get herself out of there now, if she so wished.

Taking a deep breath, Amelia made her way down the rickety stairs.

She'd done *her* part and could do no more. Hopefully, Tom would be too busy with whatever he was scheming to take any notice of the increased gut-churning wailing to investigate.

Her eyebrows knitted. Tom was up to something, that was for sure, but whatever that was, it was no concern of hers. *Not any more.*

All she had to do was stay under the radar just that little bit longer whilst she decided when to run.

The question was, how would she get Tina and Stella away? Would they even want to go? Her daughters weren't blessed with much in the brains department, plus she'd spent far too long convincing them what a good earner they were on, would they believe her when she admitted she'd been wrong?

Amelia's mind flitted back to her nephew. She hadn't read any reports of a man bleeding to death in the hospital car park, so she could only presume that Chas had been patched up. And thankfully, for all their sakes, had kept his gob shut.

But that wouldn't last. It was only a matter of time before someone said *something*. If the cops raided the Aurora, like they had several times in the past, they'd find that woman imprisoned in the attic. The one *she'd* helped keep subdued and drugged up to the eyeballs.

Amelia paused on the first-floor landing outside Deb's room.

And then there was this one...

She'd seen the paper this morning. Who hadn't? And unless she was very much mistaken, Deb had a tattoo of a daisy on her shoulder, identical to that picture in the paper. If it was Deb in that photo, then God help her if Tom put two and two together.

After all, it was *her* who'd given the girl the nod to go out last night.

STD clinic, my arse, Amelia thought. But she couldn't blame the girl for lying. She wouldn't have queued up to confide in a woman who looked the other way whilst Chas had treated her like shit either.

Making her mind up, Amelia barged into Deb's room. 'When are you planning to leave?'

Jumping out of her skin, Deb moved to the left in front of the rucksack she'd been packing. 'I... erm... Leave? I'm not leav...'

'Cut the crap,' Amelia barked. Pulling Deb to one side, she pointed to the bag. 'What's that for then? If you're going, then get a move on before Tom notices or before the Stokers find out who and where you are.' Her eyes narrowed. 'Jesus, girl, what were you thinking?'

Deb blinked, her mind whirring. 'I don't know what you mean. I...'

Amelia yanked Deb's top off her shoulder, exposing the daisy tattoo. 'These are a blatant means of identification. Not just with the cops, but for *everyone*.'

Deb pulled her top back into place, her panic growing. 'What's my tattoo got to do with anything?'

Amelia laughed hollowly. 'I take it you haven't seen yourself on the front page of the *Mail* this morning? Messing with Seb Stoker? Are you mad?'

Deb's mind raced. *There was a photo of her in the paper? With Seb Stoker? Oh, Jesus...*

'Don't worry, it's only the back of you legging it down the stairs, but it shows that tattoo clear enough. Bear in mind, the whole of Brum is trying to work out who has trashed Sam and Seb's happy relationship...'

Tears sprang from Deb's eyes. 'It's not what you think,' she blathered. Amelia would tell Tom what she'd done and she'd be put in the attic with that woman.

With nothing else to lose, she clung to Amelia's ill-fitting fuchsia top. 'Please don't say anything, *please*. I have to get out of here.'

Amelia glanced towards the door, raising her finger to her lips as she listened for movement outside. Satisfied no one was about, she moved further into the room. 'Listen, girl, and listen hard. If you're doing a bunk, then get gone. If I can recognise you from the back and your tatt, then others will too. You need to get gone sharpish and whatever you do, keep the hell away from the Stokers.'

Deb hesitated. *Was Amelia giving her a pass to flee?* 'What will you tell Tom?'

'I'll say I've sent you scouting again. You'll be long gone by the time Tom realises you've done a runner.' Her forehead creased.

'But in the event that you get caught or come back, don't expect me to admit that I knew anything about this!'

Deb visibly sagged, unable to quite believe her good fortune. 'I won't be coming back,' she whispered, grabbing Amelia's hand. 'And thank you.'

'Don't thank me,' Amelia snapped, not wanting gratitude. It only fuelled the guilt over what she hadn't done all of these years. She opened the door. 'Remember, whatever you do, stay clear of Broad Street. You'll have made enemies there!'

Deb nodded and smiled gratefully until Amelia left the room, then sank down onto the creaky bed. She'd go before Tom appeared, but she couldn't avoid Broad Street. *Not yet.* She had to meet Stacey and collect her payment. She could get nowhere flat broke.

She'd head to Broad Street, get her money and then leave Birmingham for good.

34

Seb drove up Chase Road in Harborne, scowling at the multitude of press congregating around the drive's entrance. Slamming the car down a gear, he swerved through the gate, not caring if he happened to mow a few of the reporters down.

Why couldn't they leave him alone? Hadn't they done enough damage?

He would not utter a word to them. There was only one person he wanted to speak to. And she was in *there*.

Coming to an abrupt halt in front of the house, his tyres grinding to a stop on the thick gravel, Seb jumped from the car. His hangover raged relentlessly, but nothing, not even having his leg sawn off, would delay him from putting things right with the woman he loved.

A member of the press was first up the drive, his camera busily clicking in Seb's direction. 'Mr Stoker? Can I have your side of the story?'

'Why a waitress, Mr Stoker?' another one asked.

'Mr Stoker? What do you say to the people who think you deserve this?'

Fumbling for his keys, Seb ignored the cacophony of questions and the multitude of flashbulbs – each burning into his fractured mind.

'Is your wedding with Samantha off now, Mr Stoker?'

'Do you think she'll ever forgive you?'

Seb jammed his key in the lock. *Why wouldn't it fucking go in? Come on. Come on.*

'Mr Stoker? Do you regret your actions?'

'Mr Stoker?'

'Does it not bother you that the girl was so young?'

'How long has your affair been going on for?'

Seb's anger escalated as he tried to get his key to turn. *Sam must have changed the fucking locks!* 'Sam?' he roared, banging his fist on the door amid more flashing of cameras.

'What will you do now, Mr Stoker? Will you move back to your flat above the Royal Peacock?'

'Will Sam remain living here, Mr Stoker?'

'Do you have plans to move in with your girlfriend?'

It was when a photographer shoved a camera in Seb's face as he pointlessly banged on his own front door that his will to ignore the onslaught broke.

Spinning around, he grabbed the camera lens and yanked it towards him, the strap around the journalist's neck pulling the man off balance.

Ripping the camera away as the man tumbled down the steps, Seb launched the expensive piece of kit on the floor. Bringing his boot down hard on top of it, glass and pieces of plastic flew in all directions, leaving the other journalists to pause in shock. For a split second, all questions ceased as Seb ripped the back from the ruined camera and tugged out the film.

Shoving the film in his pocket, he pulled the prone man off the floor by his lapels, then threw him onto the gravelled driveway.

Resisting the urge to rip the limbs from the man, Seb turned to the horde of press. 'All of you have five seconds to get the fuck off my property!' he snarled, his usually pristine swept back hair, flopping over his eyes. 'Go! *Now!*'

Not needing telling twice, the reporters scrambled down the driveway, the photographer on the floor scrabbling to get to his feet to beat a hasty retreat, not bothering to reclaim the pieces of his trashed camera.

Seb leant against the door of the house he'd not long purchased, panting with exertion. Pulling his cigarettes from his pocket, he lit one, his mind turning.

If Sam wasn't here, where was she? Had she gone back to her apartment or to the Orchid?

Wherever she'd gone, he would not stop until he'd made her listen to what he'd got to say. Whatever anyone said and however bad it looked, he had not betrayed Sam with *anyone.* And Seb would not let this matter rest until he had proved it.

Someone had set him up and when he found out who that someone was, he would personally beat the living daylights from them. No one fucked his life up. Someone had crossed the line and they would pay dearly.

Sitting in a chair like a waxwork, Sam stared blankly at the apartment wall. This place had once been her sanctuary, but since realising she belonged with Seb, she'd yearned for their own place. Now none of that applied, this apartment was a prison – somewhere to hide from both him and the hounding press.

She glanced up as the phone rang again. It would be bloody journalists, clamouring for inside information of her downfall, unable to hide their glee over the public destruction of her relationship.

When she and Seb had got together it had caused much surprise to ripple through Birmingham. What were the odds of the heads of two rival city firms falling in love? There had even been insinuations the relationship wasn't real – a stunt to halt the leverage people used between the firms.

But it was far from unreal. Nothing had been fabricated – at least, not from *her* side.

She could no longer say that about Seb.

Her eyes moved back to the paper's headline: *City Casino Boss Party Shame...*

She placed the paper face down on the coffee table. She'd thought it a good idea to torture herself by purchasing a paper to remind herself not to call Seb and hear his explanation.

Because she had thought about it.

Sam gritted her teeth against the continuing shrill ring of the telephone jangling the burnt-out nerve endings in her brain.

That could be him calling now.

Her hand itched to move towards the receiver, yearning to scream at Seb, but she sat still. If she heard his voice, it might break her down enough to believe the bullshit he'd have dreamt up.

Sam dragged her hand through her hair. *Who was she trying to kid?* Seb had already broken her. He'd broken *everything*.

Her relief that the phone had ceased ringing was ruined by the sudden buzzing of the intercom.

Was that Seb? Please, no!

She couldn't face it. She couldn't face his lies. She'd love to believe him, but she couldn't.

Sam tried to ignore the insistent buzzing, but whoever it was wasn't going away. Getting up, she moved to the intercom and pressed the button. She'd just listen to see if it was *him*.

'Sam? Can I speak to you?'

Sam's heart lurched at the familiar voice. That same voice that usually melted her. *Seb's.*

His voice *still* melted her heart. She longed to fall into his arms and hear that everything was a bad dream. Last night hadn't happened, there hadn't even been a party, neither had he been off his head. There had been no woman – no girl – with him in their bed.

But it was real, all right. She had seen it.

Her heart closing off once more, Sam blinked away the tears, but couldn't quite bring herself to remove her finger from the button.

'Sam,' Seb panted. 'Please! I know you can hear me. Nothing happened, I swear. I don't know who that woman was... Look, I've been set up. I don't know how yet, and I can't explain, but I know nothing happened. I love you and I...'

Sam removed her finger from the button and slumped against the wall, her jaw clenching as it immediately started buzzing again. *Please go away*, she thought. She couldn't take this.

The buzzer stopped and Sam remained tense, her breathing laboured.

Five seconds passed, then ten. Fifteen...

Had he gone?

A full minute elapsed before Sam dared to hope that Seb possessed the decency to accept she didn't want to, or *couldn't*, speak to him.

That was until loud banging at the front door vibrated through the wall she leant against.

Sam's stomach dropped to her feet. *Shit!* She should have known he'd have managed to find a way in. Followed someone entering the building or got access through blagging another resident via the intercom.

Her eyes darted around, her head pounding from the relentless banging. The last thing she wanted was more attention brought by a neighbour reporting someone was refusing to leave and causing problems.

It was no use.

Finding inner resolve, Sam took a deep breath and yanked the door open to find Seb, his usually pristine hair unkempt, his face ravaged with stress and hurt.

'Sam! Please let me explain!'

'Leave me alone,' Sam said, her voice cold and steady, when all she wanted to do was sob hysterically.

'*Please!* You have to listen!' Seb pleaded, pushing into the apartment and quickly closing the door behind him. He reached for Sam's arm.

Sam flinched at the raw pain in Seb's voice, but pulled her arm away from his grasp. She wouldn't waver. If she did, she'd disintegrate.

'I'm only going to say this once,' she said calmly. The only thing belying her true feelings was the tremoring of her hands. 'If you have any decency left, you'll walk away.'

There was a pause, then Seb spoke again. 'I'll *never* walk away from you, Sam. We can sort this out. Sam! Please listen. I love you and I'll find out who set me up. I'd never hurt you. Never!'

Sam remained silent. But he *had* hurt her. He'd hurt her more than she believed possible. How could anything make this right?

Her initial reaction was to start screaming or even laughing at the concept of this being a setup. Everything was a setup according to Seb Stoker – even when he'd been caught red-handed. But she wouldn't lower herself.

'Look at me!' Seb roared, grabbing Sam's shoulders. 'Look into my face and tell me you don't love me and that you really believe I'd cheat on you. That I'd throw away what we've got.'

Sam wanted to meet Seb's eyes, wanted to look clearly into that cold green gaze and say exactly that, but she couldn't. She'd never thought he could do that to her either. She'd believed he loved her, believed that they had something very few did.

Could it be possible there was more to this, like he said?

'Sam,' Seb repeated, gently lifting her chin. 'I love you and I *swear* I've done nothing.'

Sam tried as hard as she could not to let her eyes move in the same direction as her face, but they did anyway, the pull towards the man she loved with all her heart being too strong.

Seb's mouth crashed onto hers and her legs weakened beneath her, the fierce passion of his kiss crucifying in its intensity. Her mind raced, along with her heart and a surge of love and need. Seb wouldn't have betrayed her. He couldn't kiss her like this if his feelings weren't real. *No one* could.

Sam's arms began to snake around his neck as she succumbed to the inevitable. Then she froze.

What was she doing? She couldn't do this! She had to make sense of it all before she could do anything. This was too much.

Abruptly, she pushed Seb away. 'No! I can't!'

'Sam?' Bewildered, Seb reached for Sam once again.

'No!' Sam cried, holding up her hand. 'I need time.' He had to leave her alone whilst she learnt how to cope with his betrayal. If there was one...

God, God, God! She couldn't do anything this way. Not with him here. Not like this.

'But...'

'We'll talk soon,' Sam found herself saying. She turned away from Seb so that she didn't have to look at him again. If she did,

242

then she'd crumble for the second time. 'Please at least give me that.'

Seb stared at the back of Sam's head for what felt like centuries, his short-lived relief shattering.

The *last* thing he wanted to do was leave. What if she refused to see him again? What if she wouldn't listen and he couldn't get through to her and make her believe him?

His heart pounded. But he had to do what Sam asked if he wanted any chance of this being resolved. And that he wanted more than life itself. 'Okay, Sam. I'll do as you ask.'

Somewhere in the back of her frazzled mind, Sam heard the door shut behind Seb as he left.

She had to sort this out in her head. But how?

Seb had betrayed her – she'd *seen* it. But... but it just didn't make sense, none of this did. And she didn't have the first clue where to start in unravelling the mess in her mind.

She yet had to face the outside world and the Orchid, when everyone knew how she'd been humiliated.

Sam moved back into the lounge, snatching a bottle of wine as she went. This could be her life from now on.

Alone.

35

Tom slammed the car door and walked jauntily across the car park.

He glanced up at the façade of the Aurora that, up until recently, he'd been so proud of, but now he saw it through the eyes of everyone else. He really should have had the car park resurfaced and *definitely* should have replaced the rotten window frames – on the front of the building, at least.

The money he'd forked out on the spangly sign when he'd bought the gaff was cancelled out by the dilapidated state of the rest of the place. And yes, he might now have a leather-look desk chair in his office, but nothing escaped that the 'bar' was fashioned from off-cuts of hardboard bought from Focus DIY.

This place looked every inch *exactly* what it was. It correctly advertised the low quality of what was inside: a dump full of wizened old slappers and a handful of young 'uns. Not to forget his grizzled, drug-raddled ex in the attic...

Despite this painful awakening, Tom couldn't keep a smile from forming.

He might have failed in his dream of giving the Broad Street places a run for their money, but buying the Aurora and turning his hand to what he was good at had brought him to exactly where he'd wanted to be all along. He'd almost achieved his goal, albeit in a strange, convoluted way, but what the fuck did it matter how he'd done it?

Tom pushed open the front door, the absence of entrance staff another glaring insight into how much the Aurora's already low standards had slid, and continued up the hallway. He glanced dismissively into the room housing the motley gamblers busy losing their money as well as their will to live. Soon he could get rid of all those useless no-life bastards, along with the tarts happy to suck mouldy dicks in exchange for a couple of quid and a bed to kip in.

Now he'd secured a temporary lockup, courtesy of Bob the Knife from the Stoat and Rabbit, he had somewhere to stash the coming money. He'd even been canny enough to pop into Thomsons on the way back and check the availability of outbound flights over the next week.

Because that's when this heist was happening. He wasn't waiting any longer. Things were sliding down the pan quicker than a curry from Selly Oak, so no more hanging around. He'd be out of here soon – to where, he didn't yet know, but preferably somewhere hot.

And this time it was *his* choice to leave.

Up yours, Stoker – the joke's now on you, he thought.

Tom reached the door to his office, belatedly realising he'd seen Dan in the gaming room. He quickly retraced his steps. *Yes, it was!* 'Dan! Back again already?' *Hopefully this time the twat had cast iron info.*

Dan scrambled from his chair and gestured to Tom's office.

Tom followed, his anticipation growing. 'Well?' he said, shutting the door. 'What do you know?'

Dan grinned. 'What I fucking know is lots! Looks like we're clear to go in a few days.'

Tom raised his eyebrows. *Perfect.* 'I take it you got the info from your missus's brother? It's Wednesday now, so when? Tomorrow? Friday?'

'I don't know exactly, but...'

'Wait a minute!' Tom snarled. 'I said I wanted definite timings with...'

'Ah, but get this...' Dan grinned. 'It turns out that my missus planted a girl in Stoker's party under the guise of a waitress.'

Tom sighed. *Another of Linda's daughters being a sneaky cow? What a surprise...* 'She sent a girl to eavesdrop on Stoker?'

Dan laughed. 'That's what Grant was told, but even if Marina is a prize cunt, I've got to take my hat off to her for this one! She set Stoker up.'

Tom's curiosity overtook his irritation. 'How?'

Dan pulled this morning's *Mail* from under his jacket. 'The girl doped Stoker up and then staged it to look like she'd shagged him, just in time for that Samantha bird from the Orchid to walk in!'

'What?' Snatching the paper, Tom read the article, his face creasing into the widest of grins. *That would have pissed on his tight bitch of a daughter's bonfire. Wonderful!*

'As you can see, the press are all over it,' Dan said. 'Everyone's talking about it. I'm surprised you hadn't heard. So, Stoker will be far too busy sorting his upcoming marriage, or lack of it, to worry about anything *we're* doing.'

'Oh, this is just fucking brilliant!' Tom laughed heartily. 'I'd have loved to have been a fly on the wall. This Grant bloke must be pleased.'

Dan shook his head. 'Not particularly. All he wants is the money.'

'Oh, well, it's clearly his sister with the brains.' Tom's mouth curled into a sneer. 'Shame we'll beat them to it. Where did your missus dig this person up from to set Stoker up?'

Dan shrugged. 'No idea. Just some young hooker. From what I heard, she's not planning on paying the girl either! Marina's a hard bitch. But then, that girl will be a celebrity when everyone finds out who she is, so she'll earn a good wedge one way or the other.'

Tom started pouring two celebratory vodkas, glancing at the photograph accompanying the article. His hand paused mid-flow.

Peering closer, his face crumpled. *It was that fucking Deb bitch!* The hair was the same and he'd seen that tattoo a thousand times. *The sneaky little cunt!*

Dan frowned. 'What's up?'

Tom continued staring. *It was her. No doubt about it.* How had she got out of here to go to this party?

His eyes narrowed.

Amelia, the raddled, fat old hag!

He jumped to his feet, vodka sloshing over the newspaper. Not involved with the Stokers? Deb must have planned this all along with Dan's tart of a missus. The sly, conniving...

'Tom?'

'I'll be back in a minute.' Tom pushed past Dan. 'Have your drink and then we'll discuss our next move.'

But first he'd be having a word with Amelia and Deb.

Seb crashed into his office, his eyes wild with rage. How he'd driven from Symphony Court without ploughing into another car or mowing down a pedestrian daring to make him wait at a crossing, he didn't know. Because he'd *wanted* to.

He'd wanted to shred someone's life to pieces, the same way his had been. The press congregating around the front of the Peacock had only served to fuel his rage further.

Storming past Neil and Andrew, Seb snatched up a new whisky bottle, not bothering to mess about with the decanter.

'Get someone to remove those fucking hacks from outside my club,' Seb roared, his shaking fingers fumbling over the lid of the whisky bottle. 'If they don't leave me alone, I swear I'll kill them, and I don't care who's fucking watching!'

He glared at the bottle in his hand. He couldn't even remove the bastard top? That was the last straw.

With a guttural roar, he hurled the bottle against the wall, watching as it exploded, showering his office with glass and whisky.

'Jesus fucking Christ!' Andrew yelled. Jumping from his seat, he reached for Seb's arm.

Yanking out of Andrew's grasp, Seb marched around his desk and dropped into his chair, his fingers raking through his hair. His mood lurched dangerously between white rage and desolation. 'What the fuck am I going to do?' he cried, his voice desperate. 'I can't lose Sam, I just can't.'

He looked at Andrew and then Neil, his pain-filled eyes then reverting back to hate. 'I want whichever cunt set me up for this! Sam's my life. She's my whole fucking existence! I...'

Hearing his brother's voice trail off, Neil glanced to Andrew with mounting concern. Crunching through the broken glass to the cabinet, he took the decanter and poured a large whisky, then moved towards the desk, knowing he risked Seb's wrath, but he had to do something.

He placed the glass down, starting to believe that Seb wasn't using a setup as an excuse for what had happened after all.

Seb downed the whisky in one, the burn at the back of his throat momentarily overtaking the ravaging pain in his heart. 'Sam doesn't want to know. She said she needs time, but that's not true. She thinks I betrayed her, so she'll never forgive me. I know she won't. *I* wouldn't!'

He picked the glass up again, confused to find it empty. 'I want whoever set this shit up and I'm going to fucking kill them. Until I can prove this, things can never be right with Sam, and they *have* to be right. They just have to be!'

'We'll find out.' Andrew scraped a pile of glass to one side with his boot and sat down, coming to the same conclusion as Neil that Seb was indeed telling the truth. In a way, this was worse because this meant a very personal vendetta. *But by whom?* He looked back to Seb, not thinking he'd ever seen his brother so close to tears. 'I take it you've been to see Sam?'

'I went to the house, but Sam's changed the locks so I couldn't get in. The press loved that! She wasn't there anyway. She's left me. She's fucking left me! I'll kill whoev...'

'Where did you see her, then?' Neil interrupted, wanting to steer Seb away from his all-consuming rage.

Seb lit a cigarette and took a long deep drag, exhaling the smoke slowly in a bid to slow his ire. 'Symphony Court. By the looks of it, she's moved back there.' His right hand curled into a fist. 'She wouldn't see me at first, but I managed to follow someone else in. At first, I thought I was getting through to her and that she believed me, but then she shut down on me. Asked me to leave. Christ!'

'Tell us exactly what she said. You mentioned Sam wants time, so that's positive, isn't it?' Andrew said, not believing that at all. Seb was right. Sam wouldn't forgive this until it could be proved that nothing had happened with that woman, regardless of what it looked like.

* * *

Deb scuttled along Broad Street like a startled rabbit, deftly manoeuvring between people and making sure to stay as close to the buildings on the opposite side of the road to the Royal Peacock as possible in the hope that it offered camouflage.

The Magic Bean wasn't far, and Stacey would be waiting. *She had to be.* Deb had done everything requested and she needed the promised payment. *Quickly.*

Sweat poured from her forehead as well as down her back, despite the freezing temperature. Were all these passers-by staring at her? Did they recognise her from that picture in the paper?

Surely, they wouldn't know it was her – not from that? The only people who might recognise her were the ones who had seen her clearly last night. And there weren't many of them because she'd shielded her face when she'd done a runner. Only that woman, Samantha, had got a good look.

Deb's eyes darted towards the Peacock and the Orchid. *Just get to the Magic Bean.*

Up ahead, the light spilt from the large windows of the café. It was a good job because her feet were in agony.

The walk from the Aurora had taken forever, not helped by her paranoia of Tom coming along the road, spotting her and dragging her back to put her in the attic. This thought made her hide along the way every few yards, but she was here now, thank God.

She couldn't go back to the Aurora whether she wanted to or not.

And she didn't.

Tom might already realise she'd done a runner. He might have got it out of Amelia? Or one of the other girls could have seen her leaving. But if Tom didn't know, he would by the time the night was out if she was still missing.

Deb's pulse ramped up to breaking point and she almost fell through the doorway of the Magic Bean, her whole body shaking.

Her eyes darted around the busy café. *Shit! There was no sign of Stacey.*

She'd be here. Stacey had assured her she wouldn't let her down.

Reaching the counter, Deb shoved her hand in her pocket, finding just enough money left for a Coke.

Forcing a smile, she ordered the drink, paid and found her way to a table away from the window, but one offering a partial view of the street outside. From here, she could watch for any of the Stokers leaving the Peacock and also see when Stacey arrived.

Lighting the last but one of her cigarettes, Deb sipped her Coke, willing her hands to stop shaking. Every minute she remained in this city was a minute too long.

Wait!

Her attention sharpened.

She craned her neck, her head bobbing up and down to peer around the patches of window condensation to the street outside. She focused to the other side of the road, sure it was Stacey.

Come on, Deb prayed. *Cross the road. Hurry up!*

There was a train out of New Street to London Euston that she should still have time to catch, if she hurried. It was better than spending the night on the freezing platform, waiting for the first train to leave in the morning.

Come on, Stacey.

Deb waited with growing impatience as Stacey continued walking. *She had to cross the road soon.*

Her heart thundered harder as the woman cleared the Royal Peacock and continued. *She wasn't coming here?*

Deb frowned. Had she remembered incorrectly? Had they arranged to meet somewhere else?

No, Stacey had definitely said the Magic Bean.

Panic flooded her as the truth sank in. *Stacey wasn't going to pay her...*

Chucking her half-smoked cigarette in the ashtray, Deb grabbed her rucksack. That money was her only means of getting away from Tom, the Aurora and this city. Stacey couldn't just walk off.

Such was Deb's desperation to leave all the things she wanted nothing more to do with behind, she raced from the Magic Bean.

36

Grabbing Tina as he rounded the corner on the first floor, Tom snarled, 'Where's Deb? She's not in her room.'

Tina shrugged. 'It's not fair. I asked Mum why Deb was getting another night out and she said *you* told her to go scouting again.' She pouted. 'Mum's been weird the last few days too. Earlier, she even sai...'

'I don't give a rat's arse what Amelia said,' Tom growled. 'I just want to know where Deb has gone.'

'I've already said I don't know! Just out,' Tina insisted, wincing at Tom's hard grip of her arm. 'Look, isn't it time *I* had a chance to bring new faces in? Deb isn't getting anywhere, yet she keeps being sent to do it.'

Dropping Tina's arm, Tom continued to the next staircase. *Gone out, had she? And Amelia said he'd sanctioned it?* His eyebrows knitted. Was that fat old bitch part of whatever that little tart was up to?

'Tom,' Tina called from down the landing. 'Can you sort it? I'd be better than Deb and I got that Dan bloke in for you, didn't I?'

'Yeah, yeah,' Tom muttered over his shoulder. 'I'll sort it, okay?'

And that's what he was doing now. Sorting whatever shit Amelia was pulling. And if her slapped-face fucking daughter didn't put a sock in it, she could fuck off as well.

Tom stormed up to the second floor. Amelia wasn't in her office under the stairs because he'd already looked. This meant she'd either gone out with that silly little cow, Deb, or she was in *here*...

Not bothering to knock, Tom kicked the bedroom door open, catching Amelia stuffing clothes into a suitcase. Lurching over, he grabbed the case and launched it across the other side of the room. It landed to the floor with a thud, underwear and clothes spilling over the stained carpet. 'Off on your hols?'

Despite the shock of Tom barrelling into her private bedroom, Amelia wasn't in the mood to put up with threats.

If Tina and Stella wanted to continue being ripped off by this toerag, then they couldn't say she hadn't warned them. When they'd spoken earlier, Tina had laughed and Stella was no better. Well, let them stay if they wanted to. *She* was done. She was out of here and Tom could shove this place up his arse. She'd go with the clothes she stood up in if she had to.

She eyed her upturned suitcase, then squared up to Tom. 'I don't have holidays, Tom.'

'What do you know about Deb going AWOL?' Tom snarled. 'Word has it that *I* gave the go-ahead for her to go out tonight. I think not. So, where is she?'

Amelia sighed. *Time to lie.* She'd expected this, but it didn't matter. 'Deb's gone scouting. That's what you want, isn't it? More girls for you to earn off?'

'You're a lying bitch,' Tom barked. 'She's involved in something with the Stokers! She was on the front bastard page of the fucking paper! You're in on it and all, aren't you?' His eyes narrowed to slits. 'You stupid cow! You think I'll let her get away with whatever she's playing at behind my back? You think I'll swallow *you* being in on it either? I'll find Deb and I'll fucking kill her! Then I'll kill *you*!'

The plan was to talk Tom out of whatever he believed, but Amelia couldn't stand his fake threats and bullying any longer. No, it was more than enough. 'Leave that girl alone! I don't know what she's involved in, but *anything* is better than being lumbered with you!'

She folded her arms over her ample bosom. 'I ain't running this shithole any longer. You're a nasty piece of work and I can't believe it's taken me so long to work that out! I quit!'

Tom smiled coldly, hiding his disbelief that this fat trog had the audacity to speak to him in such a manner. He should have guessed she'd help that stupid cow. *Big mistake.*

All this time, he'd given Amelia's increasingly snotty remarks leeway because she'd done such a good job a few months back keeping things together whilst he'd been stuck in Linda's trampy flat, yet now she turned on him? *More faces than Big Ben, this one.*

'You ungrateful, snidey cow!' he spat. 'I've paid you handsomely for doing shag all these past few months. I even accepted you didn't want to get your fat arse out to pick up new girls because you're so fucking past it! Now you're helping one of my girls to bugger off?'

He caught his breath. How dare Amelia call him a nasty piece of work, like he was Dennis Nilsen or someone. 'You'd be fuck all without me, you worthless bitch!'

He laughed mirthlessly, but then just to push him further over the edge, the tortured wailing from above filtered into his eardrums, making his nerves jangle. 'She's getting worse too. Another part of your job you've slacked on. What's the fucking point of you at all? Then there's your idiot of a nephew. He could have screwed everything up for me with the crap he pulled. Did I take that out on you? No, I didn't, yet now I find you've conspired against m...'

'That woman in the attic is getting worse because I haven't dosed her up for two days!' Amelia smiled smugly. She was now on a roll, and nothing could stop her. 'As for conspiring against you, take it whichever way you wish! What you've been doing is bloody wrong! You're a fucking psycho! I've got a good mind to go to the cops and tell them how you work, what you do and how you treat everyone!'

Tom's hatred for Amelia exploded along with his rage for Linda and all of these pointless, useless cunts. It was a good job he was almost out of this. *Ungrateful, two-faced bastards, the lot of them.*

'Police, eh?' Grabbing a fistful of Amelia's frizzy hair, he dragged her towards the door.

'Get off!' Amelia screeched.

Tom pulled Amelia along with force. 'Shut the fuck up! If you don't want that bird's nest on your head ripped off, you'll move your feet sharpish!'

With searing pain radiating from her scalp, Amelia scrabbled for the wooden banister as Tom dragged her up the attic stairs, the remains of her chewed fingernails snapping as she clawed pointlessly at the wood. 'No!' she wept. She wouldn't end up the same way as that poor cow up here.

Ignoring Amelia's screeching and the ever-increasing noise from the attic room, Tom pressed on regardless, sweat liberally pouring from his brow. If this fat bitch didn't get a shift on, he'd kill her stone dead and leave her on the stairs.

Dragging Amelia into the attic room, Tom held back from gagging at the stench. He let go of Amelia's hair and she dropped to the floor, her hands moving to her burning scalp. He then grimaced at Linda writhing on the bed, her hollow, sunken eyes unaware of anything going on around her. 'You can shut up as well!' he screeched, punching her frail body. *She was next. She was fucking next.*

Seeing Amelia scrambling to her feet, he stopped her in her tracks by delivering a heavy kick to the side of her face, watching with satisfaction as she flew backwards, landing with a crash on the floorboards.

Dazed, Amelia realised the strange wailing adding to the noise of the room was coming from what was left of her own mouth.

Tom grinned at Amelia's mouth hanging slack from her newly broken jaw. 'Keep the noise down, you slut,' he snapped. 'You're as bad as this fucking corpse-like creature.'

Despite her agony and stunned state, Amelia knew she was in deep trouble. Her hands, caked with her own blood, groped at the floor, searching for something to help pull herself up. She didn't want to look, but found herself compelled to, and a strange sense of detachment fell over her as Tom moved towards her with an empty syringe.

For a split second, she thought about fighting him, but knew it was pointless. She'd seen what he was about to do once on a telly programme. She knew she was done for.

All Amelia could hope was that Deb had got away and that her daughters would see sense and escape too.

Her eyes moved to the woman on the bed, hoping for a last glimpse of solidarity, but found the returned stare vacant.

'This is what happens to two-faced whores,' Tom muttered triumphantly as he shoved the tip of the needle in Amelia's neck.

* * *

With what she needed safely stashed in the bottom of her handbag, Marina used the same process of watching the goings on, like she'd done previously when looking for Deb before.

She'd walked up and down this stretch of Broad Street so many times, she was surprised there wasn't a groove worn into the pavement.

Back and forward, up and down, over and over...

Her insides twisted impatiently. It was difficult not to steam into the Orchid and do what was required.

Thanks to Grant showing her the layout from a map he'd pinched, she knew *exactly* where Samantha's office was and how to get to it. But there was no point going in if the spoilt bitch was absent. And on that point, she was unsure.

Marina waited on the off-chance she might miraculously receive an answer via the universe, but in reality, she was putting off the inevitable. And she'd been putting it off in case her worst fears were realised and the stupid cow wasn't in there at all.

Samantha might be hiding in that posh house of hers, licking her wounds, too distraught over darling Seb's 'philandering ways' to face coming to the place she'd been handed on a plate, but she strongly doubted it. Her pseudo-sister would be devastated, all right, but she'd bet the snotty cow wouldn't hang around the house where she'd been publicly humiliated and where the press must still be camping out.

Samantha would do *exactly* what a spoilt slag would do – run to her opulent casino where she could fawn and sob so that her doting staff, all desperate to act like nothing had happened, would tend to her every whim. *Like Grant...*

Yes, Grant would be in there somewhere.

And what a two-faced bastard he'd turned out to be.

Marina's face twisted into the most horrible of scowls, her stunningly beautiful features becoming ugly.

That's why she was here. Now Grant had exposed his true colours as to where his loyalties lay, she wasn't hanging around. If he'd jumped the other side of the fence, she wouldn't put it past him to confess to Sam who he really was.

And if that happened, then everything really *would* be ruined.

Deciding she'd put it off long enough already, Marina veered off her usual route past the casinos, making sure she kept out of sight of the Magic Bean, and headed to a telephone box.

She didn't know why she was bothering avoiding the place. Not even Deb Banner would be so thick as to show her face around here tonight – or ever again. And even if she did, she'd have a long wait for her promised money. That would never happen. *Oh, whoops, had she lied? Never mind...*

What sort of saddo took on a job like that without a guarantee or a down-payment?

No one. Apart from Deb...

Chuckling with the idiocy of it all, Marina reached for the telephone box door, scowling as a teenage girl reached out at the same time. 'Fuck off,' Marina hissed. 'I'm using this, so find another!'

With a parting sneer, Marina pushed her way into the glass cubicle, her nose wrinkling at the smell. Fishing a tissue from her coat pocket, she picked up the greasy handset and tapped in the memorised number.

Thank you, dear brother, she thought as the call connected.

Drumming her fingers on the metal shelf, she glared at the screwed-up fish and chip paper in the corner of the booth, the strong smell of vinegar mixing with other unpleasant aromas within the confined space.

As the call rang out, Marina frowned. Had the number she'd got from Grant's mobile been entered under an incorrect name?

No, Grant was far too methodical for that. It was Samantha's direct line because he'd told her enough times that he'd been given it – like he'd enjoyed telling her how 'trusted' he was at the Orchid.

Fat load of good that had done as it turned out, but it would soon. *Very* soon.

As the line suddenly clicked, the ringtone changing slightly, Marina concentrated as the call was answered.

'The Violet Orchid,' a twinkle-like voice trilled.

This was Samantha?

'I'm after Samantha Reynold,' Marina said, doing her best to sound business-like.

The irritatingly sparkly voice continued, 'Miss Reynold is not in this evening. Can I take a message?'

Not in? Course she was in – she had to be. 'Are you sure she's not there?' Marina pushed. 'We had a meeting booked for tomorrow and I...'

'Miss Reynold has unexpected business to attend to,' the voice repeated. 'I'm unsure whether she'll be in tomorrow, so if you leave your name and number or call back in the morning, I can ch...'

Marina slammed the receiver down. *Fuck!* Where did this leave her now?

She stared into her handbag. She had everything ready and was primed to go. She couldn't wait another night, or worse, two. *No way.*

Sparking up a cigarette, Marina left the call box, glaring at the bright lights of the casino frontage ahead of her. She'd give it half an hour, then call back. If it was bullshit, she'd get a different excuse to the one she'd just been given, which meant Samantha *was* inside the Orchid.

If the woman genuinely wasn't there, then there was only one other place she would be – Chase Road in Harborne. Marina had seen the road name and photo of Samantha's posh house in the paper, so she'd be able to tell exactly which one it was.

A grin spread over her face as she recommenced her route up

and down outside the casinos and bars. Either way, Samantha Reynold was getting hers tonight.

* * *

Brushing himself down, Tom loped down the stairs. He'd been gone a while and could only hope Dan had stayed put. The important thing was to act normal, whilst informing the man of the change of plans.

'I was just about to give up on you,' Dan said as Tom entered the office. 'Are you all right? You're out of breath.'

'Yeah, I got sidetracked with one of the girls,' Tom winked, wishing that was true. He picked up the remains of his vodka, emptied it on the floor and poured himself a fresh one. 'I'm not as fit as I used to be.' *And wasn't that a fact.*

He'd pulled his shoulder dragging that fat bastard, Amelia, around. Shoving her body in the wardrobe after had made it even worse. Still, that was one problem out of the way. *For now.*

'What's that?' Dan pointed to Tom's hand.

Tom glanced at his hand. *Shit. He thought he'd wiped off the blood splatters.* 'Oh, the girl I just shagged has the painters in. Dirty little scrubber didn't have the manners to tell me. It's all in my kecks now as well!' He rolled his eyes. 'It had better wash out. Armani pants aren't cheap!'

Now onto the important bit... 'I've decided to move on this job of yours. Rather than waiting, we're going to do it now.'

Dan sat up. 'Now? I'm not certain the coast will be clear. Grant said th...'

'It *has* to be clear!' Tom slugged down his vodka. 'It's happening tonight. End of.' It had to be, now that stupid cow, Amelia, had made him lose his temper.

But first, he had to locate Deb and make sure she couldn't open her trap to anyone about him or anything, ever again. And he had a good idea where to look first.

There was no point dragging things out. Now he'd successfully removed one woman, he might as well get the rest done.

In an ideal world, he'd have dispatched Linda whilst he'd been in the attic too. She could have joined Amelia in the wardrobe. But the prospect of touching Linda's shit-soaked corpse was too much, especially when, in real-time, it was more important to catch up with Deb. Besides, Linda would be as dead as a doornail from natural causes very soon, so why waste the effort? Especially when so much money was on the table.

Slamming his glass down, Tom stood up. 'Right, let's get going.'

Dan blinked, unsure what to do. 'But we need to plan and...'

'Christ!' Tom barked. 'What is there to plan? It's not difficult. I'll tell you exactly how things will work whilst we're on the way. I've been in the Peacock before, so I know wh...'

'Wait!' Dan gasped, his dread intensifying. 'The Peacock? We're going to the lockup to lift the money, aren't we? Why would we go to the casino?'

'Because there's someone I want to find. And whilst we're there, I want *you* to do something. We need to ensure the Stokers are diverted.'

'But they're *already* diverted!' Dan slapped the newspaper, still sodden with the spilt vodka. 'Look! They'll be all over the shop with what went on at that party.'

'That's as maybe,' Tom snapped, not about to tell Dan *all* of his reasons. 'But we don't want any surprises and what you're going to do will make sure we get a clear run at the lockup.' He pulled his leather jacket on. 'Come on. We need to get on with it.'

37

Neil shoved his hands in his pockets as he walked from the underground car park beneath the Peacock. Taking the long way around, rather than going through the staff door from the car park, would allow a bit more time before receiving the onslaught of questions from Seb the second he got through the door.

That's if Andrew had failed in getting Seb up to the flat above, like they'd discussed. After seeing the state of their brother, both Neil and Andrew had agreed one of them should go and talk to Sam.

Neil frowned. And it had been *him* who'd got the job.

Surprisingly, Sam had granted him entry to her apartment and was in a similar state to Seb.

Despite Neil testing the water, her shutters were well and truly down, and he hadn't got far deducing whether anything could be salvaged for his brother.

Neil couldn't say that he blamed Sam, but this was so out of character for Seb. It was no secret Seb was crazy about Sam. In addition, out of all of them, Seb was the one with an unmoveable attitude on fidelity. That's why he'd never got himself seriously involved with any woman. *Until Sam.*

Although Seb's adamant stance that the incident at the party was a setup, Neil couldn't for the life of him see *how*, and that made it difficult to give the theory credence, when all he could give to Sam as an explanation was that 'he didn't know'.

Breaking the news that Andrew had okayed the release of a card shark at the Orchid last night hadn't helped either, but that was the least of his worries.

Neil continued round the corner of the side street into the bright lights of Broad Street.

What would he say about Sam's response? Seb hearing him repeat Sam's words, 'it can be nothing but over', wouldn't help the thin thread of hope his brother was clinging to.

Neil's attention was so focused on this as he continued towards the Peacock, he very nearly missed it.

He *would* have missed it, had the girl kept going, rather than stopping and doing an abrupt about turn, then breaking into a run.

Without thinking, he rushed after her. It was her, without a doubt – that girl from the CCTV who had been dragged into that red VW Golf that night.

He'd almost given up seeing her again, having not caught a glimpse since, but if he could just talk to her, there was a chance of collaring the nonce pimping these youngsters.

It was this that fuelled him to break into a run. It wouldn't solve Sam and Seb's issues, but it could mean the end of *one* unpalatable thing.

'Hey!' Neil yelled. Upping his pace, he closed the gap, catching up with the girl not five yards past the Peacock. He backed her against a wall. 'I want to talk to you, nothing more,' he said, the terrified, hunted look in her eyes bothering him.

'If you're sensible, no one will get hurt. Walk alongside me,' he said, purposefully making the tone of his voice menacing. He placed his hand on the back of Deb's elbow. 'And don't even think of trying to run off.'

He smiled inwardly as the girl moved in the correct direction beside him. Of course, he had no intention of laying a finger on her, but fear would make her comply and he had to help her. The poor cow was scared out of her wits. *And not just because of him.*

* * *

Sitting in a small office somewhere at the back end of the Royal Peacock, Deb felt her heart gradually slow from its breakneck speed.

She'd spent at least half an hour convinced she would die from fright before this lot even had the chance to kill her or ship her off to be another sex slave in one of their plentiful brothels Stacey said they owned. They'd probably take their turns with her beforehand too.

But this hadn't happened.

Deb accepted the second whisky Neil Stoker poured, grateful for something to deflect her trembling hands. Even their jittery shakiness was beginning to calm down.

All those things Stacey had said about what the Stokers were like seemed the opposite of what she was hearing.

Her first thought, on spotting Neil Stoker not five yards in front of her, was to get as far away as possible. She'd seen the recognition on his face and when he'd given chase, easily catching up with her, she'd thought the very worst.

But she'd been wrong. Neil hadn't pulled her off the street over her presence at the party or what she'd done there. He'd pulled her in over a red VW Golf. *Chas's VW Golf.*

Deb might have been correct that no one had got a good look at her face at the party, but it looked like she'd been very wrong about other things.

Neil Stoker's interrogation consisted only of what trouble *she* was in and who was behind it. He actually *cared* that girls like her were being used. This man – and apparently the whole Stoker firm – wanted to stop this practice.

They certainly weren't the psycho perverts exploiting girls for sex, like Stacey said.

Deb felt close to tears. It had been a long time since anyone had been genuinely bothered about her. She'd thought she'd found that person in Chas and then Stacey, but she'd been wrong on both counts...

Was she wrong now?

Neil eyed the girl carefully. He'd got nothing of any substance out of her, short of her admitting she slept with men for money, and he was becoming increasingly frustrated. 'Listen, love, we can't get rid of the lowlife bastard, unless you tell us who he is and where he operates.'

Placing her glass down, Deb picked at her chewed nails. She couldn't tell this man about Tom. Although she'd love nothing more than for him to be wiped off the face of the earth, it would mean the others would cop too. Amelia had been good to turn a blind eye in helping her leave and the other girls would have nowhere to go. She couldn't do that to them. Furthermore, Tom would find and kill her if she were to open her mouth and she had nowhere to run now she had no money. Her heart raced once more.

'We need to remove this scum,' Neil pressed. 'So, for a start, tell me who the man in the red car is and why you've been hanging around outside here? We've seen you on several occasions.'

Deb wrung her hands. 'The guy in the red car has gone.' *And he had. Chas was probably dead...*

'I know you're worried, but me and my brothers, as well as other people, want to stop this. We want to help.'

Deb blanched, raging guilt flooding her. They wouldn't want to help if they knew what she'd done.

These people may be hard as nails, but she *believed* this guy. How could she tell him anything, without admitting what she'd done for Stacey?

Should she be honest? After all, she had no loyalty to the woman who had blatantly used her, but regardless of this, Deb didn't think her honesty would be appreciated once this man knew what it was about.

'Are you scared of talking to me? Worried about repercussions?' Neil asked. *He was getting nowhere fast.* 'I don't even know your name. And who's that blonde woman you've been seen with? Is she part of this too?'

Deb flinched at the barrage of questions, her guilt burning brighter.

'I said, is that woman part of this?' Neil repeated, his voice rising. 'How the hell can we help, if you won't tell us who the fuck anyone is?'

Deb shrugged. 'I-I don't know who she is.'

'You're lying!' Neil spat. 'For Christ's sake! Who runs this shit? Where do you stay?' *He was making a pig's ear of this. The girl was clamming up in front of his eyes.*

He stood up. He'd got an idea and would use the phone in Seb's office to make the call. 'You stay there. I'll be back in a minute.'

* * *

Sam had no intention of answering the phone, the fear it could be Seb again burning strongly. But Neil had promised Seb would back off and give her the time she'd asked for.

Whether he did or not didn't matter because no amount of time in the world could change his betrayal.

How could she believe it was a setup, like Neil said, when no one could offer a clue as to how?

Easy. She couldn't, so that only left her with the same option she'd had before.

But she wanted to believe it because as unexplainable as it was, something or someone was involved in this. There was something about it all that was causing an insistent prodding inside her brain, but she just couldn't fathom *what*.

Oh, she was too tired to think about this any longer. All she wanted to do was go to bed and get some much-needed sleep. She was exhausted.

She snatched up the phone. 'Yes?' she said warily, then frowned. 'Neil?'

The immediate thought that something had happened to Seb barrelled into her mind, emphasising that as much as she told herself this was over, it wouldn't be easy to switch off and forget the man she loved. *That's if she ever could.*

She listened carefully to Neil's words and a spark of purpose reignited. Things may be a disaster in her personal world, but she could at least stop *this*. 'Yes, of course I will,' she said.

The girl Neil held in one of the offices at the Peacock was understandably reticent to talk to a man, but she might open up to Sam, and then they could track down and stop the filth ruining so many young girls' lives.

'You're sure it's the same girl? The one that's been seen with that... *man*?' Sam asked.

Her heart pounded at Neil's confirmation. This time, she must be 100 per cent sure they got the right man because she had the feeling the person responsible would be taking the hit for a *lot* of things presently wrong in her life.

Right or wrong that may be, but Sam couldn't think of a more deserving person to take her wrath out on.

There was just one thing...

'I'll talk to her, but not in the Peacock... No offence, Neil, but I can't see Seb right now.' Sam's lips tightened. She couldn't go anywhere where Seb could walk in; somewhere that smelt of Seb; that reminded her of Seb...

The only problem was, there wasn't anywhere that *didn't* fit into one or all of those categories.

She listened to Neil's suggestion. 'Okay. I'll make my way there now. Go to the back entrance. I'll let Kevin know you're coming.'

Replacing the receiver, Sam got to her feet. She was exhausted, but this was more important than lying awake going over things she couldn't change.

Picking up the phone for the second time, she dialled Kevin's number. She hadn't been to the Orchid today for obvious reasons, but no doubt everyone was aware of what had happened. At least Kevin knew better than to mention the party or be stupid enough to ask her how she was, and for that she was grateful.

She hastily explained the situation. 'They'll be coming around the back, Kev,' Sam said. 'Keep everyone else out of the way and take them straight to my office. I'll be there in ten.'

Putting the phone down, Sam exchanged her pyjamas for a black pencil skirt, white top and jacket. She grabbed her handbag and left the apartment.

38

Marina's perfect opportunity had dissolved into a black hole – the situation worsening bit by bit. It had been going so well, too.

Grinding out the umpteenth cigarette in the doorway, she felt her jaw might snap. For God's sake, how could Deb have been so bloody stupid?

She'd given it at least twenty minutes since calling the Orchid, but unable to stand waiting any longer, she'd called again.

She'd almost reached the phone box, when she'd heard a name being shouted.

The name she'd told Deb was *hers*...

And sure enough, heading towards her, there she was – *Deb*.

Worse than that, not more than a couple of yards in front, was one of the Stokers...

It wasn't Seb, but Marina could see from the size and stance of the man, even from behind, that it was *one* of them. This became more obvious when Deb froze in her tracks, then turned on her heels with the Stoker in hot pursuit.

Quickly darting across the road, Marina had stepped into the arched doorway of a bar, watching the man catch up with Deb.

Less than thirty seconds of inaudible conversation later, both Deb and the Stoker walked down the road into the Royal Peacock.

The stupid bitch had willingly accompanied him into their casino?

The girl was fucked. They would have pulled her in for her actions at the party, which meant only one thing...

That silly little mare wasn't the sort to keep her mouth shut and play dumb. She'd bleat like a lamb at the first whiff of a threat.

Christ!

Marina scrabbled through her handbag for a new packet of fags. She always had spares.

Dragging the packet from her handbag, careful not to expose the other vital item in there, she tore at the cellophane, her anger increasing as her fingers fumbled to open the cigarettes. She never got nervous. *Ever*. But now she was panicking – like *really* panicking.

Praying that Deb would emerge from the Peacock unscathed and that she'd somehow been blissfully wrong in her theory, things had then got even worse because then Samantha Reynold had appeared, literally materialising several feet away from her from a taxi.

Marina's hand had hovered over her handbag. She could have acted right at that very moment. She'd got a clear view, but had no choice but to sit tight.

It might have looked the perfect opportunity, but there was one major shortfall.

Marina glanced back around the busy street – just as busy now as it had been when Samantha had been in front of her – along with all those *other* people who would also have borne witness.

So, that was that.

With no other choice, Marina had impotently lurked in the doorway as her bastard of a 'sister' disappeared behind the glass frontage of her money-maker.

But Marina was still here. Correction – standing here wasting time. She couldn't be a sitting duck. Not now Deb was busy spilling every last detail about her to the Stokers, guaranteeing her place on the list for those getting their face chopped off – after Deb's, of course.

Yet Samantha was somewhere in the next building to the grassing little tart, along with the men who would soon be coming after *her*.

What to do?

Marina paced up and down the small space the doorway offered. Regardless of things going pear-shaped, there was no leeway to reconfigure the plan.

Samantha had to be taken out tonight.

Marina smiled. After she'd done it, she and Grant could rush to the lockup and get the cash. She'd already stashed some tools they would need close to the location. It would be easy.

Then, and only then, could they leave.

Yeah, Grant would be pissed off – he already was, that much was clear from the way he'd been earlier. *'Get real,'* he'd said. *'Sort yourself out. Stop being crazy.'*

Marina scowled. She wasn't crazy and this needed doing for everyone's sakes. It was obvious.

No matter how angry Grant would be for what she was about to do, he'd forgive her. He always did. She was his *real* sister and that took precedence. It always had and, therefore, always would.

Despite the dire direction this night had taken, the corner of Marina's mouth curled into a smile.

* * *

'I'm fine, Elaine.' Sam forced a smile as she walked through the Orchid's reception, not knowing which was worse: people pretending nothing had happened and that Seb's betrayal wasn't splashed all over the papers, or asking veiled questions about how she was.

What did they want her to say? Admit her heart was shattered, that she'd been publicly humiliated and didn't know what to do? Or act hunky-dory and pretend everything was fine?

Of course, she chose the latter. She didn't have the answers herself, let alone to give to anyone else.

Hastily making her way down the staff corridor, Sam pulled her resolve in check. She wasn't here to dwell on that. She was here to get to the bottom of who was the ringleader who thought he could use the area around here as a grooming ground.

She looked up as Kevin stepped out of his office. 'Are they here?'

'Yes, but I've got to tell you there's contention with the boys about a Stoker being here after, well... after what happened. And Andrew Stoker letting that card shark walk last night didn't go down well either.'

Sam sighed impatiently. 'I've always endeavoured to keep my personal life separate from work. I won't have all of this bollocks kicking off again about "us" versus the Stokers.' She raised her chin defiantly. 'Andrew made the decision last night as I was unavailable, and I back that. I also have no problem with the Stokers, short of *one*. And you know why that is. Thank the boys for their loyalty, but business is business.'

She smiled to ensure Kevin understood none of this was directed at him. She'd been unfairly hard on him since the wrong ID of the previous man he'd brought in. 'I'll go and see if I can make headway with this girl.'

Turning, Sam opened her office door, wondering about the best way to broach this difficult subject. She walked in, her customary smile dropping at the young girl in an oversized green jacket.

She'd seen this person before. It was a face she would never forget.

Her eyes darted to Neil. 'Is this a joke?'

'Shit!' Deb yelped, jumping from the chair. When Neil Stoker said they were moving to another place and she'd accompanied him down the back stairs of the Peacock and then through a couple of warren-like alleys, she hadn't realised they'd moved to a completely different building!

She'd been brought to the Violet Orchid? And the person she'd been told would help was the woman who'd wanted to kill her last night?

'You've brought this slut to my fucking club?' Sam raged, her eyes wild.

'What the fuck?' Neil looked between Sam and the girl. 'Sam, what are y...'

'I want an explanation,' Sam spat, moving forward as Deb backed further against the wall. 'This is the tart I caught in bed with Seb!'

'*What*?' Neil cried, getting to his feet. 'She's the one *we've* been looking for from the CCTV!' He grabbed Sam, and it took a surprising amount of effort to restrain her. She looked set to kill the girl.

Deb saw the murderous rage in Samantha Reynold's eyes and couldn't say she blamed her. Feeling even more guilty that she'd been part of something so underhand now she knew these people hadn't been part of any of the things she'd been led to believe, she realised she had two choices: make a run for it or tell them the truth and accept the punishment that she probably deserved.

'Please,' Deb yelped, her eyes pleading. 'Nothing happened with me and Seb Stoker.'

'It's *Mr Stoker* to you,' Sam spat, fighting against Neil's grip. Being restrained did nothing to calm her, only making her want to lash out further. 'Give me one good reason why I should believe you? You've wrecked my relationship!'

Neil watched Deb quivering. He should be equally as angry. What had happened had caused big problems – not to mention the fallout that would follow for some time – but there was something about this girl that his gut told him was speaking the truth. 'I think we should hear her out. I feel this is more than a bloke grooming young girls for his own ends.'

Sensing a lull, Deb spoke. 'I know I've done wrong, but I needed the money. She paid me to do it.'

'You got *paid* to sleep with my fiancé?' Sam screeched, her temper rising to boiling point. She didn't care what Neil said, this had gone far enough. Jerking forward sharply, her force pulled Neil off balance.

Neil struggled to regain his footing whilst keeping Sam from ripping this girl limb from limb. 'What are you talking about, you stupid girl? Who paid you?'

'Stacey. The one you asked me about,' Deb babbled.

Neil's attention sharpened. So the blonde *was* involved? 'Stacey who?'

Deb frantically shook her head. 'I don't know. I only met her the other week and she offered me thousands to...'

'Oh, Christ!' Sam's eyes bored into Neil's. 'Are you telling me you believe this bullshit?'

'But it's true!' Deb cried. Shoving her hands in her pocket, she pulled out the empty vial of ketamine. 'She gave me this. She said to put it into Stoker's drink at the party, then pretend I'd slept with him.'

'Jesus Christ,' Neil muttered. 'That would explain why Seb was so off his tits.'

Sam blinked. She stared at the small bottle in the girl's hand. *The whisky! This girl had served Seb with that whisky.*

Icy cold slithered through her veins. Was it possible that this *was* a setup after all? That everything Seb had told her was the truth and she'd dismissed it?

Guilt bloomed. Her gut instinct had shouted Seb wouldn't have done this to her, yet she'd veered towards the more plausible explanation of his betrayal. She should have known better. She should have trusted him – trusted *herself*. Where did she go from here?

Satisfied Sam had calmed sufficiently enough to safely release his hold of her, Neil steered Deb around the other side of the desk. He indicated for her to sit down and stay there. 'Okay, let's for argument's sake say we believe what you're saying. The question is *why*?'

'The money!' Tears rolled down Deb's cheeks. 'I had to get away. My boyfriend wasn't my boyfriend. I thought he was, but he lied. He's the one with the red car. He roughed me up and because you saw, he got cut up. I saw that happen too!' She began sobbing in earnest, the weight of finally telling someone – *anyone* – making her words spill out like a burst dam. 'I think he's dead. He'll have killed Chas. There's this woman in the attic who screams day and night. I'll be put there next, and I can't go back. But I haven't had my money. I'm sorry. I'm sorry!'

'Whoa!' Neil held his hands up. 'Slow down! Who killed this Chas bloke? And who asked you to drug Seb? Chas? Who?' *He'd kill the man himself.* He took the vial from Deb's shaking hands and examined it.

'No, it was Stacey who told me to do it. The blonde woman.'

Sam took the vial Neil held out and examined it. *Seb had been doped with ketamine?* 'This Stacey works with you? She's a prostitute?'

'No,' Deb said, the word prostitute in relation to herself making her flinch. 'I met Stacey here.'

'At the Orchid?'

'No, in the café opposite. I believed what she said.' Deb bowed her head, her shame complete. 'She said you people enjoyed earning off young girls.'

Neil's veins thrummed with rage. *Someone had put about that they were nonces?*

Deb finally raised her eyes to Sam. 'Stacey wanted to destroy you.'

'*Me?*' Sam cried, almost wanting to laugh with the absurdity. 'What has this woman got against me?'

'I don't know.' Deb burst into another round of sobs that racked her entire body. 'I just wanted the money to escape. I-I'm so sorry.'

'And I'm supposed to believe this?' Sam roared, her short spell of calm now reverting back to white rage. Not so much for this deluded teenager, but anger that yet again, someone nameless should want to destroy her happiness. And for what?

But the anger with herself for believing the worst remained. 'I want to know who this blonde is,' Sam yelled. 'I'm so fucking sick of this!'

Snatching a thick crystal glass from the desk, she hurled it against the wall and Deb cowered as fragments of glass exploded around the room.

'Is there a problem in h...' Entering the room, Grant stopped in his tracks, seeing the girl he'd admitted to the housewarming. *Marina's plant.* As her eyes widened, he stared at her pointedly and moved into the room. 'Do you want me to remove this girl?'

Neil sensed the sudden change in atmosphere and looked between Grant and Deb, suspicion brewing. 'Do you know this man?'

Deb swallowed, her eyes darting between the blond man,

Samantha Reynold and Neil Stoker. This was her chance to tell the truth. But would they believe *her* over a member of staff?

Before she could say anything, Grant stepped in front of Deb, blocking her from view. 'Sam, did you say you wanted me to show this person out?'

39

Marina waited in the corridor, adrenaline beating a steady pace. She'd thought for a moment back then that she was scuppered before she'd even started. She'd never thought that bloke resembling a bulldog would ever disappear.

This place didn't have its wits about it tonight. The hoo-ha surrounding Samantha's personal life had clearly thrown the staff into a muddle because they didn't know their arse from their elbow.

Marina had walked through the Orchid's reception like she was a regular here – far too aloof and confident to be questioned. She didn't know why she'd bothered making that extra effort because the dippy bitch of a receptionist and the two security blokes were far too busy gossiping to notice her.

So much for what Grant had said about this place being highly secure and running like clockwork. There had been no requests for membership cards or anything.

Marina smirked. She'd seen more organisation on a school trip!

Well, they only had themselves to blame. Any one of them had multiple chances to stop and question her, which she'd fully expected to happen, but she need not have bothered wasting energy thinking about it.

But once she'd stepped into the staff corridor, seeing a man loitering outside Samantha's office door, she'd got the fear.

Panicking, she'd ducked to the side of a cabinet and waited for the man to go, but he'd spent ages pressed against the door, listening. She'd even toyed with removing him just to get into the room, but that would have spoilt things. Thankfully, he'd eventually disappeared into another room further along the corridor.

With the coast clear, she'd been about to make her move when Grant had appeared and gone into Samantha's office.

Marina glanced up and down the corridor. Now the coast was clear again, but that wouldn't last long.

She'd stewed over this for far too long already. Her fake thief of a sister would suffer, and she would suffer *now*.

Okay, so she'd wanted Samantha on her own, but Grant would have to put up with her take on things. He'd get over it, but she had to be quick. She needed to get this done so they could go to the lockup. Timing was everything.

Marina opened her handbag, her breath ragged.

Leaving the sanctuary of the cabinet, she moved stealthily along the corridor, her senses primed.

Her fingers tightened around Grant's gun. She'd use this on anyone she had to, but there was only one real target. And *she* was in *here*.

Reaching the office door, Marina burst in. If she'd waited just a split second and listened first, she might have considered changing her mind.

* * *

'Holy fuck!' Seb gasped. 'I'm on my way!' Slamming the phone down, he turned to Andrew. 'Good job I didn't let you talk me into hiding in the flat upstairs.'

Andrew watched his brother grab his jacket, his face set like stone. 'What's going on?' He followed his brother up the corridor. 'Seb?'

'That was Kevin. Sam got a call from Neil,' Seb said as they crashed through the double doors. 'Neil's got the girl from the CCTV – the one in connection with the suspected nonce. He asked Sam to speak to her and took her to the Orchid.'

Andrew ignored the confusion on the staff's faces as he and Seb barrelled through the reception. 'What's the issue, Seb? We wanted to get to the bottom of that.'

'Yes,' Seb continued, 'but the girl's only the same one found in my bed last night...'

'*What*?' Andrew squawked. 'Are you sure?'

'Kevin overheard the commotion. Sam's going mental, that's why he called me.'

'Jesus Christ!'

'When we get there, you find Kevin. I'll go and see Sam, Neil and that bloody girl and put this fucking record straight,' Seb said as they raced from the Peacock to the pavement outside.

* * *

Tom grinned, although he was far from happy. He'd been spot on heading here instead of going straight to the lockup. His instinct never let him down, hence why he usually acted upon it and by God, he was glad he had.

He'd just sensed that conniving little bitch would come here and after reaching Broad Street and parking up, he'd been just in time to see Deb being frogmarched into the Peacock by one of the Stoker twins.

Only Deb was stupid enough to return to this neck of the woods after what she'd got herself involved in, but it showed that she was more scared of *him* than the Stokers, and that was a much-needed ego boost.

But compliments aside, there was no doubt he was on borrowed time. A further distraction was required because there could only be one reason why Deb had been taken inside the Peacock – they'd discovered her part in the setup.

Tom's eyes narrowed. He might have missed the boat in dishing out the slag's punishment for double-crossing him, but this brought another problem.

The Stokers wouldn't take lightly to what Deb had done to big-boy Stoker and Samantha, so she'd be getting the mother of all interrogations. The little cow would blab about Dan's missus's involvement and then, when they caught up with Marina – which they *would* – if she was anything like her skank of a mother, she'd blab about Dan.

After that, it really didn't take rocket science to work out that Dan would flap his gums about *him*.

Tom scowled. Yep, he needed an extra prong to the diversion.

He scanned the front of the Peacock and the alley running alongside it. His idea would cause a mega-diversion; a distraction bigger than the one the Stokers already had with the slapper they believed had fucked Mr Big himself.

Doing it would only take a few minutes. At the very least, it would delay the Stokers from doing anything that could take them to the lockup, or if that bitch had opened her trap, heading in *his* direction.

The idea was good in the first place, but now it was even more of an attractive prospect. With any luck, it would remove a couple of the people proving to be thorns in his side and threatening his general existence.

Tom's attention sharpened with movement opposite and he found himself laughing. *It just got better and better.* This bonus of two Stokers unexpectedly leaving was welcome, but how long a window they had to act was unknown. 'Now's your chance,' he hissed, jerking his head in the direction of the Peacock. 'I don't know how long we've got, so move it!'

Dan stared at the two big men racing towards the Orchid. His stomach lurched. 'Why push our luck? Something's kicked off, so let's just go straight to the lockup.'

'We don't know *where* they're heading next, so we need to ensure they remain here and not anywhere near where *we're* going!' Tom's eyes were fixed on the Stokers, now entering the Orchid. He grabbed the back of Dan's jacket. 'Go on! Get in there, do what I said and then get the fuck out. I'll meet you where we agreed.'

He shoved the carrier bag he'd propped up in the footwell into Dan's hand. 'Put that under your jacket.'

Before he knew it, Dan was shoved out of the passenger seat and Tom's motor screeched off, leaving him half in the road.

Jumping out of the way at the blast of a horn, he darted through the traffic and down the alley at the side of the Peacock before he could change his mind.

'You fucking bitch!' Marina screamed. Kicking the office door shut behind her, she pointed the Beretta at Sam.

Totally caught up in the moment, it took a second before the other figures in the room registered.

Her eyes flicked to Grant. She'd expected him, but the Stoker man and that little cow, she hadn't. They had gone into the Peacock, so how could they be here?

No, no. This wasn't what she planned.

Still, she had the gun and it was trained on Samantha's pretty face. And by God, she would use it to wipe every single feature off that grasping cow's mug for eternity. *That* was what she was here for, and nothing would stop her. *Nothing.*

'You've taken what's mine,' Marina said, her voice now quiet and low. She didn't want to bring the bulldog man running. She would deal with Neil Stoker as well as Samantha if she had to. It was no skin off her nose. Deb didn't figure. She was irrelevant.

Her lips twitched into a smirk at the people rendered into paralysis at her entrance. How she loved the benefit of surprise. *Have that, Samantha, you stuck-up slut!*

It took Sam a few seconds to process that a stranger had burst into her office with a gun. She'd like to think this was some kind of joke, but it clearly wasn't. How could this woman have got down here undetected?

The only thing to do was remain calm.

She studied the woman's face. Even though it was twisted with rage and a sneer overtook the lips, there was no mistaking the woman was stunning. Her very distinctive eyes sparked a base recognition. But recognition from where? And from what?

She'd initially thought the words spitting from the blonde's mouth were aimed at the young girl, but with rising realisation, she now knew both the words and the gun were aimed solely at *her*. 'What is this about?' she asked, amazed her voice didn't betray the steadily rising knot of fear radiating from within her.

Marina took a step forward and waved the gun in Neil Stoker's direction in case he should be so misguided as to think about moving from the wall.

No one would ruin her plan. This was happening, whichever

way. 'You asked what this is about?' she laughed, the melodic sound at odds with the situation. 'Think you're the special one? Thought we weren't good enough, did you?'

She heard her voice getting higher and louder and willed herself to keep control. 'You got all of *this* whilst we got jack shit?'

Sam shook her head in bewilderment. 'I don't understand.'

Marina threw her head back, her long blonde hair flicking over her shoulder. She aimed the gun between Sam's eyes.

'Don't do this,' Grant hissed.

'Shut up, Grant,' Marina spat. 'Don't go any further above the call of duty to take her side. We'll have what's ours soon enough.'

Grant? Sam thought. *His name was Trevor, wasn't it?* Her gaze darted to Neil.

'Cat got your tongue, bitch?' Marina's hate-filled eyes centred back on Sam, her mouth cracking into a sneer. 'No sign of your man tonight? How very sad...'

The young girl's words about the party resounded in Sam's mind like a stone. 'Wait a minute. You're Stacey?'

'*She* thinks so,' Marina grinned, smacking Deb in the head with the barrel of the gun.

Deb, who up until now had been silent, let out a loud howl as her left temple split, blood pouring down her top.

Sam instinctively moved towards Deb, but her eyes did not stray from Marina. 'Why do you have such a problem with me? What's this about?'

'Stay where you are, rich bitch,' Marina barked.

'For Christ's sake, Marina! Stop this!' Grant bellowed.

'You know her?' Sam gasped. 'You were part of this all along?'

'What the fuck is this?' Neil roared.

'Of course I know him. Grant's my brother, not yours!' Marina cried, her eyes on Sam. 'He'll never be yours. He's *mine*! And in answer to your original question, I'm Marina Devlin and I want what we should have had all along. You should learn to share, but it's too late for that now!' Her mouth cracked into an even wider smile as she cocked the gun.

Sam attempted to process what was going on as it unfolded as if in slow motion. She found her eyes darting to the man that up until now she'd believed to be Trevor Jensen, seeing in his face something that she could only describe as sadness – maybe even regret.

She'd liked this man and felt they had a connection. She'd even found herself *confiding* in him, when all along he'd wanted to destroy her?

Nausea rose.

And the woman? *Devlin?* Sam knew the name Devlin. Where did she know that name from?

These questions were pushed to one side when Neil suddenly moved from the wall. Sam didn't see Grant moving at all until the blonde became obscured by his large frame. At the same time, a shot rang out, the noise ricocheting around the room.

Someone screamed, the blonde appeared back in view, but Grant had gone.

40

Chas thought drinking that shit vodka he'd nicked from the shop had seemed like a good idea at the time. It had been the only way to give the illusion of warmth in these freezing temperatures, but now the effects had worn off, all it had achieved was to make things worse.

Hunkering down further within the boxes, Chas shivered uncontrollably, his filthy hand tracing over the rough and scabbed stitches holding together what remained of his face.

Thanks to Bedworth, he was now a freak. A fucking hideous freak, not fit to be accepted in society.

His shaking hands fumbled to unscrew a bottle of water. Raising it to his lips, he winced. Any slight movement pulled the slowly healing jigsaw of his face in all directions, causing a kaleidoscope of pain. Even the slightest breeze hurt beyond belief.

He should have remained in hospital where it was warm, but he couldn't. Two days was long enough and the minute he'd got the chance to grab a shedload of pills from the medicine trolley whilst the nurse's attention was diverted with an old duffer's morphine, he'd taken his chance.

Chas popped two more pills from the blister pack into his mouth. He might have thought twice about leaving hospital if he'd realised his car was no longer anywhere to be seen; that it was so bloody freezing or if he'd had the faintest clue he looked like a bad version of the Elephant Man.

Only on seeing the shock and revulsion as he left the hospital and walked up the road did he realise he hadn't seen his reflection.

It would have been better if he'd been left believing he didn't look *that* bad. But thanks to the glass of the drinks fridge in the corner shop, he'd seen the exact state of his mug.

Fifty stitches? His mouth slashed clean across his cheeks both sides, like he'd been in a fucking electric cheese slicer?

Chas shuddered. He made himself feel sick, let alone anyone else!

And here he was – reduced to pinching a tramp's bed for the night, whilst he got his wits together.

Lurking around the back of the Broad Street casinos wasn't his first choice, but it wasn't like any fucker would recognise him like this.

He'd wait patiently until that slut of a bitch showed her face.

Because she would.

Deb Banner would be out and about doing Tom's bidding, like always. She'd be smugly thinking she was clever and that she'd got one over on him. That she'd successfully set him up to get him out of her life.

Well, he'd see about that.

After he'd finished off that little whore for dropping him in it, he'd ensure his two-faced fat cunt of an aunt and Tom-bastard-Bedworth got their comeuppance as well.

Feeling the effect of the dihydrocodeine start to take the edge off his nerve pain, Chas managed to slightly smile without it making him gag.

He might not be in the running for male model of the year any time soon, but the scars would improve slightly with time. He might even be able to talk properly eventually.

In the interim, he'd bide his time until he could pick Deb, Amelia and that bastard Tom off the face of the planet one by one.

* * *

Marina stared at Grant's body at her feet, his lifeless eyes staring up at the ceiling. Her initial shock turned to rage.

He was dead.

Her brother was dead and all because of *this* bitch.

Samantha Reynold had ruined everything and now she'd even taken Grant.

Swinging her gun around stopped Neil Stoker in his tracks as he moved forward. 'Back against the wall,' she hissed through gritted teeth.

'Oh, my God,' Sam whispered, just able to hear her own words over the sobbing of the white-faced girl sitting in the chair. She stared at the pool of blood blooming underneath Grant's body. He'd put himself in front of the gun? *For her?*

Her eyes tracked up to the malevolent glare of the blonde, whose gun was now trained back on her. But in place of the woman's previous steady grip, Sam detected a slight tremor of her fingers.

Her brain scooted through what she had to defend herself with. She'd refused Seb's offer of a gun not long ago. How she wished she hadn't. For once, even Neil was unarmed.

Shit. What should she do?

'You killed my brother!' Marina screamed, interrupting Sam's thoughts. 'Stealing my mother not good enough for you?'

'What?' Sam's eyes darted back to Grant's body on the floor, her ears still ringing from the gunshot. 'Stacey... Marina... I...'

'Now you'll get the bullet meant for you!' Marina yelled, her eyes bulging. 'You whore, you fucking...'

'*Drop the gun!*' Seb crashed into the office behind Marina, his gun raised. In the same millisecond he noted the stranger's gun trained on the woman he loved, Neil's position in the room, the body on the floor and the young girl from last night. *This was bad...*

As the woman swung around, her face filled with rage, Seb knew he had to act fast.

The woman darted to the left, now covering both him and Sam with the gun. Seb's eyes met Sam's, but he didn't have time to read the emotion he saw there as the blonde's finger squeezed the trigger – the barrel aimed at Sam – *his* Sam.

There was no time.

It all happened in the same instant; Neil lurching forward, the blonde moving, a gunshot, his own searing pain...

* * *

Dan's cramp had increased to an alarming level whilst he'd squatted behind the trade bins down the side of the Peacock. So much for Tom saying this door was opened regularly to chuck empties out from the bar. Five whole minutes he'd been here, and his legs weren't used to being twisted at this angle.

He'd thought it best to remain poised, ready to move. That way, the second someone reached the bin, he could dash around the other side and nip inside the Peacock.

The fundamental problem with that was now he questioned whether his legs would work if the chance presented itself.

Dan moved his weight from one leg to the other, the smell of rubbish turning his stomach. But even that didn't come close to the stench of *this*...

He stared at the bottle in his hand, a rag saturated with the petrol contained within, stuffed into the top of the glass neck. The smell was making his eyes burn.

It wasn't a particularly sophisticated way of doing things, but Dan had to give Tom credit for fashioning something from the contents of his car boot in record time.

He peered through the crack of the bins like he'd done many times in the past five minutes.

Hang on, was that door even shut?

Dan squinted through the gloom, sure the metal door hadn't been properly closed by whoever had last used it. *He might as well try it.* Providing he wasn't unlucky enough to be there just as someone finally decided to ditch some rubbish, he could save time *and* his legs.

With difficulty, he used his good hand to grab hold of the trade bin's handle and dragged himself upright, hoping that what remained of his right hand would keep hold of the petrol-filled bottle.

He staggered towards the door, blood making its way painfully back into his legs. Furtively glancing around, he prised his fingers against the door.

It was open.

Opening the door enough to slip his fingers into the gap, he pulled the heavy door and went inside, making sure it didn't slam shut. This was his way out.

Standing motionless, Dan went over the directions Tom had given him. His eyes adjusting to the gloom, he felt his way along the wall towards a set of metal steps.

Refusing to think too deeply about what he was doing and what could happen should he be caught, Dan climbed the steps, wishing that he had shoes with soles fashioned from sponge to render him silent. Even the slightest sound was amplified in the cavernous space.

Reaching the top of the steps, he looked around, getting his bearings. Tom had said there was a stockroom filled with spare furniture and stuff – the perfect accelerant to get a fire started.

Dan's head thumped, his blood pressure off the scale as he headed towards a room, the Prodigy's 'Firestarter' inexplicably on repeat in his head.

He wished it would stop.

He'd never done anything like this before. To be honest, it still wasn't top of his bucket list, but the prospect of getting a clear run to the money in that lockup was. Even after sharing it with Tom, he'd be left with a wedge bigger than he'd ever thought he'd have in his life.

After that, the only thing left to worry about was getting the fuck away from everybody – including Marina and Grant.

Once he'd disappeared and when the inbred freaks finally found the money AWOL, they would know he must be behind it.

Having them and the Stokers on his back wasn't a pleasant thought, but he'd be miles away by then.

Reaching the room, Dan's heart dropped into his shoes as he peered through the gloom at a bank of chest freezers. They would hardly fan the flames.

Tom had got it wrong, the stupid bastard. What now?

Sure he'd heard a noise, Dan froze, his banging pulse worsening his growing headache.

It was okay. There was no one here, but someone would surely be along soon.

Moving to the next room, relief washed over him seeing a pile of upholstered seats and stools, as well as what looked like bags of heavy drapes.

This was it.

He stared at Tom's crudely fashioned Molotov cocktail. If he put his lighter to the end of this petrol-soaked rag, surely the thing would explode in his face?

He wasn't doing that.

Lobbing the bottle against the wall inside the room, Dan flinched at the splintering sound of breaking glass. Pulling his matches from his pocket, he then extracted his lighter and set fire to the entire box of matches, chucking both the box and the lighter into the room.

Unwilling to hang around, he made quick work of retreating back down the stairs, a massive bang resounding behind him along with a bright orange flash.

If that hadn't done it, he didn't know what would.

Barrelling through the metal door, Dan raced along the alley, only to stumble into a pile of boxes. 'Shit!' he hissed. Struggling to regain his footing, he spotted a pair of eyes glaring at him from within the cardboard shelter and to his horror, realised he'd smashed up a tramp's abode.

'Sorry, sorry,' Dan spluttered, continuing on his way, his breath now coming in gasping pants.

All he could hope now was that Tom was where he'd said he'd be.

* * *

Sam stared in horror at the scene in front of her. *He'd been shot. Seb had been shot! No, no, no!*

'Seb!' she screamed, vaguely noticing another flurry of move-ment as the young girl rushed from the room, her coat a bright blur of green through the door.

Let her go. What the girl said was the truth. Seb hadn't betrayed her.

But now he'd been shot...

Sam rushed towards Seb, seeing blood seeping from the clear hole in the upper thigh of his finely pressed trousers. *He wasn't dead, he was alive!*

Neil grappled with the blonde on the floor, his hands fighting to take possession of the woman's gun. 'Keep back!' he hissed to Sam as the barrel of the gun swung precariously close to his face. His eyes darted to Seb, now dragging himself along the floor to reach the gun that had fallen from his hands as he'd hit the deck.

Not caring about anything short of the man she loved, Sam knew she had to get Seb's gun. She'd get his gun and shoot this loony bitch herself. She'd...

'No!' Seb cried, sweat pouring down his brow, his rugged face contorted with pain. He couldn't have anything happen to her. 'Leave it! I...'

Flinching as another gunshot rang out, Sam instinctively dropped to the floor, the noise deafening her already ringing eardrums.

From her position almost face down, her senses tipping in all directions, she blindly searched the room. *Was it Seb again? Neil? Her? That woman?*

Sam felt no pain and Seb and Neil were still moving. She spotted a bullet hole in the wall a foot from where she'd been standing. Perspiration soaked her back, her top clinging to her clammy skin as she scrambled to her knees. She had to reach that gun.

Losing her grip on her gun to Neil and hearing Samantha shouting, Marina knew her time was up unless she could get out of here.

Amid the confusion, she rolled from under Neil. *Grant was dead and she had no gun. Fuck, fuck, fuck!*

Snarling with rage, there was only one option and that was to make a run for it. She had no choice but to put killing Samantha on hold because she had to get that money.

Sensing Samantha moving towards her, Marina sprang up like a cat, dealing a hefty punch.

'Sam!' Seb roared, his rage increasing on seeing her flying to the floor, the exertion of his shout causing the blood to pump harder from his wound. *He'd blow that bitch's head off for this.*

With a last surge of effort, his fingers closed around the butt of his gun.

With Neil Stoker almost on his feet and Seb readying his gun, Marina knew she had to leave. Sam might be otherwise occupied and nowhere near as defunct as she'd planned, but with any luck, she'd lost a tooth.

Sorry, Grant, Marina thought, risking one last look at the crumpled body of her brother. *It shouldn't have been like this. If he'd only followed her lead, Samantha would be dead and they'd be out of here by now.*

With agility she didn't realise she possessed, Marina raced out of the door and up the corridor, sure there must be a fire exit nearby.

She'd hail a cab the minute she reached the street.

As she slammed through the fire exit at the end of the corridor, a blast of icy night air hitting her in the face, she heard Neil Stoker roaring behind her.

She had a head start so would be gone before that Stoker man could reach her.

Too late, mate, she grinned, clattering down the steel steps. She knew the address of the lockup because Grant had told her. She'd be there in ten.

She could still do this.

41

Tom was getting fed up doing circuits. It wasn't like he had time to waste fannying about. This was the *third* time he'd come all the way down Broad Street to the roundabout at Five Ways, then driven up Tennant Street, Granville Street, Holliday Street and onto Gas Street, only to go back down Broad Street all over again.

How long would that dickhead be?

The thought that Dan had been captured wormed its way into his mind, before he shook it away. Unless something had fundamentally changed in the last few months, it wasn't possible.

The instructions he'd given Dan were bang on – a sure-fire route into the casino. The Stokers were absent, and the directions meant the chances of anyone clocking Dan were slim. Nevertheless, it was still feasible...

It should have been an in and out job. *Easy peasy.*

It was all a bit of a pain in the arse, really. If he'd got the codes for the safes out of the bloke before now, he wouldn't be waiting around for the man!

Travelling back along Broad Street, Tom saw the Peacock in the distance and what he thought might be what he'd been itching to see.

He continued in the slow-moving traffic, his eyes fixated on the building in question.

His smile widened at the hint of orange flames intermittently licking the back of the Peacock. It wasn't raging – not yet, but it would be. *Bingo! He'd done it. Dan had fucking done it!*

Almost orgasmic with excitement, Tom willed the traffic to either speed up or fuck off. He'd told Dan to meet him somewhere around the back – *anywhere*, but he needed to hurry.

'Get out of the fucking way!' he snarled, braking so a taxi could make a drop.

Almost slathering with anticipation, combined with the urge to proceed with the final part in his mission, Tom couldn't resist giving the Peacock and the Orchid his middle finger as he passed. 'Fuck you, Stoker, and fuck you, daughter!' he spat, loving how those words sounded out loud.

Turning the corner, now free of the traffic, Tom put his foot down.

A figure ran down the pavement on the dark backstreet ahead and Tom's heart skipped. *No, it couldn't be!*

It was. It was her...

Laughing out loud, Tom knew he had to do it, otherwise he'd never forgive himself for not grabbing this spectacular opportunity handed to him on a plate.

Doing a quick check in his mirrors and finding no spectators, he slammed the car down a gear and mounted the pavement.

The jolt as his car slammed up the kerb, rattling his teeth, wasn't anywhere near enough to stop him cackling with euphoria.

The figure turned as the car sped nearer, shock turning first into recognition and then to full-blown fear.

Tom thought it was one of the best things he'd ever seen.

He whooped with satisfaction as the pathetic, beseeching face of Deb Banner zoomed into close-up as his bumper smashed into her legs, sending her flying across his bonnet, her head making a resounding thud as it collided with his windscreen.

'That will show you not to double-cross me, you rancid slut!' Tom screamed, his voice wild with the sweet pleasure of revenge.

Sharply hitting the brakes, he slammed the car in reverse and swerved to the left to dislodge the useless bitch still residing on his bonnet, blocking his view. 'Get the fuck off!' He jerked forward in the driver's seat as if the movement would aid his task.

Hitting the brakes once more, the body slid from the bonnet onto the road and Tom sat still, the sound of his laboured breathing loud over the idling engine.

He glanced in his mirror again, the shaking of his hands not from fear, but exhilaration.

A sick smile weaved across his ravaged face.

Perfect! But just to make sure...

Shoving the gear stick in reverse, Tom stamped on the accelerator, the engine screaming as the car shot backwards in a haphazard line.

Changing back to first gear, he put his foot to the floor and lurched forward, gritting his teeth with the wonderful jolt of first his front wheels, followed by both back wheels mounting the crumpled body, ensuring that if there had been any hope, there was none now.

Taking a final glance in the rear-view mirror, Tom smiled at the unmoving mangled lump of green material on the tarmac.

He screeched off down the road, his blood pumping. He had almost reached the turn to lead back into Broad Street when he spotted Dan hurrying along the pavement, his pinched features luminous in the glare of the headlight's full beam.

The passenger door opened even before Tom had made a complete stop.

'Fucking hell!' Dan panted. 'That was epic!'

'Shut the fucking door!' Tom yelled, driving off with one of Dan's legs still half-out the passenger side. 'What took you so bloody long?'

'I wasn't long!' Dan cried, craning his neck out of the window to admire his handiwork. 'I did it just as you said. It's taking hold well now, isn't it?' Facing forward, he then frowned at the gloop on the glass. 'What the fuck is all that and why's the window cracked?'

'Fuck knows,' Tom muttered, pressing the window washers, giving the windscreen a liberal spray with the strong-smelling liquid. He set his wipers to the fastest speed. With any luck, it would remove the mess. Such was his happiness he hadn't even noticed it was there.

The screen wash wouldn't sort the crack across the centre of the windscreen, courtesy of Deb's thick skull, but it didn't matter. This old nail of a motor wasn't needed after tonight. 'Get the safe code ready. Erdington's our next stop. Money, here we come!'

Tom stopped at a junction, giving way to three fire engines, their blue flashing lights bright as they raced into Broad Street.

* * *

After swiping paperwork from Sam's desk onto the floor, Andrew grabbed Seb underneath the arms, whilst Kevin took his legs, and together they lifted him onto the desk.

Seeing Seb's face twist in pain, Sam followed, not wanting to let go of his hand. 'Will he be all right?' she asked as Kevin cut Seb's trousers to expose the bullet wound.

Andrew tipped a generous amount of vodka over some thin-nosed pliers. 'He will be once I get this out.'

'You're using *those*?' Sam squawked, her face paling. 'Shouldn't we get him to a hospital?'

'Hello? I'm not dead, Princess,' Seb said, the words hissing between his gritted teeth. He pushed Kevin's hand holding the bottle of vodka away. It wouldn't dull the pain in time. 'Going to hospital will spark too many questions, plus it would take too long. I'll be fine.'

He hoped so anyway. He trusted Andrew to do a good job. Both he and his brothers had removed bullets from men's limbs several times in the past. 'Neil had better have caught that psycho bitch.'

Sam clutched Seb's hand, still unable to piece together what had gone on. 'What will happen to him?' Her eyes moved to Grant's body, still on the office floor.

'I'm going to chop him into fucking pieces and throw them into the canal,' Kevin snarled. There was him feeling responsible for bringing the wrong man in for interrogation and now he'd employed the person who'd helped set Sam up, resulting in Seb Stoker getting shot? 'If I hadn't employed Trevor, then...'

'*Grant*, you mean,' Sam said hollowly. 'He fooled us all.' She'd trusted and even *liked* the man.

Wincing, she watched Andrew dig the nose of the pliers deep into Seb's thigh and rummage around. She gripped Seb's hand tighter as he stiffened with pain. 'I'm the one who should be sorry. I'm sorry I didn't believe you, Seb, I really am.'

Unable to stop it, a tear rolled down her cheek. That woman could have killed Seb tonight. She could have killed *any* of them.

Seb smiled through his clenched jaw. 'It's fine, Sam. I get it. I'd have reacted the same.'

'No, you wouldn't,' Sam countered. 'I should have had more faith. You've been so strange lately and I thought... thought you'd gone off me...'

Seb gave Sam a slight nod in Kevin and Andrew's direction. 'We'll talk about this another time, okay?'

He knew what she was thinking. It was what she'd touched on before. That she'd actually believed Liam forcing himself onto her had put him off made him angrier than ever. *Nothing* would ever put him off Samantha Reynold.

This was *his* fault for not being honest about the stress he'd been under with money. That his behaviour had made Sam feel sullied hurt more than any bullet wound could. 'We'll be fine, Sam.'

Sam smiled weakly, anger at herself worse than what she felt for whoever that woman was. She only hoped Neil had caught her. She needed answers – not the collection of riddles she'd been given.

'Got it!' Andrew exclaimed, proudly holding up a mangled bullet between the jaws of the pliers.

'Thank fuck!' Seb gasped. 'Stitch me up, then.'

Sam watched in fascination as Andrew deftly stitched the skin of Seb's thigh with a needle and fishing wire, her mind racing in the background. What if this woman came back for her? For *any* of them? She clearly had a problem and the things she'd said...

Grateful Andrew had finished, Seb pushed himself upright.

'What are you doing? You need to go home and rest,' Sam cried.

'Bollocks to that! I want the woman who's done this and,' Seb kicked Grant's body with the foot of his good leg, 'I want the answers about what she and this cunt were up to.'

'I'll make a start with getting rid, shall I?' Kevin nudged the corpse, only to look up in surprise as Neil burst in.

'Did you get the bitch?' Andrew asked. 'Where is she?'

'Forget her!' Neil panted, leaning against the door jamb to

catch his breath. His eyes betrayed an emotion that he rarely showed – *worry*.

'What? Why?' Seb barked, struggling to his feet.

'Because some fucker's torched the Peacock! It's on fire!' Neil spluttered.

* * *

Jumping out of the taxi on the A452 in Erdington, Marina buzzed with both rage and anticipation.

She walked casually until the tail-lights of the taxi had disappeared from view, before breaking into a run. Although she'd been fortunate to get a cab within seconds from Broad Street and it made quick work of getting through the city to the vicinity of the lockups, there was no way of knowing if Neil had followed or whether she'd given him the slip.

She'd like to think brotherly loyalty was more important and he would have returned to see how Seb Stoker was, but then money was their game, so not necessarily.

Now they were aware Grant was involved, they might suspect *she* knew about the lockups and the massive amount of cash stashed within and plan to head her off.

Marina continued up the road to the industrial estate, her lungs screaming from the unaccustomed exercise. She couldn't risk the taxi dropping her closer. She didn't know who was on the Stoker payroll. Probably half the city, knowing them. But after this, they'd have fuck all to pay even the milkman!

Plus, she needed to collect *this*.

Glancing over her shoulder, she ducked off the road down the side of a Chinese takeaway and crunched through overspilling rubbish to a pile of empty cooking oil drums stacked behind the trade bins. The dustcart wouldn't take those, so it had been a good place as any to hide these for safe keeping the other day.

Her eyes narrowed. *The bag better still be there.*

She'd pre-empted that once she'd dealt with Samantha, they'd make a sharp exit, but she hadn't counted on doing it entirely on her own.

But she hadn't completed her plan, had she? Samantha Reynold was alive, and her brother was dead.

Marina blinked away her angry tears and pulled out the Tesco carrier bag containing the hidden tools. Without stopping for breath, she dodged back out onto the road.

Damn Grant for leaving her. Why had he got in the way? That fucking bullet had Samantha's name on it, not his. Why had he stopped her from shooting the bitch?

Her teeth grated as her heels rubbed relentlessly in her shoes. *Why, Grant, why?* She inwardly raged. *You fucked everything up and made me shoot you.*

Reaching the industrial estate, Marina flew through the open gates. If the stupid fucks couldn't be arsed to close the gates, it wasn't likely there would be any guard dogs.

She glanced around to get her bearings, seeing a mechanic's, a frozen food unit and a self-storage place. No need for security – there was nothing worth nicking.

Apart from what she'd come for...

Her brows knitted as she clocked the unit she wanted. *Fuck you, Grant. You should have remembered where your loyalties lay.*

Reaching the lockup, Marina pulled a crowbar from the carrier bag and with a surge of strength, jacked the padlock from the metal shutter. Nothing would stop her tonight.

It didn't matter that she hadn't got the code for the safes. She'd smash them to fuck; tear them open with her teeth; do *whatever* to get inside the bastard things.

Yanking the steel doors open with strength that someone of her frame and size should not possess, she raced into the lockup, pulling a torch from the carrier bag.

Now she'd lost the gun, she had no means of defence, short of this crowbar and a wrench, so she couldn't take unnecessary chances of drawing attention. She wouldn't shut the door either. She had no intention of being long.

Grab and go, grab and go.

Spotting the line of cabinets against the back wall in the torch-light beam, Marina rushed across the large space, fishing more carrier bags out of her handbag as she went. She'd stuff as much into these as she could.

Frustration rose. Had Grant been here, he'd have brought big holdalls and they could have easily lifted the whole bloody lot. *The stupid, selfish basta...*

Marina stopped, the torch falling from her hand to hit the concrete with a clatter.

No!

Scrabbling on the ground to retrieve the torch, she staggered forward, sure she must be hallucinating.

Her mouth fell open as she shone the light back into the cabinets.

The safes were open...

And empty...

Marina moved frantically to the next cabinet, only to find the same. And the next...

Fuck! They were all empty! How? How had this fucking happened?

42

After spending the entire night impotently watching fire ravage the casino he'd been entrusted to run and maintain, now the morning had finally arrived and the fire service had done all they could, Seb limped into what was left of the Peacock and looked in horror at his beloved casino.

This was his father's goldmine and the family's front for *everything*.

The frontage was still intact and didn't look much different, but the interior told a very different story. Everything was either burnt or ruined from smoke or water damage.

'The fire chief believes it started in one of the back rooms,' Andrew said, surveying the carnage.

Sam eyed the charcoaled remains of the once splendid tables and sparkling roulette wheels, now unrecognisable. The place had gone up so quickly, she could barely believe it had happened at all.

'I want to know exactly how it started,' Seb snarled, his sadness morphing into anger. 'If it's anything to do with that bunch of sparkies who changed that fuse box a few months ago, then I'll...'

'Ah, Mr Stoker.' The fire chief moved towards the group, gingerly wading through the blackened rubble littering the floor. He looked between the three Stoker brothers and Samantha Reynold uncomfortably. 'I'm afraid it's now looking like it was most probably arson.'

'What?' Seb jumped to his feet, wishing he hadn't as pain tore through his damaged thigh. '*Arson?*'

'Someone did this deliberately?' Sam gasped.

'We will, of course, continue our investigations,' the fire chief continued. 'I'm very sorry, sir. All you can do is file an insurance claim. We'll supply our report to corroborate our findings.'

Seb nodded and shook the fire chief's hand. 'Thank you.'

He moved his weight onto his good leg. He'd sit down if he could, but there wasn't a thing to sit down on. Everything was ruined.

He dragged his hand through his hair. *Fuck.*

Sam placed her arm around Seb's waist. 'Come on, let's go to the Orchid and have a drink. You've been standing for hours.'

'I'm fine,' Seb said sharply, then took Sam's hand. 'I'm sorry. I don't mean to snap.'

Sam glanced around at the devastation once more. All night, she'd stood on the pavement next to Seb and half of Birmingham, who had appeared out of the woodwork to witness the destruction of one of the best casinos in the city. She was unable to shake the nagging thought this had to be something to do with Grant and Marina Devlin, but she didn't know how.

Marina had been in the Orchid threatening her, and Grant had been there too. Neil said Marina had run in the opposite direction afterwards and the fire was already underway by the time he'd reached the pavement.

Those names, Marina and Grant Devlin, had resonated in Sam's mind since learning them, but she just couldn't place them.

Then suddenly, at 5 a.m. this morning, the odd things the woman had said began to make sense.

Devlin. Linda Devlin – her mother...

Devlin was her mother's name from her short-lived marriage, resulting in two children by the names of Marina and Grant...

How Sam had refrained from collapsing in shock as the pieces slotted together, she didn't know, short of that she wouldn't let Seb or *anyone* down by causing further problems by flaking out and hitting the deck. Especially whilst the Peacock burnt down around them.

So, that was why she'd felt a strange connection with Grant on the occasions they'd talked? It also made sense of the handful of bitter references he'd made about his past. And why his eyes had seemed so familiar.

The man was her brother. *Had* been her brother...

And that woman – Marina, whose hate-filled vengeance had very nearly finished them all – was her sister.

Not for the first time, sweat beaded under Sam's hairline.

Jesus Christ. They were her siblings, who despised her for having everything, when they'd had nothing? If they'd only told her, rather than set her up, attacked her and tried to ruin her life, she'd have told them that wasn't the case. Neither had she 'stolen' Linda.

Linda had left them *all*...

Seb watched Sam's face becoming paler. 'Are you all right?'

'I'm just tired. We really should go somewhere to sit down,' Sam said, flustered. She'd have to tell Seb about what she'd now realised. He'd been shot and lost his casino because of a link to *her*.

Andrew picked his way over to Sam and Seb. 'I've just had word from Kevin. Everything's been rectified and cleaned at the Orchid, if you know what I mean...?'

'Then I think we should go there to take stock,' Sam said,

regaining control of her speeding mind. She could discuss everything there, rather than here where there were too many ears.

* * *

Tom had the best seat in the house. He'd had what amounted to a
ringside view of the spectacle all night – well, most of it. And he
was equally as enthralled with it now as he had been then.

Perching on a seat spanning the entire width of the floor-to-
ceiling window which stretched across one of the bedroom walls, it
offered a brilliant vista of the city. A bird's eye view, allowing him to
gloat over his resounding success.

He turned to Dan, who had now finally got out of the sump-
tuous bed to sit in a reclining armchair the suite offered, to start
early on the replenished stock of the minibar.

Tom grinned. This was how *he* would live from now on too.
Luxury was no less than he deserved. His waiting had finally paid
off. He'd pulled off the job of the century with bells on and he was
loving it.

The only slight disappointment was that the Violet Orchid had
escaped joining the Peacock in being spectacularly razed to the
ground. That would have served his bitch of a daughter right. Still,
Dan had done a sterling job with the Peacock and that alone
would ruin Samantha's life by proxy.

His eyes tracked back to the group gathered outside the
Peacock. From this height, they looked like ants. Miniscule human
beings on the face of the planet – worthless individuals to be
sneered upon from his elevated height.

Even from here, Tom could see it was *them*. The three Stokers
and his daughter.

Samantha might be standing with them in a show of false solidarity, but the whole city knew, thanks to Stoker's infidelity, that

their relationship was over. The daft bint would be even less inclined to patch things up with the man when she realised he was penniless.

His face creased into a grin. The Stokers wouldn't yet have a clue they hadn't a penny to their name. All their swish trappings in the form of their posh casino had gone up in smoke and their stash was now in the hands of someone much more deserving.

As the group traipsed dejectedly in the direction of the Orchid, Tom walked over to the large fitted wardrobe, sliding the mirrored doors open with a flourish.

He'd never get tired of looking at *this*.

His gaze fell to the three large sports holdalls sitting in the bottom, each one stuffed to the rafters with money. Money which was now *his*. He could dance with glee.

'Shit!' Dan hissed at the sharp rap of the hotel room's door. 'Is that the police?'

Tom slid the wardrobe shut, the soft-close mechanism music to his ears. 'Don't be stupid! The police aren't looking for us.' He opened the door.

'Your room service, sir.' With an ingratiating smile, the waiter wheeled a trolley into the room and made a big deal of placing silver-covered plates on the table, along with thick linen napkins and silver cutlery.

Dan watched with bemusement whilst a silver cruet set and a choice of sauces were added. As a final embellishment, the man placed a copy of the morning paper to one side.

'Enjoy your breakfast, gentlemen,' the waiter trilled, standing back from the table to admire his handiwork. 'Do you require anything else?'

'No, that's it, thank you,' Tom muttered, the smell of the full English breakfast he'd ordered making his mouth salivate like Pavlov's dogs.

The waiter shuffled from foot to foot, making no attempt to leave. Tom was about to tell him to fuck off when he remembered the etiquette. Shoving his hand into his jeans pocket, he fished out a twenty-pound note and stuffed it into the man's hand.

'Thank you, sir.' The waiter did what looked like some kind of mini-bow, before backing out of the room with his trolley.

Dan waited until the door had closed, before he spoke. 'Twenty quid as a fucking tip?'

'And?' Tom scoffed, removing the silver lid from his plate and chucking it onto the bed. 'It's not like we can't afford it.' He glared at Dan, thinking it was a shame he had to share any of the money with this prick.

Stuffing scrambled egg and half a sausage into his mouth, Dan scoured the paper. 'It's made front page news!' he beamed, proud of his accomplishment.

Tom glanced at the headline: *Top Casino Up in Smoke*, then looked at the rest of the article, jubilant at the photographs highlighting the trashed interior. His eyes lit up further: *... it is thought the fire could be arson...*

He stifled a laugh. *Arson? No, really?* Hopefully their insurance would think they'd pulled the job themselves and refuse to pay out. *Shame...*

Tom didn't read the rest of the article. He knew what the score was. He was more concerned why posh hotels insisted on putting tomato sauce in poncey bowls, rather than supplying a bottle. He eyed the thimble-sized dishes scornfully. There wasn't enough for a fucking mouse!

'Hey,' Dan mumbled, spitting a piece of sausage across the table. 'Look at this! Isn't that where we were last night?' He pointed to a small article in a side column. 'You know, where you picked me up?'

Tom glanced at the paper with disinterest until he saw what it was about.

Hit and Run Death in City Street

The body of a young girl was discovered late last night by another motorist on Granville Street in the city centre. Run over repeatedly, the young woman was left dead at the scene by the fleeing driver. The victim is described as five feet, three inches tall, with brown hair and wearing a green wax jacket.

If anyone has any information, please contact the police on…

'Did you notice anything?' Dan asked, shovelling bacon into his mouth.

'No,' Tom snapped. 'Even if I had, it's hardly like I'd go to the police and say, "Oh yeah, I was there. I was just waiting for someone who was setting fire to the Royal Peacock," is it?'

Dan laughed. 'You know, you're quite funny when you want to be!'

Tom grimaced. *Yeah, hilarious...* This bloke really was a gormless twat. Which reminded him, he had to get rid of that motor pronto. He didn't want that scuppering his new life before it had even begun. There was only so long they could hide here in the Hyatt. Being opposite their enemies, keeping an eye on their movements was fine for the short term, but leaving the country was the end aim.

Only one more day before those fake passports he'd ordered from that guy in the Stoat and Rabbit turned up and then they'd be home and dry.

43

Linda's eyes were more than accustomed to the darkness. There had been no difference between light or day for as long as she could remember. And she could remember little.

Her world had consisted of nothing short of the incessant need for release from the all-consuming cravings that had become the one and only reason for her existence. The pain and desperate torture to relieve her slaking need, like a thirst that could not be quenched; the iron grip twisting her insides, releasing the myriad creatures crawling up and down her veins and inside her brain to command possession of every thought – if that's what the continuous never-ending spirals within her mind counted as, only to be eventually ceased by someone slotting a needle into her vein.

When her need became unbearable, the screaming and howling around her made it worse. The noise grated against every single frayed nerve ending, making the excruciating pounding in her head worse.

It had only been in the last few days that Linda had realised the teeth-grinding noise had been coming from her own mouth.

Trying to make sense of this in her addled brain didn't add up.

It was like being in an abattoir consisting only of herself. It was surreal.

During her brief glimpses of logic, she'd questioned what was happening, but these questions remained unanswered as her consciousness looped back into the spiralling pain and worm-like creatures invading every inch of her body.

Linda gagged at the thought. The pain and hallucinations had peaked, then gradually dulled in their intensity. It was then that she'd noticed the stench.

That was when things started to get *really* bad...

This time, neither the pain nor the relentless urge for the saviour of a needle was the culprit, but gradual realisation.

The stench was her.

Slowly, very slowly, in the never-ending hours of being denied respite in the form of sleep, seeped the memory of what had happened to bring her to this situation.

Tom.

Tom had beat her in her flat. The flat she'd had next to her friend of old, Vera, with the two children she'd managed to keep with her. Tom had beaten her black and blue and the next thing she knew, she was shackled to this bed in darkness.

Linda blinked, panic overtaking her. It pushed its way back in at every given opportunity, but she couldn't allow it to overtake her now.

She concentrated back on what she'd remembered, the fear that her memory might elude her again, fresh.

Her firstborn – Samantha – had been back on the scene and they'd been getting to know each other, but then Tom, who'd she'd stupidly believed had finally returned for her, promising they'd be a family at last, had lied.

That bastard's only wish was to turn their daughter over. And

Linda had been beaten to within an inch of her life and jacked up on God knows what because she'd been all set to betray him.

And she had no idea how long she'd been here.

Linda stared at the oozing infected welts around her shackled wrists. A long time, by the looks of it.

That woman – her pseudo-saviour who delivered her daily release – had stopped coming.

And that's when everything had worsened.

But she'd got through most of that now. The worst had passed. She'd also eaten the majority of the food that woman had left, obviously knowing she'd get the chance to escape soon enough.

Now, she was almost strong enough to think about that.

Linda's gaze moved to the outline of the wardrobe in the darkness.

She remembered that too...

How she wished she'd had the strength and courage to do something when Tom had appeared. She'd thought it was over when he'd stepped into the room.

But she hadn't been the target.

This time, she'd been lucid enough to witness him murdering her pseudo-saviour.

Linda shuddered. When that woman had looked at her, knowing what was about to happen, she'd longed to somehow portray that she understood. To give the woman the notion that she wasn't alone, even if there was nothing that could be done to save her.

Linda felt the burn of shame. She hadn't done that, though, had she? She'd pretended she was unaware. Call it self-preservation, but if she'd allowed her eyes to register one ounce of recognition, she would have suffered the same fate.

And the body of that woman in the wardrobe was now overtaking the stench that she, herself, made.

No, she had to get out of here. She'd go home and get away from this. She'd go and find Vera, Sam, *someone*.

But she didn't dare move.

Not yet.

She was still very weak and didn't know whether her legs worked any more from lack of use during the time she'd lain in her own filth.

Either way, she had to get out without Tom Bedworth getting wind.

There were others here too – lots of them. She didn't know who they were, but she'd heard them talking. At first, she'd presumed the voices were in her own head, but they weren't, so how would she get out unnoticed?

Linda curled into a ball, desperation overtaking her before pulling her mind back on track. *You haven't come through this to give up now, Linda*, she told herself.

She would find a way. She *had* to.

* * *

Seb stretched his leg out, the stiffness grating. He took the painkillers Sam plucked from her handbag and swallowed them dry, hoping they'd kick in quickly. He hated being anything other than on form.

He dragged his fingers through his hair, weary beyond words.

How he longed for a hot shower, but even that would fail to remove the unmistakable stench of burnt wood and plastic clinging to every fibre of his being. He expected the smell would remain ingrained within his nostrils for eternity.

'I still can't believe it!' Neil muttered, shaking his head as he poured himself a whisky from Sam's decanter. He held it up.

'Anyone else?' Seeing nods, Neil filled the other glasses. 'What a fucking night!'

There was only so long they could speculate how this had happened and who was behind it. He glanced at Sam's face, her brow knitted with deep worry. Even her shocking revelation about those people being her siblings didn't answer the questions. *Nothing* did.

Seb watched Sam too. Her eyes remained fixed on the area where the dead man had lain, and he could guess what she was thinking. This revelation would hit her doubly hard, and he didn't quite know what to do about it. What *could* he do? He reached for her hand. 'Are you all right?'

Sam looked up. 'Those people wanted to hurt me, yet it was *you* and your casino which took the brunt.' She met eyes with all three of the Stoker brothers. 'I am truly sorry.'

'You can't blame yourself for this, Sam,' Andrew said. 'The situation was out of anyone's control. And you forget that unhinged bitch was aiming for you!'

Sam bit her bottom lip. *Didn't she just know it.* But even that failed to feel real. 'I should have somehow known,' she continued, sadness cascading. 'I actually liked Trevor... Grant, and that makes things worse.'

Seb swallowed the remark he wanted to make. Whether he liked it or not, if it hadn't been for Grant Devlin stepping in front, Sam would be dead. 'Going over things won't help,' he said briskly. Finishing his drink, he held it out for a refill.

'What do we do about that woman?' Neil asked. 'She's clearly got a screw loose.' He wasn't feeling great about having to make the decision to let her escape, either.

Sam picked at her fingernails. The prospect that her own flesh and blood was out to kill her was not palatable. That Marina had gone to such lengths to ruin her relationship and then kill her meant it was unlikely she'd stop there. 'What do you think has happened to that young girl?'

'If she's got any sense, she'll have got as far away as possible,' Andrew growled.

'I see the local rag didn't waste time printing this!' Seb muttered, glaring at the Peacock on the front page of the *Birmingham Mail*. 'I think we'd best get the ball rolling with the insurance. It will take months to get things back up and running,' he said, anger at the injustice of the situation returning.

Neil wanted to drag out what he'd got to say for as long as possible, but knew he couldn't. He felt sick to the stomach. 'I, erm... think there might be a problem with the insurance...'

'Oh, I'm expecting them to accuse us of doing an insurance job when it's labelled as arson, but we'll deal with that if it comes to it. I'm just glad everyone got out.'

'Yes,' Neil continued, looking slightly grey. 'But I didn't mean that... I meant, I don't think we've got insurance...'

Andrew's and Seb's eyes darted to their brother. Even Sam pulled her eyes away from the paper to stare at Neil in horror.

'We've had insurance with the same firm for donkey's years! Dad set it up, remember?' Seb hissed, his tone guarded.

Neil put his head in his hands. 'I know, but each year the premium increases. It was becoming a piss take, so I thought we'd get a better deal elsewhere.'

'Get to the fucking point,' Seb snarled.

Neil looked between Andrew and Seb. 'I purposefully didn't renew it, but I... I forgot to take out another policy.'

'*Forgot*?' Seb roared, jumping up, then clinging to the edge of the desk as the pain in his leg kicked in. 'Tell me you're joking?'

Neil's downcast eyes told Seb all he needed to know. 'Oh, fucking brilliant! I can't believe this! You stupid, stupid fucking...'

'Hang on!' Andrew interrupted. 'Yeah, Neil's fucked up, but this might not be a *complete* disaster.' He turned to Seb. 'I'm just glad you insisted we stored the excess cash in the lockup safes, otherwise that would have gone up in smoke too. And I know it's not much of a silver lining, but I think we've now got a way to lose that cash.' He raised an eyebrow. 'You know, rather than using the insurance?'

Seb's urge to punch Neil dissipated slightly. *The excess cash? Andrew may just have an idea there...*

Sam frowned. 'What's all this?'

Seb sighed and took Sam's hand. '*This* is something I should have told you about. If I had, you'd never have thought in a trillion years that I've been anything but happy with you.' He'd have much preferred the casino hadn't burnt down, but being as it had, some good might as well come out of it.

'Andrew, can you get yourself down the lockup and move at least half of the cash out? The bill for the damage will be horrific.' Seb turned to Sam. 'I'll explain later.' He then noticed her distraction. 'What is it?'

Sam pointed to a small article in the paper. 'That girl from last night... I think she's dead...'

44

Reaching the top of the attic staircase, Tina paused, the silence unnerving. So many months now, she'd put up with the screeching coming from up here, its hideous noise had become part of the usual sounds of the Aurora, but its absence was odd.

She glanced around. This area was out of bounds, but what was she supposed to do? The Aurora was like the *Mary Celeste* this morning. Oh, sure, the other girls were here, but no one else was. Chas had disappeared, Deb hadn't come back last night and now her mother and Tom had gone AWOL?

Tina frowned. Her mother had been acting out of character since Chas had left and her behaviour had been even stranger these past few days.

Yes, Tina might have thought it was a joke yesterday when her mum had gone on about getting out whilst they could, but neither Tina nor her sister had taken her seriously. How could they? This game had been their mother's life, always encouraging both of them to follow in her footsteps. *'Easy money and free bed and board,'* she'd said.

Why would she have had such an about turn?

Tina's mouth set determinedly as she continued along the attic landing.

She'd checked with the others, and no one had been paid this morning. Every Thursday they got their percentage of the wedge, but no one was here to cough up. There wasn't even any bloody milk in the fridge! It wasn't good enough.

Tina wasn't being turned over. She'd brought that Dan bloke in, hadn't she?

What if her mother had run off with Tom and ripped them all off?

She shook her head resolutely. No, she wouldn't do that. The only place Amelia could possibly be was up here, dealing with the mystery woman, like usual.

Tina edged towards a door that had a padlock on, but the padlock was hanging off. *The door was open!*

Could it really be true there was a deformed relative of Tom's locked in a tiny attic bedroom like the princes in the Tower of London?

She suddenly felt rather excited. This was like being in a mystery movie.

Hang on! What was she doing? Creeping around a no-go area of a brothel to see if a fucked-up cripple was chained to a post in the attic?

She wasn't losing her place here for something like this, especially now she was going up in Tom's estimation.

Stopping, Tina was about to retrace her steps, but curiosity got the better of her. 'Mum?' she called. 'Mum? Are you up here?'

Before she could change her mind, she pushed open the door, then froze in her tracks. 'What the...?'

Aside from the stench, a strange skeletal-looking creature stood in the centre of the room staring at her. Tina's eyes darted to the soiled bed, the empty crisp packets strewn around the floor and the empty cuffs attached to the metal bed post.

It was true! A woman was kept prisoner in here? *This* woman? But she wasn't deformed, she just looked terrible.

Tina's gaze fixed back on the woman. *There had to be a reason she'd been locked in here. She must be dangerous.*

Heart pounding, Tina backed against the wall. '*Mum!*' she screeched. 'This woman's trying to escape!'

'Shut up!' Linda hissed. 'Don't say a word.'

'Keep away from me, you fucking freak!' Tina yelped, pressing herself further against the wall. 'I don't know who you are, but...'

'You've got to listen to me,' Linda gasped, her sunken eyes wide. 'Where's Tom?'

Tina wanted to scream as the skeletal creature's bony fingers encircled her wrist. The overpowering stench of faeces and other smells she could not name clogged her throat. *What if this woman had a horrible disease and it was catching?* 'Get back to where you're supposed to be, you nutter,' she spat. 'Tom will go mad when he finds out.'

Bolstered by a new-found strength from the veiled confirmation Tom was absent, Linda knew this was the only chance. 'You've got to help me. You need to get out too whilst you still can!'

'Are you crazy?' Tina yelled. *Imagine how pleased Tom would be with her when he found out she'd thwarted this loon's escape.* 'I'll tell Tom what you're doing. I'll tell Amelia! She's my mum and she'll believe me...'

'Amelia's your mother?' Linda's eyes darted towards the wardrobe. She tightened her grip on Tina's arm. 'Listen girl, you need to leave, we both do, or Tom will kill us both!'

'I'm Tom's favourite,' Tina said proudly. *She soon would be, anyway.*

Linda's desperation snowballed. 'No! Tom's dangerous. You've got to g...'

'I've got to *nothing*,' Tina snarled. 'Mum? *Mum!*'

'She won't answer you,' Linda snapped. She felt bad for this girl, but this was the only way. 'She's dead...'

Tina laughed. 'Oh, fuck off! You really are mental, aren't you?' Her eyes narrowed. 'Get the fuck away from me and...'

'If you don't believe me, look in there. Tom killed her! I saw him do it!' Linda pointed to the wardrobe. 'See for yourself!' She had to get through to this girl. 'Tom's not here, is he? We have to leave now before he comes back.'

Tina felt like punching this creature in the face. She'd almost felt sorry for her for a minute, but not any more. Shaking her head, she dragged Linda to the wardrobe. 'Don't think I'm letting go of you. Not that you'd get very far.' She tugged at the wardrobe door. 'You can ju...'

Shrieking, she jumped back in shock, her eyes fixed on the lifeless body crammed like a bag of old clothes into the bottom of the wardrobe, the glassy eyes staring back at her. At the pool of pungent bodily fluid dripping steadily from under her mother's body over the edge of the wardrobe floor, vomit rushed up Tina's throat into her mouth. 'Oh, my Christ!'

Letting go of Linda, Tina staggered back. *Her mother was dead? Dead?*

Her panicked eyes shot to Linda. 'Did you do this?' she screamed.

'Does it look like I could manage that?' Linda cried. 'For fuck's sake, girl, I've already told you! It was Tom!'

Tina stared at Linda. It was true, this stick-thin creature, weak from drugs and lack of food, wouldn't stand a chance with overpowering her big, strong mother. *But Tom could have...*

Linda lurched towards the door. If Tom was out and she found the strength to get down the stairs, then she'd be out of this hellhole.

She glanced back at the frozen figure of Tina, still staring shell-shocked at the corpse in the wardrobe. If this girl was stupid enough to remain, then she was dead meat. 'Stay if you like, but I'm taking my chances.'

* * *

Sam had broken her cardinal rule of not drinking in the afternoon.

Another visit from the police was half-expected, but she *hadn't* expected them to turn up unannounced, otherwise she'd have spoken to them somewhere other than her office, which smelt strongly of bleach and freshly cleaned floors. One of them had even commented on it, which hadn't helped matters. Her nerves were shattered.

As usual, Seb had neutralised her fears, making it clear the police would receive a bigger than usual monthly payout to cover all eventualities and was confident no trace of a body would ever be linked back. Yet again, he'd sorted it.

But what had *she* done?

Sam's bottom lip trembled. *She'd distrusted Seb. She didn't deserve him.*

That she'd believed him to have betrayed her burnt brightly. She should have known better. 'How's your wound?'

Seb stretched his leg out. 'Stiff, but it'll be fine. I told you, Andrew's a dab hand at that kind of thing.'

Sam closed her eyes and listened to the steady beat of Seb's heart beneath his shirt... the cold dread of how she'd felt when that gun went off... seeing him hit the floor... that split second she'd believed she'd lost him...

She shuddered, grateful it had been his leg, rather than anywhere else.

'Hey.' Seb put his arm around Sam. 'What's with the long face?'

Sam shrugged miserably. 'Everything. I should have trusted you.'

Seb kissed the top of Sam's head as she leaned against his chest. 'I should have been upfront I was working out how to offload this money. That you believed my moods might be down to any reason involving you horrifies me. You're my life, Sam.'

'And you're mine,' Sam whispered. Carrying on without Seb filled her with dread. Yes, she was disappointed he hadn't levelled with her, but it seemed they *both* had things to learn. Relationships like this weren't second nature to either of them.

Why hadn't he told her about his money worries? She might have been able to help. And Seb now admitting he'd used some of that money to buy their house?

He knew how important it was to her to purchase the house together, like a *normal* couple. Yet now it was owned by the Stoker firm.

But how could she be cross about it? She loved him too much. It was only temporary and paled into insignificance with what had now happened. The most important thing was that they still had each other and this attack, aiming to trash her life, had failed. But it had sure as hell done damage.

Sam's mind tracked back to the Devlins. The confusing emotions surrounding them made her head spin. A half-brother and sister who'd wanted her *dead*.

But Grant had died, saving *her*. Yet his killer was still out there somewhere...

'That poor little cow,' Sam found herself saying. 'That girl who was part of the setup? Dead. I feel cursed.'

'Cursed?' Seb cried. 'It's down to Marina, not you.'

'Maybe, but it's unlikely we'll find out who was pimping those girls now.' Sam sat up. 'Christ, I feel so responsible. Like I said before, everything that has happened is linked to *me*. Grant Devlin is dead, that girl is dead, you've been shot and your casino has burnt down.' She paused, chewing at her lip. 'Where do you think she's gone? Marina, I mean?'

Seb pursed his lips. *Wherever she'd gone, he'd find her, but he wouldn't voice that. Not just yet.* 'Back to London? Who cares? The main thing is that we're all okay. Everything will be fine. Now, whilst we've got some time to ourselves, why don't we make up for a bit of what we've been lacking the past few days?'

Pulling Sam astride him, Seb began unbuttoning her blouse.

'Sorry!' Andrew said, bursting into the office.

'Can't this wait?' Seb muttered, pulling himself reluctantly away from Sam's mouth.

'I'm afraid not,' Andrew said as Neil entered the office behind him.

Sam clambered off Seb's lap, only grateful they'd been interrupted now, rather than later. But looking at the Stoker twins' expressions, her stomach dropped into her feet. 'What is it? What's happened?'

'It's gone,' Andrew said slowly, his voice sounding oddly mechanical.

'Gone? What's gone?' Seb frowned.

'We've just come from the lockup,' Neil said, the words sounding as hollow to his own ears as they felt leaving his mouth. 'Someone's cleaned us out.'

Seb looked at his brothers, then to Sam, the words not quite sinking in.

'The money's gone, Seb,' Andrew repeated. '*All* of it.'

* * *

Chas shovelled the last bit of the baked potato he'd bought from the roadside stand by Rackhams into his mouth, savouring every last mouthful.

It had been easy during last night's chaos and confusion with the Peacock up in flames to pick a couple of pockets of people who had appeared out of the woodwork like ghouls to gawp at the spectacle. And those people flocking from the surrounding bars in their eagerness to witness one of the city's most prestigious casinos going up in smoke weren't short of money. They were all too far up their own arses to contemplate they could be robbed without even realising it, the silly fuckers.

Chas sucked melted butter from his fingers, not wanting to waste a morsel.

He'd lifted a nice few quid – enough to see him through for a couple of days and even enough to get a room at one of the dosshouse hotels down the Chinese quarter tonight – somewhere that wouldn't ask questions or stare too long at his ruined face.

Oh, it had been a fine spectacle watching that fucking casino getting razed to the ground. He might not have spotted Deb Banner, but that disappointment was far outweighed by the thought of those Stoker bastards witnessing their place reduced to ash.

Chas smiled as he pulled the strip of painkillers from his pocket and treated himself to another couple. He'd hoped the news would reach him that the Stokers had been caught up in the flames, too, but seeing them all surveying the damage this morning, it looked like they'd all escaped unharmed.

Shame.

But he *had* overheard people talking. Word had it that it was arson.

And that's when Chas remembered the clumsy bastard who'd smashed up his makeshift bed in the alley.

That bloke had come from the direction of the Peacock's side door.

Chas smiled. He could be sitting on a goldmine here, pretty sure that if push came to shove, he 'may' just recall enough of the bozo's description, if the Stokers were interested?

However, that was for another time. He would revisit that after he'd served his revenge on the people *he* wanted.

Getting up from the bench, Chas chucked the polystyrene potato box into the bin and, sparking up a cigarette, made his way back towards Broad Street to continue his vigil from the shadows.

Deb would turn up sooner rather than later. And he'd be waiting.

* * *

As much as Marina found it almost impossible to comprehend, time had run out on any realistic window for Dan to return, so she'd no choice but to accept the unthinkable.

By this time of day, even if Dan hadn't returned the night before, he'd have sloped in long before now. But there was no sign of him.

And there wouldn't be, either.

Marina's head pounded, her anger having reached boiling point some time ago. She glanced around the smashed-up lounge of the crappy flat.

She had no recollection of ripping those horrible thin curtains from the rail, upending the table or stabbing the moulting velour sofa repeatedly with a bread knife. But she knew she had.

She just wished the recipient of her anger was one of the many people who, in the space of twenty-four hours, had trashed her meticulously arranged plans.

Marina tugged at her hair. She'd rip it clean off her own scalp if it toned down the searing rage bubbling through her system and removed the white-hot fury at seeing those empty safes...

She couldn't remember how long she'd stared at the vacant space where the money – *her* money – should have been. Neither did she have any knowledge of getting back to Bearwood from the lockups.

After taking out her rage on this shit-tip, the remainder of the night was spent stewing between resentment at Grant for firstly, spoiling her chance to remove Samantha and throwing himself in front of her gun, to secondly, working out how the bastard Stokers had beaten her to it and swiped the money before she'd got there.

Neil Stoker had been way behind her, she'd successfully crippled Seb Stoker, so how could they have managed it? She'd then thought it could have been the other one – what was his name? Andrew?

It was only by midday, when Dan's prolonged absence seeped into Marina's mind, that she considered a ludicrous possibility.

And the longer Dan had remained missing, the stronger that creeping possibility became.

Now it was clear...

Her face crumpled into a scowl.

That stupid, one-handed, pointless thick fuck of a wanker had got one over on her.

Dan had *actually* done it. He'd robbed her fucking blind.

Marina's breath caught. She didn't know which was worse: being outdone by a thick moron, or that she'd been stupid enough not to think he'd listened to everything she and Grant had discussed.

By underestimating Dan's ability, she'd inadvertently done this to herself. And that was more galling than anything.

But Dan hadn't got the balls to pull off something like this alone. *No way.* He'd always been a yellow-bellied, slimy bastard.

Her teeth grated, the noise making her want to scream.

There weren't many people willing to take on the Stokers, so who had helped him?

Marina's nails dug deeper into her palms. She needed the pain to concentrate.

Think, think. Who could it be?

And that was the problem. She didn't know. And for that, she wanted to kill everybody around her.

But she couldn't do that either. She'd lost the gun, she'd lost Grant, she'd lost the money and now everyone was on the lookout for her.

Shit.

Marina lurched up from the slashed armchair. *Fuck this!*

There was only one thing to do and, as much as the concept pained her, she had little choice.

And this time, the man had better step up.

45

Waking up stiff as a board and chilled to the bone, Linda shivered, the usual rush of dread washing over her.

Tom? Was he here?

Blinking at her unfamiliar surroundings, she adjusted herself on the cold tiles, wincing as her hip bones pressed against the hard floor.

Despite the uncomfortableness, relief cascaded over her. Tom wasn't here and she was no longer in *that* place.

A dirty cubicle in a public toilet, amid used sanitary towels and various drug paraphernalia, might not be everyone's idea of a preferable location, but to Linda, it meant *everything*. It meant escaping from her prison last night was not a dream.

With effort, she pulled herself up from the floor and used the toilet before stuffing a wad of toilet roll into the pocket of the jacket she'd stolen last night.

She'd spent the night desperate for sleep, but instead had remained on guard from the shouts and noises surrounding her.

The familiar sound of people from the other cubicles – strangers using the toilets as a base to bring punters for a quick ten-quid fumble was not new – she'd been party to that game herself back in the day, neither was the gasp of satisfaction of the delivered release in the form of whatever drug was fed into someone's veins – something else she understood.

Linda's guts had churned, the familiar cravings never far away. She'd have been lying if she hadn't thought about opening the door and offering herself up in whatever way worked in exchange for a hit, but she hadn't.

However tempting it was, she couldn't give up now.

No, she had to stay firm. She done it before, and she'd do it again. She was through the worst now, but the all-consuming need clamoured as a never-ending reminder.

Her hand faltered on the door lock. Although it wouldn't take much to kick open the flimsy wood, the presence of a lock that *she* was in control of subconsciously offered a modicum of safety.

But was Tom on the other side, waiting? Had he realised she'd escaped and followed her?

Taking a deep breath, Linda flung open the door, her stomach wedged firmly in her throat.

The place was empty, thank God.

Moving out, Linda headed to the sinks. She couldn't go anywhere until she'd cleaned herself up as much as possible.

Raising her eyes to the scuffed and chipped mirror, Linda yelped. The reflection was not her.

Except it was...

The gaunt, hollow face looking back at her was worse than she'd imagined. How could she face anyone like this?

Swallowing down her anger and humiliation, she splashed ice-cold water onto her face, as if the process would remove the pasty, yellow tinge of her skin; the dark circles under her sunken eyes; replace the missing teeth and remove the spots dotting her ravaged face.

Taking the bundle of toilet paper from her pocket, she stripped off her top and doused the paper in the sink. Scrubbing under her armpits and sluicing her arms in the water, she winced as months of ingrained filth ran over the cuts on her wrists and the swollen, infected track marks.

Whether she liked it or not, she couldn't stay in here for the time required to mend. And the chances of mending were minimal without adequate food and water.

Bearwood public toilets were the furthest she'd been able to reach last night. She'd been too exhausted to go further, but where she'd been heading, she wasn't sure.

Something else that had circled in her mind all night.

Linda's first thought was to go to her friend Vera's. But she'd decided against it.

That flat in Northfield held the terror and revulsion of what Tom had done to her. It was a permanent reminder of how he'd tricked his way back into her life and ruined *everything*.

She wasn't strong enough to face that just yet and wasn't sure whether she ever would. Plus, she'd lost her last two children to the care system – that's inevitably where her two smallest would have gone, since everyone believed she'd done a runner.

The council had probably even relet her flat by now.

Linda attempted to tame the mass of tangles, fast turning into dreadlocks with her fingers, and then pulled the silk scarf from the pocket of the stolen jacket and fashioned it over her head.

God, she looked a fright, but this was the best she could do for now.

Linda stared at her reflection once more, but this time with renewed determination.

Tom Bedworth was out there somewhere, and he'd be looking for her. Whatever she looked like, she would go to the Orchid and speak to Sam. She'd explain what had happened and pray her firstborn daughter didn't turn her away.

But first she had to get all the way up to Broad Street without Tom finding her and that thought alone terrified her more than anything.

* * *

Seb sat quietly in Sam's office, it having become a temporary nerve centre for the Peacock. His mind churned. Despite the Royal Peacock still smouldering and the press still lurking around, Sam now knew the truth and things were back on track with her, so what anyone else thought was by the by.

Even Neil ballsing up the insurance had been a blessing in disguise, until it was uncovered their millions in stashed funds had been robbed.

Seb raised his eyes towards the ceiling, willing his anger not to spiral out of control, especially after receiving the message from the Irish to say that in the light of the change of circumstances concerning the Peacock's fire, their offer of help had to be rescinded...

Andrew entered the office, his face grim. 'There's more of them in reception now. I've told them we will be in contact soon.'

'That's the third bunch this morning,' Neil said. 'I'm sorry, Sam. They're our staff. They shouldn't be coming here asking to see us.'

'I'll arrange a temporary office somewhere close by for the time being,' Andrew said, pulling out his mobile.

'No, you won't. You don't need to do that,' Sam insisted. 'I meant what I said earlier, you're more than welcome to use whatever you need here.' She glanced at Seb; she could see the worry etched deeply on his face. She stroked his arm. 'I mean it. Do whatever you need. It's the least I can do.'

Seb smiled tightly. *Sam still felt this was all down to her?* It wasn't, but even if it were, he wouldn't have her feeling responsible.

His anger simmered steadily below the surface. He'd thought everything was going so well and now look at him.

His plans had been clear. The business had enough money to be able to afford to pull back on some of the riskier dealings they'd done in the past. There had even been enough overflow to think about cutting back on the gun trade.

Okay, so it was never an option to go completely straight, but he had planned to reduce the risk factor. The less they stuck their necks out, the less people would want a piece of them. The less it put Sam, the children that he hoped might shortly follow, and the rest of his family in the firing line, the better.

He never wanted the opportunity to manifest again where someone felt they could lay their filthy hands on the woman he loved to score points or winkle out money.

No, he'd provide an existence where they could step back from the danger.

But what could he possibly give Sam now?

Sam watched Seb closely. She could see his mind turning in its internal struggle. To all but lose the Peacock and then find all that money had been snatched? What could she do to help?

'Whatever happens, I won't have any of my staff suffering,' Seb said bluntly.

Andrew frowned. 'It can't be helped, I'm afraid. They'll have to accept it will be a while before they'll get their jobs back.'

'The Orchid can take at least some of your staff temporarily,' Sam suggested.

Seb shook his head abruptly. 'Absolutely not!'

'But we run a huge risk of losing loads permanently otherwise, especially croupiers and waiting staff,' Neil muttered glumly. 'The enforcers will remain loyal, but we need to provide at least *something* to tide them over.'

'Christ, Neil!' Andrew snatched up the list of estimated rebuilding prices. 'Have you not seen the best-case scenario of costs? We can't afford to keep everyone happy. We need to...'

'Enough!' Seb barked, slamming his fist on the desk. 'No one will be going without. Everyone will be paid full whack, the Peacock will be rebuilt and the cops will be paid off. I won't have *any* family suffering because of what's been pulled on us. I'll find a way.' *The only thing that would help now was the last option he wanted.*

'What I don't understand is why the safes weren't forced?' Sam said, almost to herself.

She'd accompanied the Stokers to the lockup last night and she'd seen with her own eyes the bolt jacked off the door, but, unlike the door, the safes hadn't been forced. Whoever lifted the cash had known the codes...

Against her better judgement, her eyes slid towards Andrew and Neil. *They wouldn't have pulled an inside job, would they?*

She immediately shook the thought away, but noticed the weighted silence in the room. 'I didn't mean to insinuate th...'

'You *did* delete the safe code from your mobile?' Andrew eyed Neil accusingly.

'I've already told you I did,' Neil cried indignantly. 'I did it straight away after I deposited the tournament takings. I told you that at the time.'

'And you took your phone into the lockup with you?' Seb asked, not quite able to comprehend Neil entering the safe code into his mobile in the first place. Firstly the screw-up with the insurance and now this blatant breach of security?

'Well, yes, of cou...' Neil stopped abruptly, the confusing memory of finding his phone on the van's dashboard coming to mind. 'Shit!' he muttered.

'Oh, my God!' Seb muttered. 'You didn't, did you? You left the fucking phone in the van? That runner took you there. I remember you moaning about it.' He dragged himself to his feet, his eyes sparking. 'You stupid bastard!'

Neil dodged when Seb lurched towards him, grateful his brother's usual panther-like speed was lessened by his damaged leg, only for Andrew to grab him from behind and pin him to the wall. 'It must have dropped from my pocket when I got out of the van,' he blathered.

'You left the code for our safe in full view of a fucking runner?' Andrew yelled.

'Simon wouldn't have looked. He'd have just placed it on the dash. I...'

'Then Simon will be answering some fucking questions,' Seb spat. 'I can't believe you've been so stupid, Neil. You useless fu...'

'Guys!' Sam cried, desperately wishing she hadn't said anything. 'We don't know whether that's what happened.'

'Of course it is!' Andrew raged. 'How else can it be explained?' He pushed himself into his twin's face, his mouth twisting with rage as he raised his fist.

46

Pulling his hood down over his ravaged face, Chas kept his head down as he skirted along the side of the buildings along Broad Street.

He felt a thousand times better for having a proper bed to sleep in last night. That's if the bed at that cheapo hotel could be classed as 'proper'. Either way, it beat the hell out of a cardboard box and was also marginally better than being next to wailing bastards in a hospital ward.

That soak in the bath was long overdue too, but he hadn't got enough cash for a second night. Not unless he acquired a bit more pin money from the pockets of these dickheads poncing about here.

He'd keep that option open whilst looking for Deb.

Two nights now she'd been absent, so she'd be here tonight. There was no way Bedworth wouldn't have her scouting for fresh talent for *three* nights in a row.

Chas shoved a cigarette in his mouth, careful not to catch the stitches around the corners.

Now, where was the best place to lurk to avoid suspicious looks or attention? He couldn't hang around outside the casinos or that bloody stupid café Deb went to before, but he *could* find somewhere giving him a good view of all of those places.

His eyes tracked to the cindered skeleton of the Royal Peacock, now surrounded with a temporary construction fence. The alley down there was out, but *that* one wasn't.

Glancing left and right, Chas nipped across the road, pulling his hood even lower on spotting one of the casino security on a walkabout.

Here would do.

Chas darted into the mouth of the alley next to the Violet Orchid, jumping out of his skin as someone yelped in fright. Christ, the ugly bitch had almost given him a bloody heart attack!

How bloody typical. The only decent place to lurk and there was a resident tramp in situ. And this time, judging by its voice, it was a female one.

Well, she could fuck off...

He grabbed the skinny creature by her ill-fitting jacket. 'Get lost, will you? I need to be here.'

He glared at the woman, intending to use his scary face as leverage to back up his threat, when he stopped.

It was that creature from the attic. The howler!

'Well, well, well,' Chas sneered. 'I don't expect you recognise me because the last time I saw you, you were that off your tits you were on the bleeding moon!'

'Leave me alone!' Linda yelped, terrified. This man with the slashed-up face might recognise *her*, but she didn't know him. *But he could only recognise her from one place...*

Fear rushed over her. She shouldn't have hesitated going into the Orchid. She should have just gone straight in and demanded to speak to Sam the second she'd got here. Instead, in true Linda style, she'd freaked out and rushed down an alley to calm the threatening hyperventilation.

Tom must have sent this man to take her back to the Aurora and kill her. He'd had her followed, watched... *She'd been so close...*

Determination suddenly flooded her. She wouldn't miss this chance now. She was literally *yards* away from her daughter and she wasn't allowing this man to trash that. *No!*

Screaming obscenities, she lashed out, her grubby fingernails clawing at the man's face.

As the first fingernail tore his already sore skin, Chas dodged to the left, his dexterity surprising him.

This rancid old cow had legged it from the Aurora, so she might have news on Deb? Failing that, what about using the hideous old boot for some blackmail? This was his opportunity!

He'd grab the old witch and inform Tom that if he didn't cough up decent compensation for his injuries, then he'd take this old girl to the cops. She could tell them what Tom had done to her – what he'd done to all those women and girls.

The cunt would be stupid to risk that.

Chas slapped his hand over Linda's mouth. If she didn't shut the fuck up, she'd draw attention. 'You're coming with me, you wasted old slapper!'

Linda struggled against the man's grip, her eyes wide with terror, muffled squawks coming from her covered mouth. She kicked out wildly, her hands flying in all directions, aiming for the man's eyes, his throat – *anywhere*.

She was done with this. She was not going back to Tom Bedworth!

'Stop struggling, you bitch!' Chas screamed as Linda dragged him forwards, nearer to the mouth of the alley.

He'd knock her clean out cold if she didn't calm down.

* * *

'What now?' Seb cried.

'Yep! It's happening right this minute!' Kevin yelled as he rushed down the corridor.

Neil and Andrew let go of each other's throats and raced after Kevin, all concept of punching each other's lights out forgotten for the time being.

'I didn't catch what Kev said!' Sam said as Seb struggled to his feet and made to leave the office.

Seb moved faster than he should towards the back exit. 'Kevin said there's a bloke outside roughing up a bag lady. It's the same guy Neil ID'd on the CCTV – the one you're after. The *right* one this time!'

'The man with the red VW Golf?' Sam gasped, hatred rising. That man was here again and up to his old tricks? But this time, picking on old women and tramps?

Her mouth set, her resolve as well as her legs overtaking Seb down the corridor. Excitement burned. That young girl might not be around to tell her tale, but Sam could right at least part of that wrong.

If that bastard was the one she'd wanted to get her hands on for so long, then she might still be able to put a stop to that grooming gang.

'Stay here!' Seb barked as he all but threw himself down the steps to the pavement outside.

Not likely, Sam thought, rounding the corner just in time to see the Stokers dive into the alleyway. Rushing to keep up, she turned into the mouth of the narrow entry.

'This wanker is trying to drag this woman off,' Andrew spat, pinning the man to the wall by his throat.

'I wasn't!' Chas spluttered, his bowels turning to liquid.

In the dim light, Sam couldn't see much of the woman this piece of filth was attempting to accost, but it was obvious the poor soul was homeless. Probably a drug user too.

Her eyes narrowed. 'Expanding your horizons?' she shouted at Chas. 'Finding more vulnerable people to target? People whose desperation make easy pickings?'

'Let me see him!' Neil pulled the man's head back by his hair. 'Yep! That's the fucker! God knows what's happened to his face, though,' he winced.

'What's going on?' Chas spluttered, his hand scrabbling to take the pressure off his tearing scalp. 'I don't know what I'm supposed to have done!'

'I'll tell you what you've done! You're pimping girls – *young* ones. And you know it!' Sam pushed forward and turned to Seb. 'I want this piece of shit to pay!'

Seb didn't need prompting. Moving forward, he took over from where Andrew left off. Grabbing the man, he slammed his head against the brick wall. 'You're coming with us.'

'Take him to the Orchid. Go the back way,' Sam instructed. *It was payback time for those young girls. For Linda. For...*

Black dots flashed behind Chas's eyes and his head pounded. He'd heard the crack as his head hit the wall and it hadn't sounded good. Neither was the pain. Neither was *this...*

He saw the raw hatred in Sam's eyes, the hand of this Stoker man pinning him to the wall was also getting tighter. *He was in deep shit.* 'You must have me mixed up with someone else. I...'

'He's lying!' Linda yelled, finding her voice. 'He's been doing everything you said.'

Sam had all but forgotten about the poor woman. Making sure Seb had a good grip of the man, she approached the bedraggled creature.

Linda backed further down the alley, her burst of confidence deserting her.

'It's okay,' Sam said gently. 'We'll help. Don't worry. I...'

In the dim light, she looked into the face half-concealed underneath a headscarf and frowned.

It looked like...

No... It couldn't be...

Linda saw the flash of recognition on her daughter's face. It was only slight, but it was there all the same. She turned away from the small amount of illumination this dank alleyway offered, but it was too late.

'Linda?' Samantha whispered. 'Mum? Is that you?'

Before the words had exited her mouth, she already knew the answer. It *was* Linda. 'Oh, my God!' she shrieked.

'I'm sorry,' Linda gabbled, unable to bear the disgust on her daughter's face. 'I shouldn't have come. I... I'm sorry.' Pulling away, she made to race for the alley mouth, but Sam kept a firm hold of her coat.

A strange mixture of relief coupled with anger poured over Sam. After all this time and this worry, her mother was *here*. She wasn't dead!

Hearing Sam shriek, Seb turned, keeping one hand firmly around Chas's neck. 'Sam? What's wrong?' Her eyes were wide – almost trance-like. 'Sam?'

Sam desperately tried to process the information. Linda had disappeared. She'd deserted her twice, as well as her younger children. Seb believed Linda had set her up and was back on drugs, hence the disappearance, but look at her now.

She stared at Linda's ravaged face, the sunken eyes, missing teeth... This *had* to involve more than choosing to disappear?

'Sam!' Seb barked. 'What's that woman saying to you?'

'Please! I shouldn't have come.' Linda clutched Sam's sleeve. 'I was plucking up the courage to come in and ask for you and then *he*,' she glared over to Chas, 'stopped me.'

It was the reference to the hooded man that snapped Sam back to reality. Rage exploded. She met Seb's eyes. 'It's my mother... It's Linda.'

Seb's jaw dropped. *Sam's mother? This tramp was Linda?*

He turned back to the scrote held in his grip. He'd had enough of people like this piece of crap hurting people who he loved. Like Liam, the bastards who had robbed the safe, the Devlins, the arsonists – whoever they were. He was sick of the whole fucking lot of them.

And this cunt would pay for everything.

'Get Linda inside,' he muttered and with his brothers following him, he manhandled the man further down the alleyway, where it was darker.

* * *

Chas didn't think he'd ever experienced such crushing panic as this – even when Tom Bedworth had shoved that fucking knife across his mouth.

This was Tom's fault. If it wasn't for Tom, he wouldn't be looking for Deb or needing to use scabby bitches from attics as bargaining chips in the first place.

But maybe he still could? Maybe if he gave the right information – something for these nutters to work with – then he could walk away from here?

His mind continued to whirr as he found himself dragged into the recesses of the alley, further away from civilisation.

'Please,' he gabbled, unable to formulate words properly in his crushed throat. 'Everyone is lying. I was looking for a tart – a hooker who's been stealing things from th...'

'You mean that young girl I saw you half-strangling last week?' Neil spat, wanting to get his ten-pence worth in. 'Dump him here, Seb.'

'But she deserved it! And that woman back there... you don't underst...'

Chas's excuses were cut short when Seb threw him to the floor, his head and back taking the impact. He howled in pain, his mind racing for the right words to stop this.

That was it! The fire at the Peacock!

'Listen! I can help you. Your casino? I saw the man! I saw him running from the side door just before it burnt down. I'd recognise him. I'd...'

'Of course you did! Now, isn't that convenient?' Seb sneered. 'Forget it! You're nothing but a lying nonce!'

He put his boot on Chas's throat, his large frame towering menacingly over the prone man. He was done with excuses. Done with wankers.

With a savage smile, he ground the heel of his polished Italian shoe down, a weird choking noise escaping from Chas's mouth.

'Now be fucking quiet!' Andrew hissed, adding a hefty kick to the man's ribs.

Flashing lights strobed behind Chas's eyes and bile rushed up his throat. He couldn't breathe. *Fuck!*

'Tell me who you're working for?' Sam caught up with the group down the alley, Linda still clinging to the side of her.

'Go inside, Sam. You don't want to see this,' Seb growled.

A smile crept onto Sam's face. 'Oh, but I do.'

And she did. She wanted to see this more than anything. Whatever *this* became, it was *more* than well-deserved.

'Christ,' Linda muttered, scared beyond all wits.

The anticipation mixed with devastation on Sam's face triggered Seb. In that instant, it did something to his promise of wanting to keep his head down to forge a cleaner life for them all. He pulled his blade from the sheath under his jacket.

Old habits die hard.

White fury covered him like a shroud as he plunged the knife into Chas's chest.

'Oh, my God!' Linda squawked. Ripping away from Sam, she leant against the wall, retching.

Seb didn't hear Linda. He heard nothing, short of his own heartbeat crashing in his ears as he plunged the blade in again. And again.

Over and over and over.

This was for Sam. This man had upset her. And for that, he would pay. He would also pay for everything else that everyone had done to upset her. And *him*.

It took a good minute of this frenzied and unstoppable attack before Andrew and Neil managed to drag Seb off.

Dismissively wiping his knife down his trousers, Seb shoved it back in the sheath, glancing at the mass of puncture marks and gore covering the dead man's body below him.

Saying nothing, he pulled Sam into his arms. 'Get Linda inside now.' He jerked his head towards the mangled body. 'That wanker had nothing to say. You just take care of Linda and listen to what she has to say. We'll make good here.'

Nodding, Sam took hold of Linda's arm and walked towards the main street, a disturbing sense of calm washing over her.

Seb had butchered that man well and good.

And she was glad.

* * *

Slamming the phone back into its cheap wall-mounted cradle, Marina was sure she'd spontaneously combust. Two days now and still no word. Not from Dan, nor from the useless bastard she was trying to get hold of.

She glanced around the flat, still in the same state from when she trashed it. It wasn't like she would bother tidying it up. She was done with making things liveable. Things hadn't been liveable for quite some time and nothing anyone could do, short of torching this dump, would improve that.

Snatching the wine from the side, she glugged straight from the bottle, then wiped her mouth with the back of her sleeve. She stared scornfully at the photos of the Royal Peacock emblazoned on the front page of the *Mail*.

Was that down to Dan as well? Had he concocted a smoke-screen to divert the Stokers, enabling him to steal the money? *Her* money?

Aside from the last couple of years of her life, it wasn't the only thing he'd stolen either.

Marina's eyes moved to her handbag, perched on what remained of the coffee table.

Yeah, and as a parting gift before her useless, lying cheating scumbag of a pointless boyfriend had turned her over, the tosser had swiped her only credit card with a few quid left on it.

Fuming, she snatched up the wine once more. The only way she'd afforded this was courtesy of a bit of cash she'd got left in her purse. But now she'd got nothing.

She fumbled for the remaining cigarettes left in her packet. She didn't care about the lack of food, but having fags was a must.

Marina's hand clenched into a fist. She wanted that money and she wanted it *now*.

And then she wanted Dan's head, along with Samantha Reynold's, on a fucking stick.

This should have all worked out perfectly, but it hadn't.

Stomping back to the phone, she snatched it up once more. If she couldn't get through soon, then she'd have no choice but to trek down to London. She wasn't giving up on what had been pinched from under her nose, and what she'd specced out perfectly.

But how could she manage that when she didn't even have the money to get the bus into town at the moment?

If something didn't happen soon and very soon, then she was fucked.

And if that was going to happen, then she would certainly not let it be because of Dan Marlow.

47

Ignoring the smell permeating the air, Sam poured Linda a second brandy and continued to let the woman talk.

The stench would dissipate, as would the shock of the Orchid's staff when, with her arm protectively around Linda's shoulder, she'd steered her frail, shaking mother through the gleaming reception down to her office.

The staff could speculate and think whatever they liked, but this was *her* casino, *her* firm. She didn't have to explain herself to anyone.

Readjusting the blanket draped around Linda's shoulders, Sam took a swig of her own drink. God knows, she needed it.

The office lighting uncovered the extent of her mother's damaged appearance, and it was taking all of Sam's control not to scream with rage.

She'd heard Linda's gabbled explanation of how she'd been kept prisoner, dragged from her flat, then drugged up. She'd heard all of it. But what she *hadn't* heard was an explanation as to who had done this or why. And that, she wanted.

'I'd have never left you or my two little ones, Sam,' Linda

sobbed, still terrified her new-found safety would dissolve and that Tom would appear from underneath the floorboards.

Sam nodded. She had been relieved to hear her instincts had been right all along, but anger that someone had knocked her mother senseless, dragged her off and kept her prisoner all of this time, drugged up to the eyeballs, was almost too much to bear. And she wanted whoever was responsible to pay.

'But why did you write that letter? That letter where you asked Vera to take care of the kids and that you were back on the crack?'

'I didn't!' Linda cried. 'Well, I did. But he forced me!'

'Who? Who forced you?'

'How are the kids?' Linda ignored the burning question. 'Where are they? I've been so messed up, I haven't been able to think straight. Christ, I haven't been able to think at all.'

She looked away, reticent to hear the answer. 'H-have they been taken into care?'

Sam shook her head. 'No. They're with Gloria, my adoptive mother. They're getting on fine.'

Linda's eyes welled. 'Oh, thank you, thank you! And Vera? How is she?'

Sam faltered. 'She, erm... We don't speak. I think she believed that you'd picked drugs over your kids and felt I was stupid for trying to find you.'

Linda's eyes filled up further. 'You... you were looking for me?'

Leaning over, Sam reached for Linda's hand. 'Of course I was. I never believed you'd set me up. I just couldn't find you. None of us could. I... I wish we had, though...'

'I didn't set you up, Sam, I swear! I'd never...' Linda stopped.

'Going back to that letter, who was it that did this to you? Who forced you to write it and then kept you locked up? Was it that man in the alley?' Sam was unwilling to push Linda when she was in such a state, but she had to know. She had to know if Seb had broken the chain of this wrongdoing.

Linda pulled her hand from Sam's and unsteadily reached for her brandy. 'He was part of it, but it wasn't him who did *this*...'

'Then who did?'

Linda's hands wrung nervously in her lap, her eyes sliding to those of her daughter's.

She wasn't about to protect Tom Bedworth, but how could she tell Sam that man was her real father? How could she admit the foul creature was Sam's own flesh and blood?

That bastard had already destroyed *her* life not once, but twice, and she was damned if she'd allow him to hurt their daughter – in *any* way. She took a deep breath. 'It was Tom.'

Sam frowned. 'Tom?' *Who the fuck was Tom? A pimp? Who?* 'Who is Tom?'

'He's someone from my past.' Linda kept her eyes averted, scared Sam would read her mind. What she'd said was true, just not the *whole* truth.

'And where is this Tom now?'

'That, I don't know.' Linda glanced over her shoulder, even though she hadn't meant to.

'Wherever he is, he won't find you, if that's what's worrying you?' Sam said, eyeing Linda carefully. 'I'll make sure of that.'

And she would. Removing that scrote in the alleyway was one off the list, but this Tom person? By the sounds of it, he was the one running that filthy setup, therefore she would hunt him down until...

The office door opened and Seb walked in. He placed his hands on Sam's shoulders. 'It's all done and clear.'

Smiling, his gaze moved to Linda, wiping the shock of her appearance from his face the second it registered. 'Hello, Linda.'

Linda smiled weakly, aware that exposing her teeth only showcased the ones no longer there, and she managed to somehow override the fact that she'd just seen this man knife someone to death in the alleyway.

She watched him limp over to the drinks cabinet. 'What have you done to your leg?'

'It's a long story.' Sam shot Seb a look. Linda didn't yet know her son was dead, and it looked like *she'd* be the one to break that news.

* * *

'Stop fucking moaning,' Tom snapped. 'Jesus wept! We've only been here two nights and you're already losing the plot?'

He paced around the junior suite. 'Most people would give their right eye to spend even one night in a place like this, yet you're whining?'

Dan irritably flicked the metal cap of his eighth bottle of Stella off the table onto the floor. 'Surely we can go somewhere to stretch our legs and get some bloody fresh air? I feel like a fucking mushroom! Even if we just go around the corner to that crummy pub? Oh, what's it called?' His eyes suddenly lit up. 'How about we get a taxi somewhere?'

Walking to the huge window, Tom stared down onto the vista of Broad Street. If Dan didn't shut up, he'd launch him out of this window. That way, the prick could have as much fresh air as he wanted...

He wasn't over the moon that the fake passports hadn't turned up today like promised either, and it didn't look much like it would happen now it was so late in the day.

He stared down onto the bustle of the Friday night revellers below in full swing.

It would be so easy to punch Dan in the face, but he had to keep a lid on things. They'd be out of here soon.

Regardless, he had to get away before someone discovered Amelia's body and no doubt by now, *Linda's*, in the attic.

His mouth flattened into a grimace. If he hadn't been in so much of a rush, he'd have had the foresight to set things up so that the Aurora was razed to the ground as well as the Peacock. That way, there would be no chance of anyone stumbling across anything detrimental. He'd also have rid the world of a few more skanky whores for good measure whilst he was at it.

Still, he hadn't, so that was that.

'The passports will be here tomorrow, I'm sure,' he mumbled. *They better had be, anyway.*

Dan flicked through the room service menu for the umpteenth time. 'I hope so because I'm getting sick of these fucking pizzas as well.'

Plus, he was exceptionally bored. Tom wouldn't even allow any room service of the female variety to be booked either. *'Too risky,'* he'd said.

What was riskier was his balls exploding.

Dan grinned. At least he could take some solace in knowing Marina was up the river without a paddle. Unable to help it, he began chuckling.

How he'd have loved to have seen the look on her and Grant's faces when they realised the cash had been swiped from under their noses. And even better when they'd worked out that it must have been *him* behind it...

'What the fuck are you laughing at?' Tom barked, his patience veering worryingly to the edge.

'Nothing. Just thinking, that's all.'

Snorting with derision, Tom dropped into one of the armchairs and picked up the TV remote. Being cooped up with Dan was never part of the deal, but he only had a few more hours of this shit and then they could get out of here.

* * *

'I just can't believe it!' Linda sobbed. 'I'd always hoped to make things up with Grant. The last time I saw him, I wasn't in a good way,' she admitted, shame burning her cheeks.

Seb snorted derisively, unsure why Grant deserved *anything* being made up to him. The man was party to ripping Sam off and trying to rob him, so as far as he was concerned, Grant had received his just desserts.

'It doesn't surprise me about Marina,' Linda added, a harsh note to her voice. 'I know they're both my kids...' She put her head in her hands, as if that would rationalise this news. 'It had to be Marina's doing.' Her head swung up, her eyes fiery. 'However he came across, Grant was a good boy. He always was...'

Seb snorted once more, this time louder, shifting uncomfortably on the seat as Sam nudged him.

'He had a good heart,' Linda continued, 'whereas Marina was always a nasty piece of work.' She shook her head, the mere memory of her daughter unpalatable. 'Like her father, that one. She has his temperament. She'd have dragged Grant into whatever she was playing at, you mark my words.'

'Grant wasn't a puppet, Linda,' Seb remarked, this time ignoring Sam's warning look. 'He didn't *have* to allow Marina to dope me up, ruin my relationship and plan to rob my safe. Neither did he have to agree to that woman storming in here and trying to kill Sam.'

Linda pursed her lips. 'No, he didn't, but you don't know Marina. Being as she's like Mickey, her bloody wanker of a father, then Grant wouldn't even have been aware of anything until last knockings. A devious cunning bitch, she is.'

Linda paused, hating herself for thinking it, let alone speaking out loud, but she would anyway. Because it was true. 'I wish it was Marina who was dead, instead of Grant.'

And with that, she burst into tears.

48

'You look a lot better now,' Sam smiled when Linda emerged from the bathroom.

'I slept better than I have done in a very long time,' Linda said gratefully, her whole demeanour now having changed.

The long-standing desolation was being kept in check by the resolve borne from Sam's promises. Linda knew she could do this and she *would* succeed.

She glanced at her reflection in the wood-framed cheval mirror. She hadn't expected Sam to call a mobile hairdresser and a whole selection of clothes from Rackhams either.

She smiled at the neat trousers and jumper she'd picked from the vast selection on offer.

Sam had insisted she choose a *huge* selection. More clothes than Linda had ever had in her life. And lovely ones, at that.

Tears pricked the back of her eyes. She didn't deserve this. Not after the way she'd let all of her children down. If she hadn't been such a loser, then perhaps Grant wouldn't be dead and Marina would have been a nicer person?

'The taxi will be here any minute,' Sam said, frowning at the battle going on behind Linda's eyes. 'It's one of the best rehab places in the Midlands. They'll soon have you free from every trace of those drugs. Just think – you'll be able to see Tayquan and Shondra before you know it!'

Linda took Sam's hand. 'I don't know how I can ever thank you for what you've done for me. Both you *and* Seb. You have your own problems to deal with and...'

'Leave that side of things to us,' Sam insisted.

'If I was any sort of a mother, I'd be here for you, rather than the other way around.' Linda's self-doubt gained traction once more. 'This clinic you're sending me to is expensive, isn't it? I've heard of it before.' She looked up, wide-eyed. 'What if I fail? What if I let you down? What if... what if Tom...'

'That man will not locate you, I can promise you that!' Sam snapped. And she knew this because she'd arranged for a twenty-four-hour guard to protect Linda during her stay in the clinic until that man was found. And now, thanks to Linda, Sam knew *just* where he operated from.

Linda nodded, unsure whether she believed that in its entirety. Tom always managed to find her in the end. 'Seb's not around? I wanted to say goodbye.'

'Unfortunately, he's at a meeting about the rebuilding of the Peacock, but you won't be away for long. I'll come and visit you, okay?'

Levelling with Sam about who Tom Bedworth really was twitched against Linda's lips. Telling her daughter that Tom ran the Aurora and that she knew him from her past was one thing, but should she have admitted the man was Sam's father?

Part of her thought so, but the rest did not.

What would telling Sam achieve?

From what she'd gathered, Tom's days were numbered, so Sam

being aware of her relationship to him would only hurt her, wouldn't it?

Linda knew telling Sam might make herself feel better, but she'd be telling her for one reason only – to assuage her *own* guilt – and this wasn't about *her*, it was about Sam.

She had to take this one on the chin and keep it to herself for her daughter's sake.

The beep of a horn startled Linda from her thoughts and she looked up, her stomach churning. 'Is that the taxi?'

'It certainly is.' Sam picked up the large suitcase. 'Come on, let's get you on the road to a full recovery.' She hugged Linda tightly. 'Are you sure you don't want me to accompany you? Just whilst you get checked in?'

'You've already done more than enough! You get yourself over to the Orchid and be with your man,' Linda insisted.

* * *

Dan bristled as Tom let himself back into the hotel room. 'I thought we weren't supposed to go anywhere?' he snapped. 'I came out of the shower to find you'd disappeared?'

'When exactly do I have to explain anything to you?' Tom snarled. Dan's attitude wasn't helping his overall outlook this morning.

'I thought you'd legged it with the money,' Dan grumbled, looking pointedly at the large wardrobe the other side of the room where their bounty was safely stashed.

Tom ignored Dan's griping. He had other things to worry about. He knew something had gone pear-shaped when he'd woken up this morning. He could feel it in his water.

And he'd been right.

Taking off his jacket, he slung it over the back of an armchair, then wiped his clammy brow with the back of his hand.

'What's the matter?' Dan frowned. 'You're all pasty and grey.' His eyes widened. 'Oh, my God! The cops aren't downstairs, are they?'

'Don't be stupid!' Tom laughed, the sound sticking somewhere between his voice box and tonsils. 'You're paranoid! Give it a rest! I popped to reception to extend our stay for another night, that's all.'

And that he hadn't wanted to do either, but until they got those passports, they couldn't move. The chances of getting a flight later on today, once they'd turned up, were also slim.

His ability to sound unfazed amazed him, but *was* Dan being paranoid? Tom didn't know what made him venture to the reception, but something had, and he wished it hadn't.

No, there weren't any police, but at this rate there might be soon.

He'd only gone to the underground car park as an afterthought. He didn't even know why he'd done it. Maybe the knowledge his car was still sitting there, screaming out its oddity by being surrounded by gleaming Audis, Jags, BMWs and Bentleys, was what did it.

The car should have gone, along with the £20K payment for those two passports. That was part of the deal, but as the passports *still* hadn't arrived, so the car had remained.

Or so he'd thought.

But Tom's car, the one that had successfully mowed Deb Banner into the tarmac, had disappeared.

Who the fuck had taken it? The police? A thief?

Whoever had helped themselves hadn't done Tom any favours. The motor was destined to be crushed, but now the bloody thing was still out there, being driven round Birmingham by some twat?

It wasn't like he could report it stolen either, but when the toerag who'd pinched it for something suspect got a tug, it *would* be in the hands of the police...

Shit. Fuck. Shit.

They really had to get out of here before someone came looking.

'What's going on?' Dan probed, mystified by Tom's unaccustomed twitchiness.

'Nothing!' Tom barked. Dan didn't know about the car and neither would he. The muppet was enough of a liability as it was. 'I take it no one's been with our passports?'

Dan shook his head. 'Nope. Not yet.'

'Right, that's it!' Pursing his lips, Tom strode over to the phone, stabbing the 'o' for an outside line. He tapped in the number for the Stoat and Rabbit, hissing impatiently.

'Hello?' Tom said when the call answered, ignoring Dan staring at the side of his head. 'Is Nige there?'

If Nige was anywhere by midday on a Saturday, it would be the Stoat and Rabbit, and Tom wasn't being fobbed off with excuses about the passports any longer. It was more imperative than ever that they got out of here now.

'Oh! Erm... when will he be back? I was expecting an... erm... delivery yesterday evening, but Nige didn't show up and...'

Frowning, unsure he'd heard correctly, Tom removed the receiver from his ear and stared at it in disbelief. 'What? No! I hadn't heard. When?' *He was sure he would be sick.* 'Christ! When will he be able to sort my stuff out?'

Tom listened to the reply, then replaced the receiver. He sunk into the chair. He could not believe this. He could just not fucking believe it.

He snatched up the newspaper he'd grabbed from reception on his way back from the car park.

'What?' Dan asked. 'What is it?'

'Shut up!' Tom hissed, frantically thumbing through the pages. Stopping on the article he wanted, he scanned it, his heart sinking. *Shit!*

Knife Attack at City Pub

Drinkers out for a social evening were interrupted by a brawl at the Stoat and Rabbit public house in Yardley yesterday (Friday, 9 February).

The seemingly unprovoked attack happened outside the pub around 6 p.m., watched by horrified drinkers from inside.

The victim, Nigel Beater, 56, suffered multiple stab wounds to the chest and neck before his unknown assailants fled the scene.

Mr Beater remains in a critical condition at the Queen Elizabeth Hospital.

The motive for the attack is not known and police have been unable to get a clear description of the attackers.

Anyone with information or who witnessed the assault should call...

'Bollocks!' Tom spat, shoving the paper into Dan's hand. 'Look at this!'

Dan read the article. 'Oh, fuck! That's the guy doing our passports, isn't it?'

Tom didn't answer. Of *course* it was the bloke doing their passports. Their ticket out of here was now lying like a fucking pin cushion somewhere in the QE.

So now what? It would be days, possibly *weeks*, before the man recovered. That's if he didn't croak it.

Tom racked his brains. He didn't know anyone else that he

could ask to do passports – not anyone he trusted not to mention they were for *him*.

No doubt by now it was all over town that the Aurora had been left unattended. And that was the *good* scenario. The not so good scenario was that the police had discovered Amelia's and Linda's bodies...

With a wave of fear, Tom snatched the paper back from Dan and flicked through it again, relieved there were no reports of bodies, but that still left them with a problem. And he had to think of how to get around this sharpish before his connection with that motor came to light.

'What are we going to do now?'

Tom glared at Dan pacing the room, his whining spoiling his concentration. 'I don't know,' he mumbled. 'But we can't stay here, and we can't leave the country now either. Not yet, anyway.'

He snatched a bottle of Budweiser from the minibar, pulling the metal top off with his teeth. 'I need to think and see who can put us up for a while, or a room we can rent on the quiet.'

And he hadn't the foggiest idea where to start with that yet.

* * *

Seb shook Fletcher's hand and waited for him to leave Sam's office before sinking down into the chair.

Sam's chair. He no longer had a chair. He was in Sam's casino, offering nothing, and unless he moved fast, he could offer nothing in the future either.

He stared at the remains of the whisky in the decanter, his fingers itching for a glass. A *large* glass.

But it was Sam's whisky, and he wasn't taking any more from her than he already had.

What he'd just heard from the accountant cemented what he'd all but already decided upon. Now that decision was a dead cert.

Andrew and Neil had already accepted this was the only way forward when he'd told them his thoughts, but Seb had wanted more than anything to find another solution.

There wasn't one.

And because of that, he must give Sam the option to walk away from it all. From *him*.

The thought crucified him, but if he could give her nothing else, then he had to at least give her freedom.

Seb looked up as the door opened, surprised to see Sam. 'I didn't expect you so soon,' he said, forcing a smile.

'Linda's gone to rehab. She'll be in there for at least a month.' Sam's face was alight with happiness.

She draped her arms around Seb's neck and drank in that scent only he had. How she'd missed him, but now they could work on getting things back to normal and up and running.

Seb could have quite happily put everything he had to say aside and carried on for just that little bit longer. How he longed to forget it all.

As Sam's lips brushed tantalisingly against his neck, he removed her hands from his chest, despising himself for ruining the moment. 'I need to talk to you.'

Sam frowned. 'If you're worried about the cost of the clinic for Linda, don't be. It won't affect my promise of covering the cost of your staff.'

She moved to sit in a chair. 'You should have seen Linda, Seb! She looked a thousand times better this morning. The life's returning to her eyes already. I think the prospect of seeing Tayquan and Shondra again is her driving force.'

She paused, a frown creasing her brow. 'But we need to deal with that Tom Bedworth person. It can't be left.' Although she hadn't wanted anything to spoil the new hope for Linda, the fury of what had been done to her held no bounds. Whatever happened, the man responsible would pay. 'When are we paying the Aurora a visit?'

'Nothing will be left, I can assure you of that. It will be soon,' Seb said, his dread mounting.

It hadn't escaped his knowledge that the Aurora wasn't unheard of. It was the very place Andrew and Neil had gone to several months ago whilst on the lookout for who was behind all of that business with John Maynard. But once Maynard had been removed, it had been *him* who had made the decision the Aurora required no more thought.

How wrong he'd been.

'But there must be other women and young girls there who need our help and...'

'Sam, I *promise* you he will be dealt with, but I need to do something else first.'

Sam looked at Seb carefully. Something was wrong. *Very* wrong. He looked pale, ill. 'Wh-what's wrong? You mustn't stress about using here as your base or me taking some of your staff temporarily. I told you the Orchid can cover all of that. It will be fine and...'

'You don't understand,' Seb cut in, his face stern. 'I've just had a meeting with Fletcher. The money my firm has in the bank will cover the start of the clean-up and rebuilding process. It will also grant me a few weeks of paying all my staff's wages, but I need more funds.'

Sam frowned. 'Okay, so perhaps the bank will...'

'Neither the firm nor I have any collateral now. Don't forget that even my flat above the Peacock went up in smoke too. The bank won't lend whilst I have no means of trading, and I can't trade until the Peacock is up and running.' He took Sam's hand. 'There's something you've forgotten. Again, something that was down to *me.*'

Sam's heart thumped. *There was something else?*

'I literally have a few weeks before the creditors come knocking.' Seb's eyes met Sam's. 'And there's only one thing left of value...'

Suddenly the penny dropped. 'The house! The house belongs to the Peacock!' Sam gasped.

'I'm so sorry. This is all my fault,' Seb said, anger with himself and everything increasing once more. 'I've let you down and I didn't want to.'

'You have *not* let me down!' Sam insisted. 'How on earth could you think that? If we need to sell the house, then we sell it.'

Seb shook his head. 'That won't happen. I know how much you love it. I'm not taking that from you as well as everything else.'

Cold rushed over Sam. 'What do you mean, everything else?'

'What I have to do will put you and your firm in jeopardy, as well as mine. I'll take the hit, but I won't have you do the same.'

Scenarios whizzed through Sam's mind at an ever-increasing speed. 'Seb, you're frightening me.'

Seb put his head in his hands. He wanted to lash out at anyone and everybody who had put him in this position. He would find them all – every single one of them, but not until he got everything back on track.

He took a deep breath. 'I'm doing what I promised myself I wouldn't – stepping into the fire more dangerously than ever before at the only time in my life when I wanted to step *away* from it.'

'You're talking in riddles!' Sam cried. 'I don't like it. You're worrying me.'

'Sam, what I'm trying to say is that I'm giving you the option to walk away,' Seb said, his eyes fixed on Sam. 'Actually, I'm *telling* you to walk away. I won't have you being dragged into the repercussions this might unleash.'

Sam folded her arms defensively, astounded at what she was hearing. 'Seb, you can't tell me to walk away and expect me to go, "Okay then"! Look at what we've been through! There's nothing that would make me *ever* consider wa...'

'My option of rectifying this was the Irish, but they've pulled out. I wasn't happy involving them in the first place, but it was better than what it's left me with... And that is, I have to do a job,' Seb muttered before he could change his mind. 'A heist. And a big one.'

Sam blinked. *A heist?* 'No! You don't need to. I'll raise some capital. I have collateral on the Orchid, and don't forget I have the Symphony Court apartment. We can sell that and...'

'Even if I accepted that, which I won't, it's not enough and would take too long. I need this *fast*.' Seb pulled Sam into his arms and stared into the eyes that he could drown in. 'I'm sorry, Princess, I really am. It's been years since the Stokers pulled something like this and never on this scale, but it has to be done.'

He tucked a loose curl behind Sam's ear. 'Now you can see why you must walk away.'

Sam buried her face against the familiar broadness of Seb's chest, scarcely able to comprehend that people had done so much damage for him to be put in this position. *And now he expected her to leave?*

Raising her head, she stared into his green eyes. 'Who are you planning this on?'

Seb shrugged. 'I have a few prospects – some more dangerous than others, but none of them good. There are only certain options offering the kind of payout I need. It won't be on my doorstep, though, I can tell you that. I won't take from my own city.'

'I'm not walking away from you or this,' Sam said, her voice calm and crystal clear.

Seb pressed his lips against the smooth skin of Sam's forehead. 'You *have* to. I cannot risk anything coming back on you. After this, you'd be looking over your shoulder for the rest of your life.' He traced his thumb across her bottom lip. 'I won't allow that to happen, so *please* do as I ask.'

Sam pulled Seb's hand away from her face. 'Let's just get one thing straight. I'm not the green about the gills girl I was this time last year. I will st...'

'I will not allow you to be involved with me!' Seb barked. 'You're too important.'

Sam raised her chin defiantly. 'We stand together. On *everything*. I want vengeance on the bastard that ruined my mother's life, I want the people who torched the Peacock and who robbed you. I want to do all of it with *you*. Whatever affects you affects *me*. If you need to pull a heist to put one part of this right, then I'm helping you do just that. And you will not stop me.'

She placed her hands on his chest. 'This is about *family*, Seb. Linda's my family, yes, but so are *you*. You're going to be my husband and that still stands. I love you, so we're in this together. Whatever the cost.'

Seb swallowed the lump in his throat, his love for this woman crushing. 'But...'

'But nothing!'

Seb slowly realised he couldn't win this one. As much as he didn't like it, Sam had dug her heels in and wasn't going to back down, whatever he said. He now realised she'd do it with or without him.

Bringing his mouth down on hers, he didn't know how he'd got so lucky to have this amazing woman love him as fiercely as he loved her.

EPILOGUE

Mickey Devlin staggered through the door of his bedsit and slumped down onto his thin mattress, the bed still unmade from the last time he'd slept here, which, at a guess, was three days ago.

His mouth cracked into a smile. He'd cleared up nicely at the Bricklayers Arms on Wednesday night and it would have been plain rude not to celebrate with a pretty girl of his choice.

And, like magic, there were always plenty on hand to pick from when he was flush.

'There's a call for you,' a voice shouted through the flimsy door of Mickey's room.

Mickey scowled. Soon he'd fork out for a decent abode, rather than living in a crummy dump like this in a block of equally crummy other bedsits reserved for the dregs of society.

But then, there was always more important things to spend his money on – like women and beer.

Dragging himself off the bed, Mickey thought about not bothering answering the call. The only thing that made him do so was that one of the few people who had this shared phone number was the blonde he'd not long left. She must be rampant for him if she was calling already.

He was knackered, but best not look a gift horse in the mouth.

Walking out into the communal hallway, Mickey picked up the greasy handset dangling from the coin-operated phone. 'Can't get enough of me?' he laughed.

The smile then dropped from his face. 'Marina? Is that you?'

* * *

Mickey tugged his holdall from the top of the wardrobe. It wouldn't take long to pack. But before he did that, a drink was in order.

Opening the MDF cupboard, he fished out the quart bottle of rum he kept stashed there.

Hearing the acidic tones of his daughter down the line, he'd very nearly hung up. He'd never liked Marina much. Mainly because she looked like her mother before the old bat had turned into a wizened crackhead.

But he was glad he hadn't told Marina to sling her hook because *finally* something which had fruited from his loins was offering payment for the gift of life.

Out of all of his children scattered across London, as well as other parts of the country, Grant and Marina were the only ones with half a brain. Hence why he'd trusted Grant to do the business in getting dosh off that trout of a mother of theirs.

But Grant hadn't bothered keeping in touch about that, like he'd instructed. Clearly, the greedy prick was intent to not share. At least Marina had more brains than that.

Mickey drank deeply from the small bottle of spirits.

Should he be upset that his son was dead?

Probably, but in all truth, he wasn't.

It wasn't like he'd ever really known the kid, so Grant's demise made little difference. But what *did* make a difference was what Mickey now knew.

And who would have thought it?

Frowning, he stood up and moved to the ramshackle chest of drawers, pulling at the stiff drawer containing his meagre assortment of clothes.

Grabbing a handful of T-shirts, he shoved them into his holdall, along with some underwear. Anything that wasn't clean could fucking stay. It was all shit stuff anyhow, but once he'd got his mitts on that dough, he'd command the finest of the fine.

His eyes narrowed.

Whereas Dan would be getting more than the loss of a few fingers. He'd rip the cunt to pieces for this.

To think he'd helped that man find a way to escape from the people wanting a piece of him around here?

What a sly one Dan was.

And ripping Marina off too?

Mickey had almost laughed when his daughter told him what had happened. Until he realised how bloody insulting it was that someone as brain dead as Dan had somehow grown the nous to turn over one of his offspring!

How the hell he'd managed it, Mickey didn't know, but Marina's theory had to be correct.

Dan couldn't have done this on his own. *No way.* The thick bastard definitely had outside help.

Mickey smiled. It was fine. It wasn't like it mattered who Dan had on side, and neither did he care whose money the prick had half-inched.

The only relevant thing was, according to what Grant had told Marina, it was *millions*. And those millions had his fucking name on.

Zipping up his bag, Mickey glanced around the room he'd been stuck in for the last couple of years. That old bitch of a land-lady could chase him for the back rent if she so wished, but she'd have to find him first.

Slamming the door behind him, he made his way out of the building. There would be a train bound for Birmingham New Street from one of the stations tonight. And he'd be on it.

Like he'd said to Marina, that's what fathers were for – helping out their children in times of need.

He hadn't specified *whose* need.

And this need was *his*.

Mickey would get that money and with a bit of help from him, he'd ensure he and Marina discovered *exactly* where Dan Marlow was hiding with it.

ACKNOWLEDGMENTS

Vendetta is my third book with Boldwood and the twelfth book I have written since 2017. What a crazy few years it has been!

I cannot emphasise enough how much I enjoy developing characters from shady underworlds – some who you love to root for and others you are hoping against all hope, get their comeuppance!

Frequently, I find myself waking in the middle of the night with more ideas of what will next happen to characters and having to jot it down! My long-suffering husband is by now used to me frantically scribbling away in the small hours, as well as chuckling to myself when one of the despicable characters meets their end!

Also, if anyone happened to overhear my son asking me every day when he gets in from school as to who I've killed today, I suspect I may get some rather strange looks!

The honour of being able to write as a job is a dream come true and one I will never tire of. I'm especially enjoying that my latest series is set in Birmingham – the city I grew up in and around and one that is very close to my heart.

Huge thanks to all of the Boldwood team and, as always, my fabulous editor, Emily Ruston, who never ceases to be a pleasure to work with. Also, a special shout out to Annie Aldington who has done a superb job in bringing the characters to life in the audiobooks of this series – she's got them down to a tee!

Many thanks also go to the loyal and supportive folk I have met online, several of whom have gone a long way to restore my faith in social media.

Love to all of my family and friends and lastly, but by no means least, to all the readers out there. Hearing that you enjoy my books keeps my incentive to write strong. Thank you all so very much.

MORE FROM EDIE BAYLIS

We hope you enjoyed reading *Vendetta*. If you did, please leave a review.

If you'd like to gift a copy, this book is also available as an ebook, digital audio download and audiobook CD.

Sign up to Edie Baylis's mailing list for news, competitions and updates on future books.

https://bit.ly/EdieBaylisnews

Takeover, the first in the Allegiance series, is available now.

ABOUT THE AUTHOR

Edie Baylis is a successful self-published author of dark gritty thrillers with violent background settings. She lives in Worcestershire, has a history of owning daft cars and several motorbikes and is licensed to run a pub.

Visit Edie's website: http://www.ediebaylis.co.uk/

Follow Edie on social media:

twitter.com/ediebaylis
facebook.com/downfallseries
instagram.com/ediebaylis

PEAKY READERS

GANG LOYALTIES. DARK SECRETS.
BLOODY REVENGE.

A READER COMMUNITY FOR
GANGLAND CRIME THRILLER FANS!

DISCOVER PAGE-TURNING NOVELS
FROM YOUR FAVOURITE AUTHORS
AND MEET NEW FRIENDS.

JOIN OUR BOOK CLUB
FACEBOOK GROUP

BIT.LY/PEAKYREADERSFB

SIGN UP TO OUR
NEWSLETTER

BIT.LY/PEAKYREADERSNEWS

Boldw**oo**d

Boldwood Books is an award-winning fiction publishing company seeking out the best stories from around the world.

Find out more at www.boldwoodbooks.com

Join our reader community for brilliant books, competitions and offers!

Follow us
@BoldwoodBooks
@BookandTonic

Sign up to our weekly deals newsletter

https://bit.ly/BookandTonicNews

Printed in Great Britain
by Amazon

16212107R00220